More Praise for Lucy Monroe and her novels

"Emotional, sexy, and romantic. *Touch Me* is just plain wonderful!" —*New York Times* bestselling author Lori Foster

"Lucy Monroe is an awesome talent." —*The Best Reviews*

"Monroe brings a fresh voice to historical romance."
—National bestselling author Stef Ann Holm

"Monroe pens a sizzling romance with a well-developed plot." —*Romantic Times*

"A fresh new voice in romance . . . Lucy Monroe captures the very heart of the genre." —Debbie Macomber

"Fast-paced and sensual." —*Booklist*

"Romance as only Lucy Monroe does it . . . joy, passion, and heartfelt emotions." —*The Road to Romance*

"A perfect ten! First-rate characterization, clever dialogue, sustained sexual tension, and a couple of jaw-dropping surprises." —*Romance Reviews Today*

"An intense, compelling read from page one to the very end. With her powerful voice and vision, Lucy packs emotion into every scene . . . [a] sizzling story with tangible sexual tension." —Bestselling author Jane Porter

"Lucy has written a wonderful full-blooded hero and a beautiful warm heroine." —Maggie Cox

"A charming tale . . . The delightful characters jump off the page!" —Theresa Scott

Berkley Sensation titles by Lucy Monroe

TOUCH ME

TEMPT ME

Tempt Me

LUCY MONROE

BERKLEY SENSATION, NEW YORK

THE BERKLEY PUBLISHING GROUP
Published by the Penguin Group
Penguin Group (USA) Inc.
375 Hudson Street, New York, New York 10014, USA
Penguin Group (Canada), 90 Eglinton Avenue East, Suite 700, Toronto, Ontario M4P 2Y3, Canada (a division of Pearson Penguin Canada Inc.)
Penguin Books Ltd., 80 Strand, London WC2R 0RL, England
Penguin Group Ireland, 25 St. Stephen's Green, Dublin 2, Ireland (a division of Penguin Books Ltd.)
Penguin Group (Australia), 250 Camberwell Road, Camberwell, Victoria 3124, Australia (a division of Pearson Australia Group Pty. Ltd.)
Penguin Books India Pvt. Ltd., 11 Community Centre, Panchsheel Park, New Delhi—110 017, India
Penguin Group (NZ), Cnr. Airborne and Rosedale Roads, Albany, Auckland 1310, New Zealand (a division of Pearson New Zealand Ltd.)
Penguin Books (South Africa) (Pty.) Ltd., 24 Sturdee Avenue, Rosebank, Johannesburg 2196, South Africa

Penguin Books Ltd., Registered Offices: 80 Strand, London WC2R 0RL, England

This is a work of fiction. Names, characters, places, and incidents either are the product of the author's imagination or are used fictitiously, and any resemblance to actual persons, living or dead, business establishments, events, or locales is entirely coincidental. The publisher does not have any control over and does not assume any responsibility for author or third-party websites or their content.

TEMPT ME

A Berkley Sensation Book / published by arrangement with the author

PRINTING HISTORY
Berkley Sensation edition / April 2006

Copyright © 2006 by Lucy Monroe.
Excerpt from *Take Me* copyright © 2006 by Lucy Monroe.
Cover art by Franco Accornero.
Cover design by George Long.
Interior text design by Kristin del Rosario.

All rights reserved.
No part of this book may be reproduced, scanned, or distributed in any printed or electronic form without permission. Please do not participate in or encourage piracy of copyrighted materials in violation of the author's rights. Purchase only authorized editions.
For information address: The Berkley Publishing Group,
a division of Penguin Group (USA) Inc.,
375 Hudson Street, New York, New York 10014.

ISBN: 0-425-20922-9

BERKLEY SENSATION®
Berkley Sensation Books are published by The Berkley Publishing Group,
a division of Penguin Group (USA) Inc.,
375 Hudson Street, New York, New York 10014.
BERKLEY SENSATION is a registered trademark of Penguin Group (USA) Inc.
The "B" design is a trademark belonging to Penguin Group (USA) Inc.

PRINTED IN THE UNITED STATES OF AMERICA

10 9 8 7 6 5 4 3 2 1

If you purchased this book without a cover, you should be aware that this book is stolen property. It was reported as "unsold and destroyed" to the publisher, and neither the author nor the publisher has received any payment for this "stripped book."

With deep affection for
Debbie Macomber,
a dear friend and wonderful mentor
who both blesses and inspires me
and countless others with her unflagging determination
in pursuing her dreams

Prologue

Langley Hall
Autumn 1820

Lady Irisa, daughter of the Earl and Countess of Langley, took a deep breath and almost forgot to let it out before cautiously stepping into the drawing room.

The late afternoon sun bathed the Brussels carpet in its muted glow. Mama was terribly proud of the fact that the carpet was even finer than the one in His Grace's drawing room. Irisa took another hesitant step forward. Although the matching fireplaces at either end of the room had been lit, the heat from their twin blazes did nothing to dispel the cold that covered Irisa like an uncomfortable cloak.

Dread made a particularly chilling companion.

After almost seventeen years of trying to please her parents, Irisa knew without a doubt she would shortly be incurring their wrath, if not their utter disgust. After all, it was not even moderately proper for a daughter to blackmail her parents. Not to mention that she would be doing so in order to avoid marriage to a duke, her mama's fondest wish.

Thea, her half sister who had been raised in the West Indies and was therefore somewhat more independent than the average English lady, had told Irisa that when negotiating, one must know one's adversary. In addition, one must have something one's adversary needs or desires—and above all else, one must be willing to follow through.

Irisa knew her parents as well as they would allow. She definitely had something to bargain with. And after her awful experience the night before, she was willing to follow through, whatever the cost.

If only His Grace were a great deal younger and perhaps just a bit kinder, but no one had ever been foolish enough to label His Grace kind. From all accounts, neither of his two previous wives had been happy. Servants' gossip had it that the man could not even keep a mistress. He was cruelly arrogant, assuming his wealth and status would secure him everything he could possibly want. Right now, he wanted Irisa.

He'd made that very clear the previous evening when he caught her alone in the hall after dinner. She had taken a long bath and scrubbed herself with lilac-scented soap, but she could still feel the touch of those cadaverous hands and wet, pinched lips. The duke had grandchildren close to her age, but that didn't seem to bother him. He clearly thought it shouldn't bother her either.

It did. Very much. She shuddered at the memory of his hot breath against her ear, his rough handling.

Her parents had encouraged the old roué's courtship with embarrassing enthusiasm. Well, Papa wasn't exactly embarrassing. He was much too reserved for that, but he *did* encourage the duke's attentions.

Mama, however, made it very plain to *everyone* that the match was all she could wish for her only daughter. Irisa had finally come to accept that her own happiness was not nearly as important to her parents as the social prestige they would gain by a familial connection to His Grace. It had hurt deep inside, in a place she had tried hard to ignore since she was a very little girl and realized neither of her parents was particularly fond of her company.

If she thought that marrying the duke might actually gain

the love she wanted so desperately from them, she might even be willing to do it. Unfortunately, she was sure it wouldn't. She had tried for almost seventeen years to earn their affection, and even now, with the duke so close to coming up to scratch, Papa and Mama both continued to find fault with her.

After today, they might even hate her, but it was a risk she had to take. She would *not* marry His Grace.

She had no choice but to take immediate, drastic action. The duke had made an appointment to call upon Papa tomorrow. She had a horrible suspicion her parents wanted to announce the betrothal at her birthday ball next month. She could not fathom why else Mama had decided to have the entertainment. It certainly would be the first time any significant effort had been made to celebrate her birthday.

She stepped farther into the drawing room, pulling herself more erect. She could do this. Thankfully, both her parents were present. Mama tatted lace while Papa read some papers spread out on the table.

"Mama. Papa. I have something I need to tell you."

She spoke quietly, but such was the silence in the room that her parents immediately responded to her low voice.

"What is it?" Papa asked, looking not at all pleased by the interruption.

"I've decided not to marry His Grace."

There. She'd said it. Of course, now came the truly difficult part of following through on her intention.

"You forget yourself, young lady. It is not a decision for you to make."

She felt unaccustomed irritation rise within her at her father's words. Why wasn't it her decision? It was her life they were talking about. Papa wasn't the one who would have to put up with those cold, creepy hands touching his person.

She didn't say this, of course. "Perhaps in the normal way of things that would be true, but my situation is unique."

Mama's head snapped up from the lace she'd gone back

to tatting, her eyes narrowed. "There is nothing unique about your situation. You are a green girl who will follow the advice of her parents in the matter of marriage and that is that."

Irisa locked her hands in front of her, praying for both patience and courage. "No, it is not. I will not marry the duke. In fact, I have decided I will choose my own husband and I don't want to do it right away."

Her father stood, rage making him seem taller than his actual five feet ten inches. "How dare you speak to your mother that way? You will apologize immediately and I will hear nothing more on this matter."

Even as the familiar fear of Papa's wrath constricted her heart, the last wisps of doubt about her chosen course of action faded from Irisa's mind.

Papa never wanted to hear her, not about anything. Sometimes she got the feeling he would have been just as content had she never been born. She thought perhaps she finally understood why, now that she knew the true story of his first marriage and her part in making it impossible for the first countess ever to return to England.

Once her half-sister's presence had been revealed to the family, along with the actual date of the first countess's death, so much had been made clear. Irisa had been born and her parents had "married" years before Papa's first wife had died. Mama and Papa had lived under a cloud of uncertainty from the first day of their life together as supposed man and wife.

Their legal marriage had not taken place until this past year in the country, under the utmost secrecy.

It explained so well why Papa treated Irisa more like a burden than a beloved daughter, and why Mama worshipped at the altar of outward appearances. Nevertheless, her parents must claim some responsibility for her birth, and her happiness should carry some weight with them. They were her parents. *They should love her.*

"I'm sorry if my words upset you, Mama."

Her mother nodded her head regally and then focused

her eyes once again on the white thread in her lap. Papa returned to his seat, his attention going back to the papers in front of him, not deigning to acknowledge Irisa again.

"I will say only one more thing on this matter and then I will bow to Papa's wishes for silence." She spoke as if she had their undivided attention.

Mama stopped tatting, but she did not raise her head. Irisa could not tell if Papa had ceased reading.

"When His Grace comes to call tomorrow, Papa will decline his offer or I will be forced to make public the *unique* circumstances of my birth."

Papa's chair crashed to the floor as he stood and Mama's gasp sounded like a moan, but Irisa ignored them both as she turned and walked from the room.

One

London
1824

SIRISA FACED LUCAS ACROSS THE SMALL LIBRARY. The fog-dampened night could not intrude on the warm coziness of the room.

Lucas's mouth curved into a loving smile. "You came."

She nodded, her throat too clogged with emotion to speak.

He extended his hand. "Come here, my love."

She moved forward as if in a daze, drawn by the warmth in her lover's eyes as much as the implied command in his stance. She wanted him.

Desperately.

And he wanted her.

As soon as she was close enough to touch, he reached out and pulled her to him. The feel of his warm skin on her bare arms sent shivers down her spine. He did not stop pulling her until her body was an inch from his own.

She knew he would kiss her now. Finally. She had waited so long, but instinctively knew the wait would be worth it. Lucas's mouth settled on hers, his lips warm and vibrant against her own. She shuddered and he pulled his mouth a breath from hers.

"Are you all right, my love?"

"Yes. Please. Kiss me again."

He did so with alacrity while one arm moved around her waist. His other hand settled on her shoulder, his fingers sliding under the fabric of her gown. She blushed at the intimate touch, but did not pull away. He groaned low in his throat and tugged the tiny cap sleeves of her gown down until the swell of her breasts were exposed. Then he . . . Then he . . .

Oh, fustion! Irisa's daydream came to an abrupt halt. What *would* happen next? Authors always stopped at the most interesting parts in the novels Irisa read. For instance, she assumed a gentleman placed his fingers under the fabric of a lady's gown with the intention of baring her unmentionables, but she couldn't be *sure.*

And she certainly had no idea what said gentleman would do once he had succeeded in pushing the bodice down. She thought the bit about shuddering and groaning had been well done, considering her lack of personal experience and knowledge in this area. Not that she would shun a bit more of both, particularly if Lucas offered the instruction.

Stifling a sigh, she reluctantly brought her attention back to the Bilkingtons' elegantly appointed supper room and her partner's monologue on hunting hounds. Lady Bilkington had an infatuation with green and gold, much in evidence in the room's decor.

Irisa smiled and nodded at Mr. Wemby during a short pause in his speech. Thus encouraged, he launched into an enthusiastic story about one of his favorite hounds. She went back to her pondering, assured once again that her rejection of his suit the year before had been the right choice.

Mr. Wemby was kind, but he had far more interest in his hounds than in any person of his acquaintance. And like the other suitors she had rejected over the past four years, he did not stir her passions . . . not like Lucas.

However, the chances of Lucas offering anything more than a polite greeting were slim indeed. Earl of Ashton, he was acutely aware of his responsibility to his title and was known as an absolute paragon of gentlemanly virtue. There were even those amongst the *ton* who went so far as to call him *The Saint*.

She'd heard it had something to do with his family, but she didn't know what. Because of the unkind things said about her brother's disfigurement and her sister's unconventional upbringing, Irisa abhorred and shunned gossip. Even if it meant learning less about a man as fascinating as Lucas.

What could she possibly learn from scandalmongers but half-truths and innuendo? One day, she would ask him about his nickname . . . if they were ever on intimate enough terms to allow such a liberty. Until then, she would make do with daydreams fueled by her belief that under his perfectly controlled exterior beat a heart as passionate as her own.

Others amongst the *ton* would laugh at such a conclusion, but she just *knew* she was right about him. In all the novels she had read, gentlemen very much like Lucas seethed with hidden passions regardless of their cold outward countenance. And on several occasions when he debated issues he felt strongly about, the quiet intensity in his voice had sent shivers down her spine—and to other less mentionable regions of her body.

She had great hopes of engaging those passions on a more personal basis. Since their first meeting at a house party, he had been consistent, if not effusive, in his attentions. Upon arriving in Town for the Season, he had begun to court her with all the polite restraint to be expected of a man nicknamed Saint.

One might even suspect he was on the verge of making an offer. Much to her parents' relief. However, to *her* chagrin, he had not so much as held her hand while driving in the park. She wanted to know what Lucas's lips tasted like. She wanted to know what happened when a man put his hand under a lady's bodice, and she wanted him to be the man to show her.

As much as she wanted his passion, she also craved more of his company. She didn't want to dance with a string of boring partners only to have the monotony relieved the prescribed two times by Lucas. Tonight, he hadn't even ensured he got the supper dance, thus the one-sided conversation with Mr. Wemby over the small supper table.

It was one of Lucas's little habits, this giving up the supper dance with her occasionally. She assumed it was his way of not drawing unwanted attention to their association. At least he didn't compound the frustration his conduct caused her by asking someone else. When Lucas didn't partner her, he made himself scarce from the ballroom during the half-hour break in music.

"Lady Irisa. Mr. Wemby." The deep tones of Lucas's voice pulled Irisa from her thoughts.

She raised a startled gaze to see him standing by their table as if her secret wishes had drawn him to her side. The prospect was a pleasing one, if fanciful.

Eyes the color of blue glass were fixed on her with a hint of amusement, his black brow raised with just a touch of mockery. His sedately tailored black evening clothes molded the body of a tall Corinthian.

"Hello," she replied, her voice husky from surprise.

What was he doing here? It was wholly out of character for him. Her heart took a sudden lift at the sign that Lucas's behavior with her was not entirely predictable.

Mr. Wemby had stopped mid-sentence in his story and now blinked at Lucas as if unsure how the other man had appeared. "Good evening, Lord Ashton."

"I've just left a friend of yours in the card room, Wemby. He's looking for advice on putting a new pack of hounds together for this year's hunt."

Fairly quivering with excitement at the prospect of discussing a subject so close to his heart, Mr. Wemby stood quickly. "I'd better see if I can be of assistance then."

Lucas inclined his head. "I'll escort Lady Irisa back to her mother for you."

Mr. Wemby's head bobbed in agreement. "Kind of you.

I'll return the favor sometime." He left without another word to Irisa.

She stared after his retreating back, more amused than offended. "There is no question how conversation with me rates against the prospect of advising another gentleman on the purchase of a hound."

"With Wemby perhaps, but if you will notice, I am still here." The words washed over her with unexpected intensity and she found herself once again raising her gaze to look at him.

His mouth was still tipped in that amused way he had, but his eyes burned into her with undeniable force.

With, dared she hope, passion?

She smiled, feeling her heart race in her chest. "Yes, you are still here."

He extended his hand in a manner so like her daydream that, for a moment, she hesitated between reality and fantasy. Gathering her wits about her, she took the proffered hand and rose from her chair. Lucas transferred her grip to his arm and led her from the supper room.

"Are you truly going to take me back to Mama?" The dancing would not resume for fifteen minutes or more.

"Perhaps you would care to join me for a stroll around the perimeter of the ballroom?"

She'd rather retreat to the privacy of the terrace. But no doubt Lucas would consider such behavior shocking.

Stifling a sigh of regret, she forced her features to assume an expression of polite enthusiasm. After all, at least she would be with him. "With pleasure, my lord."

IRISA'S SMALL HAND GRIPPED HIS FOREARM TIGHTLY and Lucas fought back a smile at her enthusiasm to remain in his company. Her complete lack of the subterfuge so often found in ladies among the *ton* had been one of the first things that drew his admiration.

Her sweet face and golden brown eyes expressed her emotions honestly. They had made it obvious as he watched her from across the supper room that she found Wemby's company a trial. The socially polite smiles she had bestowed upon her supper partner had not fooled Lucas for a minute. Her unfocused gaze had said it all.

Not that anyone else would notice. Much to his own pleasure and surprise, he had come to realize that what was obvious to him when dealing with Irisa was not so clear to others.

So he had concocted a plan to rescue her. He realized that in doing so he might draw attention to their relationship, but he was willing to take the courtship to the next level. He planned to call on the Earl of Langley in the morning and ask for permission to pay his addresses to Irisa. Lucas had no doubt she would accept him. Even if she did not show such blatant pleasure in his company, a woman of twenty was considered practically on the shelf. She would undoubtedly be grateful for an offer of marriage.

He still found it difficult to believe she had remained unmarried. Admittedly, her tiny, curvaceous figure was not the current rage. However, combined with her honey blond hair and warm brown eyes, it made for an altogether lovely package. Remembering the erotic dream that had woken him in the middle of the previous night hard and aching, Lucas acknowledged that he found her more than lovely.

He found her bloody desirable.

"I must admit I am grateful to whichever of Mr. Wemby's friends sent you in search of him. Since making his acquaintance last Season, I have become an expert on hounds. 'Tis a pity I'm not at all interested in the hunt."

He knew Irisa did not mean to mock Wemby. She never indulged in that particular *tonnish* pastime. It was a mark of her sweet nature that she had indulged Wemby's passion for hounds in conversation. Lucas would be pleased to have her indulge *his* passions as well, only he was certain were she to do so, boredom would not come into it for either of them.

"I hesitate to admit this, but I made it up," he said, quelling his lascivious thoughts with strict control. "I'm sure Wemby will find a friend more interested in his discussion of hounds than yourself, but none actually awaits him."

The sound of her laughter affected his already overactive desire and he had no choice but to steer her toward the terrace before she, or someone else, noticed the growing state of his arousal. Not that he expected a lady of Irisa's sensibilities to let her gaze wander below his chin, but nevertheless, a gentleman's evening clothes left very little to the imagination.

As they stepped from the brightly lit ballroom into the shadowed world of the deserted terrace, Irisa's head snapped up and she stared at him, owl-eyed. "My lord?"

"It was getting a trifle warm in the ballroom. I thought you could use the air."

She nodded, sliding closer until their bodies almost touched. "Air. Yes, air would be very nice."

Her lips were parted as if about to say something, but she remained silent, gazing up at him.

She could have no idea just how delectable she looked at that very moment, how incredibly kissable. Her all-too-welcoming expression did nothing to aid his body in returning to less embarrassing proportions. He had to get himself under control, and quickly, or he was likely to shock the innocent right into a faint, and compromise her into the bargain.

He needed a diversion.

"I've decided to invest in your brother-in-law's most recent shipping venture." One of the things he enjoyed about Irisa was that she conversed intelligently on topics of import.

She did not pretend, as most ladies of the *ton* attempted to, that everything outside of the social sphere did not exist.

"Sh-shipping venture?"

"Yes. He told me you knew all about it. It's a sound investment."

Her hand dropped from his arm and she moved a small distance away. He breathed a silent sigh of relief. Without her nearness, he could regain control. His reaction to her innocent provocation astounded him, but he would dwell on how best to master it and himself later. He could not allow marriage, or the prospect of it, to undermine the self-discipline he had spent so many years perfecting.

"Yes. I know about it," she replied, her voice subdued all of a sudden. "I made a small outlay on the venture myself."

He would not have thought Langley the type of man to give his daughter any sort of financial independence. "Are you in the habit of investing in your brother-in-law's ventures?"

Her creamy white shoulders rose and fell in a ladylike shrug. "Actually, in the past my investments have been mostly in Thea's business dealings and the 'Change. Up until now, Drake's transactions have been too large or too risky for me to take part in them."

Lucas's ardor completely dissipated on a wave of shocked disbelief. "You invest in the 'Change?"

"Yes." She looked at him, her expression as innocent as always, except for a spark of something in her eyes he could not quite name.

If he did not know better, he would say it was defiance, but Irisa was too biddable a lady for such an emotion.

"How long has your father been allowing you to engage in such cork-brained behavior?"

She moved back another step, her posture becoming stiff.

"Papa has nothing to do with it," she replied in freezing accents, sounding for all the world as if she thought it was none of his business.

He strode two steps forward and grasped her shoulders, forcing her to face him. Even in his anger, his body registered the feel of her silken skin beneath his fingers. "Are you saying you have been investing your money without his permission?"

She lifted her head quickly, meeting his look squarely. "I spend my allowance as I see fit."

Her pin money? Either she had a very large allowance

or she made very small investments. "I'm surprised you had the resources available to take part in Drake's latest venture."

To Lucas's knowledge, Drake required a minimum outlay from even his smallest investors and it would require a great deal more than pin money. Perhaps Drake had made an exception for his sister-in-law's whim.

She bit her lip and shifted her gaze to a point beyond his shoulder, for all the world as if she intended some manner of subterfuge.

His grip on her arms tightened involuntarily. "Tell me."

Ignoring his command, she turned her attention to the point where his hands gripped the soft skin of her upper arms. He forced his fingers to relax somewhat, realizing his hold might very well be uncomfortable.

"If someone came out of the ballroom and found us here, they would assume we were in a passionate embrace," she said in a curiously wistful voice.

Bloody hell. She was right. He quickly released her arms, but did not step away. She would not distract him that easily.

"Explain to me how you were able to invest in the shipping expedition."

She adjusted first one, then the other, of the white evening gloves she wore and then smoothed her skirt as if they had been engaged in an invigorating country dance rather than standing almost completely still for the past several minutes.

Snapping open her fan, she used it as a shield for the expression on her face. "You overstep yourself, sir. I do not owe you an explanation of my actions or my finances. We are not connected in any way."

Her fan might protect her face from his scrutiny, but the icy remoteness in her voice left him in no doubt as to her frame of mind.

Without another word, she stepped around him and returned to the ballroom before he could assimilate either her surprising stubbornness or the cool challenge in her voice.

Didn't the chit realize she belonged to him? They were as good as engaged. Of course she owed him an explanation.

He followed her with every intention of telling her just that, but a return to the bright candle glow in the ballroom brought back his reason.

What was he doing?

For the second time that evening, he had very nearly lost control. This time he would have made a spectacle of himself in a way he had vowed long ago never to do. He was one Ashton who would not follow in his mother and younger brother's scandalous footsteps.

Watching Irisa join her current partner on the dance floor, he willed her to look at him. Their discussion was not finished. She refused to return his gaze, stubbornly keeping her head angled away from him and her focus entirely on the gentleman accompanying her.

He knew it was apurpose because she had once confided she did not care for Lord Yardley's company. Lucas had learned the other man had courted Irisa two Seasons ago, but her father had denied his suit. He was certain that she had agreed to dance with Yardley only because she knew to refuse would cause comment, and she was a lady in every sense. The perfect antithesis of his mother, in fact.

The image of Irisa defiantly snapping her fan open rose before his eyes.

His lovely, biddable, beautiful little paragon had sprouted a willful streak.

In high dudgeon, Irisa barely restrained herself from slamming the door upon entering her bedchamber. Only the knowledge that such behavior would be reported to her mother stopped her. Her maid, Pansy, had left only one small brace of candles burning in the room so the deep wine red of her bed curtains and coverlet looked almost black.

Which matched her mood all too well. Her irritation

with Lucas had not cooled one whit since the scene on the Bilkingtons' terrace. He had spent the next half hour watching her on the dance floor and then left without saying good-bye or asking for his customary second dance.

She would be dismayed by such an eventuality if she weren't so *bloody* angry. Even saying the swearword in her mind made her feel guilty. What would Mama say? Something censorious, no doubt.

In her current state, the thought made her feel rebellious, squashing the remnants of guilt.

She muttered, "Bloody, bloody, bloody man," in a fit of defiant pique as she tore off her gloves and tossed them onto the dressing table.

She could not believe that he had taken her to the seclusion of the terrace to grill her on how she spent her pin money. Did he have no sensibility to her person whatsoever?

She had practically thrown herself into his arms and he had ignored her every hint.

The door opened as she was kicking off her slippers with more emotion than aim so that one ended up on top of her coverlet and the other hit the heavy mauve drapes closed against the spring night before dropping to the floor with a small thud.

"Something 'appen to put you in a tizzy?" Pansy asked as she stepped forward to help Irisa prepare for bed.

"Not something. *Someone.*" Pansy and Irisa had been friends since the maid had joined her mother, a downstairs maid, in service at Langley Hall as a young girl.

Some would say that the young woman who still spoke with a rough Cockney accent was not appropriate material for a lady's maid, but Irisa could not imagine sharing her daily life so closely with anyone else. When she'd reached the age for a lady's maid to become necessary, she had asked her brother, Jared, to approach Mama on the subject of promoting Pansy to the position.

Ever mindful that Jared was Papa's one and only heir, Mama had acquiesced. One never knew when one's husband would go to his Great Reward and leave one at the mercy of a stepson. It did not do to antagonize the person who might one day hold the purse strings.

"You mean 'is lordship, The Saint?"

Irisa met Pansy's understanding gaze in the mirror and nodded. "He's so dense, I swear he could pass for one of the Elgin marbles."

For once Pansy's laughter did not bring an answering smile to Irisa's lips. "The dolt took me out onto the Bilkingtons' terrace and quizzed me on my investments."

"And I suppose you were expecting 'im to do som'thin' altogether different on the terrace, milady?" Pansy finished removing Irisa's gown and corset.

She hung the dress up while Irisa pulled a nightrail over her still elegantly coiffed hair.

Blushing from Pansy's teasing comment, she replied with great honesty and not a little disgruntlement. "Yes."

The fact was, she usually enjoyed Lucas's willingness to discuss practical matters. It was one of the reasons she was so drawn to him. Rather than treating her as an empty-headed widgeon like so many gentlemen of the *ton,* he conversed with her as an equal.

Only tonight she had wanted him to treat her like a woman. She was beginning to feel almost desperate for it, in fact. Her liking for him had deepened to something far more substantial than mere friendship and she needed him to reciprocate those feelings in some measure. That need stirred up a familiar ache; she had lived with the pain of her parents' indifference since childhood.

The maid took the pins from Irisa's hair, allowing the curling gold strands to fall in one long mass before she separated it into three parts and began braiding it. "He's a real gentleman, 'e is. I don't think 'e 'as the makin's of one of them romantic 'eroes you like to read about, Lady Irisa."

Irisa glumly wondered if Pansy was right. Had she been fooling herself to believe Lucas had a core of manly passion he kept well hidden? Remembering the look of real anger in his eyes when she had refused to answer his question, she rather thought not. No, the passion was there, but could she tap into it? Or at any rate, a more tender passion than anger.

"He's supposed to call on 'is lordship tomorrow, you know."

Irisa's head came up so fast that she pulled the lengthening braid from Pansy's fingers. Luckily her maid was used to her fits and starts and she got hold of the braid before the strands separated and she had to start all over.

"When did you hear this?"

"The second footman 'eard 'is lordship's man talkin' to the butler. The servants is all wonderin' if there's to be a match at last."

For once, she ignored the fact that Pansy had been listening to gossip. At least it had been about something harmless.

Regardless, Irisa grumbled, "You talk as if I had one foot in the grave."

A gentleman need not even begin looking for a wife before the ripe age of five and twenty, but a woman was considered quite on the shelf if she reached twenty without attaining the exalted state of matrimony. It was ludicrous.

"You're nearing twenty-one, m'lady. Most ladies is married and with a couple of children by that age and that's the truth." Pansy tied off Irisa's braid and stepped back after making that unwelcome, if accurate, pronouncement.

"Well, I'm not one of them."

"That's what's got us all so worried, m'lady."

"I do not need you worrying about me, nor do I appreciate being the subject of gossip."

Pansy didn't even blush at the reminder and Irisa dismissed her so she could find her bed.

Still too agitated to seek similar solace herself, she paced her room.

If she had not blackmailed her parents, she would be just like all those other ladies Pansy had mentioned. She had used the truth of her birth to force them into giving her some say over her future, which raised a disturbing issue she could no longer ignore. Not after discovering that Lucas planned to call on her father the next day.

If he asked her to marry him, she would have to tell him the truth about her birth. It was the only honorable thing to do. She did not expect her parents to see it that way. They would hide the scandal from their Maker if they could. The appearance of propriety was all that mattered to Mama and Papa, and on the surface, she looked like any other well-bred young lady of the *ton.*

If there was going to be a revealing, it would be up to her to orchestrate it. The prospect was not a pleasant one.

Stopping in the middle of her silent room, she hugged herself tightly and struggled not to let deeply ingrained fears get the better of her.

She dreaded revealing her secret to Lucas as much as she had dreaded the final emotional break with her parents four years ago. She had not intended the blackmail to do that, but the result had been inevitable. Mama had never forgiven her for refusing a duke, and Papa had never forgiven her for defying him. If she did not accept an offer this Season, life at Langley Hall would become unbearable.

Is that why she had allowed her heart to become engaged with Lucas despite her better judgment and his reputation as a paragon? Was her fear of returning to Langley Hall in disgrace the reason she tried to see passion in a man whose self-control was absolute? Her eyes burned as she accepted that her doubts and hopes were most likely of little consequence.

Once she told Lucas the truth, he would certainly sever their relationship.

Lucas owned twice the lands her father did and had a large personal fortune. A gentleman of his station, particularly one who took such care with his reputation, would certainly balk at marriage to a lady who could not lay legitimate claim to the title.

Saint Ashton would leave her life as quickly and irrevocably as he had entered it, and she very much feared he would break her heart in the process.

Two

LUCAS SLOWLY PULLED THE THREAD THAT raised the miniature mast and rigging on the ship within the bottle. A deep sense of accomplishment filled him as he surveyed the perfect imitation of a Brigantine vessel now enclosed in glass. Taking the last step in the months-long process, he tied off the string and corked the bottle. He had not planned to finish the ship tonight, but had been restless after returning to his town house from the Bilkington ball several hours ago.

Working on the model had relaxed him, but it had not taken his mind off the maddening Lady Irisa. His desire for her was growing too strong to deny. They needed to marry, or he was going to do something he would regret. Like seducing her on a balcony.

He could not let that happen.

The last of his line, he was fully cognizant of his responsibility to the earldom to beget heirs.

Although his honor demanded he do his duty to the line, he had no intention of tying himself to an unsuitable woman as his father had done. Lucas could still remember the blazing rows between his very beautiful, very young mother and his elder, duty-driven father. The arguments had ended when he was ten years old with his father's death.

Without her more conservative husband around to keep her under control, his mother had gone wild. She threw lavish parties, kept liaisons in such a public manner that even her two young sons were aware of them, and spent a great deal of her time in London. Both Lucas and his younger brother, James, had been forced to endure cruel and cutting remarks from their peers when they went away to school. His mother's excesses were legendary and favorite fodder for gossip among the *beau monde* and its children.

James had largely ignored both his mother's actions and the gossip they elicited. In fact, much to Lucas's private grief, his brother had shown all the symptoms of following in her footsteps prior to his untimely death at the age of one and twenty.

Lucas, on the other hand, had fought his way through school, defending the indefensible and his mother's nonexistent honor. By the time she had died eight years ago, Lucas's intolerance on the subject had become its own legend. It was rumored that he had fought no fewer than two duels over the matter. He knew the rumors were false. There had been three duels and he had won them all.

He would never again willingly link his life to a woman who required that kind of defense. He would marry a woman whose behavior was so exemplary there would be no cause for duels—a woman like Lady Irisa.

A patterncard of appropriate behavior, she was also an enticing woman who stirred his passions in a very satisfying way. She was perfect as his potential wife, even if she had a heretofore-unknown tendency toward stubbornness.

LANGLEY'S EYES MIRRORED DEEP SATISFACTION AS Lucas made the reason for his call known.

Lucas was unsurprised at Irisa's father's reaction to his offer. The man had made no secret of his desire to see his daughter wed. The only mystery was why he had allowed her to remain unmarried so long. The earl did not seem to be the sort of man to pay close attention to his daughter's sensibilities in the matter.

Yet, if rumors could be believed—and his years as a spy for the Crown had taught him they often could—her father had rejected seven offers for Irisa's hand in the last four years. One from a duke and two more from peers of the realm.

Langley poured two glasses of port. "I've spoken with Irisa and she is not averse to your suit."

There was something in the older man's voice Lucas could not quite decipher, a grim relief, almost bitterness.

"I did not expect her to be." She had never shown any indication she would find his suit unfavorable.

Handing one of the heavy leaded crystal glasses to Lucas, Langley lifted his own slightly in a toast before settling more comfortably in his chair. "We'll have our solicitors draw up the marriage settlements then."

"I've already spoken to my man and he suggested getting together the first part of next week to negotiate the terms."

"That will be acceptable. Have him contact my solicitor to set up the appointment." Langley drew himself more firmly erect in his chair. "There is one other matter we need to discuss before I have Irisa called."

Lucas idly allowed his gaze to drift around Langley's darkly paneled library and wondered if he was about to hear a lecture on taking care of Irisa. Lucas had every intention of doing so and prepared himself to reassure the older man on that score.

"I'm sure you are aware that Irisa is not my only child."

"I know you have a son and another daughter, yes."

From the information he had gathered, neither child had a close relationship with their father. Langley's heir, Viscount Ravenswood, spent very little time in London and it was rumored even less time at Langley Hall. He was not a social man, and according to tittle-tattle, there was a very good reason. Rumor also had it that Irisa had played some role in the injury that had left her brother's face disfigured when he was a young man.

Even with his skills in ferreting out information, Lucas had been unable to substantiate this particular rumor or the details of Ravenswood's injury. One day, he would ask Irisa about it, but for now their imminent marriage was of much greater import.

"They are both the product of my first marriage."

He had heard that. "Yes."

Langley nodded, evidently unsurprised Lucas would have investigated the subject. "It pains me to discuss the circumstances of my first marriage, but I'm sure that Irisa would feel the need to make some details known to you before accepting your offer. She would not want you misled."

For some reason, what should have been a compliment on Langley's part came out sounding more like an accusation.

"I'm very pleased with Lady Irisa's forthright character. It is one of the chief reasons I felt we should suit."

"Just so. However, I wish to save her the embarrassment of discussing matters that are best left unremarked upon by a lady, matters regarding my older daughter," Langley replied.

Lucas believed he knew what Langley was so worried about. Irisa's sister was married to Pierson Drake, the man with whom Lucas had just invested a great deal of capital. He was also the natural son of a duke's daughter. Lucas found no offense in the other man's birth, but imagined that Langley was not so sanguine about the matter.

He had noticed Irisa's father had a tendency toward prudery and intractability. He wondered how Lady Thea's marriage had come about in the first place. In any case, Drake's illegitimacy would have no impact on Lucas's proposal of marriage toward the man's sister-in-law.

Ingrained habit prompted Lucas to remain silent and hear what Langley planned to say. Perhaps there was more to this situation than the information he had already obtained.

"My marriage to Jared and Thea's mother was not a happy one," Langley said with what sounded like genuine regret. "I am not proud to admit that the problems were largely of my own making. I was young and foolish, allowing jealousy to cloud my thinking regarding my wife's actions."

Lucas did not see what this had to do with Irisa, but kept his silence.

"I hurt Anna, and when she had our children, she kept the birth of our daughter a secret from me. They were twins, you see?"

Nodding his head, Lucas encouraged Langley to continue.

"In a fit of pique, Anna fled England with my daughter. When she did not return to me and her son, I assumed she had died." Langley stopped speaking, his gaze going unfocused for a moment, then he seemed to collect himself.

"Indeed, she had. What I did not know is that she had left behind our daughter to be raised by friends in the West Indies. Thea was brought up in an entirely different culture than our own, although the couple who raised her were members of the *ton.* That is the only excuse I have for the fact that she married a man like Pierson Drake."

"I've just invested in your son-in-law's latest shipping venture. He's a brilliant man," Lucas inserted, intent on preventing an outright insult toward a man he now considered to be his friend.

Langley's mouth twisted, but his voice was neutral when he continued speaking. "Yes. Well . . . Be that as it may, Thea was already married by the time she made herself known to me. I have accepted her husband because I have no choice, but I would hate to see their relationship, or the fact that her sister is quite the *original,* to adversely affect Irisa's future."

Lucas thought Langley's concern a trifle melodramatic. Neither Drake's past nor Thea's originality was a great secret to the *ton.* He had long been aware of these facts and had already decided to ask for Irisa's hand.

"I am interested in marriage to Irisa. I would not presume to hold her responsible for the actions of her family."

No more than he had felt responsible for his mother or

brother's choices. For rectifying their mistakes where at all possible, yes, but he had staunchly refused to be tarred with the same brush.

Langley's face showed relief. "That's fine then. I'll have my daughter called down immediately."

ALTHOUGH SHE HAD BEEN EXPECTING THE WORDS, SHE still sat in mute shock after Lucas made his very correct proposal. She found the prospect of sharing what must be shared in the face of his passionless proposal overwhelmingly daunting. He had not spoken a word of affection, had not even taken her hand.

The weak English sun beat into the garden, doing little to warm Irisa as she sat on the stone bench beside Lucas. He had not gone down on one knee, but then she'd always thought that was a rather silly tradition. She could hardly blame Lucas for not wanting to keep it.

Irisa took a deep breath and tried desperately to focus her thoughts.

Lucas raised his brow at her lack of response. "Surely this has not come as a complete surprise to you."

She shook her head. That at least was true. "Um, no."

His smile warmed her insides, dispelling some of the chill seeping into her from the cold stone of the bench . . . or was it from the knowledge of what must be said?

She twisted her hands together in her lap. "There's something I must tell you before I can answer your question. I . . . I want you to know that if it changes your desire to marry me, I will understand."

With startling speed, he reached out and pried her hands apart, taking them in his own.

Rubbing the backs of her knuckles with his thumbs, he said, "Your father already spoke to me on the subject and I assure you, I have no intention of withdrawing my offer."

Irisa was thinking she would not mind if he caressed her in such a fashion every day for the rest of their lives. There was something so soothing and wonderfully intimate about the way he held her hands. Even through two layers of gloves, she could feel the heat of his skin warming her own.

That was why it took her several seconds to assimilate what he had said. *Her father had already told him?* Surely not. Papa would never admit to her illegitimacy. He took such pains, even among the family, to pretend the problem did not exist.

"Papa told you about the first Countess of Langley?"

"Yes."

"He told you about her death? That she did not die when he thought she did?"

Again Lucas confirmed her words. "Yes."

"But . . ." She could not believe it. She had not expected Papa to be so forthright, nor could she believe that Lucas did not intend to withdraw his offer. "You do not mind? The circumstances of my—"

Lucas interrupted her. "You do not need to speak of it. I agree with your father that it is not a matter for a gentle lady to discuss."

Even if the gentlewoman doing the discussing was the one most affected? Somehow, Lucas's attitude on the subject did not surprise her. However, she was shocked to her very toes that he could so easily dismiss the illegitimacy of the woman he wished to marry.

He gripped her hand more tightly, the intensity that so entranced her radiating from his very being. "I do not hold you accountable for the actions of your family, my dear. You are responsible for yourself alone."

Although Lucas had extended honest respect and friendship toward Thea's husband, Irisa had never dreamed he might be so understanding in regard to his future wife. Perhaps such matters were not as important to The Saint as she had led herself to believe.

She wanted to weep, she was so relieved. For even if Lucas was less straightlaced than she had assumed, surely he cared for her on a personal level. He must, to completely dismiss as unimportant the circumstances surrounding her birth. The outward evidence of his affection would undoubtedly come later, when he was certain of her.

She allowed a brilliant smile to light up her face. "I am honored to accept your proposal of marriage, Lucas."

His perceptive blue eyes widened at the familiar use of his name, but he did not rebuke her.

He smiled instead. "I'm glad, Irisa. Very glad."

He bent his head. He was going to kiss her. The knowledge bubbled through her like champagne. She closed her eyes, tilting her head slightly, and she felt the barest brush against her temple. Lucas released her hands and stood.

Her eyes flew open.

He held his hand out to her. "Shall we go inside and share our happy news with your parents?"

LUCAS ARRIVED EARLY THE NEXT DAY FOR HIS appointment to take Irisa for a drive in the park. Anticipation at the prospect of seeing her simmered through him. She belonged to him now.

As of tomorrow morning when the official announcement would be printed in the papers, the entire Polite World would know it as well. Pulling his phaeton to a stop in front of the Langley town house, he was grateful for the time it took a footman to come forward to hold the horses. If the mere thought of seeing his fiancée was going to affect him in this manner, then they had better plan for a short engagement. Six weeks should be long enough to ensure no one would label it a runaway match.

In a characteristic fashion, Irisa did not make him wait upon his arrival. She entered her mother's rather pretentious drawing room only minutes after he had been shown in, her heart-shaped face wearing an expression of charming welcome.

She curtsied, the yellow-and-white-striped silk of her gown brushing the floor while the ostrich feathers on her wide-brimmed hat waved at him. "Good afternoon, Lucas."

He bowed, keeping his gaze fixed firmly on her delectable person. "Good afternoon. Are you ready for our drive?"

She certainly looked it. The demurely cut neckline of her gown exposed a tantalizingly small amount of creamy white skin, but it was nevertheless enough to quicken his heart rate, particularly when taken in combination with the way the silk clung to the generous womanly curve of her bosom.

The short puffy sleeves both exposed and accentuated her arms until she pulled her shawl around her, smiling. "Yes, I'm ready."

They said good-bye to Lady Langley, and Lucas led Irisa outside to his waiting carriage. He helped her into the phaeton, glad he had not brought along a tiger today. There were several things he wished to discuss with his fiancée and he did not want a servant listening in. Once seated, he set the horses in motion, carefully executing the phaeton's entrance into the crowded London street traffic.

"You have a very good hand on the reins, Lucas."

"Thank you. I learned rather young."

"Do you think you would be willing to teach me?"

One of his mother's many paramours had taught her to drive within months of his father's death. His father had always refused to do so, assuming correctly that the ability would be one more way for his mother to find trouble. Lucas's mouth set at the memory of her driving exploits, and all of the carefully considered discussions he planned to have with Irisa flew out of his head.

"You want to learn to drive?"

"You needn't make it sound like I'm proposing I join the troupe at Astley's Amphitheatre. Driving is a perfectly acceptable pastime for a lady. Why, even Lady Jersey knows how to handle the ribbons."

But she didn't do it often. Perhaps Irisa didn't wish to either. He already knew she was curious. Maybe she only wished to learn for the sake of knowing how. There was no reason to believe her motivations were anything like his mother's, but then he did not see a reason to tempt her either.

"You have no need to learn to drive, m'dear. You will always have a carriage and coachman at your disposal."

Irisa popped open her parasol and set it on her shoulder. "It's not a matter of necessity. I think I should enjoy it."

"I do not know if I will have the time to teach you," he said repressively.

"Oh." The one word came out with a wealth of disappointment. "I had hoped now we are engaged, I would be seeing more of you."

He allowed himself a small smile when he realized the true source of her disappointment. "As to that, of course we will. It will now be unremarkable for you to be seen often in my company."

She brightened at that. "I'm glad."

She wanted to be with him. The knowledge further reinforced his belief that she would make a sound wife. He had no desire for a typical society marriage where he and his wife led two completely different lives under the same roof.

He decided to introduce the first topic he wished to discuss before she made another outrageous comment and sidetracked him once again. "I would like to set our wedding date six weeks hence."

He felt the sudden tension that gripped her. "So soon, my lord?"

He liked it better when she called him Lucas. "Do you have a reason for wishing to postpone it?"

"Well, no, not precisely. I just thought we could get to know each other better before marrying."

"We will have a lifetime to learn all we could wish about one another."

"Yes. Of course." Her free hand twisted in the yellow-and-white silk of her skirt. "But don't you think six weeks is rather rushing it?"

He considered that for several moments, but discarded the idea. "It's a perfectly respectable length of time for an engagement. It is not as if you had been compromised and there will be speculation about a runaway match."

"No. It's not as if I'd been compromised."

If he did not know better, he would think she sounded disgruntled by that fact. "It's settled then?"

"We'll have to discuss it with my parents. My mother may require more time to plan the wedding." She said the last sentence with unmistakable hope.

He didn't want to crush her spirits, but he had no doubt Lady Langley would be more than willing to set the date in a matter of weeks. Lucas had the definite impression that both of Irisa's parents were overeager to see her wed.

"Was there anything else you wished to discuss, Lucas?"

Another good sign. She could already anticipate his thoughts. "Yes, as a matter of fact there was. Your investment practices. You refused to answer my questions at the Bilkington ball because we had no *connection*. That is no longer true, and as your betrothed, I must insist on complete disclosure."

"You want to discuss my investments?"

Lucas could not identify the strange undercurrent in her voice. He turned to look at her and he could almost swear her eyes were filled with outrage. His jaw set. She would have to get used to his interest in her affairs. He would not allow his wife to run amok.

"Yes, Irisa. I will not assume the disinterested role your father has seen fit to take in your financial affairs and activities."

She gasped. "You would try to dictate how I spend my money?"

Why did she sound so shocked? "It would be most unnatural if I did not take an interest in how you did so."

"Are you saying that you expect me to account for every farthing I spend?"

"Do not be ridiculous. How you spend your pin money is of little import to me." He paused. "Unless you are spending it on such foolish things as investment in the 'Change."

"Are you saying you consider a new hair ribbon a more intelligent use of my money than for me to purchase stock on the Exchange?" Her voice came out low and strained.

"I consider a new hair ribbon a more *appropriate* use of your pin money, yes. You may leave the investments to me. I promise you I will take very good care of your future and that of our children."

"Thea does not leave that side of things completely to Drake and he does not appear emasculated by the circumstance."

Shock warred with sheer outrage at her audacious comment. "My concern for you is not an indicator that I fear for my masculine role in our marriage."

"You are saying this heavy-handed behavior is motivated by concern for me?" she asked.

"Yes," he ground out between his teeth.

Suddenly she seemed to relax. "I don't want to give up investments, Lucas. I like the challenge and I like the time I spend with my sister planning them." She laid her gloved hand on his forearm. "When I met Thea, we had little in common. She had been raised on a small island around people quite different from us. She has very independent ideas, you know."

An original, as her father had said. "Yes. I know."

"I wanted to get to know her better," Irisa continued softly. "I was delighted to discover I had a sister and she truly seemed happy to know me."

The underlying disbelief in her voice confused him.

"She didn't want to discuss fashion, or any of the other things my mother had taught me to discuss with other ladies of the *ton*. Thea allowed me to tell her about the books I read and my ideas on estate management."

Irisa had ideas on estate management?

"And I listened with rapt fascination when she talked about business. She's very intelligent and patient as well. Because some of the concepts were so abstract to me that I had trouble understanding them, she came up with the idea of me investing my pin money and keeping track of the investments myself. It was very illuminating. I showed an aptitude for it and Thea was very pleased with me."

There was that tone in her voice again, almost as if her sister's approval were more than she could grasp. "So, you continued with the experiment."

"Yes, and my investment capital continued to grow."

When she named the amount she had started off with and what she had amassed since then, he could not help but be impressed. "So you see, it's really nothing for you to be worried about. I won't invest our household accounts and I promise not to go dressed in rags in order to cover my little hobby."

"This aspect of your relationship with your sister is important to you?"

"Yes. Very." She squeezed his forearm, which did very little to reassure him and a great deal to excite him. "Lucas, I can't bear the thought of a marriage in which you would expect me to account for every farthing or idea in my head. Surely you understand that. Think how you would hate it if I questioned your every decision and expenditure."

Didn't she realize that men and women were different? Of course he would not tolerate her interference in his business management. The idea was so ludicrous, he refused to respond to it.

However, he could be understanding when the need arose. "You may continue making investments with your sister after we are married so long as you limit yourself to the capital you have already secured."

Irisa did not think it would be wise to inform Lucas that she had no intention of giving up her investments regardless of what he said. She bit her lip to keep from saying something scathing in that regard. After all, she could sense that Lucas was trying to understand.

She had known when she agreed to marry him that he was somewhat stuffy, but she did not consider him rigid.

Not like Papa. It would be her job as his wife to help Lucas soften toward new concepts.

She removed her hand from his forearm. "Thank you, Lucas. That is very generous of you."

If he heard the sarcasm in her voice, he gave no sign. But then, the man was as dense as the evening fog sometimes.

She had been so sure that he wanted to discuss his finer feelings with her this afternoon. She had noted the lack of a tiger in the back of the phaeton. Such an occurrence could only mean that Lucas had something private he wished to share with her. A woman could be forgiven for believing that the day after she agreed to marry a gentleman, such a discussion would revolve around emotions, not money.

It had all started so well, too, with Lucas wanting to set the wedding date quickly. Although the prospect of a speedy marriage made her nervous, his eagerness could be taken as a very good sign, she staunchly reminded herself. Just because he had not yet kissed her properly, there was no reason to believe he did not return the attraction she felt.

Perhaps, like one of the romantic heroes in the novels she read, he wanted to wait until after their marriage because he feared he would overwhelm her with his passions if he kissed her before. The thought held a certain romantic flair, but it did nothing to lessen her frustrated feelings.

She wanted to be kissed by Lucas, to experience the transcendent bliss the poets wrote about, and if it took every bit of the keen intelligence Thea insisted she possessed, Irisa was going to make it happen.

Three

However, although they spent a great deal more time together over the next few days, Lucas showed no inclination to pursue a physical bond with Irisa. He had kissed her lightly once, but his withdrawal had been immediate and she still wasn't sure she had felt his lips against hers.

While their time together might not be doing anything to spark his ardor for her, it was having a disastrous effect on her emotions. She grew more and more convinced that she felt far more for him than mere liking and physical desire, while she became simultaneously certain that his feelings for her were limited as to the first and sadly lacking in the second.

She was contemplating that rather depressing truth when Lucas arrived to claim his second dance of the evening, a waltz.

She put her hand on his proffered arm, but hesitated to join the other dancers in the center of the ballroom.

He looked down at her questioningly.

"I would rather take a stroll around the garden if you don't mind. It's very warm in here." She had no desire to circle the room in his arms while all sorts of excitations affected her person and he remained as cool and calm as ever.

He considered her request, his expression not pleased at the prospect. No doubt he was trying to determine whether or not it would be entirely correct to take a walk in the garden with his fiancée.

"Are you sure you would not rather dance?"

"I am certain."

Disappointment flickered in his eyes and she almost changed her mind, but he had already started walking.

He led her out through one of the many sets of double doors along the perimeter of the room.

The cooler air outside did feel good and she breathed deeply, enjoying the freedom away from Society's ever-watchful eye. She spent so much time behaving correctly that sometimes she felt more like a life-size marionette than a woman of flesh and blood. Perhaps that was how Lucas saw her.

Bothered by her thoughts, she stepped away from him.

"Are you feeling quite the thing, m'dear?" His voice was tinged with genuine concern. "Perhaps you should ask your mother to take you home."

"That's not necessary." Not to mention impractical. Her mother giving up on an entertainment because Irisa felt slightly under the weather was as likely as Prinny taking on a monastic existence. "I'm simply a bit warm. Besides, it's pleasant to be private for a moment, don't you think?"

"Being in a dark garden is no guarantee of privacy."

"It's an improvement over a ballroom full of the *beau monde,* you must admit."

"There are times when a room full of people affords greater privacy than a secluded garden."

They were obviously considering different types of privacy. She could not imagine kissing him in a crowded ballroom, but the prospect of doing so in the dark garden made her pulse race. However, his words intrigued her. "What times?"

"It is easier to make certain a private conversation is not overheard in a room filled with people, than in a garden filled with shadows and places for listeners to hide."

"Who would want to hide in the shadows?"

"Any number of people. Thieves intent on observing the movements within a household, a couple hoping to have a tryst, intelligence agents looking for information."

"I suppose you know all about it?"

"In fact, I do."

"You've had a garden tryst?" The possibility made her chest squeeze tight with pain. He had dismissed his sense of correctness for another woman, but had no desire to do so for her.

"No." He sounded scandalized by the idea.

"Well, you haven't been a thief," she blurted.

"No, but I have been a spy."

"You cannot be serious." Her Lucas?

"I'm afraid so."

"But you're the heir to the title. You take your responsibilities so very seriously."

"Which is precisely why I worked as an intelligence agent during the war. I had a responsibility to my country to do what I could. Going into battle was not a possibility, but gathering information was."

"Surely it was just as dangerous."

"At times, but there are times when being a nobleman carries more risk than being a commoner. Some risks simply cannot be avoided."

In one respect his admission shocked her, but in another it made sense of some character traits that did not seem at all in keeping with a man who had spent his entire adult life seeing to the management of his estates and little else. He had an aura about him that was both dangerous and intense at times. It drew her like a moth to flame, though she wished it did not.

"Were you ever hurt?"

He shrugged, the movement discernable only because he stood with his back to the house and was silhouetted in the darkness against the lights from the ballroom. "On occasion that sort of thing cannot be avoided."

"I suppose not."

"I learned much during that time. I discovered that the appearance of innocence is nothing compared to the reality, that people whom you believe to be your friends can in fact be enemies."

"That must have been hard."

"It was worth it to serve my country's needs."

He said the words so dispassionately, but how many noblemen had left the war effort to others? How many had refused to help in any way? Her father had, just as he had ignored the plight of returning soldiers, some wounded, all in need of a way to make another life. She knew Lucas had responded to that need as well. Her maid had told her that most of the male servants in Lucas's employ were former soldiers.

After scolding her maid for gossiping again, she had hugged the knowledge of Lucas's goodness to her heart. He was a true gentleman among his peers.

"How could you tell friend from foe?"

"I learned to rely on my instincts."

"Were they ever wrong?"

"Rarely."

She hoped hers were as infallible, because it had been her womanly instincts that had dictated she accept his proposal of marriage. She could only pray they had not led her astray.

IRISA CONFIDENTLY TOOK THE REINS FROM HER SISTER'S hands and, remembering Thea's instructions, concentrated on guiding the carriage through Hyde Park. Traffic was light because it was well before the hour when the *beau monde* came out en masse to see and be seen.

"You're doing very well, Irisa. You have a natural ability with the ribbons," Thea praised her.

Irisa smiled, a warm glow invading her heart. Her sister was so different from the rest of the family. With Mama and Papa, she had always felt unworthy. Thea never made her feel that way. She acted as if she was truly glad to have a half sister.

To be fair, Irisa knew Jared was fond of her as well, but she would never forget that it was because of her that he had withdrawn from society. His face carried permanent marks that testified to both his bravery and *her* formerly impetuous nature. Society's cruel gossip had ensured he would never willingly embrace a life amidst the *ton* again.

Jared had never been lighthearted, but after he rescued her and sustained the wounds that left lasting scars in the process, he had grown almost forbidding—she did not think he needed anyone. Not like she did. She had always craved a closeness her family had been loath to provide . . . until Thea.

Spending time with the Drakes and their two small children was the highlight of Irisa's time in London. Being an aunt had turned out to be one of the most satisfying experiences of her life. Her niece and nephew loved her without reservation and accepted her love in the same manner.

"Driving is every bit as enjoyable as I had hoped it would be," Irisa said as she neatly maneuvered the carriage around an obstruction on the path.

"You should have asked me to teach you sooner," Thea chided her.

"Papa would have thrown a fit. He has such old-fashioned ideas about ladies. Besides, the idea that I wanted to learn did not truly form until recently." She bit her lip and concentrated on avoiding a rather wide landau coming from the other direction. "I had hoped that Lucas would teach me, but he informed me he did not have the time."

Thea chuckled. "I find that hard to believe, sister mine. The man is engaged to you."

Irisa smiled at the endearment, but shook her head. "I certainly don't feel engaged."

"What do you mean?"

Thankful for the distraction of handling the reins so she did not have to look at her sister when she spoke, she admitted in a rush, "Lucas has never really kissed me."

She felt Thea's steady stare. "What do you mean *really* kissed you?"

"You know, like a man does with a woman he desires. Like Drake kisses you when he thinks no one is looking."

Thea coughed. "I see. And I assume you want Lord Ashton to kiss you this way?"

Irisa nodded her head vehemently. "Very much."

The carriage jolted and she realized she had allowed her attention to wander.

Thea reached over and took the reins. "I think I had better drive while we have this conversation."

Relieved at the lack of censure in her sister's voice, Irisa did not protest losing the ribbons.

"I'm terribly fond of Lucas, but I'm not sure what he feels for me." In truth, she was almost certain she loved the man and that scared her witless. Love made one vulnerable, and she'd spent too much of her life in that condition already.

"Papa told him about the unique circumstances surrounding my birth and he did not withdraw the offer, so I assumed he had *some* tender feelings, but you would never know that by the way he has treated me these past two weeks."

"Langley told Lord Ashton about that?" Thea sounded stunned.

"Yes. I know it is a shock. I did not expect it. I had thought I would have to do the deed, but apparently Papa realized my intent and took matters into his own hand."

"That's astonishing."

Irisa agreed, but she did not want to discuss their father's aberrant behavior. She was much more concerned with Lucas's lack of interest in the more intimate side of courtship.

"I admit that I have no personal experience in these matters, but I've read several novels. It seems to me that if

Lucas did hold me in affection, he would have given some indication by now of his attraction to me."

Thea appeared to mull that over. "Life is not like a novel, you know."

She appreciated her sister's practical approach to the matter. If she had attempted to have such a discussion with Mama, the older woman would have collapsed in a fit of vapors.

She opened her parasol and twirled it in a most unladylike fashion. "Are you saying that I'm wide of the mark in assuming Lucas should express some physical desire for me before the wedding?"

"Well, he is a very correct gentleman. I think you would be safe in assuming he intends to rein in his passions until after your marriage."

"Did Drake wait until after your marriage before expressing his desire for your person?"

For the first time she could ever remember, Thea blushed. "Not precisely."

Irisa nodded more in resignation than agreement. "That is what I thought."

Surely it was not so unreasonable for her to expect some small sign of Lucas's attraction before they were wed.

IRISA'S NERVE ALMOST GAVE OUT WHEN THE FOOTMAN reached for her cloak upon arrival at her sister's town house a week later. She had a desperate urge to snatch at the fabric and stay safely covered. The plan that had seemed so perfect in the privacy of her bedroom now required every bit of courage she possessed.

Even with only her mirror and Pansy for company, her neckline had made her feel exposed, but she had believed the eventual outcome would outweigh her minor discomfort. Under the bright illumination of Thea's new gaslights, Irisa's discomfort was anything but minor. She felt the heat of a blush spreading upward from her very exposed bosom.

Flipping open her fan, she waved energetically, hoping to rid herself of the hot color before Lucas noticed. Any moment now he would turn to escort her to Thea's drawing room. They were to eat dinner with the Drakes before attending a ball elsewhere. What would Lucas do when he noticed the altered neckline and close fit of the iridescent gown?

The shimmering fabric clung to her every feminine curve, though she hadn't gone so far as to dampen the muslin of her underskirts. She did not have the boldness required for such a move, even to tempt Lucas to passion.

And she had waited to put this particular plan into action until she was certain not to spend the evening under her mama's ever-watchful eye. Since Lady Langley did not socialize with the Drakes, tonight had seemed the perfect opportunity.

Biting her lip, she wondered if perhaps she should have listened to Pansy. Her maid had maintained that rather than being overcome with passion at the sight of her in such alluring clothing, his lordship was more likely to think she'd lost her mind and take her straight home.

She sincerely hoped Pansy was wrong. Irisa could no longer wait placidly by for Lucas to notice her womanly allure. They had been engaged for three weeks and he had yet to kiss her with anything more than brotherly affection. Although there had been one instance the previous week at the Hadley soirée when she had been certain Lucas was feeling more than mild interest.

Complaining that the room was too hot and she felt light-headed, she had convinced him to once again take her for a walk in the garden. This time she had been prepared to act to ensure they did more than talk, as fascinating as she found conversation with him to be.

Unlike the week before, this garden had been lit with attractively hung lamps. She had planned to use the light to her advantage and imitate the heroine in the novel she was currently reading. Faking a stumble, she had managed to plaster herself against Lucas. Then, she had parted her lips invitingly, just like the heroine in her book, licking the top one very slowly.

Lucas's eyes had turned so dark, the blue was the color of the night sky. He'd bent his head and she was sure he was about to kiss her when some silly idiot giggled nearby. Lucas had jumped back from Irisa so quickly she'd almost lost her balance for real. He insisted on taking her home immediately, citing his concern for her light-headedness as the cause.

As frustrating as the whole failed enterprise had been, it had given her hope and the impetus to try this new scheme. Lucas had desired her, she was sure of it. Well, almost sure anyway. Thus the plan.

She needed to *know* that Lucas wanted her.

While she was comfortable discussing any number of subjects with him, personal matters were another thing altogether. Even in the novels she read, the ladies were not so bold as to discuss passion with the men they loved. And she'd spent far too many years behaving with perfect decorum to break the habits of a lifetime to ask him to kiss her . . . or even to ask if he wanted to.

He was courteous, caring of her welfare almost to a fault, but he had not shown that he wanted her, and how could she marry him if he did not? The prospect of a typical society marriage in which the husband satisfied his passions with a series of discreet liaisons repulsed her.

Lucas turned his body toward her, offering her his arm. He did not flicker an eyelid at her altered gown. Why should he? He had not so much as glanced at her, and that was the problem. She would not spend the rest of her life being ignored in this most basic sense by her husband. She was beginning to fear that Lucas had a very prudish view of the relationship between a husband and his wife.

When Lucas led Irisa into the drawing room, Thea came forward to greet them. "You two are right on time." She smiled at Lucas. "It's nice to see you again, Lord Ashton."

As she turned to her sister, Thea's smile froze in place and her eyes widened.

However, being Thea, she merely said, "Hello, Irisa," and gave her younger sister a hug.

Drake motioned to Lucas, and her fiancé excused himself without looking her way. Irisa frowned at his retreating back. How was she to entice him if he took no notice of her at all?

"I take it this very daring evening gown has something to do with the concerns you voiced to me during your driving lesson last week?"

Irisa turned her attention from Lucas's retreating back at her sister's words. She couldn't help the huge sigh that escaped her, or the irresistible urge to tug at her bodice. Had the neckline been quite so close to her nipples at home?

"Is it awful?" she asked her sister, truly worried now.

Thea's smile was both devilish and reassuring. "It is not awful, but it is not in your regular style either. I have noticed that many ladies of the *ton* wear a similar neckline once they marry."

Although she knew the words were meant to reassure, Irisa felt anything but. After all, she was not married yet.

Sighing again, she muttered, "Once Mama sees this gown, she's going to throw a terrible fit, and it will all have been wasted because Lucas appears determined to ignore me this evening. Do you know he has not once even glanced at me since we arrived?"

Thea laughed, not one of those ladylike tinkles one heard among the *ton,* but a genuine sound of amusement. "If he had, you would not still be standing here. He would have bundled you back into your cloak, and then into your carriage."

Irisa's spine straightened. "I think not. I'll not tolerate Lucas taking such a possessive approach when he refuses to follow through on his other obligations as my betrothed."

Thea tried to smother her amusement, but Irisa heard it anyway.

"You may laugh. Drake makes no pretense of his feelings for you. He is so affectionate that there are times he heats the room with the way his eyes devour your person."

Her sister's humor turned to sympathetic understanding. "I'm sure Lord Ashton will be all that you require after marriage as well, Irisa. You must be patient."

She closed her fan and gripped it with both hands. She did not feel like being patient.

She would have expressed as much to Thea, but the butler came in to announce dinner. Lucas turned from his discussion with Drake to offer his arm to Irisa and became motionless. He stared at her as if she had suddenly grown a second head rather than simply exposed a bit more of her skin than perhaps was strictly proper.

It was not a look that said he was experiencing an overwhelming fit of desire. In fact, the expression transforming his face more closely resembled fury than anything else. With nothing left to do but brazen it out, Irisa walked toward Lucas as if he did not look in the least like he wanted to throttle her.

In what she thought was a truly courageous act, she took his arm and attempted to step forward. "Shall we go into dinner, my lord?"

Lucas did not move, effectively halting her progress as well. "Where is the rest of your dress?"

The question was so ridiculous, she was sure he didn't truly expect an answer, so she did not give him one.

After a moment of continued silence, she said, "The others are waiting for us, my lord. Shouldn't we go in?"

Lucas turned his ferocious scowl toward Thea. "Mrs. Drake, do you have a shawl for Irisa to wear? I do not want her to catch a chill over dinner."

"Don't be ridiculous, Lucas," Irisa hissed, "I don't need a shawl. I'm not in the least bit cold."

Indeed, embarrassment had her so warm, she was practically perspiring. Drake had noticed her dress as well and he was watching Lucas with an expression of unholy glee. Gentlemen could be quite irritating.

Shifting his glittering gaze to her, Lucas did not bother to mute his reply. "Either you put on a shawl or we will leave before the first course has been set."

She stared at him in disbelief. "You are making a scene."

"This scene is not of my making," he replied in a hard voice that would have no doubt intimidated Wellington had Lucas chosen to be a soldier rather than a spy during the war. "Choose. A shawl or we leave."

If the choice of leaving hadn't meant a carriage ride with nothing but Lucas's company, Irisa would have gladly opted for departure. However, she did not trust herself alone with him right now. She might try to kill him.

She let go of his arm and turned to face Thea and Drake. "I would be most grateful for a shawl."

When Lucas handed her into his closed carriage two hours later, wearing both the borrowed shawl and her own cloak, Irisa had her ire under tenuous control. It was not only his heavy-handed behavior in demanding she wear a shawl that had her silently seething, but the obvious failure of her plan as well.

Lucas's order to his coachman destroyed her forced calm.

"We were supposed to attend the Barringer soirée after dinner with my sister, or had you forgotten?" she asked in frigid tones after Lucas instructed the driver to return to her parents' home.

Lucas shot her a dangerous scowl. "Impossible. The shawl would be bound to shift were you to try to dance."

All of her nervousness and feelings of being exposed in the gown evaporated in the light of such male arrogance. "Not at all, my lord. The shawl cannot shift while I am dancing if I'm not wearing it—and I can assure you I will not be wearing it at Barringer House this evening."

Lucas reclined against the squabs with an altogether deceptive casualness. For although he appeared relaxed, Irisa had the distinct impression she was sharing the carriage interior with an untamed beast ready to spring.

"You are quite right, my dear. You will not be wearing the shawl to the soirée because you will not be attending. I'm taking you home, and if you ever attempt to wear such an immodest garment in public again, I will not be responsible for my actions."

She had an almost irresistible urge to scream and then to laugh. It was that or cry, for she had no doubt the actions he threatened had nothing to do with the passion she had hoped to ignite. Oh, he was *passionate*, all right, but only in anger. He had not found the gown in the least enticing. He found it objectionable.

"May I point out that my gown is no more immodest than those of a great many ladies of the *ton*?" she asked in scathing accents, uncaring that her anger would undoubtedly only fuel his own.

"They are not betrothed to me."

"Lucky them," she muttered.

"Are you so unhappy with our betrothal, Irisa? I had the impression that you enjoyed my company." His silky accents no doubt had served him well when extracting information from the enemy, but she had no desire to answer such a loaded question.

She enjoyed his company all too much.

She frowned at him in a mute refusal to answer.

He returned her stare, his blue gaze probing in an expressionless face.

Why did she have to love such a stubborn, unbending *gentleman*? And she did love him, idiot that she was. She'd allowed herself to fall helplessly in love with a man as destined as her parents not to return her tender feelings.

"Tell me, Irisa. Do you wish to cry off?" His voice had softened to a tone of puzzlement laced with hurt.

Shocked at his interpretation of her actions, she exclaimed, "*No!*"

She was not entirely sure she could marry him if he did not even desire her, but she was equally unsure she could live without him. It was a quandary she had no hope of solving at this particular moment.

"Then *why*?"

Despite her upset at the misunderstanding between them, she could not make herself admit the true reasons for wearing such a revealing dress. "I am not unhappy, my lord."

"I see. You are certain this little display is not an attempt to subtly tell me that you no longer think we shall suit?"

A cold wind blew through her insides, dissipating the last of her anger and leaving a feeling of hollowness behind.

Four

"I THOUGHT YOU WOULD LIKE THIS DRESS." Well, if not like, then at least be inspired by. "I was told it was very flattering to my figure."

She did not mention that Pansy had made the comment after nearly keeling over in shock from the sight of her mistress in the low-cut gown.

"In the future you will do well to grace a different modiste with your patronage. The one who made that dress appears to cater to another sort of clientele entirely."

"What sort of clientele do you mean?" she asked, feeling quite dangerous all over again.

After all, she had altered the dress and it might be a tad risqué, but it was not scandalous.

Lucas's narrowed eyes chilled her to the bone. "The indiscreet sort. Women who are not mistaken for ladies."

He uttered the insult in a flat, cold tone that told her more effectively than words that he expected his fiancée to be entirely above reproach. While the circumstances of her birth might be suspect, Lucas nevertheless had found her to be an acceptable candidate as his wife because of her impeccable manners and ladylike decorum in all situations.

That decorum had been compromised tonight.

Her efforts to please her parents had not been sufficient

to gain their love, but her pains had gained Lucas's attention and approval. He wanted the image just as her parents did, not the living woman underneath it. Her anger drained away once more as a sense of hopeless loss filled her.

What a fool she had been to try to draw from Lucas what he clearly did not possess—a passionate desire for her.

"You need not concern yourself in the area of my dress further, my lord. Tonight's *indiscretion* will not be repeated."

She had made enough mistakes in dealing with Lucas—and she feared accepting his proposal had been the biggest one.

LUCAS HEARD THE DEFEAT IN IRISA'S VOICE . . . AND SHE was calling him *my lord* again instead of Lucas. He didn't like it and wanted to demand that she not do so again, but it would sound too petty. Why had she pushed him like this tonight? She had denied his assumption she was trying to tell him without words that she no longer thought they would suit.

If not that, then what had prompted her to wear that damned gown? It did not fit with her usual ladylike ways.

Irisa was not a flirt.

"Why?" he asked again, needing more than ever to understand what had motivated her uncharacteristic behavior.

She did not pretend a lack of understanding, but when she averted her gaze, he thought she would refuse to answer yet again.

"I set out to learn something." Her soft voice gave no indication whether or not she had succeeded.

He was unaccustomed to such a toneless response from his usually animated fiancée. "And did you?"

Her lovely shoulders slumped. "Yes."

"What?" That he would not tolerate his lady dressing the part of a courtesan?

She should hardly be surprised at that news.

"It isn't important." She tugged the cloak more tightly around herself.

"I don't like games, Irisa." He didn't like her current unhappy demeanor either. He felt guilty and could not understand why. "I want you to explain what you hoped to accomplish dressing in that manner."

"There appear to be a great many things you don't like, my lord. Perhaps you would be so kind as to make a list before we are wed. I would not wish to inadvertently misstep again."

Bloody hell. She made it sound as if he were some kind of ogre for having a perfectly natural reaction to his fiancée wanting to be seen in public in such an enticing dress.

He had been too angry at first for the expanse of her exposed silken flesh to affect him, but throughout dinner, images of what the shawl now hid tormented him. Even now, he ached to pull her across the squabs and let his hands discover what he had denied his eyes. He'd been in a state ranging from semiarousal to full throbbing need for the past two hours, and it had not done a bloody bit of good for his temper.

"I assumed after our courtship that such a thing would not be necessary," he said, his voice harder than he would have liked. "You have always behaved in an exemplary fashion. I can only surmise that tonight's deviation from good sense was prompted by an excess of nerves brought about by our recent engagement."

The bitter laugh that fell from her lips was unlike any sound he had heard her make before.

It completely lacked the vitality and warmth that so marked the woman he intended to marry. "You could certainly say that, my lord."

"Stop calling me that!" His own loss of control shocked him. *What was she trying to do to him?*

"Come, my lord, even you cannot object to such a correct form of address."

He wanted nothing more than to grab her, pull her onto his lap, and kiss her until she could say nothing but his name. He did not dare. In his current state, he would have her skirts around her waist and her legs spread within a few short moments. The idea was too bloody appealing. His only safe course of action now was silence.

Evidently Irisa felt the same way, for she said nothing as the coach made its slow progression toward the Langley town house.

Too soon, the silence grew unbearable. Oppressing him with its near physical weight, he tried to mentally shrug it off to no avail. He had wounded her and he did not know why or how, only that what should have been an entirely expected reaction on his part had not been. She had wanted something different from him, something he had not given her.

And for the very life of him, he could not figure out what.

They were already engaged, so she could not be trying to entice him into a deeper commitment or angling for an expression of his intentions. He'd made them clear enough.

Yet he felt as if a chasm had opened up between them, one that he was responsible for, and he hated the feeling. Perhaps if she understood his past, she would understand better why he was so concerned by the semblance of impropriety.

"My mother pursued notoriety like some fashionable women pursue a good match."

Irisa looked at him again, shock apparent in her lovely brown eyes.

"Surely you heard of her?"

"No."

"She died eight years ago, long before your first trip to Town, but the rumors persist in some circles."

"I cannot abide gossip." The intractability of Irisa's voice implied she meant what she said in the fullest sense of the words, and he felt his respect for her climb another notch.

"That is commendable, but perhaps it would have been better in this instance if you had known a little about my past."

"I'm not sure it would have made a difference, my lord."

He did not agree and his teeth gritted on the despised

my lord. "Mother was twenty years younger than my father and they fought constantly."

"I'm sorry. That would have been difficult for you." Her softly spoken words, lacking any sort of guile, were like a key turning in a very rusty lock, and he knew that he would tell her everything.

About his mother.

"She wanted a life filled with excitement and pleasure. My father wanted to ensure his line. He married her and she gave him two sons. He was content."

"But she was not," Irisa finished for him.

"No. She wanted to live in London during the Season and travel from house party to house party the rest of the year. He refused, insisting on the need of living on the estate and training me to take his place. She wanted to play, to pursue pleasure. While my father lived, he managed to keep her wildness under control, but when he died, she did as she pleased."

He took a deep breath, refusing to allow the pain of a ten-year-old boy, who had effectively lost both father and mother in one blow, overcome him. "She dressed to attract men and she succeeded. She took lovers and she made no attempt to be discreet about it. She traveled constantly. My brother and I rarely saw her, but we heard about her. The entire Polite World heard about her."

"That must have hurt you a great deal." Irisa's voice was husky with emotion.

He did not deny her claim. "I became responsible for the title at a very young age, too young to curb her dissolute ways. But when I left school and took over management of the estate entirely, I felt the time had come to try. I spoke to her about the impact her behavior had on the reputation of our family."

"She did not listen, I imagine."

"She was offended her son would have the temerity to lecture her. Unfortunately, she found me as tedious as she found my father before me. We were never close, but after that conversation, a chill developed between us."

"I'm sorry." Irisa's sweetly compassionate voice reached deep inside to a place he had kept closed to others since his father's death.

"Mother was the first person to call me Saint Ashton. She frequently mocked my tendency toward dullness and respectability. Her friends took the name up and soon the rest of the *ton* knew me as The Saint." But he was no saint. He was merely a man who wanted to do right by his title and the people who relied on him for their living.

A soft sound of distress came from the other side of the carriage. It reminded him how very unalike his fiancée was from the woman who had given him birth. Irisa hated to see others hurt; she would never mock anyone, much less her own son.

He gritted his teeth against memories that should no longer have the power to wound. Ridicule had been one of his mother's favorite forms of amusement, and her eldest son, who both looked and sounded so much like his father, had been her chief target. "I vowed never to be like her."

"You promised yourself you would not marry a woman like her either, didn't you?" Irisa asked in a low whisper.

He turned his head and flipped back the curtain to look out the carriage window into the foggy London night. "Yes."

A small rustle of silk was all the warning he had before Irisa landed on the seat beside him, her little hand clutching his bigger one tightly. "I'm sorry, Lucas. Please believe that I didn't mean to hurt you tonight."

He returned the pressure of her hand. He did believe her, just as he was absolutely certain that she had not dressed in her low-cut gown to attract other men. Irisa's honor ran bone deep.

"Were you testing the bounds of our relationship, little one?" It was the only explanation he could come up with.

"You could say that." She sounded resigned.

Had she expected more freedom? Did it upset her that he had drawn a line on her behavior? She had not responded favorably to his attempt to guide her regarding money.

Her father ignored too much and she had become accustomed to a surfeit of independence. Once they were married, she would accustom herself to their respective roles and learn that hers was not an unpleasant one.

"We will be happy together, little one. Trust me."

She did not answer.

LUCAS WATCHED HIS FIANCÉE DANCE WITH WEMBY AND frowned.

She wore the same expression of polite interest she had worn in his own company for the past week, ever since the night she had donned that outrageous dress. The dress that had taken over his dreams. No, not the dress. Irisa.

He had woken up sweating and stiff as a spike several times. Images of his hands peeling the gown away from her tantalizing curves tormented his mind and body. Had the dress been cut a half an inch lower, he would have been able to see the color of her aureoles. Trying to imagine what shade of pink they were had been driving him mad.

He wanted her with a hunger that he had never known before, but that was not what bothered him at the moment. He had almost accustomed himself to this constant state of arousal. What bothered him now was that he knew that expression on Irisa's face covered boredom when she was with Wemby.

What did it cover when she was with himself?

They were to be married in a matter of weeks, and yet he felt an insane urge to spirit her off to Gretna Green. A persistent fear that he was going to lose her plagued him, but he had been unsuccessful in pushing the wedding date forward.

Langley and his lady treated Lucas's suggestions to that effect as a joke. Irisa had been right when she said her mother would require significant time to prepare for the wedding. He had not taken into account Lady Langley's social stratagems when assuming she would fall in with his plans. She had made it clear, in a very civilized way, that she intended to get the maximum social benefit possible from her daughter's wedding.

It occurred to him that he did not particularly care for either of his intended's parents. And although she was clearly fond of them, Irisa held a part of herself back from them as well. She did not talk freely as she did when she was with her sister. The knowledge that now she treated him much the same way as she did her parents clawed at Lucas's insides.

He could not understand it. He knew it had something to do with that night and his reaction to her gown, but he did not know how to fix it. He felt as if he had failed some test.

It galled him to admit it, but he would almost be willing to let her dress in such a fashion if it would bring back the open warmth of the woman he had proposed to. This card copy of his fiancée was driving him mad.

He watched with bitter resignation as she took her leave of Wemby and turned to make her way toward Lucas, that damned polite smile pasted on her face.

IRISA DID NOT LET HER SMILE FALTER, EVEN THOUGH her fiancé's look was certainly less than welcoming.

His scowl was as black as the hair on his head. He had been short-tempered ever since her disastrous attempt to discover his true feelings toward her. She could not decide if she had given him a complete disgust of her, or if the incident had been forgotten . . . in his mind at least.

His behavior had grown very confusing. He spent more time than ever at Langley House, but was moody and edgy while he was there. She could always rely on his escort during the evenings, but he did not appear to enjoy himself at the balls, routs, and musicales they attended.

He extended his arm to her and she settled her hand against the solid muscle of his forearm before joining him on a stroll about the ballroom. He ignored attempts by others to gain their attention and continued walking, which was most unlike him.

Thus far she had pretended ignorance to his fits and starts, but her patience had evaporated along with his deteriorating temper. Her own mood was not the most fortuitous. The Duke of Clareshire, the aged lecher whose suit she had refused, had come to Town for the Season and had made it very clear he found the company of any member of her family objectionable.

His hatred for her was so pronounced, there were already stories circulating amongst the *ton* speculating as to its cause.

Despite her imminent marriage to a well-placed peer of the realm, Papa and Mama were furious with her and she'd spent the afternoon listening to a rant on what a terrible daughter she was. At one point, she had been certain Papa was going to strike her as he had on a few occasions when she was little, but he did not.

All in all, she felt raw and miserable, and she refused to politely ignore the angry cast to Lucas's face one moment longer.

Flicking open her fan, she waved it slowly in front of her. "Is anything the matter, my lord?"

His eyes narrowed at her formal address and she stiffened her spine. It had been his decision to maintain a certain level of distance during their engagement.

"Nothing is the matter. I just find I am not eager to spend the evening amidst the *ton* tonight."

She fought to hide her disappointment at his words. She did not believe him for one moment. His black mood was not limited to tonight's ball. His refusal to share the true reason for it hurt her. The one thing she had been able to count on to this point with Lucas was his openness in talking to her.

"That would explain your lack of enthusiasm for this evening's entertainment, but not your rather morose behavior these past days, my lord."

"You find me morose, little one?"

She did not know what amused him about her opinion, but there was a definite spark of lazy humor in his eyes.

"Well, perhaps morose is doing it a bit brown, but you have hardly been in a congenial mood lately," she admitted.

He covered her hand with his own, brushing it with his thumb. "Perhaps I am merely impatient for our wedding and finding the wait chafing."

She looked into his eyes, trying to decide if he was teasing her.

"From your behavior toward me these past weeks, I find that difficult to believe." She could barely credit she'd said the bold words aloud, but found she did not regret them in the least.

His brows rose. "What do you mean? Have I neglected you in some way and offended your womanly sensibilities? I assure you that I am most impatient for the wedding to take place."

It was an effort to keep her expression serene. How could he be so dense? Did he expect her to spell it out for him?

"*Why* are you so eager, my lord?"

He shrugged. "For the usual reasons that a gentleman wishes to claim a lady for his own."

She would not be so easily fobbed off. "What reasons are those? I admit to ignorance in this area."

"Which is as it should be. Do not worry, my dear." He ceased stroking her with his thumb and patted her hand with the affection Mr. Wemby might have shown one of his hounds.

Although, come to think of it, Marcus Wemby was more loving toward his dogs than Lucas was toward her. Anger bubbled under the surface of her ladylike façade.

"After we are wed, you will learn all you need to know regarding these matters." Even his tone was condescending. "For now, you will have to trust me when I say that I eagerly look forward to making you mine."

His attitude pushed her beyond caution. "I find that most difficult to believe, Lucas. Your actions thus far do not indicate any sort of eagerness on your part for the more intimate aspects of marriage."

At least the infernal patting stopped. In fact, Lucas ceased movement entirely. It would have caused a small commotion were they not that very moment standing in almost concealment by a large potted plant. The green fronds brushed the black fabric of Lucas's coat. His immobility and shocked frown made her nervous.

She snapped her fan closed. She would not be intimidated. "I grow weary of you looking at me as if I had grown another head, Lucas."

"Perhaps the problem is I cannot fathom what is going through the one you've got," he replied, sounding confounded.

That did not make her feel one whit better. It had already come to her attention that Lucas did not understand her. If he did, he would have handled the days of their engagement in a far different manner.

"Is it so perplexing for a lady to want some token of a gentleman's affections?"

He frowned. "Have I not given you that?" He looked meaningfully down at the betrothal ring he had given her the morning the official announcement had come out in the papers.

She gritted her teeth and counted to ten, but it did no good. The man insisted on remaining obtuse. "I am not speaking of *things,* my lord. What I allude to is much more *intimate* in nature."

There. She could not get any blunter than that. If he still chose not to understand, she would cry off the engagement because of sheer denseness on his part. She would not risk having stupid children.

She need not have worried. Lucas understood perfectly. His entire being seemed to swell with outrage. All of a sudden, the height she had found so masculine seemed intimidating.

"A lady does not consider such things, and she never speaks of them."

He sounded just like her old governess. How dare he presume to know what ladies *thought* of? The Polite World might dictate what she could acceptably talk about, but did he truly believe even her thoughts were governed by the appearance of empty-headed perfection ladies of the *ton* were obliged to put forth?

"This lady definitely thinks of those things, and I can tell you my thoughts during our engagement have not been pleasant ones." She frowned up at him, more words pounding inside her with the demand to be uttered. "The prospect of a cold marriage bed is not in the least appealing, I assure you."

Without responding to her outrageous statement, he started walking again.

"Where . . . where are we going, my l-lor-Lucas?" she asked, correcting her address of him when he glared at her with eyes that reflected a fury she'd never suspected he was capable of.

"We will make our excuses and return to Langley House," he bit off. "There are several details regarding our marriage that apparently need to be discussed."

His voice could have etched steel, and she had no desire to be the one cut up by it.

It was bad enough to contemplate discussing such embarrassing matters with him, but she was certain she did not want to do it when he looked and sounded so terrifyingly angry. She had to get hold of the situation. Lucas was simply not rational enough for a conversation of this magnitude.

"I think not, my lord. I have promised several gentlemen here a dance this evening. If I were to leave after the way you've monopolized me this past half hour, it would invite comment of the worst sort."

The spine of her fan bit into her fingers through her gloves and she realized she was gripping it much too tightly in her tension.

He frowned and looked around, seeming to finally become aware of the curious glances directed their way.

"Very well. I see that you are well taken care of. I think I will repair to my club for the rest of the evening. We will continue our discussion later, in privacy."

"That would no doubt be best."

He inclined his head. "As you say."

Although angry with him, she was nevertheless grateful he wanted to finish the conversation. However, perhaps she should not be surprised. From the very beginning of their association, Lucas had shown an unexpected willingness to discuss uncommon subjects with her. She should never have hesitated so long to bring this one up.

A small voice taunted her that it was not merely the thought of discussing things of an intimate nature that had made her hesitate. If she were honest with herself, she would admit she had also been more than a little afraid of what Lucas would have to say, *or not say,* on the subject.

He silently escorted her to her mother's side and then took his leave of them both. Irisa had to stifle an urge to sink into the nearest chair. She felt as if she had barely averted disaster. She could only hope that when she and Lucas talked later, she would be able to keep a rein on her tongue.

She wanted answers, not to bait the man, and she did not wish to say anything that would expose her own vulnerability without first finding out the extent of his feelings for her.

Her partner came to claim her for the next dance and she was forced to fix her attention on him and the protection of her toes. The silk slippers that matched her pale pink gown would not stand up to being trod upon by his rather zealous feet. Cecily Carlisle-Jones was in their set and Irisa's already beleaguered emotions took another beating as the girl gave her sidelong glances and then said things to her current partner which caused the gentleman to look at Irisa.

At one time, Cecily had been Irisa's closest friend. Unfortunately, when Thea had come to England, Cecily made it clear she had no intention of consorting with a lady who had chosen to marry the illegitimate son of a duke's daughter. Irisa had no choice but to sever their connection.

Losing her friend had hurt, but not as much as knowing Cecily had spent the last four years saying catty things behind her back. The only respite had been the year Cecily had spent in mourning after her young husband died from influenza.

Irisa shuddered to think what would happen if the other woman ever learned of Irisa's own illegitimate status at birth. She forced herself to look away from Cecily and concentrate on her own partner throughout the remainder of the country dance.

Several sets later, she moved around the ballroom floor in search of Mama. She had left her partner, Mr. Wemby, again, discussing hounds with a genuinely enthused debutante. Irisa would not be surprised if a match was declared before the end of the Season. She was happy for him and relieved for herself.

His attentions had become marked again and he had grown almost flirtatious since the announcement of her engagement. Some gentlemen found married ladies more congenial companions than debutantes, but Irisa could not imagine Mr. Wemby in the role of cicisbeo. Frankly, she did not want to imagine any man in that role in relation to herself.

Mama was gossiping with Lady Preston and did not notice Irisa's approach. Irisa did not immediately make her presence known. Mama's opinion of the fast young widow was less than favorable, and finding them together in a low-voiced tête-à-tête rendered Irisa momentarily mute.

"Really, I cannot imagine why you think I would be interested in such spurious gossip," Mama said with well-bred disdain.

"Come now. It's no secret among the *ton* that Ashton keeps a mistress. You make yourself appear goosish attempting to pretend ignorance," Lady Preston replied, her voice amused.

"What if he does? For all his reputation as a saint, he is

still a man and not yet married. He will no doubt give the creature her walking papers well before the wedding."

Mama's words spun in Irisa's head like a whirligig and her heart refused to beat. Lucas had a mistress? Surely not.

"The liaison is a long-standing one." Lady Preston was speaking again. "I have heard rumors that she has been under his protection for the last four years, or more. I would not count on Lord Ashton ending it merely because he has chosen to do his duty to the line."

Five

STRANGE. UNTIL THAT VERY MOMENT IT HAD not occurred to her that Lucas might have proposed merely out of duty. He was only eight and twenty. Surely he had several years before he must needs worry about setting up his nursery. Yet the presence of a mistress in his bed would explain the lack of intimacy between him and Irisa.

Did Lucas see her as merely a means to an end? Among the *ton,* it was certainly common practice for gentlemen to regard ladies as little more than ornaments to grace their homes and brood mares to fill their nurseries.

Irisa's head spun and she forced a deep breath into her lungs.

"Ashton is a gentleman. He knows what is expected of him."

Mama's questionable championship of Lucas did nothing for Irisa's precarious emotions. Her words made it sound as if it were a foregone conclusion that Lucas would indeed have a mistress.

Lady Preston shrugged her beautiful, fully exposed shoulders. "Perhaps. I believe when there is a child involved that gentlemen are less circumspect in these matters."

The satisfied malice in Lady Preston's voice sickened

Irisa. It could not be true. Lucas would not become engaged to her while carrying on an association with another woman. He could not possibly have a child.

It was unthinkable.

Not *The Saint.*

Why not? a voice in her head taunted. *Many gentlemen of the* ton *do so. Look at your own papa's past.* But Lucas was not her father.

"I am sure you are mistaken," Mama said in freezing accents, whirling around, clearly intent on making a grand exit.

The effect was spoiled when she ran straight into Irisa.

Irisa hastily stepped back. "Hello, Mama."

"Lady Irisa. We did not see you standing there. I hope our conversation did not upset you," Lady Preston said.

Schooling her features into a polite blankness, Irisa inclined her head. "I assure you, had I been listening, nothing you could have said would have overset me." She refused to give the gossiping harpy the satisfaction of knowing she'd hurt her. Irisa turned to her mother. "I believe you told me to be ready to go after this last dance."

Mama nodded in agreement to the lie without twitching so much as an eyelash.

Irisa did not bring up the subject of Mama and Lady Preston's discussion on the way home and neither did her mother. It was as if by not speaking about it, they could pretend nothing important had been said. Irisa would not ignore the horrible accusations Lady Preston had made, however.

She would discover the truth.

IRISA SPENT A SLEEPLESS NIGHT TORMENTED BY thoughts of Lucas in another woman's arms. She made several decisions as the dawn chorus rose in crescendo outside her window. The first was that until she had proof otherwise, she would assume Lady Preston had been mistaken. That did not mean, however, that she would bury her head in the sand like the flightless birds she'd read about inhabiting the Australian colonies.

No. She would ferret out the truth, she'd decided. Lady Preston had said that the whole *ton* knew of Lucas's fabled mistress. If that were true, then surely the servants would have heard something. Irisa would quiz Pansy about it this morning when the maid came to help her dress.

Her third, and by far most disconcerting, decision was not to put off engaging Lucas in an intimate discussion about their feelings. All three decisions took a certain amount of courage, but she did not gammon herself. The third one took all that she had. However, she would rather face the specter of rejection now than go through life married to a man who found her no more inspiring of passion than blancmange.

PANSY STARED AT HER MISTRESS. "YOU WANT TO KNOW if 'e keeps a ladybird tucked away? *Why,* milady?"

Irisa repeated the conversation she had overheard at the ball the previous evening.

Pansy's face turned pensive. "I don't know, milady. I 'aven't 'eard anything, but that's neither 'ere nor there. I'm not one for much gossiping, as you well know. I could ask Cook. She's got a fair ear for scandal."

Irisa adjusted the jacket over her amber silk carriage dress before turning to meet the maid's gaze. "I think that would be best, but Pansy, you must be careful. I do not wish to stir up any more tittle-tattle. You must not allow her to get the impression you believe the rumor, and do not under any circumstances repeat what I told you about the words between my mother and Lady Preston."

Pansy contrived to look offended. "I said I wasn't one for much gossip. I didn't say I don't know what I'm about when I choose to participate, milady."

"Good." Irisa smiled. "We can discuss your discoveries when I return from my driving lesson with Mrs. Drake."

* * *

IRISA URGED THE HORSES, PULLING HER SISTER'S BRAND-new high-perched phaeton to a slightly faster clip as she tried to determine how best to bring up the subject dominating her thoughts.

Lucas's alleged mistress.

She had graduated from driving in the park to negotiating traffic in the less-congested streets of London and found it challenging to focus on both her thoughts and the horse and foot traffic surrounding the phaeton.

She finally decided the direct approach would be best. She could trust her sister with her secrets. "Thea, I would appreciate your advice on a delicate matter."

"Of course. Anything."

For a second time that morning, Irisa repeated the awful conversation she had overheard the night before.

Thea shook her head decisively. "I don't believe it. Pierson likes Lord Ashton, and my husband is a very good judge of character. He also has a strong moral streak. He would never like a man guilty of such a thing, and the very idea that there might be a child is absurd."

Irisa grimaced. "As absurd as Papa fathering a baby outside the bonds of matrimony?"

Thea laid her hand on Irisa's forearm and squeezed gently. "There were unique circumstances then, sweeting. Besides, Lord Ashton is not Langley."

Irisa certainly would never have agreed to marry Lucas if she had believed he was like Papa. "How would I go about finding out if Lady Preston was mistaken?"

Thea sighed. "You aren't going to give this up, are you?"

"No."

"I suppose you could make discreet inquiries," Thea said after a few moments of pensive silence.

"Pansy is talking to Cook even as we speak."

"That is a start. Do you want me to ask Pierson? Although I must say, I think if my husband had heard anything of that nature, he would have told me immediately."

"I'm sure you are right. What else can I do?"

"I suppose if you knew the supposed mistress's name, you could inquire into her finances. There are ways of discovering if Lord Ashton is paying her bills."

"In that case, I will have to wait to hear what Pansy learns from Cook."

"Are you certain you wish to investigate this, Irisa?" Thea asked again. "I truly cannot see your gentleman behaving in such an amoral fashion."

Irisa sincerely hoped Thea was right. "If he does not have a mistress, looking into the matter will do no harm."

Unexpectedly, Thea shook her head. "I'm not sure that is true. At the very least, I can foresee Lord Ashton finding out about it and being quite angry that you do not trust him."

"It is not a matter of trust. He will have to accept that I had no choice but to investigate Lady Preston's claims. A lady cannot close her eyes to unpleasantness and expect it to go away. I learned that by watching Mama all these years."

It had not made Irisa any more legitimate that her mama chose to ignore the truth of her birth. And Irisa refused to be a coward; hiding from bitter reality would do nothing to change it.

LUCAS STIFLED A CURSE WHEN THE BUTLER INFORMED him that Mrs. Drake had taken Irisa for a drive in her new phaeton. Having already called upon his fiancée at Langley House and discovered her gone, he did not feel amiable at the news that he had once again missed her. Was she avoiding him after their argument the previous evening? Perhaps the things she had said embarrassed her.

"When do you expect them back?"

The butler, who looked more like a pirate than a proper English servant, rubbed the side of his nose. "Well, me sight ain't what it used to be, but that bright yellow carriage coming up the street be them, I'm thinking."

Lucas turned to see where the butler indicated. The two women riding in the fashionable conveyance were indeed familiar. The amber of Irisa's gown contrasted nicely with her golden blond curls, and Lucas felt a tightening in his chest at the sight. How could she worry that he did not want her?

His lips had started to curve in a smile of greeting when he noticed who handled the ribbons. Irisa.

Lucas tensed, but reminded himself to stay calm. He had not actually forbidden her to learn to drive. He would have to take this circumstance as an example and be clearer about his wishes in the future. Making an issue of it now would be a waste of time. She obviously already knew how to drive and Irisa would never engage in the dangerous pastime of racing as his mother had done.

Waiting until the last possible moment to slow the horses, Irisa pulled the phaeton to a stop in front of the Drakes' town house with a flourish. Mrs. Drake clapped her hands in appreciation and Irisa smiled with pleasure at the praise.

He stepped forward to assist the ladies from the carriage. "Well done, little one, though I could wish you were a bit more cautious when reining the leads in."

Irisa turned her head in a startled fashion. "*Lucas.* I did not expect to see you here."

He handed Mrs. Drake out of the carriage. She headed into the house, and he reached for Irisa. He ignored her extended hand and chose instead to take a more secure grip on her waist and swing her down. He did not immediately let her go either.

He ached to touch her, and even this small intimacy was better than nothing. "How could you when I did not know myself I would be here until I called at Langley House to discover you were out?"

Pink tinged the translucent skin of her cheeks. "I had an appointment for a driving lesson with Thea."

Unable to help himself, he bent down and kissed the tip of her nose. "So I see."

Ignoring the look of bemusement on her face, he turned and led her into the house. They found her sister in the drawing room giving instructions to a footman regarding tea.

Lucas settled Irisa on a small sofa, taking his place next to her. She shifted to give him more room when his thigh brushed hers.

He raised his brow in silent mockery and turned to her sister. "It appears I owe you my gratitude, Mrs. Drake."

"Whatever for?" Mrs. Drake asked.

"Evidently you have taught my fiancée to drive."

"I asked you for instruction first, if you will remember," Irisa said.

He deliberately brushed her arm, delighting when she jumped. There was no reason for him to suffer alone. And he did suffer, regardless of what she thought.

"So you did."

Drake and the children joined them for tea. As always, the sight of Irisa interacting with her nephew and niece gave Lucas pleasure. She would be an excellent mother. Her patience with the children and obvious delight in their company marked her as different from his own mother and most other ladies in the *ton*.

"You aren't angry, are you, Lucas?" Irisa's quiet voice carried above the clip-clopping of hooves on the street as they traveled toward Langley House.

"Why would you think I was angry, Irisa?"

She sighed. "You did not sound overly taken with the idea of me learning to take the ribbons when we discussed it before."

"I'm sorry."

"Then you aren't angry?"

"No."

"That's good. Lucas?"

"Hmm?" He turned toward Hyde Park.

"Why didn't you want me to learn to drive?"

"My mother died while racing her curricle." And had added the last fillip of notoriety possible to her name.

"I'm sorry," she said, compassion filling her voice, "but surely you realize that I would never do something so foolish as to enter into a race?"

"Yes. You are the perfect lady in every way, little one."

She frowned. "No one is perfect, Lucas."

Rather than argue with her, he shrugged. They were in the park now and Lucas handed her the reins. "Show me what you have learned, my dear."

She hesitated, but then accepted the ribbons with a sure hand. "I've found that I truly enjoy this."

It showed on her expressive, heart-shaped face. "I'm sorry I did not offer to teach you."

"I forgive you. I enjoyed the time with my sister. She's quite patient."

Before Lucas could reply to that comment, Irisa slowed the horses and stopped alongside another carriage.

The man in the carriage had hawklike features wrinkled with age. The Duke of Clareshire.

"Lady Irisa." His glaring countenance turned from Irisa to Lucas with no appreciable lightening of his expression. "Ashton."

Tension emanated off Irisa in almost physical waves. "Your Grace."

"I read the announcement of your engagement." That was all he said; no congratulations were added.

"Yes," Lucas said, forestalling Irisa's answer. "I made sure it was printed in both our respective shires the first time the banns were read and here in London as well. I am quite happy for the rest of the *ton* to know Irisa has agreed to be my bride."

She smiled up at him, gratitude for his championship in her eyes. The duke's dislike of her family after his suit had been rejected was well known. What Lucas found surprising was the fact the man had waved at Irisa to stop the carriage to converse.

"Humph." The old man's eyes narrowed evilly. "She could have been a duchess rather than a mere countess. Silly chit."

Irisa drew herself erect beside him. "I am more than content with my upcoming marriage."

The duke made another disgusted sound and motioned for his driver to move on without another word.

"I could not imagine being married to him."

"A sound notion for any woman with common sense."

"My thoughts exactly, Lucas." She grinned and set the carriage in motion again.

However, they had not gone ten feet when she was obliged to halt the carriage again. Perhaps the park had not been the best choice of venues for her to show him what she had learned.

Lady Preston, a woman who showed every sign of following his mother's destructive path in widowhood, acknowledged them. "Lord Ashton. Lady Irisa. What a pleasant happenstance."

"Lady Preston." Lucas inclined his head. "Yardley," he said to the gentleman sharing the widow's carriage.

Irisa nodded her head, but said nothing. That was unlike her. She was usually perfectly correct in her address. She had even greeted the duke with a civil tongue. While Lucas found Lady Preston too much like his mother to be comfortable with her, she was still accepted in all the drawing rooms of the *ton*. Therefore, Irisa's marked lack of effort to pursue the pleasantries surprised him.

Yardley and Lucas exchanged a few remarks while Lady Preston smiled smugly and Irisa remained still and mute. She set the horses in motion the moment Lucas indicated an end to the conversation.

"Why did you stop?" he couldn't help asking after the way she had ignored the other woman.

"She waved at me and I did not wish to give her the cut direct. It would have been cause for speculation."

That explained why she had stopped, but not why she

had been so reticent in her speech. "Has she said or done something to offend you?"

"Not precisely, my lord."

He winced at the formal address, but he thought he understood what motivated Irisa now. She had not wanted to draw comment by cutting the widow, but neither was she comfortable with the other woman's company. Like Lucas, she did not approve of Lady Preston's scandalous behavior.

"I commend your taste. She is not a good companion for a lady like you."

"Why is that?" Irisa asked almost belligerently, making him wonder if his assumptions had been far from the mark.

"Surely you know of her reputation."

"She's a widow, Lucas. Widows are afforded a certain amount of freedom among the *ton*."

"Regardless, I am glad you show no inclination to form a friendship in that quarter."

"Will you avoid association with Lord Yardley? If she's so bad, then surely her companions cannot be any better." Irisa bristled, as if his attitude offended her.

Perhaps it did. She had some odd notions for a female, but as she had said, no one was perfect.

"It is not the same thing," he chided. "A gentleman's reputation can withstand what a lady's cannot."

Irisa knew the ways of the *ton* as well as he, and he could not see a reason for the escalating argument unless she was using it to avoid continuance of their discussion at the soirée.

"Are you saying that you ascribe to the double standard common among the Polite World in regard to a gentleman and a lady's behavior?" Irisa asked in a voice filled with more emotion than their discussion warranted.

Once again he sensed he was missing something important, but there was only one answer possible to her question.

"Not ascribe to, but accept." It could be no other way. "It cannot be helped and you know it. If Lady Preston continues on her present course, it will not be long before many drawing rooms are closed to her, while they will remain open to the gentlemen she cavorts with. A man will be granted leeway in his behavior that a lady cannot begin to hope for. It is the way of the world."

"You are right, of course." She remained quiet for the rest of their drive through the park.

Lucas could not help feeling as if he had failed yet another test, and just as on the night she had dressed so provocatively, he had not the vaguest idea what the test had been.

When they arrived at her home, he did not accept her invitation for refreshment as it was so obviously given grudgingly. Now was hardly the time to discuss his desire for her.

"Will I see you tonight, my lord?"

Bloody hell. They were back to *my lord* again. "I'm afraid not. I have other plans this evening."

Perhaps an evening without his company would improve her attitude toward him.

She stared at him for a long moment, as if trying to discern his thoughts, but finally nodded and turned to go inside.

Bloody hell. He wished he could rid himself of the feeling that he was losing her.

IRISA MADE HER WAY UPSTAIRS, HER MIND FILLED WITH confusion. To what extent did Lucas accept the *ton*'s double standards for gentlemen and ladies? Far enough to justify keeping a mistress while engaged to another woman? He expected such exemplary behavior from her. He wanted a paragon for a wife . . . the perfect lady.

Although he was willing to marry her despite her illegitimacy, he had made no secret of the fact he wanted her to be above reproach in her behavior. No doubt he expected even more circumspection in her behavior than he would from a woman who had no blemish on her past.

Even so, her heart insisted that Lucas would not impose such high standards on his wife if he were not willing to live up to them as well. Had he not told her he had vowed never to become like his mother?

Pansy was waiting when Irisa entered the bedroom. "We'll 'ave to rush to get you ready, milady. 'Er ladyship has plans for dinner at the Bilkingtons before going to the musicale."

Irisa did not move to undress. "First tell me what you learned from Cook."

Pansy did not meet Irisa's eyes. "No time to talk about that now. You'll be wanting a bath before dressing."

"Tell me."

Pansy wrung her hands. "Now, milady, servants' gossip is not proof of anything. 'Tis still gossip just the same."

Irisa's stomach plummeted. "Enough. I want to know what you learned."

"It seems one of the kitchen maids is sweet on his lordship's underfootman."

Right at that moment, Irisa could not work up even the slightest interest in the budding romance. "So?"

"So, they've been steppin' out like."

"And?" Didn't she realize that drawing it out like this was making it worse?

"'E told 'er that 'is lordship visits a woman what used to be an actress. The underfootman didn't know if they had relations or not, seeing as how Lord Ashton does most of his visitin' during the day, but 'e knew the woman's name and direction."

Irisa reeled at the news. It was true. *No. No.* It couldn't be. There must be an explanation for Lucas's behavior. But she could not think of a remotely plausible excuse for her fiancé to visit the home of a former actress other than some sort of illicit relationship.

She briefly considered facing him with the question directly, but dismissed it as impossible. If he were innocent, he would be furious she doubted him, just as Thea had said. Besides, if he thought ladies were not supposed to discuss their own legitimacy, as he'd said the day he proposed, he would surely disapprove of her asking him about such an unmentionable matter.

And all that aside, could she trust him to tell her the truth? If he were the sort of man who hypocritically expected perfection from his wife while living a life of licentiousness in secret, he would feel no compunction about lying to her as well. She could not believe her Lucas was such a man, but she had to *know*.

Blind faith in a gentleman's honor was a recipe for disaster. Hadn't her father shown her that well enough? He pretended to be so perfect, when in truth he had betrayed his first wife most horribly.

Lucas had said she would not see him later, that he would be busy. Did he plan to visit the former actress tonight?

Years of perfect behavior and rigid self-control melted away under the onslaught of fear knotting her insides. Acknowledging her love for Lucas had made her vulnerable in a way she had spent the past four years trying to avoid. She could not bear it if she were to discover after marriage that she had set herself up for a lifetime of the same painful rejection she had known from her parents.

She had to see for herself if this very night her fiancé had plans to betray her. Being the perfect paragon he expected her to be could not compare to the importance of knowing whether she was marrying a man who could be trusted, or a philanderer in saint's garb.

"Pansy, tell my mother that I've come down with a sick headache. Then I need you to get me a disguise." A sense of freedom she had not known in years pervaded her being as she feverishly began plotting. "I think the stable boy and I are a similar size. See if you can't get hold of his clothes."

Pansy looked poleaxed. "You want me to borrow the stable boy's clothes? *For you, milady?*"

"Yes. Hurry. We must plan." Despite the painful uncertainty prompting her actions, a thrill of pleasure at the prospect of going on an adventure shivered through her.

It had been so long since she had let the other Irisa out,

the one who feared nothing, least of all Society's conventions. Her parents did not approve of this Irisa. Indeed, Lucas would be shocked were he to realize she even existed, but Irisa knew that this impetuous creature was the true woman who lived beneath the façade of the paragon she worked so hard to be.

Six

IRISA TUGGED AT THE UNFAMILIAR SCRATCHY fabric encasing her legs. Breeches were much less comfortable than she had supposed.

Pansy had ensured that the stable boy's clothing was clean, being his Sunday best, but Irisa had had no idea that the rough wool would chafe the tender skin of her thighs so thoroughly. How did gentlemen stand such daily discomfort? Perhaps the finer fabric of their clothes made for greater comfort, but did they not feel terribly exposed in breeches and pantaloons?

She certainly did. It did not help that the coarse linen top clung to her upper body now that the thick fog and drizzling rain had soaked it through. It was a good thing the darkness and aforementioned fog would keep her well hidden. Her curves were too rounded to be mistaken for anything but feminine under the now-revealing fabric.

If she ever did something like this again, there were several things she would do differently—not least of which would be to wear a coat. She shivered with cold as she tucked her blond hair more firmly into the cap on her head.

Bloody hell, these clothes were uncomfortable. Irisa's mind wrapped around the curse with satisfaction. She had spent years trying to act the part of the perfect lady, and what had that gotten her? Had it earned her Mama and Papa's respect and approval? No. And it certainly hadn't earned her their love. While her ladylike ways were her chief attraction to Lucas, that knowledge hardly comforted her at the moment.

If behaving a little more outrageously would have prevented the heartache she now experienced while standing in the rain outside a small house in an unfashionable, but not seedy, part of London, she wished with all her might that she had done so. There was still the slim possibility that Lucas's relationship with Clarice de Brieuse, the woman who lived in the house, was innocent, but it seemed unlikely. Lady Preston, with her own scandalous ways, was in a position to be in the know about things of this nature and she believed the French woman was Lucas's mistress.

Though she had tried to ignore them, Irisa had heard whispers that Lady Preston had had no fewer than six lovers in the past two years. For a moment Irisa found herself diverted from her situation to consider that piece of information.

Did the woman's affairs last four months apiece or had some been shorter while others lasted longer? How did one go about having affairs? Papa and Mama would know, or she would not be here, but neither was likely to share that information with her. If she asked, Mama would think Irisa had taken leave of her senses.

It just seemed that since her life had been affected quite unpleasantly by the concept, she ought to at least know the basics of how an affair was conducted. Pain lanced through her as she realized that, unfortunately, she was probably about to find out. All abject curiosity fled.

This was not just an interesting exercise in gaining knowledge. She did not want to see Lucas in another woman's arms, but she could not bear to remain ignorant of the truth. She had tried to convince herself that her spying would result in proving Lucas's innocence, but it had not worked.

Logic stood firmly in the way.

What possible reason could he have for a relationship of such duration with a former actress, other than an affair?

Four years was a long time. Perhaps Lucas loved the other woman. He could not marry her. His sense of duty was too strong for him to take for his countess a woman of questionable reputation, much less one who did not belong among the *beau monde.* Were the circumstances of Irisa's birth well known, she had no doubt he would never have sought her acquaintance, never mind courted her.

But they had met and he had pursued her. She could still remember the way tingles had shivered through her body and her heart had picked up its rhythm when his bottle blue eyes met hers for the first time. He had taken her hand to bow over it, and even through the gloves covering her fingers, she had felt a connection that had shocked her.

Those same fingers were now almost numb with cold and her heart beat a nervous tattoo of unpleasant anticipation. The excitement of her adventure had palled as she waited in the damp night for him to make his appearance at the home of his supposed mistress.

She could not believe another woman had a claim to Lucas's passions. Because her own heretofore unknown passion had been so violently aroused by Lucas, prior to accepting his proposal, she had naïvely convinced herself that he was similarly affected, even though he did not express it. It had been easy to believe he was protecting her from a compromising situation until after their wedding.

However, the growing suspicion that Lucas did not exhibit passion in her presence because she did not inspire it was all but settled in her mind. He did not want her because he did not love her and he did not love her because he loved someone else. His mistress.

The sound of carriage wheels and horseshoes scraping the street sent Irisa farther into the shadows of the building. She waited with dark premonition for the carriage to stop and its party to alight. A figure clad in gentleman's garb stepped with familiar grace to the cobbled street and Irisa's heart seemed to stop beating. The many-caped greatcoat did nothing to disguise the broad shoulders of Lucas's tall figure.

Numb horror invaded Irisa's being as she acknowledged that, up until this very moment, she had continued to hope the rumors had been just that.

But it *was* Lucas who knocked on the door. It *was* Lucas who stepped inside the house as if he had every right to be there.

Forcing herself to face the full extent of the awful situation, Irisa inched toward the light that spilled from a small crack in the drapes covering the parlor's window and peered in.

A breathtakingly lovely redhead sat calmly on a sofa next to the fireplace. She looked up with a warm smile when Lucas was shown into the room. He had removed his greatcoat and Irisa found that an additional act of betrayal. He clearly meant to stay awhile. He leaned over and kissed the creature's cheek, and that act of casual intimacy was more than Irisa could take.

She slid to the ground, her back against the cold stone of the house, and let tears course down her cheeks unheeded. She had committed the unpardonable act of falling head over heels in love with the man she intended to marry, and in doing so had exposed herself to the pain of a woman betrayed.

CLARICE PULLED LUCAS DOWN ONTO THE SMALL SOFA next to her, her face wreathed in a brilliant smile. "Thank you for coming by this evening, Ashton. I know you are busy with the Season's activities and your fiancée."

In truth, Lucas did not mind a break from the whirling round of social commitments. Watching Irisa dance in the arms of other gentlemen was becoming increasingly difficult, particularly when her mood toward him had become so distant.

"Do not concern yourself. You said you had something important you wished to tell me."

"*Oui.* Oh, Ashton, Maurice has proposed," Clarice said, her soft voice vibrating with happiness.

Lucas smiled. "That's wonderful news. I cannot think of a man more worthy of your company. Have you accepted his offer?"

The joy in Clarice's eyes dimmed a little. "No. I could not without speaking first to you."

"Surely you realize that I would be pleased by such an event."

Maurice was another French ex-patriot like Clarice. He had come to England during the French Revolution. The younger son of a noble family, he had decided that starting over in England was preferable to death by guillotine. He was several years older than Clarice, but she did not appear to mind.

"He wishes to return to France."

The words hung in the air with the weight of a heavy blow.

Lucas should not have been so shocked. Now that the war was over, many of France's nobility were returning to the home of their birth. The fact that Maurice wanted to marry Clarice and take her home with him spoke clearly of his deep affection for her. That did not ease the pain in Lucas's chest, however. If Clarice returned to France, she would undoubtedly take her daughter as well. The thought of not seeing those clear blue eyes so like his own again for a very long time, if ever, staggered him.

Clarice was watching him, tears in her crystal-clear eyes. She understood his pain. "Ashton, you have been more generous than any other gentleman would be. Your brother, had he lived, would have offered me money to see my baby placed elsewhere, and that would have been the end of it."

Lucas wanted to deny it, but he knew she spoke the truth. James would not have considered the child of his mistress anything more than a temporary inconvenience.

"That would have been his loss."

Clarice swallowed and nodded. "I don't know if I have

ever told you how much I appreciate what you have done for me. When I first came to you, I was terrified, certain you would either deny my claim, or if you did believe me, that you would take my baby from me."

"Yet you came to me anyway."

"I was desperate."

Yes, she had been desperate the first time she had met him, desperate enough to try to seduce him. She had also been pregnant.

"I have never regretted taking responsibility for you and my niece. You have been an exemplary mother."

"Merci."

"You will have Maurice contact my man of affairs to discuss the terms of your settlement."

Clarice's eyes grew round. "I have no dowry. Maurice understands and has accepted that."

"On the contrary. You have a very respectable dowry and I will be settling an appropriate sum on my niece as well. You will bring her to England to visit occasionally, won't you?"

Clarice threw her arms around him. "Of course I will and you must come to visit us as well. Maurice would be very happy to see you again."

She let him go and sniffed. He handed her his handkerchief and she dabbed at her eyes. "I hope Lady Irisa knows what a truly wonderful man she is marrying."

He wasn't at all certain that she did, but he could hardly ask Clarice to tell her.

IRISA DID NOT KNOW HOW LONG SHE SPENT SITTING outside Clarice de Brieuse's home. She had stood up, driven by an inexplicable compulsion, to peek once more into the drawing room, only to see the redhead throw her arms around Lucas in a very intimate embrace, a far more intimate embrace than any Irisa had ever shared with him.

She had slid back down the wall and once again given in to her emotions. Her tears had finally ceased and her body was no longer racked with silent sobs, but she could not seem to make herself move. The misery of Lucas's betrayal and rejection weighed her body down as surely as if the stableboy's clothes had turned into one of the heavy suits of armor in Langley Hall's long gallery.

She did not want to think of what Lucas and the beautiful auburn-haired woman were doing, but images of them locked in one another's embrace tormented Irisa until she feared her tears would start all over again. The sound of the door opening and Lucas's leavetaking finally galvanized her into action. She slowly stood, feeling like a very old woman, as the sound of Lucas's carriage moved off into the distance.

The fact that he had not seen fit to spend the entire night with his mistress afforded no consolation to Irisa's shredded emotions. Even if she had not loved him, the fact that he found another woman desirable when he was so neutral toward her person would have been enough to decimate her feminine pride.

The fact she did love him increased her pain a hundred times.

She had to go home.

Sneaking back into the house turned out to be easier than she had expected, but she had not considered what she would do regarding her chilled state when she had managed to gain her own room. She couldn't very well call for a hot bath or tea at this late hour without arousing suspicion, but her body was now shaking with cold.

She would have to make do with drying off and dressing in her warmest nightrail. She did so, hanging her damp clothes over the back of the chair behind her privacy screen. Pansy would discreetly take care of them in the morning.

Pulling an extra quilt onto her bed, she burrowed under the covers, seeking warmth and relief from the painful shivering of her body, but there was no relief for the pain in her heart. Although her body eventually warmed, she did not sleep. Her mind was too active to allow that blessed respite from her emotional pain. The future stretched out before her like a Greek tragedy.

If she married Lucas, her heart would die bit by bit as she attempted to live with the knowledge that the man she loved had given his heart and body to someone else. It was not to be borne. She would rather be alone than married to a man who could not love her.

Lucas approved of her, which was a far cry from the tender affection she craved. She understood now—his deep sense of duty had instigated his desire to marry, and that same sense of duty would insist he marry well. Irisa's place in the *ton* was irreproachable because no one knew of her illegitimacy. She was well born, proper in her behavior, modest in her dress, and mindful of her duty as a daughter and future wife.

In her ill-fated attempt to earn her parents' approval, she had allowed herself to become little more than a paper image of a woman. And it was that paper image that had drawn Lucas, not the heart that beat within.

Thea defied convention to run her own business, although she did it discreetly. Miss de Brieuse faced being a social outcast to have a relationship with the man she wanted. Even Lady Preston had more courage than Irisa. The young widow lived for her own pleasure, not the approval of the *ton.*

It was time for Irisa to show the same sense of daring. An idea began to form in her mind, a plan that would rid her of her faithless fiancé and her dull reputation at the same time. She realized that, in all likelihood, it would not be merely Lucas who would no longer wish to marry her—no gentleman in the *ton* would link himself with a notorious woman.

Irisa considered that an additional benefit to her plan. She didn't want to get married, not ever. She could not imagine loving anyone else as she did Lucas, had absolutely no desire to do so. Nor did she desire to enter into a marriage of convenience. If she could not trust Lucas, a man whom she esteemed above all others, to be faithful, what chance could there be that any other gentleman of her acquaintance would be any better?

She wasn't completely naïve. She knew mistresses were a way of life for many members of the *ton,* but she had believed that The Saint was different. She had been wrong.

As she considered her plan, she realized it would probably give Mama and Papa a complete disgust of her. But then, that would hardly represent a significant change from the current cold disapproval she felt in their presence. Perhaps Drake would agree to her coming to live with him and Thea. Irisa was good with the children and would make herself useful in their household. They would not mind that she was no longer socially pristine.

It took nearly another full week for Irisa to put her plan into action. Bedridden with a head cold for the first three days, she had to rely on Pansy to get the information she needed. Although the cold caused her some physical discomfort, it gave her the perfect excuse to avoid her fiancé and the rest of her family.

Even when she was no longer confined to her bed, she still refused to attend soirées or to entertain callers with the excuse that she was not yet completely well.

Lucas sent flowers every day, the blackguard. As if she wanted his paltry tokens of a lukewarm affection when she knew he was giving something far more important to another woman—himself! Saying that they made her sneeze, she refused to allow the flowers to remain in her room. When he sent her candy, she said she couldn't abide the thought of sweets right now and gave it to the servants.

Her mother, who had a horror of getting sick, did not even come to Irisa's room to harangue her about her ill-mannered behavior.

On the fifth day, Irisa put her plan into action. Pansy had discovered that Miss de Brieuse made a trip to the lending library with her maid every Wednesday morning. Irisa planned to be there when the other woman arrived.

She was perusing one of the stacks nearest the door when the beautiful redhead entered the building. Irisa waited until the other woman's maid went off to chat with someone in the common area before approaching Miss de Brieuse.

"I see that you like novels. I'm particularly fond of Mrs. Demsey's. Have you read her?" Irisa asked innocently as she moved to stand in such a way that prevented the other woman from leaving.

Miss de Brieuse lifted her head from the book she was looking at, a smile on her face. When she saw Irisa, her smile faltered and then disappeared altogether. "No. I haven't. If you will excuse me?"

So she knew who Irisa was? That made sense. Irisa was fairly certain that if she were a gentleman's mistress, she would make an effort to know his fiancée by sight as well.

Irisa did not move. "I would like to speak to you."

"I can't imagine what you wish to speak to me about. We have never met."

It was a credible performance. She could almost believe the surprised innocence in the other woman's voice, but then Clarice de Brieuse had been on the stage at one time.

"Although we have never met, Miss de Brieuse, we do share a mutual acquaintance."

The woman's gaze darted around. Irisa was certain that she saw what Irisa did. Several interested looks were directed their way and the hiss of whispered exclamations could be heard.

"This is not wise, my lady. You are drawing attention to yourself. Our mutual acquaintance would not like that."

Miss de Brieuse did not know it, but those words served to firm Irisa's purpose as nothing else could have—and they told her that her plan was working.

"It is unfortunate, but I assure you, necessary," she replied. "I really must insist on speaking to you."

"If you have anything to say, surely you can discuss it with our mutual acquaintance," Miss de Brieuse said, her voice sounding quite firm.

Irisa smiled politely. She could be very stubborn when the need arose. Had she not stubbornly clung for years to the belief that if she tried harder, she would gain the affection she needed from her family?

"Impossible. Speaking to him will not serve my purpose at all. If you are uncomfortable here, perhaps we can move to the privacy of your carriage."

An open curricle was hardly private, but she was counting on the other woman believing it was an improvement over making a spectacle of themselves in the lending library. She smiled in satisfaction when Miss de Brieuse signaled for her maid.

"If you insist on speaking to me, I believe you are right that it would be better done in my carriage where prying ears cannot hear."

The curricle seat was too small for all three women, and Lucas's mistress was forced to leave her maid behind to take a hansom cab home. Perfect.

"You're very good with the ribbons," Irisa said as Miss de Brieuse headed the carriage toward a less-crowded side street.

"*Merci.*"

"Did our mutual acquaintance teach you to drive?" Irisa could not help herself from asking.

Miss de Brieuse gave her a sidelong glance. "*Non.* I had learned to drive long before we met."

Well, at least that was something. She did not know what . . . but something.

"I have just learned to drive myself. My sister is teaching me."

Miss de Brieuse looked confused by the direction the conversation had taken. "It is enjoyable, *non*?"

"Yes. Very. However, I've never driven a curricle. Thea has a phaeton, you see. I don't suppose you would allow me to take a try with the ribbons?"

Looking even more confused, but not yet wary, Miss de Brieuse nodded. "*Oui.* All right."

She handed the reins to Irisa. It was a bit different from

the phaeton, but not enough to make it difficult. Irisa turned the horses up the next street, starting on the roundabout route she had planned earlier.

Irisa drove in silence for several minutes, allowing the sounds of London to surround her. Small boys hawked meat pies by the side of the road while a young girl pushed a cart with posies for sale.

"You said you wished to speak to me."

Irisa flicked a glance at the other woman. "Yes. I did."

"Was it about our mutual acquaintance? I think perhaps you have a mistaken view of the relationship between him and myself."

"I would rather not discuss details of your association." Irisa filled her tone with enough frozen intractability that it would effectively discourage further confidences. "Should I have any questions on that score, I will pose them to our mutual acquaintance."

Silence reigned again for several more minutes. Irisa took a side entrance into the park and had guided the carriage to Rotten Row before Miss de Brieuse realized where they were.

"You are mad. *Allez. Allez. Nous devons partir.* Take us out of here *rapidement.* Before we are seen together." In her distress, the other woman's French accent became quite marked.

Irisa ignored the command and nodded pleasantly to an acquaintance. It was Cecily's mother. The older woman's eyes bugged out of her head like a newly caught fish. She had always been an avid theatergoer. Her reaction indicated she most certainly recognized the former actress.

There was no question in Irisa's mind that news of her drive with Miss de Brieuse would spread rapidly among the *ton.*

Satisfaction in using Mrs. Carlisle's social snobbery for her own purposes filled Irisa. "If we leave right now, my intentions would be defeated. Why would I do something so foolish?"

"*Vous êtes folle!* This thing you do is foolish," Miss de Brieuse gasped, her agitation clear.

By the time they had reached the exit from the park, Irisa had seen and been seen by numerous members of the *ton*. Many had recognized the woman next to her. Miss de Brieuse had given up begging Irisa to leave and subsided in silence on the other side of the carriage, her face averted from those they passed.

When they exited the park, she roused herself. "*Why?* Why did you do that?"

Irisa sighed. "I'm sorry if I upset you, but it was necessary."

Miss de Brieuse shook her head. "Ashton will be furious with us both."

"I will explain to him that it was my doing, if you like."

"You are not concerned about his anger toward you? How can this be?" Miss de Brieuse asked in amazement. "He is a gentleman with a highly developed sense of dignity."

Irisa was counting on it. "I know."

"Yet you purposefully set out to make yourself outrageous. My lady, you make no sense."

Now that Miss de Brieuse had calmed down, Irisa could barely hear the French undertones in the woman's voice.

"I'm afraid that others will agree with you, but what is done is done," Irisa said.

They did not speak again until Irisa pulled the curricle to a stop in front of Langley House. She turned to Miss de Brieuse, intent on asking the one question that burned in her mind before a footman came out of the house.

"Do you love him?"

She had to know. Had Lucas given his passion to a woman who saw him as merely a means to an end—or was he loved? Somehow she could not bear the thought that mercenary motives had been the cause of her losing Lucas.

Miss de Brieuse met Irisa's gaze, her own eyes intent, but remained silent. A footman came out of the house and offered his assistance to Irisa so she could alight from the curricle.

She turned for one final glimpse at Lucas's mistress and was shocked by the look of understanding now filling the other woman's eyes. "*Oui.* I love him, but not as you do, I think."

Irisa nodded and turned to go. Miss de Brieuse's voice stayed her. "My lady, you would not listen to me regarding the details of my association with Ashton. *S'il vous plaît.* I beg of you. Ask him. It is not what you think."

Irisa acted as if she had not heard. She could not bear the pain of discussing such a thing with Lucas. She doubted she would be given the opportunity, regardless. Once he had heard about her notorious behavior, he would withdraw his offer and she would never see him again.

Which was exactly what she wanted, she told herself fiercely, even as those bloody, bloody tears once again burned her eyes.

Seven

LUCAS LOOKED UP FROM THE PLANS HE WAS drawing for a new model at the sound of Clarice's agitated voice in the hall.

She burst into his study with a torrent of French. "*Elle est aliénée. Votre fiancée est devenu folle. Je ne peux pas le croire. Il est incompréhensible! Ashton, vous devez faire quelque chose ou tous seront détruits!*"

He stood up and walked swiftly across his study to greet her. Her torrent of words did not cease, but she was speaking too quickly for him to understand what had her so agitated. It sounded like she said something about a fiancé.

He gripped her by the shoulders. "Calm down. Tell me what has happened. Has something happened to Maurice?"

Clarice's eyes were damp from weeping. She took a deep breath and then let it out slowly before speaking again. "*Non.* It is Lady Irisa. She took me for a drive in the park. It was awful. Oh, *sacré bleu*! You must do something, Ashton, before she destroys her reputation."

"Irisa took you driving?"

How? Irisa had never met Clarice, and if she had, she would not go driving in public with the other woman. It simply wasn't done—although to Ashton's way of thinking, Clarice would make a better friend for Irisa than Lady

Preston and her ilk. Unfortunately the Polite World would not see things that way.

"*Oui.* She has heard rumors about me. Only I think they were to the effect that I was your mistress. It is all so terrible, Ashton. Her eyes were filled with the daring that comes from desperate pain—it frightened me very much."

Could that explain Irisa's strange behavior these past weeks?

"Tell me what happened," he commanded and stood, listening in stupefied silence as Clarice told him about Irisa meeting her at the lending library and the carriage ride that followed.

"Why did you let her into your curricle?" he asked when Clarice had finally finished speaking.

She gave him a long, level look. "I think, Ashton, that your fiancée is not nearly so biddable as you may believe."

Lucas had begun to have his doubts on that score as well. Irisa had a latent courage and boldness he was just beginning to see and appreciate.

"But why would she take you driving through Hyde Park?" It was a recipe for disaster. Irisa's reputation would be ruined.

"*Je ne suis pas sûre.* I cannot be certain, but it was as if she wanted everyone to see us together."

"But why?"

Clarice frowned. "I really don't know. She acted very strangely. I thought she wanted to ask me about our association, but she told me very firmly that she didn't want to hear the details."

"You did not tell her that you aren't my mistress?"

"*Non. Je suis désolée.* I'm so very sorry, Ashton. It was a most upsetting course of events. I could not seem to think clearly and she was very insistent about not wishing to hear about it from me."

He could understand Clarice's confusion. Irisa's actions bordered on the insane . . . or the notorious. Damnation. Why had she done it? Surely she realized that if she insisted on making a spectacle of herself like this, he could not marry her. He had told her enough about his mother and his vow not to marry a woman like her for Irisa to be aware he could not tolerate such outrageous behavior in his fiancée.

Which is exactly what she planned. The knowledge seared his gut. She wanted to end their engagement. There could be no other explanation.

Was it because she felt betrayed, or had her suspicions been a convenient excuse? Even if she wanted to end their association, her actions were beyond foolish. If Irisa thought he had been unfaithful, why didn't she just cry off? And why in the bloody hell hadn't she talked to him? How could she believe him capable of such dishonorable behavior?

Rage filled Lucas at this proof of her lack of trust in him. He didn't care what the rest of the *ton* found acceptable. He would never do something so despicable as carry on a liaison with Clarice while *courting* Irisa, much less during their engagement.

Still, she must have felt very betrayed to act so unthinkingly. For her to have such a strong reaction, she had to be motivated by more than a passing fondness for him. It was that thought alone that allowed his temper to cool enough for him to consider the alternatives.

He could not let her do this to herself. He would not lose her to a misunderstanding or her own outrageous behavior. It was time she accepted that she belonged to him, and learned to trust him in the bargain.

IRISA SAT IN CURIOUSLY NUMB SILENCE WHILE HER PARents took turns ringing a peal over her. News of her drive with Clarice de Brieuse down Rotten Row had reached their ears shortly after the occurrence.

Papa had heard about it at his club and come home in a towering rage, much worse than any anger she had witnessed in him before. Irisa wondered if this was the way he had behaved toward the first Countess of Langley. If it was, it was no wonder Anna had run away to the West Indies to raise Thea.

So far, Papa had called Irisa horrible names, accused her of unspeakable deeds, and proclaimed to her and the rest of the household within shouting distance that he wished she wasn't his daughter.

The words would have hurt if she'd felt anything, but blessedly she didn't.

Mama's tactics were not nearly so loud, but they were intended to be just as hurtful. She had been calling on an acquaintance when Mrs. Carlisle had arrived. Evidently Mama had fainted upon hearing the news, and then revived enough to return to Langley House for a bout of hysterics. She sobbed into her hanky, calling Irisa an unnatural daughter.

"After all I sacrificed for your welfare, to be stabbed in the back like this. How could you do such a thing to me?"

Irisa's eyes narrowed and some of her numbness wore off. "You did not sacrifice anything for me, Mama. I was the sacrifice for your upward movement among the Polite World. Papa would never have married you, legally or otherwise, if you had not been pregnant with me." Not when he had still been married to someone else.

Mama's eyes widened in shocked disbelief and she gave a very creditable imitation of a swoon. It was too well timed and convenient for it to be real. Mama fell directly onto the fainting couch with a dramatic little sigh.

Papa did not seem to notice the fakery. He turned even more furious eyes onto Irisa. "How dare you speak to your mother like that? She risked her own reputation to give you a home, to see you raised with my name. Your lack of gratitude is as appalling as your sluttish behavior."

Irisa met his accusation with silence. She would not attempt to defend herself to Papa. He had never loved her, and now he clearly hated her. There was nothing she could say or do to change that.

"What? You have nothing to say to me?"

She mutely shook her head.

Her silence seemed to taunt him and his rage exploded. "I will teach you to sit there in silent defiance!" he roared.

He swung his arm in a wide arc, and in the split second before impact, Irisa realized he was going to strike her. Then his hand connected with her cheek and the blow knocked her off the small velvet chair. A roar sounded from near the doorway, but her vision was filled with small sparks of light, and a ringing in her ears prevented her from fully comprehending what was happening.

However, even her dazed condition could not disguise the loud thud of her father making bodily contact with a nearby wall.

She turned her head toward the sound, trying to see through the stars floating before her eyes. Sure enough, Papa sat against the wall like a naughty child in the nursery. Mama recovered miraculously from her faint and flew across the room to her fallen mate.

Slowly, so as not to exacerbate the pain now exploding in her head, Irisa turned to see who had landed Papa such a facer. A pair of Hessians topped with buff riding breeches blocked her vision.

She raised her head, again with meticulous care. "Lucas?"

He leaned down on one knee next to her, his beloved, traitorous face filled with concern. "Are you all right, little one?"

"Yes." Her face hurt, but no more than her heart.

"I would kill him, but he's your father," Lucas said grimly.

She believed him. "He wishes he wasn't."

"What?" Lucas's eyes were filled with wrath, but his voice was gentle.

"Papa. He said he wished I wasn't his daughter. I always knew it, but he never said so before."

"Hush, sweeting." Lucas hooked one arm under her shoulders and the other under her knees and then stood.

The feel of his arms around her was infinitely comforting. The knowledge that as soon as he heard of her notorious drive through the park she would lose this closeness hurt more than the throbbing pain in her face. It was the first and last time Lucas would ever hold her so intimately.

She refused to waste one second of it. Turning her face into his shoulder, she inhaled the masculine scent that was uniquely his. She would treasure this memory for the rest of her life. It was almost worth the agonizing soreness in her head. She wasn't aware they were leaving the drawing room until Mama's tear-filled voice reached her.

"Where are you taking her, Ashton?"

"To the Drakes. You can send her clothes and personal belongings there. She will stay with them until our wedding."

Irisa forced herself to stir in his arms at the pronouncement. She longed to see Thea, to be cosseted by her sister, but she could not bear the thought of going there now. Thea would see the bruise that must be forming on her cheek. The very thought of what Drake might do when he learned Papa had inflicted the wound sent chills down Irisa's spine. Drake adored Thea and would protect those she loved with fierce determination.

If Irisa were going to stay engaged to Lucas, disaster might be averted. Drake would trust Lucas to protect and defend her, but Lucas would withdraw his offer once he learned why Papa had been so upset. With no one else to champion her, she knew Drake would take up the challenge on his wife's behalf.

"Please. Not Thea's. Not yet," she whispered against Lucas's neck.

"Where then? You will not stay here. You will never again spend a night under your father's roof."

A loud gasp followed that pronouncement, but Irisa ignored it. Where could she go?

"My great-aunt, Lady Upworth, keeps a house here in town."

"Did you hear?" Lucas asked, his attention fixed over Irisa's head.

"Yes," Mama replied, her voice husky with an emotion Irisa did not recognize. "I'll have Irisa's things sent over."

Irisa's heart squeezed in pain at the speed with which her mother agreed to be rid of her. Oh well. She had expected something like this. Perhaps not the violence of Papa's reaction; it had been so long since he had lost control like that. However, she had known that neither he nor Mama would forgive her outrageous behavior.

LUCAS WAS FORCED TO WAIT IN THE HALL WHILE SERvants brought the Langley carriage around to the front of the town house. He had ridden over and could not very well take Irisa to her aunt's house riding double with him on his horse. There had been enough activity today to keep the scandalmongers occupied for the rest of the Season.

Irisa's ride through Hyde Park with Clarice was bad enough, but the violent row in the Langleys' drawing room would fuel gossip in several others before the day was out. Lucas knew it was a foolish hope that the servants at Langley House would keep the day's events to themselves. Even if they did, news that Irisa had removed to her aunt's was bound to get out and cause speculation.

Irisa lay in his arms, her head still tucked into his shoulder. She had not said anything else since asking him not to take her to her sister's home. Later, when she was feeling more the thing, he would make her tell him why she hadn't wanted to go to the Drakes', but right now that was the least of his worries. He was still dealing with the overwhelming fury he felt upon walking into the drawing room to see Langley slap his daughter right out of her chair.

Lucas had been too far away to stop him and could not rid himself of the knowledge that if he had arrived just one minute earlier, Irisa would not now be bruised and hurting. He wanted to take out his frustration on her father, but he couldn't. Right now, Irisa needed Lucas more than he needed to pound Langley.

"The carriage is ready, milord."

Lucas looked up at the sound of the butler's voice and nodded.

He started forward and Irisa spoke. "Put me down, Lucas. I can walk."

"No." He needed to hold her, to assure himself that she was all right.

Besides, if he put her down, the temptation to return to the drawing room and finish what he had started with Langley would be overwhelming.

She twisted uselessly in his arms. "Please. There will be enough gossip as it is."

Now was a fine time for her to become concerned on that score. "I'm not putting you down, so you might as well cease your struggles, little one. If you don't, anyone watching is liable to think I'm kidnapping you."

She stopped moving immediately and he laughed.

"I don't see anything even remotely funny about this situation, Lucas."

He squeezed her more tightly to his chest. "I know you don't. It's going to be all right, sweeting. Trust me."

Saying the words reminded him just how little trust she had shown in him thus far, and pain mixed with the rage coursing through him. True to form, her next words exhibited that same lack of faith in him.

"It won't, you know. I don't think it can ever be truly all right again."

The only reason he didn't start shouting at her was that she sounded so bloody forlorn. From what he'd heard when he entered Langley House, she'd also been yelled at enough for one day. As much as the idea irritated him, he should probably wait until later to confront her about their relationship. There would be plenty of time to set her straight tomorrow.

FOR ONCE THE ENGLISH SUN SHONE BRIGHTLY INTO THE small, well-tended garden attached to Aunt Harriet's town house. Irisa sat with her legs curled under her on a quilt near the box hedge and enjoyed the warmth of the spring day, letting it soak into her skin and relax her. She had let the shawl she had worn over her raspberry muslin gown drop in a pool of fabric around her.

It had been three days since her notorious ride through the park and subsequent banishment to Upworth House. Aunt Harriet and Pansy had both done their best to coddle and cosset her, but even their tender affections could not lighten the burden of her emotions. She missed Lucas.

She knew she shouldn't, but she couldn't seem to stop herself—any more than she could stop herself from remembering Miss de Brieuse's final words to her. *My lady, you would not listen to me regarding the details of my association with Ashton.* S'il vous plaît. *I beg of you. Ask him. It is not what you think.*

It was almost as if Miss de Brieuse had been trying to tell her that she was not Lucas's mistress, that the evidence of Irisa's own eyes had been false. Not that it mattered now. Lucas might not have known about Irisa's mad escapade when he rescued her from Langley House, but he was bound to have heard all the details by now.

So why had he sent her flowers yesterday? Pretty yellow rosebuds that she had wept over. Why had he called three days in a row, to be turned away by Aunt Harriet? Surely he would not insist on ringing a peal over her as well. Could he not handle the dissolution of their engagement through the solicitors?

Both Pansy and Aunt Harriet were determined that Irisa should rest. They seemed to think the bruise on her cheek incapacitated her. She acquiesced because she didn't want to face Lucas. It was cowardly, but she was still smarting from her parents' complete rejection. She could not face another verbal barrage, this time from the man she loved.

She wished she could stop loving him, but even the memory of Lucas holding the lovely Miss de Brieuse could not kill Irisa's feelings for him. Who knew better than she that the strength of one's emotions did not depend on the actions of the person loved? She had loved her parents all her life.

However, her love did not mean that she would marry Lucas, or that she would ever return to live in her parents' home. She was through trying to earn affection where none existed. Knowing she was right to turn away from both her parents and Lucas did not make it hurt any less, however. She missed Lucas terribly.

As if her thoughts had conjured up his image, suddenly he stood looming over her. "Good afternoon, Irisa. Your guards have finally relaxed their vigil enough to allow me entrance."

She did not want to look up and see the expression of disgust sure to be on his features, nor did she particularly want him to see the ugly mark on her face. However, putting off the inevitable would not make it easier to face. The last three days had shown her that.

She raised her head, keeping her expression blank. "Good afternoon, my lord."

He cursed and reached out to touch her cheek. She knew what he saw and it wasn't a pretty sight. A purplish blue mark already going green and yellow around the edges covered almost the entire left side of her face. Papa had big hands.

She barely felt the brush of Lucas's finger as he examined the damage to her face. He cursed again. A word she had never heard a gentleman say before, though she had once heard the stable master at Langley Hall say it after being kicked in the unmentionables by a horse.

Lucas dropped to the quilt beside her. "I'm sorry, little one. I wish I had gotten there soon enough to prevent this." He brushed her cheek again with almost painful tenderness.

She opened her eyes wide in surprise. Lucas was not behaving at all as she had expected him to. "You cannot blame yourself for this. I brought it on myself with my foolish actions."

He put his finger under her chin and tipped her head until

her eyes met his. His expression was so intent, it was almost frightening. "Listen to me. You did nothing to warrant such an attack from the man who should protect you from the world. Langley is a fool with a fool's temper, and he well knows now that he should never have unleashed it on you."

Irisa reached up to grip Lucas's arm. "What do you mean? What have you done?"

"Nothing that need concern you. It is just as I said. Your father will not make the same mistake again. Ever."

"You did not call him out?" she asked, voicing the unthinkable.

"No." Lucas flexed the fist that was not holding her chin. "There was no need. He has seen the error of his ways."

Irisa could see from his implacable expression that Lucas would not say any more. She shivered. *And she had been concerned about telling Drake.*

"Now. Let us discuss your *foolish* actions."

She tried to draw her head away, but Lucas would not let her.

He gripped her chin gently, but firmly. "Why did you do it?"

"Does it matter? Surely my actions speak for themselves."

"If you mean, does it matter to our future together, then no, it does not. But your actions do not speak for themselves, and I want an answer."

He didn't ask why again, but simply waited for her to answer him. His fingers against her chin were warmer than the sun beating down from the sky, and it was all she could do not to move her head and turn his gentle hold into a caress. How she longed to feel his hands on her body, his mouth covering her own. Why had he given his passion to another woman?

Sudden, aching tears wetted her eyes and she blinked, trying desperately not to let them fall.

Without warning, Lucas's mouth covered hers in the gentlest caress she had ever known. Her mouth parted on a gasp of surprise and Lucas fit his lips to hers in a sensual mating that sent her senses scattering to the four winds. His mouth tasted unlike anything she had ever experienced. There were no words to describe it. It was just *right.* She had always imagined that lips would be soft, but Lucas's were firm and mobile. With each fractional movement, she succumbed more deeply to his kiss.

Without conscious volition, her hands moved to grip his shoulders, her fingers curling into the solid muscle.

He groaned and she found herself in his lap, her body nestled against him from where her bottom rested against his thighs to her breasts crushed against his waistcoat. It was the most delicious sensation she had ever known. Lucas's tongue caressed her lips and then dipped inside her mouth before retreating. She moaned and opened her mouth wider.

He repeated the teasing foray over and over until she wanted to scream. Feelings she did not know she was capable of washed over her body like a wave crashing against the shore. She felt both stunned and thoroughly soaked by them.

Lucas drew his mouth from hers and pressed her head against his waistcoat, where she could hear his rapid heartbeat. His breathing was every bit as ragged as hers as well.

"Now, tell me why."

"I don't know if I can explain it to you," she said against his chest.

"Try."

She actually found herself smiling at his wry command. He was so arrogant and he didn't even realize it.

"I wanted out of our engagement." As soon as the words left her mouth, she realized what a lie they were.

She wanted to marry Lucas more than anything else in the world. Perhaps that was why she had really done what she had done. She had been afraid she would not have the courage to cry off, so she had acted in such a way as to force him to do so.

He sighed and she felt it in the rise and fall of his chest

under her cheek. "Why didn't you just jilt me if you were so set on ending our association?"

She wasn't about to share her new insight with him. She told him her original reason instead. "I don't want to marry. Not ever. Once I realized that, I looked for a way to both end our engagement and put a stop to Papa and Mama's efforts to see me wed."

"You accomplished one goal at least. Your parents will not be doing any more matchmaking on your behalf." His rueful humor took some of the sting from his words and what they represented. "But after the way you just responded to my kiss, I find it difficult to believe you don't want to marry me."

She felt the embarrassed color creep into her cheeks, but remembering why she had decided not to marry brought an entirely different emotion to the surface.

She sat up and glared at Lucas. "You can make me respond to your kisses, but you can't make me trust you, and that's why I never want to marry. I won't be a gentleman's ornament and brood mare, expected to hide my feelings and tolerate my husband's infidelities while I remain chaste and neglected."

He gripped her arms, the touch of his fingers translating the tension in him to her. "That's been the problem all along, hasn't it? You don't trust me, and because of your lack of trust, you've done damage to your reputation, hurt an innocent woman, and forced a rift with your family. Not that I see that last bit as a great loss."

"What innocent woman have I hurt?" Surely he was not speaking of Mama. He had made his feelings for her parents abundantly clear.

"Clarice de Brieuse."

That was too much! For him to call his mistress an innocent woman and accuse Irisa of hurting her, he might as well have slapped her as her papa had done.

She yanked away from his loose hold and scrambled off his lap. "How dare you bring up your mistress's feelings as if they are of more import than mine? You may not love me, Lord Ashton, but you have the obligation of a gentleman to protect me until such time as our engagement is at an end."

She was practically shouting at him, but she could not make herself care. What was one more notorious incident to add to her undoubtedly growing reputation?

"Since the only way this engagement is going to end is in marriage, I will continue to have a responsibility to protect you—even if that means protecting you from your own idiotic plans and notions," Lucas returned in a fair imitation of a lion's roar.

She settled her fists on her hips like any fishwife and scowled at Lucas's too-bloody-tempting male beauty. "If you think I'm going to marry you after finding out about Miss de Brieuse, you are indeed a fool, my lord."

Lucas came up off the quilt with such speed she could not even think of running, much less act upon it. He put his hands around her waist and lifted her against him until they were eye level.

"You are going to marry me and you are going to trust me, and if you ever call me *my lord* again, I won't be responsible for my actions." Each word came forth like a bullet.

Then his mouth slammed down onto hers. Where the other kiss had been gentle, exploratory, and sensually alluring, this meeting of their mouths was nothing less than a possession.

Lucas demanded her surrender with his mouth while his hold pressed her against the tightness of his masculine form. Rage that he had waited to share his passion with her until it was too late warred with another equally powerful emotion . . . desire.

Eight

Irisa struggled against Lucas's hold, tearing her mouth from his and inciting his frustration to a higher pitch.

"Let me go!" she demanded.

"Never." Wanting to bring an end to her denials of his claim on her, he caught her soft lips once again and ground his mouth against hers.

He could taste the anger on her lips, but he could also taste her desire. He wanted to stamp out the one while setting fire to the other. Her anger, based as it was on mistrust, infuriated him. He had done nothing wrong with Clarice, and Irisa should never have believed otherwise. She belonged to him, and he would never betray that bond.

Seeing her father strike her had called up fierce feelings of both protectiveness and possessiveness in Lucas. Those feelings denied duty to his line as the primary reason for his proposal of marriage to Irisa.

He would never let her go. Never. Tightening his grip, he pressed her closer to his hardening body. She whimpered and the sound of distress bought him a modicum of control.

Damn it, what was he doing? She had suffered enough at her father's hand. To think he was adding to her pain made

Lucas as angry with himself as he was at Irisa's lack of trust.

Softening the kiss, he teased her lips with his tongue while he altered his hold from rough possession to gentle seduction. She responded immediately to the change and ceased her struggles, allowing her body to mold itself to his.

Placing one hand around her waist, he used the other to hook under her knees and carried her back to the quilt.

He laid her on it, coming down beside her without allowing their clinging lips to separate. Her breathing was now as rapid as his and he doubted it was from anger. She lifted herself closer when he let a small distance separate their bodies. The desire that he'd held in check for the months of their courtship and the weeks of their engagement exploded.

He forgot they were not yet married. He no longer cared they were in full view of the house. The soft translucence of Irisa's skin beckoned him. He trailed his fingers along the demure line of her muslin gown, allowing them to dip beneath the fabric and brush the upper curve of her creamy feminine flesh.

Irisa squirmed against him, her mouth finally opening on a gasp to his questing tongue and he took full advantage, plunging inside to sample the warm honey that beckoned. He ached with the need to taste not only her mouth, but the rest of her feminine softness as well.

He brushed his lips over her cheek, down her neck, into the hollow of her throat, and ultimately to the silken skin exposed above the raspberry muslin. Pressing the undersides of her breasts until they swelled against the fabric, he kissed the enticing crevice between her swollen flesh before allowing the tip of his tongue to trace the path his lips had already taken.

She shivered, her body arching in innocent abandon, and he could not stop himself from nipping gently at the exposed curves.

"Lucas."

The sound of his name on her lips, spoken with such aching need, made him throb with the desire for release.

"That's it, little one. Let me taste you."

He tugged the sleeves of her gown down until the upper swells of her breasts were fully exposed and her nipples were covered only by the fine lawn of her chemise. *Damnation, she was beautiful.* While his tongue dipped more deeply into the cleavage between the two delicious mounds, he trailed a shaking hand down her side, over her hip, and then gripped the fleshy curve of her bottom.

The scent of her delicate skin pushed the last remnants of his control from his mind as he squeezed her bottom convulsively. "I want you, little one."

"You want me?" she asked, her voice breathy and vague.

The hungry touch of his hands and mouth could leave even an innocent like her in no doubt as to what he wanted. "Yes."

In a flurry of movement, Irisa's hands came up to push against his chest while she attempted to sit up. "Lucas, you must stop."

"No. I must not." Did she think he could turn off his desire like a street lamp when dawn cast London in its glow?

Covering her mouth with his once again, he meant to quiet her resistance. It worked. Her lips softened under his and her fingers curled into his waistcoat rather than pushing him away. Using the hand on her bottom, he pushed the apex of her thighs against his hardened sex and rocked against her. He groaned from the pleasure of it and wondered how long he would last once he was inside her.

She whimpered again and tore her mouth away from his. "Please. Stop. Lucas, we cannot do this."

He disagreed. His hardened sex was evidence that they could do this, and very effectively, too. All he had to do was pull down his breeches and lift her skirts. Denied her mouth, he returned his attention to her breasts, this time taking one taut nipple into his mouth through the fabric of her chemise. The already hardened bud swelled in his mouth.

"Stop," she said, but had her fingers buried in his hair. "You mustn't do this. I can't stand it."

"You're stronger than you think," he promised before moving his mouth to her other breast.

She moaned and arched against him. He had to feel her heat. Reaching past the hem of her muslin skirt, he tunneled his hand under the layers of fabric to caress her stockinged leg. Impatient to touch her intimately, he lightly caressed her leg upward until he felt the naked skin of her thigh.

She shrieked and began kicking her legs in agitation, which opened her to his touch. He took advantage and slid his fingers into the soft and definitely damp curls of her femininity.

She pounded on his shoulders. "Stop! Bloody hell, Lucas. You must stop. You must not touch me there. It isn't decent. *Someone is going to see.*"

Her words finally registered and sanity returned in a blinding flash of awareness. He was lying with his fiancée in full view of the house where any passing servant—or Lady Upworth—could see, and he'd been on the verge of tossing Irisa's skirts up and making love to her. He couldn't believe he'd let one kiss go so far, so fast.

Bloody everlasting hell! Where was his famed self-control? He released her and rolled away, covering his eyes with his forearm. He should help her right her clothes, but he couldn't move. He was in too much pain and the hardness that was causing it was not fading fast. Taking several deep breaths, he forced himself to focus on something besides his fiancée's tempting body.

Like the fact that he'd almost dishonored her in Lady Upworth's garden.

No. Concentrating on that was dangerous. He chose instead to think of what he could say to soothe her. An apology at the very least, but he could not lie and say it would not happen again. Taking a cleansing breath, he sat up and took stock of his surroundings. Irisa perched on the very edge of the blanket, her shawl drawn around her shoulders and wrapped in front of her like a shield. She stared at him with an unreadable expression.

"I'm sorry." The words were inadequate after the way he'd practically ravished her, but they were all he had.

She nodded, but remained mute.

Had he terrified her? "Damnation, Irisa. Say something. I wasn't going to rape you."

Her eyes widened at his words. "I didn't think you were."

That was something, at any rate. "At least you trust me that much," he muttered.

She cocked her head to one side and studied him. He felt like a beast on display at the Tower of London.

"Tell me about Clarice de Brieuse, please."

"If you had asked me that question earlier, you would have avoided a great deal of hardship."

"Perhaps. Are you going to answer it now?" Her voice was soft and her lips were still swollen from his kisses.

He didn't want to talk. He wanted to carry her off to the nearest bedroom and make slow, sweet love to her. He forced his attention to their discussion and away from his returning ardor.

"Clarice was my brother's mistress."

OF ALL THE EXPLANATIONS SHE HAD TRIED TO CONCOCT in her head to justify Lucas's behavior, this one had never occurred to her. Irisa sat in stunned silence as Lucas continued his tale.

"My brother was two years younger, and though I tried, I could not prevent him from following in our mother's footsteps. By the time he was nineteen, he had a reputation as a rake and a scoundrel." The pain in Lucas's words reached out and touched Irisa as nothing else could have.

Without conscious volition, she found herself scooting closer to him. Offering the solace of her nearness, she placed her hand on his arm. Lucas acted unaware of the light touch, his thoughts clearly in the past.

"When he was twenty, he allowed me to purchase him a commission in the army. I hoped that the move signaled his willingness to change, to live a more responsible life."

When he did not continue, Irisa asked, "Did it?"

He pulled on the cuffs of his blue superfine jacket and straightened his cravat. "We'll never know. He died a year later in the Peterloo Massacre."

"I thought only citizens died in that tragedy."

"It's true that the army murdered numerous innocents at the peaceful gathering, but some of our military paid the ultimate price as well. My brother was one of them."

She squeezed his arm. "I'm sorry, Lucas. So very sorry."

He met her eyes, and incredibly, he smiled. "You're so gentle, Irisa. I mistook that trait for compliancy earlier in our association."

She felt her cheeks heat. "I can be quite stubborn."

"Yes."

She smiled at his ready agreement. "So how did you end up responsible for your brother's mistress?"

She had no doubt that was what had occurred. What she still didn't know was whether Miss de Brieuse had become Lucas's paramour as well. Their intimate embrace the other night would indicate she had, but Irisa was determined to hear him out on the subject.

"She was carrying his child when he died."

"How did you find out?"

"She came to me."

"And you believed her?" Somehow that seemed too simple.

"It was easy enough to verify that she was indeed under my brother's protection, such as it was. As mistresses went, she had an impeccable reputation. There were no rumors of her taking other lovers."

"And the child."

"Is a beautiful little imp of four who has both her mother and me wrapped entirely around her pudgy little finger. She has the Ashton eyes and her mother's ruby hair."

Lucas would be a wonderful father. Unlike her papa, he would not ignore his offspring until they were of age to be socially beneficial.

She smiled. "I should like to meet her."

Once the words were out of her mouth, she realized how unlikely the occurrence, but Lucas nodded, a touch of sadness coming into his eyes. "I shall see that you do so before she and her mother sail for France."

"They're going to France?" Irisa asked, feeling dazed.

"Yes. Clarice is to be married and the gentleman, Maurice Brun, wishes to return to their homeland."

"You're going to miss her." It was a statement. Not a question. There could be no doubt from the tone of Lucas's voice that the move would hurt him. Did he love Miss de Brieuse?

"I shall miss my niece, but hope to have my own children to fill the emptiness her leaving will cause," he said meaningfully.

She would not be so easily sidetracked. "What of Miss de Brieuse?"

Lucas met her gaze, his own stern. "She is my friend and I will miss her as such, but that is all."

"She has not been your mistress?" Irisa probed, unable to leave it alone.

"No." His tone brooked no doubt. "She was so desperate when she came to me that she attempted to seduce me, but I could sense her fear and managed to get the truth out of her."

He made it sound as if it had all been quite simple and ordinary, yet under the circumstances Irisa did not see how that could be. No doubt his experience as an intelligence officer had stood him in good stead the night he first met Clarice de Brieuse.

"But what of the other night, when she embraced you?" After the words slipped out, Irisa realized she should not have said them.

How could she explain knowing of their embrace without admitting the truth of her own outrageous actions? She was fairly certain that Lucas would not look kindly on her dressing up as a stable boy and spying on him.

His eyes narrowed. "What are you talking about?"

"Nothing. Please disregard my question."

"That is impossible. If you set servants spying on me, I will hear about it now."

He had given her the perfect excuse, but she could not take it. "I don't want to lie to you."

"Then don't," he replied implacably.

"I overheard some gossip the other night at a soirée."

"Gossip?" he asked, his voice cold as the Scottish highlands in winter.

"Yes. Another lady was speaking with my mother. She wondered what you planned to do with your mistress after our marriage."

Lucas looked perilously close to anger, so she rushed on.

"At first I could not believe that you would be unfaithful. It was so out of character for The Saint."

"I am not a saint, Irisa, but neither am I a libertine."

She nodded in agreement. A saint would not have bared her bosom in her aunt's garden, and a libertine would have taken what Miss de Brieuse offered in her desperation.

"Mama has always hidden from the unpleasant realities of life and, in doing so, hurt the people around her."

His brows drew together. "What does that have to do with you sending servants to spy on me?"

"I did not send servants. I went myself, but that comes later. Are you going to let me finish my story, or not?" She'd almost tacked on the hated *my lord,* but felt she'd pushed her luck enough.

"By all means, continue. This is more interesting than a French farce."

"Better that than a tragedy," she replied with some asperity. "In any case, I would not allow myself to hide from the truth like Mama. If you were being unfaithful, I had to know. So, as much as I deplore tittle-tattle, I asked my maid to investigate the servants' gossip."

"I see."

She doubted it. While he might want to marry her, he did not love her as she loved him. He could not possibly comprehend the level of pain she had experienced at the thought of him in another woman's bed.

"Much to my dismay, your underfootman verified that you visit a certain former actress regularly."

"Impossible. My servants know better than to breathe a word of my association with Clarice to anyone."

"Apparently not this one. Perhaps he is new."

The tight line of Lucas's jaw did not bode well for the hapless servant. "My rules for conduct are well known amongst my staff, even the newest hires."

"He cannot be the only one, Lucas." She felt compelled to defend the unsuspecting underfootman. "Lady Preston heard about it from somewhere."

"When I discover where she came upon the *on dit,* I shall ensure the source no longer deems my affairs worthy of discussion."

Irisa hated gossip, probably more than Lucas, but she had a feeling he dealt with it in a far more intimidating fashion.

"You must do as you see fit."

"Yes. Pray continue your explanation."

She took a deep breath and did so. "The morning before I, um . . . spied on you, you had told me not to expect you at any of the soirées. I surmised that you would be visiting Miss de Brieuse."

"An interesting assumption."

"I was correct, if you will remember."

"Yes."

"And I saw you kiss her cheek. Later, she embraced you." She finished her explanation with the accusation.

"How did you see all this?" His voice had gone dangerously soft and it sent a shiver down Irisa's spine.

"I'd prefer not to tell you the particulars, if you don't mind, Lucas. What's done is done," she said, repeating what she had told Miss de Brieuse after the ride in the park.

"I do mind, very much. You will explain how you were in the position to see me with Clarice when I was told the next day that you had stayed home the night before with a sick headache that had turned into a nasty cold."

"Really, I don't see why I need to explain myself to you,

Lucas. You still have not made clear why Miss de Brieuse embraced you if she is not your mistress."

He leaned forward and the civility that usually cloaked him fell away to reveal a predator intent on its prey. "Tell me the truth about that night, Irisa," he demanded.

"I disguised myself as a stable boy and waited in the fog outside her house for your arrival. When you came, I could not help peeking in through a crack in the draperies. You kissed her cheek with more warm affection than you had shown me thus far in our association. I looked away and then later, when I took another peek, she was embracing you as if she had every right."

Lucas's glare was dark enough to eclipse the sun. "She did have the right. A woman whom I had treated as friend and sister for almost five years had just told me she was to be married. She was very happy and wanted to share her joy."

"I don't quite see why she had to share her body," Irisa muttered under her breath.

Lucas ignored her. He wasn't finished discussing the other topic from the furious look on his face. "Why did you not simply ask me for the truth?"

"I could not be certain you would give it. Many gentlemen of the *ton* think nothing of keeping a mistress."

"I am not other gentlemen."

"No, you are not, but I had to know the truth, and really, Lucas . . . you've made it quite clear you don't approve of ladies discussing things of this nature."

"We are discussing it now."

She could not contradict him. They were discussing it and he was being incredibly forthright with her. Perhaps he was less of a stickler for proprieties than she had thought.

"I suppose I may have acted a trifle hastily."

"A trifle hastily? No, my dear lady, you acted bloody foolishly! Do you have any idea what could have happened to you that night?"

"I was careful to keep my disguise." She saw no need to mention the way it had been compromised by the wet night. "My reputation was quite safe."

"*Your reputation?* That is all that worried you? You could have been attacked by footpads. You could have been raped or killed, or both. As for your reputation, you've shown you've got little enough concern for it." Although he started his tirade in a near roar, he ended it in a calm tone, laced with disgust.

Irisa felt tears prick the backs of her eyes. She did not want him to see her weak emotions and averted her face. When had she turned into such a watering pot? She never cried.

At least she hadn't before meeting Lucas. "I will, of course, understand if you choose to withdraw your offer, my lord."

Her mind registered the fact she had said the phrase that Lucas found particularly annoying a split second before he loomed over her, all outraged male.

His arms caged her in, his body so close she could feel his heat. "What I am going to do, *Lady Irisa,* is marry you as soon as possible. If I don't take you in hand, there's no telling what sort of trouble you might get yourself into. I'm doing the rest of the *ton* a favor by accepting responsibility for you. Heaven knows your father and mother are incapable of doing a proper job."

The first thing that registered as Lucas talked was that she did not like Lucas using the more formal address either. Close on the heels of that discovery came the second one. *He had insulted her.*

"I do not need taking in hand," she said with outrage. "Surely you must see that recent events have been quite out of the ordinary. I made it to the age of twenty without so much as a single incident marring my pristine reputation."

"For which we can only be grateful to Providence."

She did not appreciate his sarcasm one bit.

"There is no need to take that tone with me, sir." Her words were less effective than she would have liked as they came out in an almost breathless whisper owing to the fact that he had inched forward and his upper body now touched hers.

Her shawl, gown, and chemise might not have been there for all the notice her body took of them. "Furthermore, it appears you are the one who has no care for my reputation now."

He glared but backed away, and she took a steadying breath. She did not move as he stood up and once again adjusted his clothes to proper order.

He extended his hand to her. "Come, it is time we returned inside. Too much sun is bad for a lady's complexion and you've forgotten your parasol."

Indicating her cheek, she said, "My complexion is already quite ruined right now and I'm enjoying the sun."

He did not withdraw his hand. "Come now or I will once again join you on the quilt and I make no promise to take care with your reputation or your feminine sensibilities."

With blinding clarity, she realized he was not bluffing. She had pushed The Saint past the point of his control and she could either retreat or pay the price of surrender. She stood without his assistance. Nothing was settled between them, but in his present mood it wasn't going to be. They might as well retire to the house.

"Come inside then and visit with my aunt. She rarely gets out anymore, but she adores company."

LUCAS HAD ALREADY DISCOVERED THE ELDERLY woman's preference for company. Although she had refused his requests to see Irisa, claiming his fiancée needed rest more than company, Lady Upworth had not allowed Lucas to leave her town house without taking tea on each occasion he'd called over the past three days.

"Good afternoon, my lord. I trust you and Irisa had a convivial visit in the garden." The mischievous sparkle in Lady Upworth's eye made Lucas wonder just how much she knew about what had transpired between him and her niece outside.

He felt unaccustomed heat in his neck.

"Irisa and I smoothed out some wrinkles between us,"

he said as he seated his fiancée on a small sofa and then, as had become his custom, took his place next to her. "Has anyone else attempted to call on Irisa since we spoke?"

"Her mother came by yesterday, but as per your instructions, I had my butler tell her that Irisa was not yet receiving visitors."

A small gasp came from the woman beside him and he turned to face Irisa. "Did you want to say something, sweeting?"

She frowned. "Do not call me endearments in front of my aunt. It isn't proper."

He smiled and did not state the obvious—that she was a little past worrying about such paltry considerations. "Is that all?"

"No. I don't like you giving orders where I'm concerned. It should have been my decision whether or not I saw my mother. I'm sure she was terribly offended to have Aunt Harriet turn her away. It would upset me greatly if my presence here caused a rift between my aunt and my parents."

"And it would upset me if Lady Langley had been allowed to interrupt your recuperation with another tirade."

"Ashton is quite right, Irisa, dear. You needed your rest," Lady Upworth said.

"My face is bruised. I am not convalescing from the fever or a war wound."

"What's done is done," Lucas replied, earning him a set of narrowed golden brown eyes for turning her words back on her.

"I suppose you're right. I'll send a card to Mama, inviting her to call again, or perhaps I should call on her. It would soothe her dignity for me to make the effort." Irisa bit her lip, clearly deep in thought on the matter.

Lucas felt irritation swell and tamped it down. She still did not understand the full extent of her new circumstance.

"Impossible. You will not call on your mother." When it looked like Irisa would argue, he compromised. "You may invite her here, if you wish, but I will be present."

"That is absurd, Lucas. Mama will be much more likely to forgive Aunt's offense if I call on her."

"You will not go to Langley House. Is that clear?"

"No, it is not clear. You cannot dictate to me in this fashion. I won't tolerate it."

Lady Upworth laughed, a soft melodic sound. "Children. Calm yourselves. Irisa, you must realize that Ashton is only looking after your best interests."

Beside him, Irisa stiffened. "I can look after my own interests perfectly well."

This time Lucas laughed. He could not help it. She sounded so sincere. There she sat with a shiner that would make Gentleman Jackson proud, her reputation in tatters, and yet she claimed she could look after herself. She did not appreciate his amusement and let him know with an elbow in his side. There was nothing for it but for him to slide one arm around her waist and pull her against him, thus preventing further attacks from her sharp little appendage.

"You belong to me, and you might as well accept that I take my responsibilities seriously. You will not see your parents again unless I am present."

This time Irisa's gasp of outrage was drowned out by the sounds of new arrivals in the hall. The sitting room door flew open and Mrs. Drake rushed inside closely followed by her husband. She made a beeline for Irisa and fell on her knees in front of her younger sister. "Sister mine, are you all right?"

Irisa looked helplessly at Mrs. Drake, and Lucas could feel the tension in her. He saved her the effort of answering. "She is fine, but for one nasty bruise."

Drake met Lucas's gaze. "Is it true? Did Langley hit her?"

Suddenly every pair of eyes in the room was on Lucas. Lady Upworth looked curious as to how he would answer. Irisa looked pleading and Mrs. Drake looked as if she was about to be sick.

Nine

"He lost control, but as I was just explaining to Irisa, he will not have the opportunity to do so again."

Drake nodded, his eyes mirroring masculine understanding. "I tried to call on him today and was informed that he is indisposed. I assume he will take longer to heal than Irisa?"

"Lucas, you did not beat Papa?" Irisa's tone echoed her inner turmoil.

Entirely too tenderhearted, she would not understand the need for his violent response to her father's despicable behavior. He could not resist the emotional appeal in her voice or the worried frown marring her pretty features.

"I did not beat him, little one." He did not lie and say he had not hurt Langley, but a few solid punches and a harsh warning did not constitute a beating.

The man had still been able to walk afterward.

"I do not understand. Why did Langley hit you, Irisa?" Mrs. Drake asked, still kneeling in front of her sister.

"It's a long story and I'd rather not go into it."

Mrs. Drake did not look pleased by the answer and Drake asked, "Did it have anything to do with the drive you took through the park with Clarice de Brieuse?"

"Yes," Irisa said with a sigh.

Mrs. Drake looked confused. "Who is she?"

Lucas realized that the questioning would not end until she had her answers. For Irisa's sake, he decided to give them to her. "Drake, seat your wife and I will explain everything."

Irisa turned so that she could whisper close to his ear. "I don't want to talk about it now, Lucas."

"Putting it off will not make it any easier," he replied.

She gave a disgruntled sigh. "You are probably right, but I hate all the fuss."

He did not say that she'd brought it on herself. Somehow he did not think she would appreciate the reminder. Once Drake had seated both himself and his wife in chairs, Lucas gave a succinct, edited version of the events.

"Irisa overheard some gossip to the effect that I kept a mistress. She did not want to believe it, but being the curious creature that she is, she decided to talk to the woman in question. Her name is Clarice de Brieuse and she is my niece's mother. Irisa chose to do her talking in an open curricle in Hyde Park. Lord and Lady Langley did not approve of her curiosity or the manner in which she assuaged it."

His fiancée sagged against him in obvious relief that he had not divulged the more awkward details of her adventure.

"Oh, Irisa," Mrs. Drake said.

"My dear niece, when one is satisfying one's natural penchant to *know,* one must use circumspection. It is, I fear, a skill that develops with age and is often lacking in the young. You are very lucky to have such an understanding fiancé in this matter." Lady Upworth reached out to pat Irisa's arm in an obvious attempt to soften the rebuke.

"I suppose," Irisa grumbled.

Lucas had the distinct impression that his lady did not agree with her aunt's assessment.

"This *understanding fiancé* has decided to be married by special license in three days' time to prevent further occurrences like this one."

His words were met with varying reactions. Drake

nodded in complete understanding. Mrs. Drake looked thoughtful, but Lady Upworth shook her head sadly. "That just won't do. Irisa's reputation has already taken a beating. If you cancel the wedding, you are as good as announcing to the *ton* that her parents have disowned her."

Mrs. Drake nodded. "That's true. The best thing to do would be to act as if nothing has happened, to have the wedding on time and show a unified front as a family."

"But Papa *has* disowned me. He said he wished I wasn't his daughter and I know he'll refuse to come to the wedding." Irisa turned to meet Lucas's gaze, her own troubled and filled with lingering pain from her father's callously uttered words. "Not that I'm going to marry you in three days. We still have a great deal to discuss."

She could talk until she ran out of words, but she was going to marry him. Her aunt and sister's opinion had merit, however.

"How do you suggest we go about pretending nothing has happened?" He knew how he had done it with his mother, but he hoped to avoid the scandal of a dawn appointment.

"You will have to be seen at entertainments in one another's company and in the company of Langley and his wife," Mrs. Drake said.

"That could be a problem right now," mused Lady Upworth, looking at Irisa's bruised face.

"Well, I suppose you could stage a trip to Langley Hall to make arrangements for the wedding. That would only be natural," Mrs. Drake responded.

"No. Irisa will not stay at Langley Hall." Lucas had no intention of backing down on that particular issue and they might as well know it now.

Irisa grumbled something, but it was too low for him to hear. "What did you say, sweeting?"

She scowled. "You're dictating again."

"Do you want to stay at Langley Hall?" he asked.

"No."

"Then why are you complaining?" he asked with barely concealed exasperation.

"Because I think it should be my decision," she retorted.

"Regardless of whose decision it is, it leaves us looking for other alternatives," Lady Upworth said with some asperity.

"What about a trip to Ashton's estate?" Drake suggested.

"I suppose that would be expected this close to the wedding. It's quite common for a prospective bride and her parents to make such a visit," Lady Upworth said.

Mrs. Drake nodded. "Yes. That would do the trick. There will still be talk, of course. However, Ashton's place in the *ton* is unassailable, if I understand these things correctly, and once it is clear he still intends to go through with the marriage, the tittle-tattle will die a natural death."

IRISA BREATHED A SIGH OF RELIEF AS SHE QUIETLY closed the door to the tower room. Her ear to the weathered wood, she waited for sounds indicating her escape had been discovered. She thought one of the footmen might have seen her and gone to alert Pansy or Lucas to the fact that she was unaccompanied, but she heard nothing on the other side of the door. No rushing footsteps. No masculine voice raised in irritation.

Alone at last, she relaxed and glanced around the sparsely furnished room. It would make a wonderful private sitting room with its round walls and romantic atmosphere. Like most English country houses, Ashton Manor had bits and pieces of several past eras in its sprawling architecture, including two matching towers, both of which had roof walks. She had escaped to the east tower and not without a certain amount of ingenuity.

Pansy thought she was riding with Thea and Drake. Thea, on the other hand, believed that Irisa had gone to her room to rest . . . with her maid.

Thea's children were napping in the nursery and Lucas was closeted in his study in the west tower going over estate business. Mama was hiding in her room trying to pretend that Thea, Drake, and their family did not exist, and Papa had gone for another of his brooding walks. He hadn't spoken a word to Irisa since Lucas had carried her from Langley House.

She thought that might be because Lucas refused to leave her alone and Papa would not berate her in front of witnesses. It would be beneath his dignity. And for that reason alone, it had taken Irisa more time than usual to chafe against the uncommon strictures Lucas had imposed on her.

He had allowed her parents to come to Ashton Manor, but only with the understanding that Irisa was not to be alone in Papa's company. She had readily agreed, not wanting another ugly scene with her father, but she had not anticipated Lucas interpreting her agreement to extend to no time alone whatsoever.

Lucas refused to take the slightest chance that Papa's aberrant behavior at Langley House would be repeated—thus Irisa's need to escape.

Irisa liked her own company. Alone, she did not have to live up to the expectations of perfection placed on her by others. Since coming to Ashton Manor, she had not even been allowed to sleep by herself. Lucas had insisted Pansy be installed on a cot in her bedchamber. Irisa had spent a great deal of her life in her own company and felt stifled by the constant presence of another person—particularly since that other person was not Lucas.

He had avoided her almost as assiduously as her papa since arriving at Ashton Manor, and absolutely refused all efforts on her behalf to discuss the termination of their engagement. It irritated and amazed her that she had not realized in all the time she had known him how stubborn he could be. She was certainly aware of it now.

He insisted with absolute assurance that their engagement stand. And because he was so adamant, no one listened to Irisa when she said she wasn't sure she wanted to marry him. Her mother thought her an ungrateful wretch after the way she'd made a spectacle of herself. That was no more than she had expected, but even Thea was convinced Irisa was suffering no more than typical bridal jitters.

Perhaps if she had spoken more forcefully, at least Thea would have paid attention, but then that was the problem. She wasn't sure she didn't want to marry him either. She simply was not sure about anything right now. She needed uninterrupted time to think. So she had snuck away. No one would be the wiser until Thea and Drake returned from their ride, and from the way Drake had been looking at her sister, Irisa assumed that would not be for quite a while.

With a novel and quilt tucked under one arm, she climbed the circular stairway. Placing her burdens on the top step by her feet, she pushed the heavy bar from its loops and opened the door leading to the roof walk. Her book and blanket once again tucked under her arm, she walked out into the afternoon sunlight and her breath caught at the glorious stillness surrounding her.

Breathing in the fresh spring air, she let her gaze sweep over the rolling hills surrounding Lucas's estate. She felt as if she could see for miles, and perhaps she could. Was that not the church spire from the local village? She walked the entire circumference of the tower roof, soaking in both her solitude and the magnificent view, before spreading the quilt and sitting down with her back propped against the stone wall.

The similarity of her position to the one she had been in when Lucas found her in Aunt Harriet's garden reminded her of that consuming kiss. The word did not seem adequate to encompass the level of intimacy she and Lucas had shared, intimacy that still left her blushing whenever she thought of it, but which had not been repeated in any shape or form since their arrival at the manor.

Lucas could not have made it plainer he had no desire to repeat the experience. She bit her lip, wondering if her unladylike response in the garden had given him a complete disgust of her.

The heroes in the novels she read liked their lady loves to respond to them without inhibition, but then they never got much beyond a very enthusiastic closed-mouthed kiss. How would those same heroes react to a heroine who allowed her bosom to be bared in the afternoon sun? Who not only allowed it, but had shamelessly reveled in the experience?

When Lucas had said he wanted her, images of her naked body entwined with his had started swimming behind her closed eyelids. It had been the shock of those images that had brought her to her senses and her first attempt at calling a halt to the devastating kiss.

A true paragon of virtue would never have allowed it to get that far in the first place. Another disturbing thought that nagged at her was the fact that thus far Lucas's passions had not become stirred unless he was well and truly angry. It was a depressing notion, but the truth could not be altered. She wished she knew more about this aspect of a man and woman's relationship. Perhaps she should ask Thea about it.

Thea had a very affectionate marriage with Drake and she'd had two children. Surely she could advise Irisa on the matter. On the other hand, it did not appear that Drake ever needed anger, or anything else for that matter, to bolster his affection for her sister. Thea might be as stymied by Lucas's behavior as Irisa.

No matter how long she brooded, she could not come up with a clear understanding of Lucas's treatment of her. Sighing in defeat, she opened her novel and was soon lost in a world of crumbling castles and lurking menace. She was not aware of the passage of time, although her rooftop perch grew chilly and she was forced to draw the quilt around her shoulders.

It was not until she shifted a third time in as many minutes, trying to cast better light on the pages of her novel, that she realized it had grown quite late. And cold. And dark.

Clouds now covered the rapidly waning sun, and the gentle breeze had turned into a biting wind. It looked as if a spring shower was budding. She reluctantly closed her book, stood, and stretched. Her muscles ached from remaining in one position so long and she groaned.

Funny that no one had come looking for her. Perhaps

she could make it back to her room before anyone even noticed her absence. At the thought, she hurried toward the door. Reaching it, she pulled on the large wooden handle. It did not budge. It must be stuck. She put her book and the blanket down and tried again, this time pulling with all her might. Still, the door did not even rattle on its hinges. Could the bar have fallen back in place?

It did not seem possible. It had been so heavy. Yet the door would not open. She continued to yank on it for another five minutes before giving up, her arms aching from the strain.

All the while shadows grew around her and she tasted the dampness of impending rain in the air. Soon she would be in complete darkness. It was a moonless night and the clouds would block even the meager illumination from the stars. After the hours she had spent reading about ghosts and dark, dangerous passages, she did not look forward to a nightlong vigil on the tower roof.

There was nothing for it. She would have to call for help. Mama would be appalled that she was once again making a spectacle of herself, but Irisa saw no alternative. She walked to the wall facing the other tower. Perhaps Lucas was still in his study and would hear her.

She shouted his name over and over again, but no answering cry came. The darkness descended around her as her voice grew hoarse from yelling for help. She could no longer make out the shape of the other tower, and she realized that a light would be burning in the small window if Lucas were in his study.

How soon would Pansy notice she was missing? Surely her maid expected her to dress for dinner. Would anyone think to look for her on the roof walk? She peered over the wall in the quickly fading light. The nearest roof looked sickeningly far away. She would rather wait out the storm than break her neck jumping.

Wind rushed over her skin and cut through her light muslin dress. Shivering, she edged around the roof in search of the blanket she had left on the ground near the door. Her foot kicked something soft and she said a quick prayer of thanksgiving as she realized it was the quilt. She hastily picked it up and wrapped it around herself, hugging the thick fabric to her body.

Huddling down against the wall beside the door, she tried to find some protection from the cold wind and prayed Lucas would find her soon. She put the blanket over her head when the raindrops began to fall.

LUCAS OPENED THE DOOR TO THE EAST TOWER ROOM, fear riding him hard. Where had Irisa gone? Since it had become apparent she had disappeared, they had searched the entire house and still found no sign of her. Bloody hell. What had his fiancée gotten herself into now?

She had said that she wasn't sure she wanted to marry him, but he refused to believe that she had run away.

The feeling of uneasiness that had been growing for the last hour became acute. Something had happened to Irisa and he had to find her. Now.

He looked around the tower, but just as the underfootman had said, it showed no signs of occupation. He lifted the branch of candles he carried toward the winding staircase. The door to the roof walk was shut, with the heavy bar firmly in place. He considered the closed door. Irisa had shown marked interest in the roof walks when he'd given her family a tour of the house. But she couldn't be out there. Not with the bar blocking the door.

He turned to leave the room and stopped. Bloody hell. What would it hurt to look outside? They had looked everywhere else.

Knowing it would be a useless exercise and yet unable to stop himself, Lucas loped up the stairs and opened the door in short order. He kept the branch of candles inside, away from the wind and driving rain, but near enough to the door to cast light onto the roof walk. Just as he thought. There was nothing there but a pile of rags. Then the pile moved and he realized it was a quilt. Covering a person.

"Irisa."

The water-logged cover slid down to reveal Irisa's blond hair, damp but not soaked from the rain. Thank God she'd had the blanket. She blinked, brown eyes dark and huge in her white face, and got shakily to her feet. "L-Lucas?"

"Irisa," he said again. "What the bloody hell are you doing out here?"

"I-I'm c-cold." Her teeth chattered and her body shook violently.

Damnation. He had to get her inside. "Come here, little one." He couldn't risk letting the door shut again.

She obeyed, allowing the wet blanket to drop and bending to scoop something up from where she had been sitting. When she reached him, he saw that it was a novel. The book, at least, appeared dry. He reached out and pulled her to him, wrapping her dampened form in his arms.

"Th-that f-feels s-so g-good. You're w-warm, L-Lucas."

He tugged her inside and pulled the door shut, blocking out the storm. Irisa shook too much to walk. Unfortunately, she was in no shape to hold the branch of candles while he carried her either. Reaching down, he retrieved the candle branch and settled Irisa over his other shoulder in one swift movement.

"L-Lucas, you c-can't c-carry me like this. It isn't d-decent."

"I've got to get you warm, little one."

"B-but, Lucas . . ." She let her voice trail off and didn't finish the complaint, apparently realizing he had no intention of stopping.

He carried her to her room, barking orders at servants along the way.

"Have a hot bath brought immediately to Lady Irisa's room. Pansy, have Cook prepare warmed, spiced wine and a pot of tea. Someone get Mrs. Drake. Inform Lady Langley that her daughter has been found."

He handed the branch of candles he'd been carrying to one of the upstairs maids and lowered Irisa into a more secure hold in his arms.

She looked up at him with eyes heavy-lidded from her ordeal. "I knew you would find me," she whispered before her eyes closed.

His heart constricted. From her chilled and soggy condition, he had to admit that he had almost found her too late. Hell, he had almost not even looked. The prospect of Irisa spending the night on the tower roof, unprotected while the storm raged around her, filled Lucas with impotent fury. How had she gotten locked up there?

He would find whoever was responsible—and God help him when he did.

IRISA AWOKE THE NEXT MORNING FEELING UNEXPECTEDLY clearheaded, particularly when she considered the two mugs of warmed, spiced wine Lucas had insisted she drink the night before. Perhaps the large pot of tea he had also ordered her to drink had had a mitigating effect on the alcohol in the wine. Whatever the reason, she felt disgustingly healthy and alert after her misadventure.

Sun streamed in through the windows, attesting to the fact that the storm of the previous evening had moved on.

About to toss back the coverlet and get up, she was stayed by the sound of a peremptory knock on the door. Looking around the room, she realized she was alone. Pansy must have gotten up and left. Irisa wasn't about to answer the door in her nightrail. She waited, and was not surprised when it opened seconds later to reveal Lucas.

He did not look quite as well as she felt. In point of fact, he looked rather tired and irritated. She stifled a sigh. She really did not wish to argue this morning. Scooting to a sitting position against the headboard, she tugged the sheet and coverlet up to her chin and held them in place with both hands.

"Good morning, Lucas." Should she mention that it wasn't quite the thing for him to be in her bedroom?

"Not really. It's been a bloody frustrating morning and now it is almost afternoon."

No wonder she felt so well rested. She'd slept half the day away. "I'm sorry your morning hasn't gone well. Estate business?"

Lucas frowned and sat down on the bed next to her, reaching out to tug one of her hands away from the sheet and hold it in his own. "Not likely. The only thing in my life that can frustrate me to the level I have experienced this morning is my headstrong, impulsive little fiancée."

Well. Really. Lucas could not be blaming her.

She tried to free her hand from his grasp, but he would not let go. "I just woke up. How can I have been causing you problems in my sleep?"

"I think, little one, that you could cause me untold complications regardless of your conscious state. As to how you managed to upset my morning, let me enlighten you. First, it came to my attention that you deceived both your sister and your maid in order to lose yourself on the tower roof."

Irisa huffed. She had not lost herself. It had hardly been her fault that the door had been barred from the other side.

He went on as if she hadn't made a single sound of protest. "Second, when I tried to discover who had locked the door with you still on the roof walk, I could find no one who admitted to going into the east tower room yesterday. Not one single person, servant or family member. I'm rather proud of my ability to discover necessary information and this morning's setback has put me in a black mood."

He needn't make it sound as if his black mood were all her fault.

"But someone must have replaced the bar. I could hardly do so myself from the other side." One of the servants must have done it, but was afraid to admit to it and face Lucas's wrath.

He rubbed her palm with his thumb. "That is certainly true, and leaves us to draw some rather disturbing conclusions."

Small shocks were traveling from her palm up her arm,

and she found it difficult to concentrate on Lucas's words. "What conclusions?"

"Well, either one of my servants is lying to me, which is a troubling thought, or—it was not a servant. The other possibilities are few: your sister, her husband, your mother, or your father."

"My family would have no reason to latch doors in your house, Lucas. I'm sure it was a servant who forgot doing it until I was found." Even to her ears the excuse sounded lame.

"Perhaps it was done on purpose. Your parents are both very angry with you for causing them distress."

Irisa was incensed. Her family would never do anything so despicable. "What about you, Lucas? I've caused *you* a great deal of trouble as well."

He didn't even flick an eyelash at the accusation. "You know it wasn't me."

"How can I be sure?" she asked, not knowing why she baited him. Of course she knew it wasn't him. Lucas would never hurt her, but his suggestion that it was one of her parents was too awful to face.

"You trust me."

She refused to acknowledge the truth of his words. He had things far too much his own way as it was.

He leaned over and brought his face close, his mouth hovering over hers in an intimate challenge. "Admit it, little one. You trust me. You said last night that you knew I would find you."

She retreated against the headboard, but Lucas followed her. "Tell me."

"No. You are already far too arrogant."

"It is not arrogance to desire your trust. It is necessity," he said, his deep blue eyes compelling her to speak.

She wanted to keep the words inside, but the underlying vulnerability she sensed in him swayed her. "Yes. I trust you." She turned her head away from him.

"Are you satisfied?"

He tipped her face back toward him. "No, but I will be. In one week I will be very satisfied, Irisa."

She looked into eyes darkened by desire. "Oh."

He smiled briefly before touching his lips to hers in a short kiss. "Just one more week and you will be mine."

Ten

His low voice made her shiver. "I think we need to talk about that, Lucas. I'm not sure marrying so quickly is a good idea."

"I am." He moved back a little but left one arm over her lower body. His hand rested on the coverlet near her leg.

It must be nice to be so certain. "I think we need to discuss this."

Irritation replaced the desire in his countenance. "We need to discuss why you disobeyed my orders to be in your sister or your maid's company at all times, Irisa."

"I'm not one of Mr. Wemby's hounds to perform on command." She would not spend her marriage being alternately dictated to and ignored by her husband. If he wanted her in someone's company, he could bloody well take care of the job himself.

Lucas cocked his brow. "Are you saying that you don't intend to obey me in our marriage, Irisa?"

"Had I thought you wanted to wed a well-trained hound rather than a woman with her own mind, I would never have accepted your proposal in the first place," she informed him rashly.

"I want you."

"Well, *I* have a mind and I can think for myself. I

wanted some time alone yesterday, and if I hadn't been forced to use subterfuge to get it, that dreadful experience on the tower roof would never have happened."

Lucas looked momentarily taken aback. "That is one way to look at it, I suppose. There is another alternative. If you had been with your maid or your sister, you would not have been locked outside in the midst of a storm."

"I didn't want to be with anyone else."

"Why?"

"I just wanted to be by myself."

The heat of his body burned her through the coverlet where his hip rested against her thigh. "Clarice told me that she did not think you were nearly as biddable as I had led her to believe. I am fast drawing the conclusion that you are not as biddable as *you* led *me* to believe either."

"You discussed me with Clarice?" she asked, outraged.

He shrugged. "Yes. She is the only thing resembling family that I have. It only seemed natural to tell her about my perfect paragon of a fiancée."

"I'm not exactly a perfect paragon any longer."

"No, you are not, but you are interesting." Humor sparkled in his eyes.

"Are you laughing at me, Lucas?"

"I wouldn't dream of it, little one."

She would have pulled away, but his position made it impossible. "I don't think I'm as biddable as I led myself to believe either," she admitted, returning to their earlier conversation.

"Why?"

"What do you mean?"

"You changed. I want to understand why. I've been thinking about it for the past week. It occurred to me that you had begun withdrawing from me before you overheard that gossip about Clarise and me. What happened, Irisa? You seemed content with our bargain when you accepted my proposal."

"I did not precisely see it as a bargain."

"Label it what you like, but I thought we were both

getting what we wanted out of our association. Yet you became distant, and now you are attempting to withdraw your promise to marry me."

There he went, thinking with as much insight as a box hedge again. Really, were all men so thick when it came to matters of the heart? "I was . . . disappointed."

He was back to rubbing her palm with his thumb. "How did I disappoint you?"

"I had assumed a certain warmth of feeling on your part when you asked me to marry you, but your actions during our engagement gave evidence to the contrary."

"Your welfare is of utmost concern to me. I am"—he paused as if searching for the right word—"fond of you, Irisa. Quite fond."

"I am looking for a sensibility of feeling beyond mere fondness, Lucas." Particularly a fondness he had found so difficult to utter.

"What exactly are you getting at?" he asked with a wariness she could not mistake.

"I want your love, Lucas." There. She'd said it.

He could make of it what he wished, but she would not withdraw her words. She loved this dense, stubborn man and wanted nothing less in return.

Releasing her hand abruptly, he surged to his feet and began pacing the floor, his expression every bit as black as it had been when he found her on the tower roof the night before. "*Love?* You have withdrawn from me because of a romantical concept even the poets cannot agree upon defining? I do not believe this."

"Is the thought of loving me so horrifying?"

He turned and faced her, his body drawn in stiff lines, the grim expression in his blue eyes its own answer to her plea.

"Our relationship is based on factors much more lasting and concrete. Love need not come into it."

What could be more lasting than love? "How can you say so? We are discussing marriage, not a business investment."

He ran his fingers through the black silkiness of his hair

as he towered over her bed. "You are not a green girl, Irisa. You are nearing one and twenty. Old enough to have put such romantic nonsense behind you."

"Wanting to marry a man who loves me is not nonsense." She was so incensed that she threw back the coverlet and leapt from the bed in order to face him squarely.

"People in our world marry for a lot of reasons, and love is rarely one of them."

She put her fists on her hips and glared up at him. "It's going to be one of the reasons I marry; the chief one, in fact!"

"You should have thought of that before you agreed to marry me. You've given me your promise, Irisa. How can you honorably withdraw it? I never misled you in this area and I haven't changed my expectations."

All right, perhaps he had a small point. She hadn't realized love was a motivating factor for her either, right at first, but she knew it now.

"In fact, I've been bloody accommodating about your fits and starts," he added when she didn't answer immediately.

Fits and starts? His arrogance knew no bounds.

She stormed across the room, not wanting to be near enough to throttle him. She just might try. "I assumed you must have a strong degree of affection for me when you asked me to marry you even though you were aware of my family's scandalous past," she ground out.

If he felt he had been misled about her expectations, he was not alone.

Lucas didn't answer, but his expression shifted from annoyance to something else altogether, and Irisa became aware of three things simultaneously. The first was that her nightrail was a very thin, fine lawn. The second was that by moving in front of the window, she had succeeded in rendering it completely transparent. The third was that Lucas had also noticed. She turned to dive back under the covers, but was not quick enough.

Lucas moved with the speed of a panther striking. She was still several steps from the bed when his hands gripped her shoulders and spun her around. She barely had time to register the wild desire on his face before his lips took hers in a hot, consuming, and wholly possessive kiss.

He backed her up to the wall, pressing his body against hers, and she realized that Lucas did not need to be ragingly angry, merely annoyed, for his ardor to be aroused. As soon as the knowledge registered, she stiffened in his tight embrace. Not again.

She shoved against his chest and broke her mouth away from his. "Stop."

He complied only insofar as that he did not return his lips to hers, but instead kissed a sensitive spot under her ear. The caress sent all manner of sensations pouring through her, but she would not give in to this false passion again.

She struggled. "You must cease your attentions, my lord. I insist."

When she realized that she could not break his hold and even the use of the hated title did not faze him, she began to despair. She was fast approaching a state of not wanting to fight, and that way lay disaster. There was nothing else for it.

She kicked him in the shin and sharp pain shot up her foot. "*Ow.*"

He made an exclamation of surprise and she decided the pain had been worth it when his arms loosened.

She wrenched herself away from him, scooting from her position between him and the wall.

He spun to face her, looking bewildered but still quite dangerous. "Why did you do that?"

She glared at him. "You deserved it. I will not allow you to mislead me in this fashion again."

LUCAS'S SEX ACHED. PERHAPS THAT WAS WHY HER words made no sense to him, but what in the bloody hell was she talking about? "Explain yourself."

She limped over to the bed, her expression aggrieved.

She yanked the coverlet off, and then wrapped it around herself. His muscles tensed with the desire to rip it right back off again. He controlled the savage urge with difficulty.

"The only time you want to kiss me is when you are angry. I won't tolerate that sort of pretense of affections. If you cannot bring yourself to want physical intimacy unless your other darker passions are aroused, then I prefer you to keep them to yourself."

"You think I only want to touch you when I'm irritated?" he asked, unable to believe what he had heard.

"Do not bother to deny it." She faced him squarely. "You have not shown the least interest in a physical relationship with me otherwise."

He shook his head. "You're mad."

"I am not. I am being logical, though I don't expect you to see it. Gentlemen can be quite dense, I have observed."

All of those darker emotions she was so bloody concerned about came rushing to the fore. Irisa had been pushing him since the beginning of their engagement and he'd had enough.

He backed away from her, knowing if he did not, he would kiss her again. He wanted to settle this issue of his lack of desire for her once and for all. It should not be necessary, would not be with any other lady of the *ton,* he was sure, but Irisa insisted on being unique.

"If you're so damned logical," he gritted out, "then by all means, enlighten me. Why, if I do not want you, do I wake from dreams about you naked and writhing in my bed every bloody night with my sex hard enough to drill wood? What, other than an almost ungovernable desire for you, could explain why I spend the majority of the time we are together fantasizing about the moment when I can finally claim your body?"

Her eyes widened in shock until the golden brown depths were almost swallowed by the blackness of her pupils. "Really, Lucas. There is no need for that kind of talk."

"According to you, there is every need or I will be

accused of wanting you only when I allow my anger to overcome my good sense."

She tugged the coverlet more closely about herself, her face scarlet. "I never said anything about good sense."

"I did. And I've lost what little I had upon entering this room." He started toward her.

She put a hand out, the palm toward him. "Stop, Lucas. This is exactly what I was talking about."

"What?" He stopped when her outstretched hand touched him.

She quickly snatched it back. "You are annoyed with me."

"Yes." He could hardly deny the truth.

"There. You see." She looked triumphant.

"What the hell am I supposed to see?" he demanded.

"That you only want me when you are angry."

How did the female mind work? "I've wanted you for a very long time, Irisa. If you will recall, I was the one who wanted the wedding date moved forward."

"That proves nothing."

"Are you really so naïve?"

She opened her mouth, no doubt to argue with his assessment of her sexual knowledge, and he raised his hand. "Please. Let us not have yet another argument about your naïveté, or lack thereof."

This crazy conversation wasn't getting them anywhere. He had himself under control again. Barely. The fact that the coverlet hid her too tempting curves helped, but his desire was on too precarious a leash for him to tempt fate once again. After they were married, he would have sufficient time and privacy to prove to the maddening woman that his ardor did not require the spark of anger to ignite.

Until then, they would both have to live with the frustrating limitations of their relationship.

At the moment, making arrangements for her safety was of paramount importance. He contemplated the fading bruise on her cheek. It was almost gone. She could easily hide it with powder. As much as he preferred to stay in the country, living under the same roof with her parents was a risk he refused to continue to take.

"We will return to Town tomorrow."

She sighed. "We're through discussing passion, aren't we?"

He leaned down and kissed her softly on her slightly parted lips. "We will discuss it to your heart's content on our wedding night, little one. I promise."

She gave him a disgruntled frown. "You are taking a lot for granted in assuming there will be a wedding night."

"No, I am not. The one thing that drew me to you above all else was your strong sense of personal honor. Once you make a promise, you keep it—and you have promised to marry me."

"You sound very certain of me, Lucas."

"I am. You risked your own reputation and the wrath of your parents because your sense of commitment would not allow you to cry off, even believing I had been unfaithful. You attempted to force me into withdrawing my proposal by acting outrageously."

"Not that it worked." She frowned.

"Lucky for both of us, I realized what you were about." He smoothed the furrowed skin between her brows with his finger. "I have accepted that by not telling you about Clarice, I'm partially responsible for your reckless behavior."

"Is that why you are still insistent on marriage?" Her soft brown gaze held his own. "You believe you are at fault for my besmirched reputation?"

"There are many reasons I want to marry you." He dropped his hand, turned, and headed toward the door, stopping to look back at her when he reached it. "You must trust me, Irisa. We will have a satisfactory marriage."

"Will we?"

"Yes. We share many common interests. Apart from your aberrant behavior of late, we also have a mutual respect for our place in Society and the responsibility it entails. And as you will learn after we are wed, we share a deep passion uncommon amidst our peers."

Lucas believed that would be enough, but the doubt that shadowed Irisa's dark brown eyes told him she was not so sure.

Eleven

LUCAS RODE TOWARD HIS ESTATE MANAGER'S cottage, enjoying as he always did the lush green lands surrounding his home and the fresh breezes untainted by the many smells that polluted London's air. Returning to Town held little appeal.

Once he and Irisa were married, they could retire to the country for a year or more without being considered recluses. As newlyweds, it was expected they would focus on establishing a nursery to protect the title. He would enjoy rusticating, but would not make his father's mistake of withholding all Town pleasures from his wife.

Lucas wanted Irisa to be happy with him. Did her happiness lie only in a union based on mutual love?

His father had dismissed love as unnecessary in a Society marriage, saying that integrity and respectability would do. Irisa had rock-solid integrity and her respect for him was not in question, at least not now that she had learned Clarise had never been his mistress. However, it now seemed those two elements were not enough to guarantee a pleasant marriage.

Why had he ever believed they would be?

His parents had not been the most convivial of couples, but he had always dismissed the unpleasant facets of their marriage. Weighed against the fact his mother had not started down the path to her own destruction until she no longer had the bonds of matrimony to restrain her, those aspects had seemed minor. She had not been ecstatically happy, but she had been alive.

For the first time in all the years since her death, Lucas wondered if the trade had been worth it. His father had not loved his mother, and from that lack of love, he had found it easy to refuse her every wish for a style of living that would please her.

Lucas reined in his huge gray stallion. The same hills and valleys that gave him, and his father before him, such pleasure had been prison walls to her gay spirit. Had the lack of love in her marriage accounted at all for her obsessive search for it in widowhood?

She had bandied the love *word* about with disturbing frequency as she flitted from one paramour to another. Lucas distrusted so fleeting an emotion, but Irisa believed herself in love with him.

She must, he reasoned, or his love would mean nothing to her.

He could not believe Irisa identified love with the spurious and temporary emotions his mother had so madly reveled in. However, he was unsure what the true emotion, if indeed it existed, consisted of.

It could not be the insatiable passion of a new sexual liaison. That palled too quickly. Nor was it the desire to control another's life as his father had done to his mother. But what was it?

A better question might simply be to ask what exactly he felt for his fiancée.

He wanted her, more than he'd ever wanted another woman, and her happiness meant more to him than his own comfort. She belonged to him on a level he did not understand, but he suspected was more primitive than gentlemen of the *ton* were supposed to desire. The thought of losing her made him feel as if he'd swallowed ground glass.

He needed her.

Was that love? If he told Irisa he loved her, she would cease balking at the prospect of marriage; he was sure of it. Only his innate sense of honesty prevented him from turning his horse around and seeking his fiancée out to tell her just that. Until he was sure this amalgamation of feelings burning inside him was what she considered love, he must remain silent.

He knew only that, love or need, it did not matter . . . he would never let her walk away from him.

IRISA ATTEMPTED TO STUDY THE INVESTMENT PORTFOLIO in front of her. She wanted to diversify some of her holdings, but she could not summon her usual keen fascination with the process of putting together snippets of information from several different sources in order to make wise investment outlays.

Her mind insisted on fixing on her and Lucas's relationship.

Plans for the wedding moved inexorably forward. Mama moaned about the imprudence of going through with the big wedding breakfast every time she visited Irisa at Aunt Harriet's town house. She insisted that after Irisa's scandalous behavior, no one important among the *ton* would attend. That did not stop her from sending out invitations and ordering an exorbitantly priced buffet prepared by a hired French chef.

If Irisa cried off now, her mother would never forgive her. Not that Mama had been particularly warm toward her since the fiasco last week, but at least she was speaking to Irisa again. She had unbent enough to give Irisa the talk that she was sure most mothers dreaded and a great many daughters might prefer to do without. She would not have minded avoiding it herself.

Until this point, Irisa had looked forward to the passionate side of marriage very much. She still did . . . at least after the first night. Mama had been more candid than consoling about this aspect of marriage, encouraging Irisa to bring something to the marital bed to set her teeth into so that she might be able to accept her duty without protest.

She had said that while many aspects of this side of marriage could be quite pleasant and even lead one to believe the first time would be similar in nature, it was better to be prepared for an altogether different experience. Mama had then comforted her with the news that intimacy improved over time.

However, she had ended her lecture with the admonishment to prepare for significant pain during initiation into her conjugal duties and not to plague her husband with a waterfall of tears afterward.

Irisa was almost certain Lucas would never allow her to be hurt to that extent, but Mama said men's passions could not always be controlled. On one or two occasions lately, Lucas had left just that impression with Irisa.

Before leaving, Mama assured Irisa that Papa would be in attendance at the wedding even though he had not seen fit to visit Aunt Harriet's town house since Irisa had moved in.

It was his duty, after all.

Irisa's heart constricted at the knowledge that her own father would come to her wedding out of nothing more than a sense of obligation. Could he not summon even a smidgen of tender feeling for her?

A footman entered the small library, interrupting her gloomy thoughts.

She looked up from the papers strewn on the desk in front of her. "Yes?"

"A message has come for you, milady." He handed her a sealed white envelope of heavy parchment.

"Thank you." She nodded her head, dismissing the footman before opening the envelope and pulling out a single sheet of white stationary.

It took her a moment to assimilate the words and she had to read them twice before she accepted that they truly said what she thought they did.

Lady Irisa,

One might think congratulations on your upcoming marriage are in order, but do you really think a man of The Saint's impeccable standing amongst the ton *could find happiness with a woman such as yourself?*

You have fooled the Polite World for twenty years with your fakery—but you aren't really a lady at all, are you? The saintly Lord Ashton would be appalled to discover you are no more than Lord Langley's bastard daughter. As would the rest of the ton.

Your drive through Hyde Park with a former actress would be nothing compared to the news that your parents' legal marriage occurred less than four years ago, not the twenty-one the Polite World believes.

If you wish to keep this secret safe and your family's reputation intact, you will cry off from your engagement and stay away from The Saint. After all, could a man so far above reproach ever find his happiness with a woman such as yourself?

It was unsigned, but who would put their name to something so foul and cruel?

Irisa's first thought was that another lady had set her cap for Lucas and, having discovered Irisa's secret, was intent on using it to dispose of the competition.

Could Miss de Brieuse be in love with Lucas? No. She had marriage plans herself and was moving to France. Surely she would not attempt to circumvent Lucas's plans now. Besides, she'd been much too upset about the drive through Hyde Park. If she wanted an end to Lucas and Irisa's engagement, she would have been pleased by Irisa's notorious behavior—not scandalized.

There were other ladies of the *ton* who would be pleased to marry an earl as wealthy as Lucas, her former friend, Cecily Carlisle-Jones, among them. Her husband had lived for but a single year of marriage and the other woman's plans to better her station with a more advantageous second marriage were not exactly a secret.

She had a personal dislike of Irisa and her family, but how had she, or anyone else for that matter, discovered the scandalous truth?

Papa had been so careful to keep the second wedding hush-hush. No one outside of the family and the elderly vicar who had performed the ceremony should have known about it. It was on the parish records, of course. It would not have been legal otherwise, which would have made the whole thing a pointless exercise, but how had anyone known to look?

Perhaps they had not known. Perhaps discovery had been a fortuitous circumstance for someone wanting revenge, or as she'd first considered, to get Irisa out of Lucas's life. Whatever had led to its discovery, the fact that someone in the Polite World knew her secret changed everything.

She could not marry Lucas, and in that moment wondered how she'd ever believed she could. The blackmailer had got at least one thing right. A paragon of male virtue like Lucas would eventually find marriage to a woman of her past a liability. The secret would come out one day, just as Aunt Harriet had warned her parents so many years ago.

Irisa would always be the bastard daughter of a man who did not want her, and no amount of proper behavior could change that.

Lucas had said he did not care, that she was not responsible for her family's actions, but she *was* responsible for her own. In her reckless desire to break off their engagement, she had already damaged her reputation.

Out of a sense of duty and honor that she could not help admiring, Lucas was prepared to wed a lady almost as notorious as his mother. Irisa could not let him make such a sacrifice.

The blackmail letter put everything into perspective.

She must cry off from the engagement—not because

she was afraid of marrying a man who did not love her, but because she loved him too much to saddle him with an improper wife.

She set aside the piece of white parchment with hands that shook, and she drafted her own note to Lucas asking him to call on her at his earliest convenience.

LUCAS ARRIVED AT LADY UPWORTH'S TOWN HOUSE A scant half-hour after receiving his fiancée's summons. Although her note had been polite and brief, he had sensed an underlying agitation. If her father had been visiting and upset her, Lucas would not be responsible for his actions. He still thought Langley the likeliest culprit for locking Irisa onto the roof walk.

He was shown into the library and was surprised to note that Irisa was alone. She stood with her back to him, seemingly wholly occupied by the book-filled shelves. The yellow silk of her gown fell in graceful folds from the high waist, accentuating her femininity in an utterly charming way.

"Where is your aunt?" They had taken enough risks with Irisa's reputation.

Besides, the presence of the white-haired dowager would keep his lust in check.

Irisa turned to face him, her body stiffly erect. "I told her I needed to speak to you privately."

"What is this about?" He hoped she wasn't going to insist on another discussion regarding their mutual passion. He did not think his self-control was up to it.

She indicated one of the chairs near the fireplace. Though the day had been warm, a fire blazed in the grate. "Please, sit down, my lord."

His eyes narrowed at the formal words, but her subdued air discouraged him from taking issue with it. Something was terribly wrong. He waited for her to take her own advice before seating himself.

She fixed her gaze on the clasped hands in her lap. "I am afraid that I have decided we will not suit, my lord. I have no choice but to end our engagement."

He could not react. Not yet. Had she sounded even a trifle hesitant, he would know what needed to be said. Her blank certainty tore at his insides like the sharpest rapier blade.

"May I ask why?"

"It would be a misalliance, my lord."

"Look at me, damn it. If you are going to break your vow to me, the least you can do is look at me while you explain your reasons for doing so." Fury and fear fought for supremacy. The mere thought of losing her made his insides feel hollow. "Is this because I don't spout romantic nonsense? Do you want me to tell you I love you?"

Her head came up and her eyes were glassy with unshed tears. "Do you love me?" she asked and then shook her head. "It would be better if you didn't."

Why? "I'll take care of you, Irisa. I will be faithful and you will have my protection. Is that not good enough?"

"Thank you. You honor me with your willingness to align your life with my own, but it cannot be." Her voice broke and she had to take a deep breath before going on. "I'm very sorry, Lucas. I should never have allowed you to court me. I can see that now."

She sounded miserable, and that was the only reason he didn't shake her. What was going on in that muddled brain of hers? "You aren't crying off from our engagement, Irisa."

She took another deep breath and then met his gaze squarely. "Yes, I am. It's the only honorable thing to do."

"Is this about your ridiculous idea that I only respond passionately to you when I am angry?" he demanded, feeling as if he had been pulled into one of those awful plays that guests put on at house parties—one for which he had not been given the script and he bloody well did not know his lines.

"No. It has nothing to do with that." She bit her lip and

then tensed as if shouldering a heavy burden. "I'll place the announcement of the end of our betrothal in the paper tomorrow."

"If you do, I'll sue the paper for printing lies about a lord of the realm."

Her eyes widened. "You can't do that. It isn't a lie."

"It is. You're going to marry me. You gave me your word."

"I can't," she whispered, and then the wetness swimming in her eyes spilled over.

He jumped up and pulled her from her chair as well, then took his seat again, tugging her into his lap.

She buried her face in his waistcoat. "Please, Lucas. Do not make this any harder than it already is."

"Are you still concerned about my relationship with Clarice?" he asked.

"No," she said, her voice muffled by his chest.

That left only one alternative. Wedding nerves. He had heard that many brides were subject to them and Irisa's engagement had been more eventful than most.

"It's all right, little one. You will overcome this upset and our marriage will go forward as planned in four days' time."

"But, Lucas—"

He wouldn't let her finish. "Trust me." He tipped her chin up with his index finger. "You can, you know."

"I know. You are the most honorable of men."

He smiled. "Then how can you help marrying me, my love?"

"I don't know."

IRISA PACED THE DRAWING ROOM CARPET, WAITING FOR her sister to arrive. Thea was in the nursery, tucking the children in for the night. Normally, Irisa would have gone up to tell her nephew and niece good night as well, but this evening she was too agitated. Children had a way of sensing upset in an adult, and Irisa did not want to disrupt bedtime.

So she waited in the drawing room, and tried to formulate her plans.

She'd already decided she needed to share the blackmail letter with someone in the family.

Her brother would have been the best choice, but that wasn't an option. Jared had forgone the Season and was not due to arrive until the next day for her wedding. By then, she hoped to be away from London.

Thea, with her practical approach to life, seemed the best alternative. Besides, Irisa could admit to herself that she was a coward. If she told her parents, they would blame her. It was, after all, her fault. If she told Lucas, he would insist on marrying her anyway, if only out of a continued misplaced sense of duty.

She could not bear to think he might love her. It hurt enough to turn her back on a life with the man she loved more than her own life—to think she was also giving up his love would be too much to bear. However, she could not allow him to make the same mistake his father had made in taking an inappropriate bride. She had to protect Lucas from his own chivalrous nature.

Drake came into the drawing room with his wife, and Irisa considered that complication. It was difficult enough to expose her guilt and pain to her sister, but she was not prepared to reveal her secrets to her brother-in-law. Still, she did not see a polite way of disposing of his presence.

Perhaps he would have insight on how to deal with a blackmailer. Thea said that Drake could be quite ruthless, and dealing with a blackmailer required that trait. Ending her engagement would protect Lucas, but the rest of her family needed to be sheltered from the scandal coming to light as well.

Drake looked at her questioningly. "I thought you had plans to attend the Wickham ball with Lucas tonight."

"I am in bed with a sick headache." Now that she'd tried it on two occasions, even amidst her pain, it awed Irisa how exceedingly easy it was for a lady to fake illness and sneak from the house.

"You do not look ill to me, but you do look worried," Drake remarked, his eyes seeing far too much.

Irisa nodded. She was trying to stay calm, but the knowledge that someone knew her family's secret kept eating at her composure.

She had to hold her hands and knees together to keep from falling apart. "I need to leave Town immediately."

Thea's eyes narrowed. "Why?"

"I cannot marry Lucas, but he won't let me cry off."

"I think I'll leave you two with some privacy," Drake offered.

Irisa shook her head, realizing that his presence could only help. "No. Please. If you do, it is likely I will not find the inducement I need to hang on to my composure," she admitted with a shaking voice. "Besides, I would welcome your advice."

She was trying to be strong, but it was so hard.

Thea forced Irisa to take a seat before taking one herself. Drake remained standing. His towering presence was almost as comforting as Lucas's. The thought brought a fresh wave of sadness and she blinked away the tears that came to cloud her eyes.

"Are you entirely sure you want to cry off?" Thea asked.

Irisa removed her gloves, concentrating on the task in a bid to gather her composure. "I have no choice."

Her sister looked as if she was about to argue, but Drake laid his hand on her arm and she remained silent.

"Tell us why, Irisa," he instructed gently.

She didn't think she could say it out loud without breaking down, so she pulled the blackmail letter from her reticule and showed it to them.

As they read, Drake's face tightened with rage and Thea gasped. "This is awful. Who could do such a thing?"

Irisa twisted her hands together, mangling her gloves. "I don't know. I cannot imagine how they found out about Papa and Mama's recent wedding or why they care if I marry Lucas, but they have and they do. I won't let him be hurt."

"You've decided to accede to the blackmailer's demands?" Drake asked.

"Yes. I have no choice. If I don't, *everyone* will be hurt again *because of me* and I could not bear it." She choked on the last words. She had never been much of a crier, but lately it seemed as if she had no control over her wayward emotions.

Thea left her chair and wrapped her arms around Irisa. "It's going to be all right, sister mine. Even if this person tells the *ton* about the Langleys' marriage, it will not be the end of the world."

Irisa could not respond. Thea didn't understand. She'd only lived among the *ton* for the past few years. She did not know how cruel they could be. Papa and Mama would be ostracized. Jared, Thea, Drake, and even their children would be hurt as well.

"Did you tell Ashton about this?" Drake asked, pulling his wife back into a chair. He seemed to sense that Irisa needed some distance right now.

"No. He would insist he still wants to marry me, but I realize now I should never have encouraged him in the first place." Her voice came out barely above a whisper.

"Why do you say that?" Thea asked. "I was sure you loved him."

"He deserves more than what I am."

"How can you say that? You are a wonderful woman! Ashton is very lucky to have snagged you." Thea's staunch loyalty touched Irisa, but it did not sway her.

She turned to her brother-in-law and she saw understanding in his eyes.

"You believe that because you are illegitimate you aren't worthy of The Saint."

"Irisa could not possibly believe something so preposterous, Pierson." Thea glared at her husband.

But he just shook his head. "Ask her."

Thea turned to face Irisa. "Is that true?"

"I will always be a potential source of embarrassment for Lucas, just as I am for Papa. Whatever fondness Lucas may have for me now will eventually be snuffed out by the reality of my circumstances."

"That is not true," Thea insisted.

"It happened with Papa." Irisa's feelings were choking her, but she forced herself to go on. "Even if no one ever discovers the truth, it will always stand between us. He wants to marry a paragon and I am nothing but a bastard."

Her sister gasped in outrage. "How dare you call yourself such a name?"

Drake actually smiled. "Your sister has an aversion to that particular phrase, especially when applied to someone she loves."

Irisa sighed. "I am sorry. I don't mean to upset you, Thea. I thought about leaving Town without coming by here first, but I wanted to warn you about the blackmailer. I know I am weak, but I hoped Drake would inform Papa. I don't think I could face him knowing that I am once again causing my family distress."

Thea frowned. "That's the second time you've said that. I get the feeling you are not talking about your drive through Hyde Park with Miss de Brieuse."

"I believe your sister holds herself responsible in some way for past hurts in your family, Thea."

"It's not important." Irisa wanted to focus on the matter at hand. Dealing with the blackmailer. "I must make arrangements to leave Town tonight, tomorrow morning at the very latest. I will have to ask you to take care of sending an announcement of the broken betrothal to the papers."

Before either Thea or Drake could reply to Irisa's statement, a familiar voice interrupted their discussion. "I thought I made myself clear this afternoon on that matter. There will be no announcement. No broken engagement, and *you bloody well aren't leaving Town before the wedding.*"

Irisa turned stricken eyes to the doorway. "Lucas."

Twelve

LUCAS IGNORED HER EXCLAMATION AND turned to Drake. "Thank you for sending for me. I see my presence is indeed required." The civility in his tone was at complete odds with the banked fury in his eyes.

"How could you have known to alert Ashton that Irisa would be here this evening?" Thea asked.

"When the footman told us she waited in our drawing room, I sent for Ashton."

"You had no right," Irisa said, anger and a sense of betrayal adding to her already overset emotions.

Drake looked wholly unrepentant. "Ashton is entitled to know what has happened and to make his own decisions accordingly."

Lucas moved into the room, taking a leaning stance against the fireplace mantle nearest where Irisa sat. "Perhaps you would care to tell me what this is all about."

"Someone is trying to blackmail Irisa into crying off from your engagement," Drake replied.

"I see." Lucas turned to her. "What precisely is the blackmailer using to threaten you?"

Irisa felt skewered by Lucas's regard. If she did not tell him, Drake would, but she could not make her mouth form the words.

"Read this." Thea handed Lucas the letter.

Irisa wanted to snatch it from his grasp. It said such awful things about her—but they were true, and she could not hide from that reality any longer.

Lucas's eyes narrowed as he read. Finally, he finished and raised his gaze to her. Instead of condemnation, she saw confusion. "I realize that these threats are ugly, little one, but surely with no proof to substantiate them, they cannot do you or your family any real harm."

"The marriage is recorded in the parish register. That is proof enough, but if someone cared to, they could send word to Thea's former home in the West Indies and find record of the first countess's death six years after I was born."

Lucas's face lost all expression. "You're telling me this is the truth? Your parents' marriage twenty-one years ago was a sham because the first countess was still living?"

Sudden, sickening realization poured through Irisa. "You said you knew. When you asked me to marry you, you told me Papa had discussed the matter with you. You said it didn't matter."

"Langley spouted some idiocy about the embarrassment of your sister marrying Drake."

"You mean you didn't know that Irisa is illegitimate?" Drake asked.

Lucas answered Drake's question without shifting his regard from her. "No."

"Well, now you do and we need to decide what's to be done regarding this matter of blackmail." Thea's tone implied it was all very simple.

Irisa knew it was anything but. Her father had tricked her and Lucas. She wasn't sure how, but she knew he was responsible. Which meant that Lucas had not known her awful secret—and now he did.

Pain and grief crushed her heart. At least before, when she had believed Lucas knew the truth, she had drawn comfort from the fact that he cared enough for her not to be swayed by it. Even if she had to give him up, she had that. Now, she had nothing.

She dropped her gaze, unwilling to watch Lucas's countenance change to one of contempt.

"The first thing to do is to discover who is doing the blackmailing. We will have to draw up a list of potential suspects. Ravenswood comes to Town tomorrow, is that not correct?" Lucas asked.

"Yes, Jared wants to be here for the wedding," Thea replied.

"Good. We'll call a family conference at Lady Upworth's tomorrow afternoon."

"We'll be there," Drake said.

"An excellent idea." Thea sounded quite pleased. "Jared and the Langleys should be warned about the potential scandal once you and Irisa go through with the wedding."

"Yes."

Irisa's head snapped up and her eyes flew to Lucas's face. He watched her as if he'd been waiting for her to once again meet his gaze.

"There isn't going to be a wedding," she said, "I've already explained that. Besides, now that you know the truth, you will want to withdraw your offer. I'll cry off, of course. It's the least I can do."

"The least you can do is to keep your word. I will accept nothing less."

"But you cannot wish to marry me now."

"Why not?"

"Because I'm a . . ." Stopping herself in time, she did not say the word that would send her sister into another tizzy. "Because my parents weren't married when I was born. I'll be a constant source of embarrassment for you, Lucas—worse than your mother. Once the blackmailer makes good on his threats, I'll be more notorious than she ever was."

"Tell her she's being ridiculous, Ashton," Thea said.

Drake laid his hand on his wife's shoulder. "Hush, darling. Let the man speak for himself."

Oh, this was awful. Drake and Thea would force Lucas to pretend to accept things that a man of his nature simply could not.

Irisa jumped to her feet. "I don't *want* Lucas to speak. I'm not going to marry him and that's final." Desolation fought with rage as she glared at her sister and brother-in-law, wishing she had not given in to the urge to come here.

Lucas said, "All right."

Though she had expected them, the two words nearly shredded her composure and she could not make herself respond for the life of her. Thea stared at Lucas with a ludicrous expression of shocked disbelief. Drake maintained a watchful silence.

After several shaky breaths and a long silence, she said, "I can return to Aunt Harriet's tonight, but I must make permanent living arrangements soon. I do not believe that Papa and Mama will want me back in their house."

Not that any of this was Lucas's problem, but she did not know what else to say. She could not quite bring herself to thank Lucas for allowing her to break their engagement.

"You will be living with me," Lucas said in a voice as hard as petrified rock.

"You just agreed to cancel the wedding," Thea said when Irisa once again found herself incapable of response.

"Yes, but your sister will be living with me." His eyes held Irisa's, the message in his almost frightening. "Four nights hence, you will sleep in my bed whether or not there has been a wedding."

He'd gone mad. She could not live with him without the bonds of marriage. Then an awful thought registered. *"You plan to make me your mistress?"*

"I plan to make you my wife, but you refuse to marry me. I am not about to give up my wedding night just because you refuse to give me a wedding. I must admit it surprises me you are willing to cause the scandal, though. I realize your reputation is not quite as important to you as I first believed, but I had thought you were somewhat conventional."

"I am conventional! I am certainly not coming to live

with you unless we are married." She might be illegitimate, but she was no lightskirt.

"Good. I admit that was my preference, but you were so adamant."

As the meaning of his words registered, Irisa scowled. "I did not agree to marry you."

"It sounded that way to me. You said you didn't want to be his mistress." Drake matched Lucas's mad complacency.

Irisa turned to Thea. "Please, help me convince them this is the only way. I cannot marry Lucas and bring scandal down on him and the family."

But Thea's eyes were alight with humor, not understanding. "I think it would be much more scandalous for you to live with Lucas as his mistress, sister mine."

"I'm not going to be anyone's mistress!" She was sure the scullery maid in the kitchen could hear that pronouncement.

Suddenly Lucas's hands were there on her shoulders, his body so close she could smell his masculine scent. "No. Little one, you aren't going to be my mistress, but you will be my wife. If it requires compromising you beyond redemption, then that is what I am prepared to do. You belong to me."

"But you don't love me," she wailed.

He frowned. "You told me this afternoon that did not matter."

"I said it wasn't the reason I was crying off. I did not say it didn't matter." Did he only hear what he wanted to?

"I have thought about this love business a great deal and it is not the romantical nonsense I have always believed."

"What are you saying? Do you love me?" she asked, dazed.

"That is not something I wish to discuss in front of your sister and her husband."

Irisa's gaze skittered from one occupant of the room to the other. "Of course."

"I want you, and you promised yourself to me. I'm

holding you to that promise. Whatever it takes," Lucas said with utter implacability.

"But you can't want to marry me. I'm everything you vowed to stay away from in a wife. Don't you see?"

Lucas tipped her chin up and his eyes burned into hers. "If that were true, I would never have courted you in the first place. Do you remember when I asked you to marry me?"

She nodded.

"I told you that I held you accountable for your actions, not those of your family. Your parents are responsible for your illegitimacy. You are responsible for keeping your promise to marry me. Do you understand?"

She understood that Lucas would not give up. The man was as bendable as iron.

LUCAS CALLED ON DRAKE THE NEXT MORNING. HE wanted the other man's impression of the Langleys. Drake had known them for four years, plenty of time to get a realistic assessment of the other members of his wife's family. Lucas was shown into Drake's study immediately upon arrival at the town house.

Drake offered him a seat. "I was expecting you."

Lucas nodded. "I would have stayed to talk last night, but I had to see Irisa home. She took a hansom cab to your house."

Drake's eyes narrowed. "I trust you informed her how dangerous such an action could be for a lone woman at night."

"I tried." Remembering Irisa's uncommunicative state on the carriage ride home last night, he frowned. "I'm not sure she listened."

Drake smiled. "She's a lot like her sister."

"When I first met her, I thought she was the perfect, biddable female," Lucas admitted ruefully.

"And now?"

"She's not biddable."

"But she's perfect for you?"

Lucas smiled wryly. "Yes. Not that I ever would have expected a desire to tie myself to an impulsive, reckless, and only-sometimes-proper lady. But there it is."

"She's honorable."

"Yes." Unlike his mother or his brother, Irisa had a great deal of honor. "Even when she's trying to renege on our marriage agreement."

"She's trying to protect you and her family."

Lucas nodded. "I'm worried about her. This blackmail attempt seems too damned convenient right after that scare on the tower roof at Ashton Manor."

Drake leaned back in his chair and tapped his palm with the pencil in his other hand. "You're right, but it doesn't make a bit of sense. No one staying at your house had any reason to harm her and even less reason to want the scandal of a broken engagement."

Which was the same wall Lucas hit in his reasoning every time he tried to cast Langley as the villain. "After the way Langley reacted to her escapade in the park, I thought he might have done it to punish her, but I can't see him wanting the marriage canceled unless he's trying to get back at me."

"He's a cold bastard, but I wouldn't have thought him capable of that perfidy."

"Tell me about the first countess. She was Thea's mother, wasn't she?"

Drake nodded. "Thea and Jared are twins. Jared was born first and Langley whisked him out of Langley Hall within minutes of his birth, promising Anna she would never see her son again. Then Thea was born and Anna was desperate to keep her hidden so she would not lose her, too. When it became obvious that staying in England increased the risk of losing her daughter, Anna fled to the West Indies. She died there when Thea was thirteen."

"After Langley had already remarried and had another child," Lucas concluded for the other man.

"Yes. He had never bothered to search for his runaway wife and therefore had no way of knowing whether she was dead or alive. He told Thea he had assumed Anna was dead because she never returned to see her son. He and the current countess went through a second wedding ceremony after Thea arrived in London and revealed the date of her mother's death."

Lucas was sickened by the lack of moral character Langley had shown. "So he deceived the current countess into marriage?"

Drake shook his head. "More like she trapped him. She was pregnant with Irisa and willingly took the risk of marriage knowing that Anna might still be living. Langley told her the truth, although Jared and the rest of the *ton* believed Anna had died due to complications from childbirth."

"You're right. Langley is a cold-hearted bastard."

"Irisa called herself one, too. Last night before you arrived."

Lucas's insides twisted. "She's innocent in all this."

"She doesn't feel that way."

"Bloody hell. What a mess."

Drake smiled. "Welcome to the family."

"A family that eats its young."

"Maybe, but Langley is too socially conscious to risk the scandal associated with a broken engagement. Besides, he would never threaten to reveal Irisa's illegitimate birth. It reflects too poorly on him."

"Then who is trying to blackmail her?"

Drake frowned. "I don't know. I've been thinking about that ever since she showed us the note last night, and I can't come up with a single name."

"I'll find him."

"You sound certain."

"I have some experience in this sort of thing," Lucas said simply.

Drake raised his brows in question.

"I played the part of domestic intelligence agent during the war with Boney."

"You would have been damned young."

"It was a matter of duty to my country." Lucas shrugged. "My youth made me appear harmless."

Drake's smile turned feral. "You'll pardon me for saying so, but I can't imagine a time when you appeared harmless. You've got too much killer instinct."

Coming from his future brother-in-law, Lucas took the words as high praise. "Whoever is playing these games with Irisa is going to learn just how dangerous I can be."

LUCAS'S FIRST IMPRESSION OF IRISA'S BROTHER WAS that he was bloody glad to have the giant on his side. Though he was only an inch or two taller than Lucas's own taller-than-average frame, the man carried enough muscle to overshadow even Lucas's Corinthian build. The scar that ravaged one side of Viscount Ravenswood's face only enhanced the man's natural air of intimidation. Black hair hung down his back to just below his shoulder blades and his eyes were emotionless pools of onyx. He exuded an air of dark menace and Lucas liked him on sight.

Ravenswood glowered at Lucas. "You will be good to my sister."

Lucas returned the man's look, stare for stare. "Yes."

Ravenswood nodded and then turned to Irisa. His expression lightened, although he did not smile. "I'll know if he isn't."

She smiled at her brother and reached up to kiss his cheek. "Lucas is the best of men, Jared. You need not worry on that score."

Lucas warmed under Irisa's certainty. She'd spent enough time showing hesitancy at the prospect of marriage to him that he had begun to have a few niggling doubts regarding her feelings toward him. He started to lead Irisa to a small sofa, but she pulled back.

"I would rather stand, Lucas."

"You want to be ready to bolt?" he asked, not without some amusement.

She did not smile when she nodded her head. "Yes."

He brushed her cheek. "You know I won't let Langley hurt you again, don't you?"

She did not get an opportunity to reassure him of her faith in his ability to protect her because Ravenswood interrupted.

"Langley hurt you?"

Irisa frowned at Lucas and then put a soothing hand on Ravenswood's arm. "It was nothing. I did something that upset Papa and he lost his temper."

"He knocked her right off her chair and left a bruise that lasted more than a week. If his fist had been closed, he might have broken her jaw."

"Lucas." Irisa looked ready to do a fair amount of damage herself.

Ravenswood cocked his head to one side. "You took care of it, I assume."

Lucas shrugged. "He won't touch her again."

Ravenswood did not reply. He simply turned and walked away. He ended up sitting in a chair that, although it was part of the grouping around the fireplace, gave the appearance of being separate, just as Ravenswood did.

"I can't believe you told him that. Jared already barely tolerates Papa. Now, he's going to hate him and it will be all my fault."

Lucas would not let that pass. He gripped Irisa's chin in a gentle but firm hold and forced her to meet his gaze. "You are not responsible for your father's lack of self-control. If his son hates him, it's because he earned it. Got it?"

Irisa's warm brown eyes were still troubled, but she agreed. "Yes. I've got it. I still wish you hadn't told him."

"I'm sorry it upset you."

"But you aren't sorry you said it?" she asked, clearly disgruntled.

"No." He would not lie.

She sighed. "I suppose that's the best I can hope for. You're a very arrogant gentleman, you know."

"So you've said before."

"Only because it's true."

He shrugged. "Perhaps."

They had more important things to discuss than his arrogance. He pulled Irisa into his side and turned to face the rest of the room. She tried to pull away, but ceased her struggles when he squeezed her warningly.

The entire family had gathered in Lady Upworth's drawing room. The white-haired dowager rested on a brocade chair and oversaw the gathering with the regal bearing of a queen. Lady Langley sat to the older woman's right, doing her utmost to keep her gaze averted from Mrs. Drake. Irisa's sister and brother-in-law were ensconced together on a settee. Thea seemed to take impish delight in trying to catch the current countess's eye. Langley stood behind his wife's chair, his expression grim.

"I don't see why this little family gathering is necessary. I've a great deal to do in readying for my daughter's wedding. This is most inconvenient," Lady Langley complained.

"Someone is trying to scare Irisa into backing out of our engagement," Lucas answered.

Lady Langley gasped. "That's ridiculous."

"I agree. Anyone who knows me at all would realize that once I set a course of action, I stick with it. I find this attempt at blackmail personally offensive." He looked directly at Langley as he spoke, but the older man's face remained stony.

"Let's hear the details," Ravenswood inserted.

Irisa stiffened beside him and Lucas took a moment to give her a reassuring squeeze before he went on. He spoke to the room at large, watching each face for a change in expression. "Irisa received a note yesterday threatening to reveal the mockery of her parents' initial marriage if she did not withdraw from our betrothal."

Langley's eyes narrowed in anger and his wife looked shocked. Lady Upworth sighed and shook her head. Ravenswood looked ready to kill someone. Lucas approved the reaction. Drake was also watching the other occupants of the room intently while his wife sent a look of commiseration to Irisa.

"Where is the note?" Langley asked, speaking for the first time since Lucas's arrival.

Lucas removed it from his coat pocket. "Right here."

Ravenswood moved with the speed of a striking viper and had the stationary in his hand before Langley could reach for it. He read the words and then tossed the paper in Langley's direction in a casual move filled with contempt. Langley reached to pick the paper up off the carpet.

Ravenswood returned to his seat. "You're going to go through with the wedding."

It was not a question, but Lucas answered anyway. "Yes."

Six months ago, the thought of tying himself to a woman with Irisa's secrets would have been ludicrous. That was when he had been looking at marriage to an ideal, a faceless paragon of a woman. His fiancée now had a face, that of an angelic blond beauty, and the only ludicrous thought was contemplation of life without the impetuous little baggage at his side.

Lady Langley looked up from the note her husband had just handed her. "You cannot possibly. At the very least, the wedding must be postponed. We cannot risk the blackmailer making good on his threat."

"If there is a blackmailer," Langley said.

Lucas glared at the other man. "What do you mean?"

"How do we know that Irisa did not write this herself?" he asked, pointing to the note now in Lady Upworth's frail hands.

"Because she said she did not," Lucas replied, not understanding why the question had even been asked.

"Thank you," Irisa whispered.

"That is hardly enough evidence. Her mother and I have personal experience with Irisa's willingness to resort to base behavior like blackmail."

Lucas could not believe what he was hearing. "Explain yourself and do it quickly, or you'll be meeting me over a brace of pistols at dawn."

Langley's face paled, but he did not apologize. "Irisa

was on the verge of betrothal to a duke when she took it into her head that she did not wish to marry him. She threatened to tell the *ton* of her illegitimacy if we pressed the issue. She has absolutely no sense of family loyalty or honor."

"That's a bloody lie. Irisa's loyalty to those who care about her is absolute and her honor is beyond reproach." Ravenswood's voice vibrated with anger.

"The duke was old enough to be her grandfather and she was barely out of the schoolroom. Your willingness to sell her into such a marriage to advance your own social position says little for your own character," Lady Upworth admonished in regal tones.

Lucas intervened before the discussion could get any more out of hand. "Irisa's ingenuity in protecting herself from your schemes is not at issue here. There *is* a blackmailer and he has threatened to reveal *your* past peccadillo when she marries me. Since the wedding will take place as planned, I thought you had the right to know the probable outcome."

"That's just it, Ashton. Are you quite sure the marriage is going to take place, or has Irisa decided she doesn't want to marry you either and has reverted to her *ingenious* methods of *protecting* herself?"

Thirteen

PAPA'S WORDS HUNG IN THE AIR LIKE A THUNderclap, harsh and deafening.

She supposed, in his own bitter way, Papa was justified in his suspicious. After all, she had blackmailed him once in the past, but could he not see the difference between then and now? Lucas was not some lecherous, aged duke whose very touch left her feeling nauseous.

And she was no longer a green girl barely out of the schoolroom. She would never revert to such tactics to end an unwanted engagement now. She didn't need to. Thanks to her sister's sage advice on investments, Irisa had resources of her own. "I did not write the note."

Lucas hugged her. A warm embrace full of comfort. Right there in front of everyone and she didn't care. "We know that, little one."

He trusted her. He believed her. She loved him and it took every ounce of self-possession she had not to blurt the words out right then and there.

"Langley is an idiot and I'm sorry you had to live so many years in his company."

Drake chuckled at Lucas's words and Thea coughed. Jared grunted a sound of approval, but Mama looked scandalized and Aunt Harriet appeared sad and terribly fragile.

Lucas turned his attention back to Papa. "I assume you do not wish to cooperate in gathering the information necessary to identify the blackmailer."

Papa's mouth tightened. "I will not waste my time pursuing a phantom."

Lucas nodded. "Then it would be better for all concerned if you and Lady Langley left."

Mama gasped loudly. "We aren't going anywhere." The warm feeling Irisa experienced at her mother's show of concern turned frigid with Mama's next words. "I am not leaving this house until I have your promise that the wedding will be postponed or canceled. Irisa has brought enough shame to our family's name. I will not allow her to bring more."

Lucas muttered something about parents eating their young, but Irisa did not understand it. Releasing her, he moved to where Mama was sitting.

He casually lifted her right out of her chair and she shrieked. "It really is time you left, Lady Langley. We will see you at the wedding. If you are not there, I will assume it is because you wish to sever your connection with my title and position."

Mama's mouth opened and shut, but no sound came out. Lucas maneuvered her toward the door.

Papa followed, his expression sullen, but he stopped in front of Irisa on his way out. "If you have a shred of decency in you, you will protect your family's name."

Then he strode forward and took Mama's arm, leading her from the room.

Irisa's knees wanted to buckle, but she remained standing by an effort of will. Lucas returned, took one look at her face, and led her to a chair.

Once she was seated, he turned and met the gaze of each person remaining in the room. "Does anyone else believe Irisa and I should postpone our wedding?"

Aunt Harriet's sigh caught everyone's attention. "Secrets have a way of outing themselves. It would be foolish to take action based on the fear of it happening now rather than later."

"I agree. Drake is in a similar position to Irisa and the *ton* does not ostracize him. I believe her marriage to you will protect her from a great deal, Ashton." Thea nodded her head for emphasis when she finished speaking.

"My wife is quite correct. While Irisa is bound to face a certain amount of nastiness, your position will make her place in society almost unassailable," Drake added.

"What about Papa and Mama? There will be awful gossip about them, and many of Mama's friends will cut her when they learn the truth." Irisa could not believe that her family was blinded to the cruelties her parents would face.

"Langley married her, even if the legitimate ceremony occurred a bit late. In the eyes of the *ton* that makes everything all right." Jared's voice implied he did not share the *ton*'s views.

Irisa did not think he would ever forgive Papa for what he had done to the first countess.

Lucas smiled. "Then I can assume the rest of you will be in attendance at the wedding three days hence."

Irisa listened in silence while they discussed the blackmailer.

"What about Langley?" Drake asked.

"I thought you were of the opinion that he was too self-serving to threaten the revelation of his secret," Lucas replied.

"I don't mean I think he's the blackmailer. What about his enemies? He's a bloody harsh man when he wants to be. It's hard to believe he hasn't made some pretty strong enemies."

"Why attack Langley through Irisa?" Jared asked.

"Because anyone who knows Langley well knows how important social prestige is to him. Irisa's connection to such a powerful title would be a coup he would relish and any opponent of his would know that," Thea pointed out.

"That still doesn't explain how Irisa got locked on the tower roof," Lucas said.

Then Jared had to be told the story of her mishap at Ashton Manor. He didn't take it well, but Irisa was not up to soothing him. She was trying to understand the connection Lucas seemed intent on drawing.

"Why would you think the two events are related? Getting locked on the roof was surely an accident. I know you hate to think your servants would lie to you, but I'm certain one of them must have done it and been afraid to confess later," Irisa said.

"It's all rather confusing," Aunt Harriet said, her face wan with tiredness.

The revelations about the blackmailer, the altercation between Lucas and Papa, and the subsequent discussion had all been too much for her. Irisa wished she could have spared her great-aunt all of the unpleasantness. Aunt Harriet was the kindest of women and deserved to enjoy her old age, not be plagued by family secrets and scandal.

Lucas noticed her aunt's condition as well and turned to Irisa. "Call a maid to escort your aunt to her rooms."

"That won't be necessary. I'll take her up." Jared stood and, ignoring the dowager's protests, gently scooped her into his arms and carried her from the room.

"What of your enemies, Ashton?" Thea asked. "Drake told me that you played the role of intelligence officer during the war. Surely you have enemies from that time."

"If they were my enemy, then they were the enemy of the Crown and are dead or reside in prison. Besides, that was years ago. We need to look for someone whose anger is fresh enough to still want revenge."

"We can't be sure that revenge is the motivating factor," Jared said, returning to the room. "There is also money."

"But the blackmailer didn't ask for any blunt," Irisa argued.

Jared shrugged. "Not this time. Might be testing the waters, so to speak. If you called off your wedding, then they'd know you were vulnerable to them. Could turn you into a nice steady source of income."

"It would seem, if that were the case, that the blackmailer would be happy for Irisa to wed Ashton. He has much deeper pockets than the unmarried daughter of an earl of moderate estates," Thea volunteered.

"Maybe. Or maybe the blackguard realizes that once Irisa is under Ashton's protection as his wife, the threats won't hold much water." Jared sat down in the chair he had used earlier.

"I had also considered the possibility someone wanted me out of the way so Lucas would once again be on the marriage mart, but this sort of blackmail seems so extreme, even for a lady who does not like me," Irisa said, thinking of Cecily Carlisle-Jones.

"What of it?" Jared asked Lucas.

"There are always marriage-minded females interested in a bachelor with both wealth and a title, but no one I can think of who has been marked in her efforts."

"What of His Grace, the Duke of Clareshire?" Thea asked.

"He rusticates in the country," Jared said.

"He's in Town for the Season," Thea said, proving she wasn't completely oblivious to what went on among the *ton*. "He came soon after Irisa's engagement was announced and he hates the whole family since Irisa's refusal."

"If we're considering rejected suitors, then there are several more men worth mentioning," Irisa said doubtfully.

"Name them." Lucas's tone brooked no argument.

She had no desire to give any. "There is Mr. Wemby, for one, and Lord Yardley. There are a couple of gentlemen who have since married: Sir Roger and Viscount Atworth. And I suppose we had best put Cecily Carlisle on the list. She was once a close friend of mine, but we had a falling-out and now she hates me."

Thea made a disgusted sound at this, but Lucas looked as if he was committing each name to memory.

He frowned. "Each one of them is a peer of the realm, or highly placed in Society. I know from past experience how difficult it can be to investigate members of the nobility without raising suspicion. Servants talk, and undue interest is noted quickly."

"I trust you have a plan," Jared said.

"Not yet, but I will soon." Lucas's mouth narrowed into a thin line. "While this is an avenue worth pursuing, I don't see any way of luring the blackmailer out before the wedding. I think we're all going to have to be prepared for the worst and expect him to make good on his threats. If Ravenswood is right and demands for money come later instead of revelations, we'll be prepared."

LUCAS'S HAND ON HER ARM KEPT IRISA CLOSE TO HIS side. He had insisted on attending the Bickmore rout as intended, saying that Thea's original plan to prove to the *ton* that all was well between them after Irisa's drive through Hyde Park with Miss de Brieuse still stood. She had agreed, not wanting to alert him to her plans to leave Town.

She'd thought and thought and *thought* about everyone's willingness to pay for her happiness. She simply could not bear to let them. Her family had already paid too high a price for her place in it. Her own honor would not allow her to continue to pursue a path toward her heart's desire that required everyone she loved to be humiliated by their association with her.

It would be different, perhaps, if Lucas did love her. The pain her leaving would cause him would weigh on the side of her happiness, but another lady of the *ton* would do just as well for his wife. After all, he'd said often enough he wanted to wed a perfect paragon and *she* was not that lady. If he could set aside his unbending honor for just one moment, he would see that.

Despite knowing she was doing the right thing in leaving Town, her emotions were in such a state, she had considered attempting to avoid this evening's entertainment.

However, after the debacle of being discovered by Lucas in her sister's drawing room when she was supposed to be in bed with a sick headache, she had not dared try that excuse again. Although it was, in fact, very close to reality. She felt sick to her stomach at the thought of never seeing Lucas again and her head pounded from trying to keep a serene façade in the face of the speculative stares being cast her way.

Lady Wickham bore down on them and Irisa pasted a smile of welcome on her face. "Good evening, Lady Wickham."

"Good evening, Lady Irisa. I'm so glad to see you feeling better. We missed you at our ball last evening."

Irisa gripped her fan more tightly, but did not lose her smile. "Thank you. My indisposition came as a great disappointment to me as well. Your entertainments are always so lovely. One truly regrets missing them."

Had she done it too brown?

Lady Wickham smiled. "You're too kind, my dear."

"Not at all. Lucas was just telling me what a lovely evening I missed," Irisa added, lying through her teeth.

Lady Wickham's gaze traveled to Lucas. "I'm surprised he noticed. He barely stayed long enough to hear the hired orchestra play their first tune."

"Not because the soirée wasn't all that it could be."

Just like a gentleman, he didn't feel the need to explain himself while Irisa felt compelled to babble excuses left and right. She stifled a sigh.

"Your parents seemed to enjoy themselves," Lady Wickham said, her eyes narrowed in consideration.

"Yes, one cannot help noticing that when her parents were present, Lady Irisa was absent, and now that she is present, they are absent. Interesting, isn't it?"

Irisa's attention moved to the woman who spoke with such thinly veiled innuendo. Lady Preston. The spiteful gossip was at it again.

"The wedding is in only three days' time, and one can certainly understand both my fiancée and her mother succumbing a bit to the pressures of planning such an important event," Lucas said smoothly. "The only surprise is that either woman has managed to attend anything at all this week."

Lady Wickham laughed, sounding much like a friendly, braying horse. "Nonsense. The gel and her mother aren't nearly so weak as all that. You, my lord, have a limited view of ladies. Why, I remember my youngest daughter's wedding. We hosted a month-long house party. What a time that was."

Once launched, there was no way of stopping the story. Not that Irisa wanted to. She found it preferable to listening to more gossip, but what she truly wanted was time alone with Lucas. Time to store up one more memory to keep her company in the lonely years ahead without him.

IT WAS THAT THOUGHT THAT PROMPTED IRISA TO SPEAK as Lucas led her from the third entertainment they had attended that evening. It was quite late, almost three in the morning, and she was tired from smiling and chatting with nosy, gossip-minded people, but Irisa did not wish to go home. Not yet.

"Lucas, could we not go for a small drive before you return me to my aunt's home?"

He stopped in the process of handing her into the carriage. "You look tired enough to fall asleep on the squabs. Why do you want to go for a drive now?"

"Perhaps I merely want some conversation in which I do not have to meticulously weigh every word I utter. Please, Lucas?"

He stared at her for an uncomfortably long moment and then turned to give instructions to his coachman.

"We will take a circuitous route to your aunt's town house." He settled in the opposite seat, his long legs brushing the folds of her cloak.

She affected a shiver. "It's quite chilly tonight, don't you think, Lucas?"

He shook his head. "Not particularly. Are you cold, little one? Would you like a lap blanket?"

So much for subtlety. "I would rather you share your warmth with me," she blurted out.

Although her cheeks felt on fire with her blush, she did not retract the words. She wanted a last kiss from Lucas and she had already discovered to her dismay that subtle hinting did not work well. He was far too much The Saint to be so easily swayed.

Even in the dim light cast by the carriage lantern, she could see that his smile was anything but saintly as he asked, "Do you want me to kiss you, Irisa?"

She nodded, embarrassed to have to admit it.

He put a hand out to her. "Come here, then."

She took his hand and he pulled her onto his lap. She savored the feel of his hard, muscled body beneath hers for several seconds before raising her head to meet his eyes.

"I think I know what this is about."

Dread snaked through her. Had Lucas divined her plans? "You do?"

He nodded. "You are attempting to discover if I feel passion for you when I am not under the influence of darker emotions. I assure you I will give you sufficient proof of my desire for you on our wedding night, but I don't mind giving you a small sample now."

She swallowed. "You don't?"

"No." His mouth lowered and covered hers with the faintest of caresses.

Her eyes fluttered closed and she soaked in the sensations surrounding her, memorizing the feel of Lucas's lips, the warmth of his body, and his sharp, clean scent.

He slid his tongue along the seam of her lips and she parted them without thought. He slipped inside and kept up the leisurely exploration of her mouth. It felt so good. This kiss was different from any he had given her, and yet no less satisfying. The gentleness in him made her want to weep, because under it she could taste his passion—genuine passion not prompted by anger or any other dark emotion.

Lucas did want her.

She needed to feel his skin. Just this once. Tearing off her gloves, she squirmed in his lap.

His hand gripped her hip and pressed down. "Stop moving, love, or I'll forget this is only supposed to be a kiss."

His mouth covered hers again, this time not quite so gently. She moaned as his tongue found hers. How could she go the rest of her life without the drugging pleasure of Lucas's kisses? Pushing the thought away, she undid the buttons on his waistcoat and touched his rock-like chest through the silk of his shirt. His heat burned against her fingers through the sheer fabric, but it was not enough.

With two sharp tugs, she undid the simple knot of his cravat. The hand on her hip was no longer restraining her, but moved in a circular caress that made her want to press her bottom against his thighs. When she followed through on her desire and felt his growing hardness against her hip, he growled. Taking advantage of his preoccupation with her moving bottom, she opened his shirt with greedy fingers.

At the first touch of her fingertips against his skin, he shuddered and the knowledge that she could affect him so profoundly filled her with bittersweet satisfaction. She brushed her hands over his hair-roughened chest, lightly skimming the small hard buds of his male nipples.

"Bloody hell, that feels good. Too good. Little one, you've got to stop."

She kissed the underside of his chin and flicked her tongue out to taste the skin there. "I don't want to, Lucas."

His hands tightened on her, and then suddenly, they were under her cloak, undoing the tapes on her gown. One hand caressed the aching swell of her breast and she shivered. The other one tunneled under the skirt of her gown, moving with swift assurance up her leg. Unlike in the garden, this time she made no attempt to stop him. She wanted to know what it felt like to have Lucas touch her most intimate place. If that made her a hopeless wanton, she did not care.

"You're so soft, sweeting. So perfect." He spoke against her neck as he used tiny kisses to trail a path down the column of her throat.

Somehow her cloak had come undone, and with her opened gown, her bosom was completely exposed to the exploration of his lips. Moving the hand that had held her breast around her back to support her, he closed the distance to her nipple with his mouth. She waited in almost painful anticipation for that jolt of feeling she remembered from the first time he had taken such liberties. When it came, she barely stifled a scream.

Sensations traveled down her body and pooled deep in her belly. She rocked against his lap, trying to find relief for the pressure building, and her legs relaxed, falling open in a wanton *V.* Lucas took immediate advantage of her position and slid his hand to rest against the hair-covered mound between her legs. The sensation was so unexpected that this time a small shriek of shock managed to escape her lips.

"I could not have said it better myself." Hot air from Lucas's mouth fanned her breast when he spoke.

She slid her hands onto his sturdy shoulders and gripped with all her might. "Lucas, I do not know what is happening. I feel so strange." She moved against his hand. "I want . . . I want . . ." She did not know what she craved, but she knew he alone could give it to her.

He slid one finger between the sensitive folds of her intimate flesh and brushed against the swollen nub. Her body arched and she would have come off his lap if his hand did not hold her down. She whimpered, her feelings spiraling out of control.

"Lucas, do something!"

His laughter sounded strained. "I am, little one. Trust me."

Her head swung from side to side as she mindlessly sought . . . she knew not what. "Now, Lucas. *Now.* I cannot stand it."

If he heard her demand, he gave no indication. His mouth continued to suckle her breast, ravaging her with delicious torment, and his finger moved in small, maddening circles over the nub of sensitized flesh between her legs. Then, without warning, her entire body convulsed and she felt as if every nerve screamed with the same incredible pleasure. The pleasure went on and on until she was mad with it and begging him to stop. Then her body went completely limp against him, and she tasted the salt of her tears on his bare chest.

"I love you, Lucas. I love you with all my heart."

LUCAS WAITED IN THE DARK OUTSIDE LADY UPWORTH'S house, the hour not quite dawn, his closed carriage stopped out of sight around the corner. Something about the way Irisa had said good-bye to him after their passionate interlude in his carriage alerted him to the fact that all was not well with her. She had told him she loved him with sweet abandon, but the joy of sated physical desire in her voice had been muted.

She should have been pleased that her experiment had been such a success. He had proven beyond the smallest doubt that his passion for her was based solely on her person. So, why had her eyes been filled with both despair and a determination that she tried to hide when he said good night?

His instincts warned him she planned to run.

A hired carriage rolled to a stop near Lady Upworth's town house. When no one alighted from the vehicle, Lucas's suspicions rose. The driver's repeated glances up and down the street cinched it.

Lucas approached him. "Are you waiting for a young lady?"

"Wot's it to you if oi am, guv?"

Lucas pinched a sovereign between his thumb and forefinger, holding it aloft. "This."

The driver reached out his hand to snatch the coin, but Lucas pulled it back, just out of reach. "Answer my questions first."

"Make it quick like, guv. The lidy'll show soon."

"Who are you waiting for?"

"Don't know. The one wot 'ired me said she needed things secret like. Probably runnin' away to a lover, you ask me."

Since that had not been one of Lucas's questions, he ignored the man's suppositions. The only lover Irisa wanted was Lucas. He was sure of it. No, her decision to run had nothing to do with treachery—and everything to do with blackmail.

"Where are you supposed to take her?"

"Don't know that either. 'Ired me for a week at a bloody good wage, so don't care much either."

Lucas asked what Irisa had promised in way of pay. When the coachman told him, Lucas offered a substantial increase over the amount for the coachman to disappear. The man took the money and did as suggested, moving his carriage at a fast clip down the street, having said something about the gentry being easy on a man's gin rations for once. The sound of the horses' hooves on the pavement had barely faded when Lucas spied two cloak-covered figures coming around the side of Lady Upworth's town house. Although a hood covered her head, he had no doubt the smaller one was Irisa. The other must be Pansy, her maid.

They both carried portmanteaus and a small trunk between them. Irisa's reticule dangled from her wrist over the portmanteau's side. She looked up and down the street, then turned to say something in a low voice to her maid.

Although he could not hear what Irisa had said, her maid's reply came distinctly through the night-chilled air. "I 'ope 'e didn't come, milady, and that's the truth. What you think you're about running off like this, I don't know."

Irisa said something else, her words again indistinct, but the agitation in her voice was apparent.

Lucas decided he might as well make his presence known. Stepping away from the shadow of the building, he said, "If I were a distrustful man, I might think Langley's accusations yesterday afternoon had some merit."

Fourteen

In the days since their return from Ashton Manor, Irisa had gotten almost no sleep, instead spending her nights restless with worry. Added to her overtired condition was an emotional turmoil of storm-like proportion, and she was not sure the voice she had heard was real, or a conjuring of her desperate imagination.

She had experienced the most overwhelming event of her life in Lucas's arms not an hour since and her determination to leave had wavered. However, she could not make sense of her own thoughts anymore and had been following her plan in an almost trancelike state.

"Have you nothing to say, Irisa?"

He was not a realistic creation of her overtired mind. He was here. All her well-meant convictions crumbled in the face of the terrible grief tormenting her at the prospect of losing Lucas, and it all became too much.

Dropping her valise with a plop, she did the same to her end of the trunk, resulting in a thud as it hit the ground and an exclamation from Pansy. Then, she picked up her skirts and flew across the ground separating her and Lucas. Throwing herself against his chest, she wrapped her arms around his waist and held on with all her strength.

"Oh, Lucas. I'm so glad you are here. I know it is horribly selfish and I'm not at all noble to feel such relief. You deserve so much more than my besmirched reputation and the scandal sure to result from our marriage, but the very idea of another woman touching you has tormented me since leaving your carriage earlier. I cannot bear it." Tears clogged her throat and she squeezed her eyes shut, pressing her face into his solid chest.

"I should leave for the sake of my family," she choked, "but you won't let me and *I'm glad.*" That knowledge wracked her with guilt. "I'm every bit as dishonorable and weak-willed as Papa believes."

With that shameful admission, she burst into tears.

Lucas's arms came around her and his hold was as tight as her own. "Hush, love."

She could not obey him. Tears made her feel pathetic, but she could not stem their flow. Not this time.

"Pansy, see that your mistress's things are returned to her room, but leave the trunk. I will take it with me now. You will begin moving your mistress's things to my town house today anyway."

"Yes, milord."

"I'm taking your mistress with me." He was forced to pry Irisa's arms from around his waist because she couldn't seem to let go of her own volition. Then he lifted her into his strong embrace and spoke to Pansy over his sholder. "You are to tell the rest of the household she is still abed. I will return her via Mrs. Drake and no one need be the wiser."

"Yes, milord."

"Where are you taking me, Lucas?" She didn't really care, so long as she remained with him.

"You and I need to talk. I'm taking you someplace safe and private to do so."

"That's nice." She was so weary, she did not think to argue or ask for more particulars.

Lucas placed her on the carriage seat before turning around to retrieve the trunk. She heard him give instructions to his coachman through an exhausted haze. When he stepped up into the carriage, he took the seat next to her and then pulled her close. His warmth enveloped her, making her feel safe, and she slipped into a light doze.

A FEW HOURS LATER, LUCAS STUDIED IRISA'S SLEEPING form. Blond curls framed her heart-shaped face. She looked so bloody sweet. So innocent. Not like the siren who had come apart in his arms. Not like the stubborn little baggage who snuck away from her companions to read by herself on his tower roof and ended up locked outside during a storm. Not like the enraged fiancée who had accused him of wanting her only when he was angry. And not at all like the impulsive, reckless female who had tried to run away rather than marry him.

Dark lashes fluttered and her eyes opened. He waited silently for her to wake fully and become aware of his presence.

According to Clarice, Irisa had slept the entire time he had been gone. He had returned to his own town house for some much-needed rest. He did not want to conduct the coming interview in an exhausted state, and he had not trusted himself to sleep under the same roof with her. He wanted her too much.

Irisa turned her head on the pillow and the golden brown depths of her eyes focused on his figure sitting next to the bed. "I suppose you want an explanation."

He stood up. "Not yet."

Turning, he retrieved the breakfast tray Clarice had brought in earlier. He motioned for Irisa to sit up in the bed and she did so, keeping the quilt tucked under her arms so it covered her bosom. He raised his brows at that bit of modesty. Such an innocent little siren.

He put the tray across her knees. "Eat first."

"Thank you." She picked up a piece of toast and took a bite, following it with a sip of chocolate. He didn't let her stop until she'd finished all the food on the tray. When she had, he took the tray and placed it outside the door.

Turning around, he found her watching him. "Where are we?"

"Clarice's. She has no live-in servants so your arrival was unobserved. Her daily woman believes you are a friend arrived from the country last evening after she had gone home."

"I see. Miss de Brieuse does not mind me being here?"

"No."

"Why did you bring me here, Lucas? I was too tired to question it this morning, but now my mind is functioning properly and it doesn't make any sense."

"We need to talk."

She pleated the blanket between her fingers. "Surely I could have slept in my own bed and talked with you later."

He caught her gaze and held it. "I wanted to be sure you would still be here when we were both rested enough to have a coherent discussion."

She looked away from him. "I deserve that, I suppose."

"You tried to run away. I could not be sure you would not waken with a renewed determination to do so."

She blushed and he knew his caution had not been misplaced.

"And yet you did not act disappointed when I caught you trying to sneak away."

She grimaced. "No. I did not. I suppose that is because my relief was too great."

"If you were so bloody relieved to be stopped, why were you trying to go in the first place?" It bothered him more than he wanted to admit that she could have been planning to run after giving herself so freely to him in his carriage.

She released the quilt and clasped her hands in front of her, letting her eyes once again focus on him. "I would rather be dressed for this discussion."

"I'd rather you stayed right where you are, the way you are. It gives me an advantage, and with an obstinate little thing like you, I need one."

Her mouth tightened and he knew she didn't like his pronouncement, but she did not jump out of the bed and start yelling at him. Unfortunately. Would this nightrail be as transparent as the one she wore at Ashton Manor?

"Tell me why you tried to run away."

"I told you at Thea's, but you would not listen."

"Tell me again. I'll listen more closely this time."

She went back to pleating the quilt and bit her lip. Finally, she spoke. "I'm so tired of feeling guilty, Lucas. I don't mean to hurt my family and I didn't want to cause you grief." She sighed. "It seems no matter how hard I try to be proper and biddable, I can never make up for my birth."

"Why would you think you had to make up for your birth? It is hardly your fault your parents made the decisions they did."

She shook her head. "You don't understand. If Mama had not become pregnant with me, Papa and the first countess would surely have reconciled. Thea would have been raised here and had her proper place in society. Jared would have known his mother."

"Those are events over which you had no control." He could not believe she thought otherwise.

"That is true, I suppose, but my birth caused them nonetheless."

"You, however, did not cause your own birth."

"You are right, of course, but I am used to feeling it is all my fault."

"Why?"

"Because my brother's disfigurement is my fault. He shuns society because my actions have made him an oddity. Were it not for me, he would still be living at Langley Hall where he belongs, in the bosom of his family."

Lucas couldn't follow her faulty reasoning and sat in stunned silence. It was obvious to the most casual observer that Viscount Ravenswood had little use for society and no desire to fit in amongst the Polite World, scar or no scar. He also had no love for his father, and considering the man's treatment of the first countess, that was entirely understandable.

"Irisa, you take far too much on yourself," he said finally.

"No, I do not. Because of my stubborn recklessness, Jared is a societal outcast."

"I doubt your brother considers that much of a burden."

Her eyes took on a faraway look, as if she were seeing something he could not. "When I was a small girl, I did not obey my nurse at all. Sadly, Papa and Mama indulged me. One day in early spring, I wished to play outside, but Nurse told me I must take a nap instead. It had been raining for days and it was the first bit of sunshine we had seen. I can still remember looking out the nursery window and longing to play in the sun."

"And?"

"I allowed Nurse to put me down for a nap. I was devious, and as soon as she left to attend to other chores, I snuck out to play. I wandered far into the fields of Papa's estate, and little did I know it, but my disappearance had been discovered. A search party was sent out. My brother found me, but so had a starving wolf. Jared saved me almost at the cost of his own life."

"That is how he became scarred?"

"Yes."

"I'm sure he feels the scars are a small price to pay for your life. I would suffer much worse for the sake of my small niece."

Irisa winced and her eyes turned black with haunted agony. "There was so much blood. Jared's pain-filled cries still echo in my mind sometimes. I ran, Lucas. I was terrified and I ran, leaving my brother to face the wolf alone."

"How old were you?"

"Six," she said in a dead voice.

"Too young to be anyone else's protector, and your brother did not die."

"No. We were found by Papa and the servants came. Someone shot the beast, but I thought Jared had already been killed. He lay so still on the blood-soaked ground."

"You were allowed to see this?"

"Yes. Papa wanted me to be fully cognizant of what I had wrought with my willful disobedience."

Even with what he knew of him, Lucas could not believe Langley's cruelty. "The bastard."

She didn't hear him, her attention too focused on the past. "Papa shouted at me that I had killed my brother and then he took a stick to me, so I could share in my brother's pain."

"He beat you?"

She shrugged. "I don't remember much until Mama came to my room later. I was in bed and it hurt horribly all over, but all I could think was that Jared was dead and it was my fault. I deserved the pain." She started to cry, silent tears running down her face. She swiped at the wetness. "When Mama came to me, I was crying then, too. She told me to stop, that I'd brought it all on myself and my brother. She told me Jared lived, but that I should not be surprised if he hated me."

"Both your parents deserve to be horsewhipped."

She shuddered. "Jared didn't hate me, but everything changed after that. Papa no longer loved me and Jared grew quiet, as if something inside him had died."

"He probably learned of your beating and felt responsible."

Irisa's gaze flew to his, her eyes wide with shock. "Why would he think that?"

"For the same reason you felt responsible for his suffering. You were both children and not mature enough to realize that what happened was no one's fault."

"I disobeyed my nurse and Jared was nearly killed because of it. Every time I behaved in a wayward fashion after that, my parents reminded me what my willful disobedience could cause. I know very well whose fault it was."

"Small children disobey on occasion. It is the way of life. What happened to your brother was unfortunate, but it was not malicious on your part and you are not to blame for the estrangement between Ravenswood and your parents.

All responsibility for that lies squarely at your father's door."

"My parents—"

"Behaved abominably."

She looked at him with an expression both infinitely sad and terribly vulnerable. "I have often thought I could not treat my own child so harshly."

Unable to resist the temptation any longer, he moved to the bed and pulled her into his arms. She sobbed into his neck and he was glad because he knew she needed to release these tears. She'd carried a false burden of guilt far too long.

When she eventually calmed, he asked, "Is that why you tried to run again, even though you knew I didn't want you to go and neither did the rest of your family?"

"Papa and Mama would have approved my decision."

"They are unnatural parents, in my opinion."

"I think perhaps you are right." She sighed and snuggled closer to him. "I could not stand the idea of hurting you as I had hurt my brother. The scars might not be visible on your face, but marriage to me will mar your pristine reputation beyond redemption."

"To hell with my reputation. I cannot let you go."

"But you want to marry the perfect paragon."

"I love you, Irisa. To me, you are everything that is perfect."

She shuddered against him. "I was so glad you stopped me from leaving Town this morning."

It was not the reaction he wanted to his declaration, but he had to allow for the fact she probably did not believe him yet. It would take time. Her parents had done her a huge disservice and she was only slowly coming to realize how wrong they had been.

"Why were you glad?" he asked, trying to draw her out.

"Because I love you." She raised tear-drenched eyes to his and spoke with a conviction that went to the very depths of his soul. "I want to marry you. I want to bear your babies and help you with your estates. I want to experience the indescribable pleasure I find in your arms and I want to give you pleasure. Lots of it. I never again want to worry you are another woman's lover, because you will be mine. I want to sit across from you at the dinner table and discuss all of life's important subjects. I want to grow old with you."

Lucas could not move. He could barely breathe. He pressed his lips to hers. She sighed and responded sweetly, twining her arms around his neck. It was a kiss of commitment. A promise. A vow. And when it was over, they were both shaking.

He released her and stepped away from the bed along with the temptation it represented. There were still things that needed to be said.

"Irisa, you are not responsible for your family's troubles and you aren't selfish for wanting to marry instead of giving in to the blackmailer."

"But everyone is going to be touched by the scandal, Lucas. Thea and Drake, Jared—they all pretend it doesn't matter, but it does. I'm bringing disgrace to my family and I can't seem to stop myself."

Black rage churned inside Lucas, but he kept it hidden. He wasn't angry with Irisa. He was furious with her parents for making an innocent girl bear the burden of guilt for their sin.

"You aren't bringing disgrace on your family. Your father is the one who terrorized his wife into running away. He's the one who never went after her and married another woman while the first countess was still living. You didn't do any of that and you aren't responsible for making it happen."

"But if Mama had not gotten pregnant with me, she could not have trapped Papa into marriage."

"If Langley had not been unfaithful, your mother could not have gotten pregnant. But regardless of how it happened, I'm bloody glad it did. I want to marry *you,* Irisa. Your honor and courage far exceed those of any other lady I know. You will make *me* a very suitable countess."

She flew off the bed and hugged him much as she had that morning. He wrapped his arms around her and returned the embrace, and that was how Clarice found them when she came to help Irisa get dressed, Lucas's chubby niece in tow.

A TENTATIVE NEW HAPPINESS BUBBLED INSIDE IRISA AS she carefully organized her papers and ledgers for movement to Ashton House, and she reveled in the sensation. She was marrying the man she loved, and he said he loved her.

She was not sure she trusted the words. After all, not so long ago he had scoffed at the very idea as romantical drivel. And she could not shake the fear that what he loved was an image of perfection that went only as deep as the façade of her behavior. Not the real Irisa Sellwyn, illegitimate and somewhat headstrong daughter of the Earl of Langley.

Even so, if he was willing to overlook the episode with Miss de Breiuse, Irisa vowed she would never again behave in a way that would invite comment by the *ton.* She would not make him sorry he had married a woman with a less than pristine past.

Tomorrow, she would become the Countess of Ashton, and even if her illegitimacy were exposed, nothing would change that. As her sister and Drake had pointed out, among the *ton,* marriage covered a multitude of sins and she was determined to add no more to feed the gossip mill.

She looked up at the sound of a light tap on the door. Pansy had gone to Ashton House to oversee Irisa's things being put away in the countess's bedchamber.

"Enter," she called as she closed the lid on the traveling case full of papers.

One of her aunt's upstairs maids walked in and curtsied, then handed Irisa an envelope. The thick white linen paper looked all too familiar and Irisa almost shrank away from it before silently admonishing herself not to be a coward. It was one thing to refuse to dwell on the blackmailer's threats; it was another thing entirely to hide from them. She was not her mother. She would face whatever problems might arise and do so with her eyes firmly open.

Reaching out for the note, she was about to dismiss the maid when she realized that, unlike the other one, this note had not been franked. It had not come via the post.

"Did you see who delivered this?" Her voice came out harsher than she'd intended and the maid's eyes widened.

"No, milady. Cook said it come to the back door. A boy delivered it. One what runs errands and such for small bits o' change."

Irisa's heart sank. "Thank you."

The maid curtsied again and left.

Irisa's hands trembled as she opened the envelope and pulled out the missive. The virulent words made her ill, but soon her discomfort turned to satisfaction. The blackmailer had given her all she needed to defeat his nefarious schemes.

SHE SMILED WITH ANTICIPATION AS FIRST LUCAS, AND then Jared, read the note. She had sent for Lucas immediately after having received the second threat. Jared had arrived at Aunt Harriet's at the same time as Lucas, and she decided to take him into her confidence as well. They were seated around a table in her aunt's small library. The same table she had been sitting at when the first note arrived.

Lucas looked up from the note and met her eyes. "You do not seem upset."

She grinned. "How can I be upset when the blackguard has given us such a prime opportunity?" She clasped her hands in delight. "We will set a trap with myself as bait and catch him before he can do any damage. The family will be safe and I will have my wedding."

"You'll have your wedding regardless." Lucas's tone did not suggest she argue the point and she didn't.

Touching his arm, she soothed him. "Of course."

"You believe Ashton will allow you to set yourself up as bait?" Jared made it sound like her plan was as rickety as a three-legged stool.

She frowned. "Naturally. How else are we to catch him?"

"He demands you come alone carrying a great deal of blunt," Lucas reminded her, not looking at all as if he was falling in with her plan as she had expected.

Crossing her arms, she sat back in her chair and fixed both her brother and her fiancé with a look that told them she meant to have her way. "I assume that between the three of us we can be sufficiently clever to outwit one little blackmailer."

"I will not allow you to be put at risk." Lucas's expression was every bit as set as her own.

"Then protect me."

Jared rocked back on the legs of his chair. "I know that expression. We either agree to help her, or she'll go on her own. It'll take tying her to the bed to keep her here."

She did not consider this in the same vein as behaving with impeccable decorum. She had no choice but to stubbornly insist on taking action. It was for Lucas's own good.

His expression was unreadable. "And who said I was averse to tying her to the bed?"

She gasped in outrage. "Lucas, that is a terrible thing to say." Turning to her brother, she said, "You can quit your laughing. You should be offended on my behalf."

Jared shrugged. "I'm thinking your marriage bed might be bloody interesting if your husband isn't averse to tying you to it."

It was Lucas's turn to laugh, but her face felt as if it had caught fire. She could not believe her brother had said that. Did ladies and gentlemen truly do such things? She wasn't about to ask Lucas in front of Jared. Enough was enough.

"The topic under discussion is our plan to catch the villain trying to prevent me from marrying Lucas, not my marriage bed." Even saying the words in front of Jared mortified her, but she could pretend to be as casual as they.

Lucas gave her a wickedly sexy grin and winked. Thankfully, his next words did not match his teasing actions.

"You expect me to protect you while you wait in the middle of Hyde Park in the dead of night?" He sounded merely curious.

"Yes. Surely for a former intelligence agent, such an undertaking should not be too difficult." She gave up trying to shame him into it. "Please, Lucas. We have to try."

"No, we don't. Your aunt was right. Secrets do have a way of getting out. I'm not going to put you at risk to keep this one. It isn't worth it. You're too precious. Do you understand me?"

The words and the intensity with which they were spoken went straight to her heart, but she couldn't give in. She tried to formulate an argument in her head that would sway him, but before she came up with anything, Jared spoke.

"If it were just the gossip, I'd agree with you. But what about the incident at Ashton Manor? We don't know if the bastard is dangerous to Irisa, but we can't take the risk of letting the blackmailer roam free indefinitely."

Lucas's expression turned chilling. "You're right, but there are too many variables in this circumstance we cannot control. She could be hurt despite all our efforts to protect her."

"Let us discuss what we can control," Irisa said, refusing to be left out of the conversation. It was her plan, after all.

"You are instructed to arrive in a hansom cab. It would take very little to arrange the use of one and have either Jared or myself disguised as the driver."

She considered that, looking first at Lucas and then Jared. "I don't think so. You are both rather distinctive in your size."

Lucas narrowed his eyes while looking at Jared. "You're right. It will have to be me. Ravenswood's bulk is unmistakable."

She had said they were both too big, but would not quibble. She assumed Lucas knew how to disguise himself.

Jared shrugged. "I'll get to the rendezvous point early and conceal myself as close as possible."

"We'll bring Drake in on this and he can do the same."

Irisa smiled. "There. You see. With you, Jared, and Drake nearby, nothing could possibly happen to me."

Lucas did not return her smile. "Does it strike you that

your impulsive nature must be quite well known amongst the *ton*? You will notice the blackmailer thought nothing of demanding you come to Hyde Park in the middle of the night. Alone. Most ladies would faint at the very idea."

She wrinkled her nose. "Poor-spirited creatures."

But his words touched on a nerve. Perhaps he was right and the impulsive nature she thought she'd suppressed so well had shown itself once too often. After this adventure, she would do her best to curb that tendency once and for all.

LATE THAT NIGHT, IRISA RODE IN THE CAB, ACCORDING to plan. It stopped. Taking a deep breath and saying a quick prayer for courage, Irisa opened the door and stepped down. The park looked very different at night, with its trees casting ominous shadows in the moonlight. The fog had rolled in during the carriage ride from Aunt Harriet's house, and soon it would be difficult to see Lucas and the hansom cab at all.

He had instructed her to return to him if no one showed up before the fog got too thick. She shivered in the cold air and was reminded of the night she spied on Lucas and Clarice.

At least tonight she had a warmly lined cloak covering an equally warm gown. Lucas had insisted she wear something woolen, which was not at all fashionable, but imminently practical.

She walked along the path that led to the dictated meeting place, the satchel full of money banging against her leg. Lucas had insisted she carry the money in case something went wrong. Her gaze darted to the right and left of the path, but she could not make out Jared or Drake. Good. With any luck, neither would the blackmailer. When she arrived at the well-constructed replica of a ruin that was her destination, it was empty except for a piece of white stationary held in place on the ground by a rock. She stepped forward and picked the paper up. It gave detailed instructions for a secondary meeting place farther along the path.

Should she go on? If she wanted to catch the blackmailer, she had no choice. It would not hurt to go to the next rendezvous point, not if she stayed on the path and hurried before the fog became so thick she was entirely cloaked in its pooling brackish mass. Irisa stepped out of the ruin on the opposite side from where she had entered it. She could only hope her movements were observed by Jared or Drake.

Walking swiftly, she reached the fork in the path indicated on the paper. She saw no sign of anyone. Nor did she see another note. Had the blackmailer changed his mind? As the thought entered her head, a hand landed heavily on her shoulder.

"So you decided to show up after all, Lady Irisa." The voice was low and gravelly, but the accent was cultured.

Stifling the shriek that crawled up her throat, she tried to turn around, but the hand on her shoulder stayed her.

So did the hard object poking into her shoulder blade.

"Do not make a sound and I won't have to hurt you."

Fifteen

RAGE LENT STRENGTH BY FEAR SWEPT through Lucas as Irisa and the darkly clad figure behind her started moving down one of the side paths.

What did the little idiot think she was doing? He had told her not to move from the ruin. He had abandoned his position by the hansom cab the moment Irisa walked out the other side of the ruin, but he was still too far away to stop them. Bloody hell.

Where were Ravenswood and Drake? They should have intervened already, but Irisa and her companion were drawing farther away unimpeded. Her silent acquiescence bothered Lucas. Either she was being a bloody fool and straying from the plan willingly, or the cloaked figure behind her had threatened her in some way.

Lucas moved with the silent tread he had perfected in his younger days, steadily closing the gap between himself and his quarry. He picked up his pace, realizing that with the gathering fog he would be unable to see them in a few minutes unless he got much closer. The sound of their voices floated back to him and he tried to make out what they were saying.

"Where are you taking me?" Irisa asked.

"It is imperative you maintain your silence, Lady Irisa.

I will have to ask you not to speak again." The cultured voice had an unreal quality that put Lucas further on his guard.

"Why do I have to be quiet? There's no one around this time of night to hear me." Irisa's voice rose slightly, sounding irritated. Good girl. Her next words, however, made his blood run cold. "There's also no need for you to hold a pistol on me. I've brought the money and you're welcome to it." She stopped walking. "Don't you want to see it?"

Then a multitude of things happened at once. Two familiar figures rose out of the fog and rushed Irisa and the man standing behind her. Drake grabbed her and lifted her away in one clean move. Ravenswood didn't give the blackmailer a chance to react, but kicked the gun from his hand and then cold-cocked him with a single powerful punch.

Lucas arrived in time to watch the blackguard fall to the ground. He would have liked the satisfaction of hitting the bastard, but he would settle for questioning him once he woke up from his forced sleep.

Lucas bit back the urge to ask Irisa what the bloody hell she thought she'd been doing when she left the ruin. The fog was so thick now, he couldn't see anything beyond a few feet and there was no reason to believe the blackmailer worked alone. His cohorts could be waiting close by in the shrouded darkness. Ravenswood and Drake's silence said their thoughts ran along the same lines. Irisa, however, showed no such reluctance to speak.

"Well. That takes care of that."

Lucas wished he could agree, but instinct told him their villain did not lie on the ground at his feet. Drake clamped his hand over her mouth. When she struggled, he bent down to whisper low in her ear. She stopped struggling and Drake let her go.

Though he wanted nothing more than to verify she was unhurt in any way and then yell at her until she promised never to take such a foolish risk again, Lucas stood motionless, listening. He focused on the immediate vicinity, ignoring the sounds of late-night horse and carriage traffic on the London streets.

He would have liked to send Drake back to the carriage with Irisa, but could not be certain that was the safest course of action. The blackmailer's cohorts could be waiting there. This time of night, footpads could be waiting just as easily. Lucas remained motionless for a quarter of an hour, but heard not so much as a blade of grass bending.

Ravenswood's victim began moving as consciousness came back, and Lucas decided there was nothing to be gained by remaining on the path. He motioned silently for Ravenswood to bring the blackmailer, and for Drake and Irisa to head back toward the hansom cab.

Ravenswood, having bound the man while Lucas listened for evidence of associates, swung him up over his massive shoulders and carried him down the path. Lucas let Drake lead the way and followed behind Irisa. Her patient silence had impressed him, and the way she now attempted to move without sound as her brother and brother-in-law were doing reminded him just what a unique creature she really was. They reached the hansom cab without incident. If the blackmailer had come to full consciousness, he had made no attempt to call for help.

Drake climbed to the driver's box and Ravenswood joined him after depositing his burden on the floor of the carriage. Lucas helped Irisa inside and then joined her on the narrow seat, pulling the door shut behind him. He rested his feet on the blackmailer, exerting pressure to keep the man in place.

"There is no need for this sort of behavior, I assure you."

Lucas ignored the slightly slurred speech. He didn't want to question his captive in the dark interior of the cab. He wanted to see the blackmailer's face when he answered Lucas's questions. Irisa seemed to sense his reluctance to speak and remained silent as well, but she slipped her small hand into his for the remainder of the carriage ride.

* * *

THEA WAS WAITING FOR THEM IN THE LIBRARY WHEN they arrived at her and Drake's town house. She flew across the room and checked first Drake, then Irisa, then Jared, and finally Lucas for signs of injury. Lucas stepped back from Thea's ministrations with ill-concealed discomfort.

Irisa smiled reassuringly at her sister. "We're all fine and we've caught him," she said with a flourish of her hand indicating the bound man standing between Jared and Lucas.

He didn't look like a blackmailer at all. He dressed like a dandy, though the fabric and cut of his clothes were clearly not from Weston's. Brown hair fell in disordered curls around his face and he held himself with feigned relaxation. Irisa knew it was feigned because his eyes darted about as if gauging the possibilities for escape.

She shifted her focus to her fiancé. Why did he look so grim? Lucas's attention was centered on the mischief maker, but there was no sense of satisfaction or victory in him.

He turned to Thea. "Please take your sister to the drawing room. We will join you there when we've finished questioning this scoundrel."

"No." Irisa could not believe he would try to exclude her from the final outcome. "I want to hear why he has been threatening me and how he learned my secret."

"I want to stay, too," Thea said. "We all have a vested interest in hearing what this awful man has to say."

"My dear lady, to have one so charming refer to me in such terms is indeed a blow. Please, hear me out before rendering your judgment."

Irisa glared at the blackmailer. "There's nothing you can say that will justify your odious behavior."

Suddenly Drake was in front of the bound man. "If you speak to my wife again, much less call her a dear, you'll be swallowing your teeth with your next breath."

The man blanched. "I did not mean to offend."

Lucas looked at the blackmailer consideringly and then

at Thea and Irisa, his expression remote. "You may stay as long as he cooperates and you remain silent. If your presence hinders my interrogation in any way, you will leave the room without further argument."

Irisa could not help shivering at the chill in his voice and let him know she agreed with a nod. Thea did the same.

"Sit over by the fireplace."

She and her sister moved quickly to obey Lucas's instructions.

Lucas shoved the villain into a chair and then moved to stand threateningly over him. Jared took a position to Lucas's left and Drake took one to his right. The blackmailer turned absolutely pasty. Irisa thought she would have, too, if she was faced with such a show of brute strength—Lucas and the men beside him each exuded an aura of menace.

"Who are you?" Lucas's words cracked in the air like gunshots.

"Th-Thaddeus P. Brandon at your service, and I assure you there has been a monumental misunderstanding."

"Oh? You did not hold a gun to my fiancée's back and attempt to kidnap her tonight?"

As Lucas asked the question, Irisa realized that particular aspect of the situation had escaped her until now. Why had the odious little man held a gun to her back?

Thaddeus was back to looking sickly. "Well, as to that. I was merely following instructions, sir. You cannot mean to take offense over the fact I take a certain amount of pride in handling my work professionally."

Lucas's expression turned deadly. "Oh, but I do. When it involves threatening my fiancée, I take grave offense. You might even say fatal offense."

Irisa stifled the urge to shout a denial of Lucas's implication. She would not allow him to kill anyone on her behalf, even a sniveling, blackmailing villain.

Thaddeus groaned. "I assure you, sir, I had no intention of hurting your lady."

"Tell me about your instructions," Lucas demanded.

"I was told to meet your lady at the park and remove her from the premises before her lover arrived. My client said he was her guardian and had discovered she planned an elopement with an unsuitable *parti* this evening."

"What the hell are you talking about?" Jared's voice boomed out, causing the blackmailer to jump in his seat.

Lucas turned to her brother and glared him into silence. Really, Irisa thought, the man acted as if he was the only one with any say in this situation. Jared's question was perfectly understandable; Thaddeus's words had confused her, too. But by the way Jared went back to hulking menace, he didn't seem to mind Lucas's high-handed tactics.

"Who hired you to meet my lady in the park?"

Hired? Lucas didn't think this man was her blackmailer. She tried desperately to fill her lungs with air as the probability that the ordeal was not finished washed over her.

"I don't know." Before Lucas could make good on the threat that came over his features, Thaddeus went on. "I never saw his face. Many of my clients prefer anonymity. He came into my place of business, a little tavern near the river, and approached me. He had heard I had a reputation for delivering good service, you see."

The man was actually preening. Irisa frowned in astonishment.

"What were you supposed to do with my lady when you left the park?"

"I was to deliver her to a waiting carriage at the West Entrance."

Drake cursed. Jared looked ready to explode.

Lucas met Thaddeus's look with a narrow-eyed gaze for several seconds and then nodded once. "That much at least is true."

Thaddeus's eyes widened. "I assure you I have not lied to you, sir."

Lucas's smile was feral. "Oh, you've lied all right, and you're going to tell me the truth or you'll end up food for the rats that frequent the area around your *office*."

"It's true, guv. Every word. I didn't see the bloke's face

wot 'ired me and that's the 'onest truth, it is." Lucas's threat had succeeded in making Thaddeus lose his cultured accents.

"Why did he hire you to fetch my lady rather than do it himself if she was his ward?"

"I don't know, guv. I don't ask me clients their reasons when they offer me a lot 'o blunt."

Again, Lucas grew silent. "Have you ever done work for this particular client before?"

Thaddeus shook his head. "Never saw 'im before. I'd remember. Got a good ear for voices, I do."

"I should kill you for what you tried to do tonight." Lucas's voice had taken on a conversational tone that, at first, made it difficult for Irisa to appreciate the import of his words.

Thaddeus had no such trouble. He started shaking. "I made a mistake, guv, and I'm that sorry. Please, don't kill me."

Did Thaddeus really think Lucas was going to murder him in her sister's library? She had to admit that Lucas had taken on a chilling aspect that was quite frightening, but couldn't Thaddeus see her fiancé's innate honor?

"There is one way you might begin to make up for the insult you have done to my lady," Lucas mused.

"Anything, guv."

"I want the name of the man who hired you."

"I'll take it on as me most 'igh-payin' job."

"It is. The payment will be your life."

LUCAS STEPPED INTO THE LIBRARY. IRISA SAT QUIETLY gazing into the fire, her expressive face for once devoid of emotion. Was she going to plead with him to postpone the wedding?

He'd seen the look of horror that came over her as she realized Thaddeus Brandon wasn't the blackmailer. She still worried about how the revelation of her parents' secret would affect her family. Lucas would do a great deal to spare her pain, but he would not cancel their wedding. Irisa needed his protection and he couldn't give it effectively while living in a separate residence.

"Drake and Thea have gone up to bed. You should do likewise, little one. Tomorrow will be an eventful day." Their wedding day.

She turned toward him and the firelight cast her face in shadows. What was she thinking? Her thoughts were often incomprehensible to him since logic did not usually appear to play a large part in them.

"I know," she said, "but I wanted to talk to you first."

"We are not postponing the wedding." He hadn't meant to sound so harsh, but she might as well understand he could not be moved on this.

Her spine stiffened. "I was not about to suggest we should, but you needn't come all over bossy with me like this, Lucas."

He crossed the room and pulled her from the chair. He had to see her face, to read her eyes. When the shadows fell away and he could do so, what he saw there transfixed him. Warm approval. Love.

"Perhaps you will find this less objectionable," he said just before pressing his lips to hers.

He was careful to keep the kiss light, not wanting to test his self-control too much. She nearly undermined his good intentions when she melted against him and parted her lips in invitation. He allowed himself the pleasure of touching her tongue in a brief caress before pulling his mouth from hers.

"What did you want to discuss, sweeting?"

She blinked little brown owl eyes at him. "Discuss?"

"You said you did not wish to go to bed before talking some things over with me," he reminded her with a trace of amusement.

He savored the knowledge that his kisses affected her so strongly.

"Oh. Yes." She blushed prettily. "I wanted to thank you.

I know you were not overly fond of my plan, but you went through with it and I'm grateful."

"We did not catch the real villain in this piece."

She sighed, playing with the buttons on his waistcoat. "I know. I suppose I knew somewhere deep inside that would be too easy, but we tried and you helped me even though you didn't want to and I'm most appreciative."

"Is that why you aren't begging me to postpone the wedding, because you're grateful for my help tonight?"

Her gaze flew to his. "Of course not. We had already agreed not to do so. Tonight had nothing to do with it."

Something inside of him relaxed at her words. "I'm sorry we were not successful."

She smiled understandingly. "We caught that Thaddeus person. Do you suppose he will succeed in discovering who hired him?"

Lucas doubted it. Once the blackmailer realized his attempt at kidnapping had failed, he would avoid any connection to the person who might identify him.

"Perhaps," he hedged, unwilling to crush the hope in her expression entirely.

She wrapped her arms around him in a tight, brief embrace. "Thank you."

He pulled her to a chair and sat down, tugging her into his lap as he did so. "I'm glad you waited up to talk to me. There are a few things I wish to discuss with you as well." And he'd rather argue with her about them now than on her wedding day.

She nestled against him and her sweet, womanly scent surrounded him. "All right, Lucas."

"Someone tried to kidnap you tonight."

She nodded her head where it rested against the lapel of his jacket. "I know."

He hadn't expected hysterics. Not from Irisa, but he had not anticipated this nonchalant reaction to the dangerous situation either.

"Until we catch the blackmailer, you are at grave risk."

She stilled. "I had not thought of it that way."

He had, and the thought had been enough to turn his hair gray. "We will have to take precautions to keep you safe."

"What kind of precautions?" she asked, wariness evident in her voice. She appeared far more concerned about the steps necessary to keep her safe than the reality of the threat.

"Nothing too difficult," he tried to assure her, though he knew she would not like his dictates. "You will simply have to be with someone at all times, and I do not want you to leave the house unless I accompany you."

She gasped and pulled back until she was glaring into his eyes. "I do not wish to become a prisoner in my own home, Lucas."

"There is no need for melodramatics. You are not going to be a prisoner."

"Like I wasn't a prisoner at Ashton Manor?" she asked accusingly, her agitated fingers digging into his waistcoat. "If you are intent on ignoring me after our wedding like you did then, I will never be allowed to leave the house. I will not live like that. I cannot bear to have someone with me all the time either. It is too stifling."

The mulish tilt to her chin let him know she was prepared to stand her ground. Bloody hell.

"I did not ignore you at Ashton Manor. I merely avoided spending time alone with you." If he hadn't, there was every possibility that they would have anticipated their wedding vows.

"When you wanted to yell at me for finding some time to myself, you were quick enough to come alone to my room."

"And came all too close to losing my self-control, if you will remember."

The anger in her eyes did not diminish. "You are alone with me now."

It suddenly occurred to him that his behavior at Ashton Manor had hurt her feelings. Did she truly believe he had avoided her company because he had not wanted to be with her, that he would behave similarly after their wedding?

"I'm holding on to my desire to lie naked with you by a strand, little one. And that is exactly how it was for me at Ashton Manor. The only thing saving you tonight is the knowledge that tomorrow I will make you mine completely."

He shifted her in his lap until he knew she could feel the evidence of his words against her hip.

Her eyes went round and the flush in her cheeks intensified—but not from irritation, if he read her expression correctly. "Oh."

"I will not avoid your company once we are wed, and you can be assured I will be available to escort you on any necessary excursions."

The dazed expression receded from her eyes as they narrowed. "And what do you consider necessary? A trip to the lending library? A call on Thea, or one of my other friends? A drive in the park? A visit to the museum? Going to see my man of affairs? For I do all of those things and more, on a moment's notice sometimes."

He smiled. "You will have to arrange the trips beforehand, and perhaps for a time ask some of those people to call on you, but it will not be so bad. Trust me."

"I do trust you, Lucas. I wouldn't marry you otherwise, but I'm not going to agree to this kind of confinement. Even Papa gave me more freedom."

Did she think she had a choice? "You will agree, because it is the only way of assuring your safety until the blackmailer is caught."

He squeezed her hip when she opened her mouth to argue. "It is my responsibility to see to your safety and I will do so, even if it means locking you in your room."

She tried to jump off his lap, but he wouldn't let her.

She settled for sitting at the very far edge of his knees and glowering at him. "You will not attempt to intimidate me in this fashion, my lord."

He knew she used the title just to annoy him, but it still worked. "I am not making threats, I am informing you of a certain outcome if you put yourself at risk like you did on the tower roof at Ashton Manor."

She hissed with outrage. "I did not close that door, Lucas, and it's the perfect example of why your plan will not work. If I hadn't been forced to subterfuge, I would not have been in any danger."

"You were not *forced* to subterfuge. You chose to go off on your own and the results should have at least made you realize your peril. However, your actions indicate you will continue to blithely ignore the truth of your circumstances and behave in a wholly reckless manner." He realized the term might cause her pain after what she had told him the day before, but he could not think of a better description for her behavior. "For that reason alone, precautionary measures must be taken."

"What do you mean? I have done nothing to warrant such sarcasm from you. *I am not reckless.*"

"You left the ruin."

"I had no choice. There was a note telling me to meet Thaddeus Brandon further up the path."

"You chose the wrong alternative. You agreed you would not leave the original meeting place."

"If I had not, we would not know about Thaddeus Brandon."

Lucas did not consider that sufficient reward for the risk she had faced and told her so.

"I was safe at all times. You and my brothers saw to it."

"The man held a gun to your back." The feeling of desperate fear he had experienced when he realized she was in such peril came back.

Irisa's anger suddenly drained from her countenance and she laid her hand on his chest in supplication. "But he did not have the opportunity to use it. I am fine."

"And you will stay that way."

She surprised him by nodding. "Yes. I will. May I have permission to leave the house with my family?"

The quick about-face disconcerted him, but he appreciated it. "If Ravenswood or Drake is with you, yes."

She smiled and patted his chest. "Thank you. Now about the matter of having someone with me at all times while I am home . . ."

He shook his head. "I cannot compromise on that, little one. Will it be such a sacrifice to spend a great deal of time in my company?"

Her smile dazzled him. "Will it be in your company, Lucas?"

"Yes." And feeling the way he did right now, much of that time would be spent in bed.

He wondered if Irisa would show herself to be as adventurous in this aspect of marriage as she had shown herself to be in so many other ways of late.

A man could only hope.

Sixteen

IRISA WASN'T THINKING OF HER WEDDING night the following morning as she prepared for her marriage ceremony. There were too many other worries filling her thoughts.

Aunt Harriet had taken her aside early that morning to give her the talk, believing her mother would have neglected it because of the strained relations between the two of them. Irisa had not had the heart to tell the dear old lady that Mama had indeed already done her duty. Her aunt's advice had been much like her mother's, with one alteration.

She said a woman must always consider her duty in the marriage bed to be sacred despite the discomfort and embarrassment a lady faced when her husband exercised his conjugal rights. According to Aunt Harriet, things did not improve upon practice when it came to the passionate side of marriage.

Irisa was sure she was wrong, but trepidation toward the consummation of her marriage grew inside her with each moment that drew her closer to becoming Lucas's wife.

Then, much to everyone's surprise and Irisa's personal dismay, Mama had arrived two hours ago to oversee her daughter's toilette. So far she had managed to rout Thea from the bedchamber, made Pansy re-dress Irisa's hair three times, iron her petticoats, and apply rouge and powder to Irisa's strained features.

"You look like you are going to a funeral, and though under the circumstances it is understandable, we can't have the *ton* believing you are anything but pleased about your marriage."

"I am pleased about my marriage," Irisa replied.

"How you can be when you know it will bring certain ruin to your family's standing amidst the *ton,* I cannot fathom. That I managed to raise such a selfish, willful daughter with so little concern for her family's honor is a blow no mother should be expected to face." Mama dabbed delicately at the corner of her eyes with an embroidered handkerchief.

Irisa refused to be goaded into an argument. She hadn't wanted her marriage to bring grief to her family, but surely it would be better for the secret to out when she was a countess than if she were still the unmarried daughter of a moderately placed earl.

She had tried to protect her family and catch the blackmailer, but her plan had failed. Just as her attempt to leave Town had failed. The best she could do for them now was to follow through on her plan to marry Lucas and rely on the protection of his title when the scandal exploded. She only hoped Lucas would not regret overmuch his insistence on going through with the wedding.

Thea came back into the room, looking absolutely beautiful in a gown of peacock blue silk. She took one look at Irisa and walked to the water pitcher, where she wetted her own handkerchief. Coming to stand in front of Irisa, she began wiping at the powder and rouge Pansy had applied.

Not deigning to speak to Thea, Mama glared at Irisa instead. "One would think that, as your mother, I would have the final say in your toilette the morning of your wedding. Some people have absolutely no manners or sense of social courtesies."

Irisa clenched her teeth in an effort to hold in her temper.

"Some people would do better seeing to their own appearance than worrying about that of a lovely young girl," Thea retorted. "For instance, a mother's tears might cause the smudging of her kohl and render her ridiculous."

Irisa stifled a hysterical giggle as her mother gasped and spun to face the mirror. Seeing that Thea was right, she immediately set about repairing her cosmetics.

Taking advantage of her preoccupation, Irisa went with Thea and Pansy to the other side of the room to don her white silk gown. Gold ribbon accented her neckline and the fashionably high waist, while the hem had been tucked in scallops revealing an underskirt of gold as well. She pulled on long white gloves and slipped her feet into the white kid slippers fashioned to match the dress.

Thea stepped back and surveyed her with a smile. "You do look lovely, sister mine."

Pansy nodded and sniffed. "That you do, milady."

Irisa tried to smile in return, though her stomach was knotted with tension. "Thank you."

Thea turned to Pansy. "Help Lady Langley finish the repairs to her appearance and I will take Irisa to the drawing room to wait for the coach."

When they reached the drawing room, Thea poured Irisa a glass of brandy. "Here. I think you need it."

Irisa took the snifter without a word of protest. Her sister was right. She needed something.

Taking a large sip, she immediately started coughing. "I didn't realize it would burn so much."

Thea made her finish the brandy, but she drank it in much smaller sips. Her insides, which had felt chilled with nerves, began to warm. "Mama is angry with me for going through with the wedding."

"Lady Langley is too concerned with her place in the *ton*. She is foolish if she believes that now the secret is known it will remain private. She should be grateful you are marrying someone as well placed as Lucas. When the scandal hits, his consequence will help to mitigate it."

Irisa nodded and took another sip of her brandy. "That is precisely what I was thinking this morning."

"Then why are you so upset?"

"Who said I was upset?" Irisa hedged.

"Before your coughing fit over the spirits, your face was as white as your gown, and you've got a wild, desperate look in your eyes. Don't you want to marry Lucas?"

"I want it more than anything in the world," Irisa admitted, "but I'm scared. What if he comes to hate me as Papa has done because I am a source of embarrassment for him?"

Thea squeezed Irisa's arm. "You know, I have never once regretted marrying Drake."

"You are not like Lucas. The mores of society mean very little to you."

Her sister shrugged. "This is true, but I still think you are silly to worry about Lucas coming to hate you. He is nothing like our father."

"You are right." She took another fortifying sip of brandy. "May I ask a rather personal question?"

"Of course."

"Mama has intimated that initiation into lovemaking is not always pleasant . . ."

Thea bit her lip. "It can hurt the first time."

"That is what Mama said." But she'd hoped that her mother had been wrong.

"It is nothing to worry about. I'm sure Lucas will take good care of you."

Irisa hoped her sister was right, but her fears on that score were far from vanquished.

LUCAS HELPED IRISA DOWN FROM THE CARRIAGE, THEN swung her into his arms and carried her up the steps to her new home.

Nerves and embarrassment beset her. "Really, Lucas, I don't think this necessary. I can walk."

His face taut with some undefined emotion, he held her with a grip of iron. "Hush, little one."

His command for silence came out sounding like a caress and he did not stop to greet the assembled servants.

She gripped his shoulder and tried to shake it. "*Lucas.* Put me down. It is time you made me known to my staff."

He stopped, his expression pained. "You are right, but this is the final delay I will tolerate," he growled.

His tone and words so surprised her that she did not protest when he kept her anchored to his side after he lowered her with obvious reluctance to the floor. Although his impatience was palpable in the tense line of his body against hers, he did not hurry through the introductions, taking time to make every servant feel their worth in the household.

Irisa had met some of them before, during her stay at Ashton Manor, footmen and a valet that traveled with Lucas, but the majority of the men and women standing in the hall were unknown to her. She took pains to commit each face and name to memory, wanting to make a good impression on her staff in the days to come. She liked the round little housekeeper and smilingly accepted her invitation to tour the town house, but when Irisa attempted to pull away from Lucas in order to follow the other woman, he did not let go.

"There will be plenty of time tomorrow for your new mistress to become familiar with her home." As Lucas spoke to the housekeeper, he once again swung Irisa into his arms.

She caught her breath in surprise and automatically clutched at his shoulders for balance. "Lucas, what are you doing?"

The question was rather moot as his intention was obvious to her and everyone else in the hall. Lucas was taking her to bed. And somehow, in this intense mood, she could not see him taking care of her as Thea had said he would.

He'd mounted several stairs before stopping to turn and instruct the now grinning housekeeper to have dinner delivered to his bedchamber later. "Until then, I will expect you to take care of all household issues with your customary efficiency."

The housekeeper bobbed her mobcapped head.

Turning toward the austere butler, he said, "In the event that anyone should have the temerity to call upon a new bride and groom on their wedding day, we are *not at home.*"

That elder personage nodded without a hint of emotion.

Irisa buried her face against Lucas's neck in mortification. She could not believe her husband had made his intentions so clear to the staff, and her earlier embarrassment returned tenfold. He might as well have stood on the top step and shouted his aim to bed her to anyone within hearing distance.

She hissed as much to him as he continued his ascent on the stairs.

"Irisa, it is our wedding night. The servants expect me to share your bedchamber."

She pulled her face back and glared at him. "It is not our wedding *night.* It is still our wedding *day* and I'm not at all sure we are supposed to engage in this sort of activity yet."

He stared at her as if she were the one behaving like her brains had gone to let. "We are married now, sweeting. We can engage in *this sort of activity* anytime we please."

"But Pansy was supposed to ready me for bed."

"I'll help you out of your clothes." The look in his eyes when he gave that promise made her shiver.

"I have a new nightgown Thea gave me to wear. You aren't supposed to see it until I have it on."

His eyes devoured her like a voracious beast. "You won't need a nightgown."

"If you're trying to soothe my nerves, you're not doing a very good job," she informed him, feeling very much like a cornered fox facing a hound.

He blinked. "You expect me to soothe you?"

"Yes." She really must ask Thea if all men were prone to moments of such thickheadedness, or if it was just Lucas.

"Why? You know you like what you feel in my arms. There's no reason for you to be nervous. You're the one who wanted me to show more passion toward you." He truly sounded perplexed. And frustrated.

"Sometimes, you remind me very much of a stone statue." She muttered the words, not bothering to hide her exasperation.

His eyes positively burned with wicked amusement. "I assure you, there are portions of my body that feel a great deal like a stone statue at the moment."

As the meaning of his words sank in, she went absolutely rigid in his arms. *"Lucas."*

He ignored her shocked exclamation and pushed open the door to his bedchamber. Stepping inside, he shoved the door shut with his foot. He released his hold under her knees and slowly lowered her once again to a standing position, groaning as her body rubbed the portion of his anatomy he had just referred to. Frissons of excitement and fear shot through her in equal measure and she pulled from his embrace, hastily stepping away.

He turned and locked the door, his action settling on her nerves like a threat.

She moved back toward the window, taking in her surroundings as she went. Lucas's room reflected his character. The furniture was made of sturdy walnut, his four-poster bed the hugest she had ever seen. Even Jared would fit comfortably in it. The walls, draperies, and bedding were muted shades, masculine yet elegant. She brushed against the draperies and stopped, their velvet roughness rubbing against the bare portion of her left arm. Sunlight warmed her back through the window.

His eyes narrowed at her retreat and he looked even more like a predator.

"This is a lovely bedchamber, Lucas. Is mine done in the same style?" Irisa couldn't believe she'd just asked such an inane question.

Of course the countess's chamber would not be done in the same masculine tones and simplicity. Indeed, Pansy had already told her that it was a charming room filled with finely carved pieces and done in light shades of mauve.

"Perhaps I could see it," she said with sudden inspiration.

His answer was to walk over to the door that must lead

to her room and lock it as well. The sound of the tumbler clicking into place echoed in her mind.

She bit her lip and sighed. "I suppose not."

He shook his head, but said nothing. She watched in frozen fascination as he began to undress. First, he sat down and tugged off his Hessians. Then he untied the intricate knot of his cravat and removed it, taking time to lay it across the corner of the bed.

"Are you sure you don't want to call your man to help you?"

He glanced at her. "You can help me if you like, wife."

She swallowed. Help him undress? "I don't think so, but thank you for offering."

She sounded like a twit.

He began unbuttoning his waistcoat and her temperature rose with each button he slipped through its hole. Soon the garment lay open and he shrugged it off along with his coat, leaving him clad only in his breeches and shirt. She could see the dark hair of his chest through the fine silk, and his skin tantalized her where the opening had been revealed by the removal of his neckcloth. She wanted to touch that skin. Taste it. But for some reason she could not seem to move.

She still feared the reality of culmination. He had touched her before. She knew the pleasure she could find in his arms, but today she knew it would not stop at mere touching. He would join her body with his, and the memory of her mother's words kept her on the other side of the room from the man who tempted her beyond bearing.

He began unbuttoning his shirt and she held her breath, waiting for a glimpse of the muscular contours of his chest. She had never seen him like this, though she had touched him, had felt the hardened muscles beneath her fingertips. She had not known the mere sight of his male torso would enthrall her so completely.

"You are beautiful," she said as the last button came undone and the shirt separated to reveal his body to her heated gaze.

He smiled. "I think not, little one."

She shook her head. He did not understand and she could not explain it, but he had a male beauty she had never expected. Perhaps she should have said *handsome,* but the word did not convey the richness of Lucas's attraction to her.

He put his hand out. "Come here."

She could not move.

"Are you afraid?" he asked, his voice filled with unmistakable desire, but laced with concern.

Was it not obvious? She'd retreated like the besieged before a marauder.

"I think a little." But even as she said the words, she began moving toward the siren's call of his body.

When she was two feet away, she stopped. "I'm here."

He did not make fun of her whispered statement of the obvious. "I'm glad."

He reached out and pulled her the rest of the way to him. She pressed her hands against his chest and immediately regretted the barrier of her gloves. She wanted to feel him. She remembered the sensation of touching the short, curling hair that covered his chest and the male nipples that felt like small pebbles on his heated skin that wonderful night in his carriage.

She wanted to know that pleasure again. Using her teeth, she drew off first one glove and then the other. He smiled his approval, but the expression held no humor. Then she used her bare hands to push Lucas's shirt over his shoulders and off his body, reveling in the texture of his skin under hers. She brought her fingers back to his chest in order to rub small circles around his hardened nubs.

He groaned and the hand that undid the tapes on her gown trembled where it brushed against her back. "Little one, you don't know what you are doing to me."

He was right. She didn't. She had no experience in this area other than what she had shared with him, but she could imagine. If he shared the feelings of pleasure and lightheaded joy coursing through her body, then she had a very good idea what her touch was doing to him.

Remembering how she had felt when Lucas's mouth covered her breast, she leaned forward and flicked her tongue over his hardened male nipple. He jerked against her and the sound of rending fabric reached her ears at the same moment she felt the skin of her back exposed to his caress. Gently closing her teeth over the same nipple she had just tormented, she tugged.

Lucas gave a feral shout and pushed her away.

His hands tore at her gown and petticoats, removing the beautiful clothing from her body with passionate abandon. One moment she was fully clothed in the layers required for modest dress among the *ton* and the next Lucas had stripped her until all that remained were her garters tied to her stockings. Her garments lay around her feet in a puddle of torn silk and muslin while every private part of her body was exposed to his hot stare. She felt his eyes, deepened to the blue of the night sky, fix on the soft blond curls of her feminine mound before they rose to caress her breasts with a hungry glance.

Even as her nipples beaded under the look of untamed desire in his eyes, her earlier fears rushed back and she turned to run. Where she was going, she had no idea, but she could not stand that look of intense need on Lucas's face. Her gaze fell on the bed and the relative safety the coverlet could provide.

She dove for it and burrowed under the sheets and covers even as she sensed him right behind her. He landed on the bed a scant second after she did and fingers as strong as steel bands tunneled under the covers to lock around her wrist and hold her in place. Soon his body followed and she found herself panting for breath beneath his hardened, almost naked male form.

"Lucas. Please." Fear made her voice high and thin.

He smiled a buccaneer's smile. "I'll please you until you're screaming my name, Irisa. Trust me."

Those two words pounded in her head and kept her from hysterics. She did trust him. Completely.

"You're going too fast. It's . . . it's all so overwhelming," she admitted, her voice barely above a whisper and tears burning at the backs of her eyes.

His size, which usually comforted her, now made her feel weak and helpless.

Lucas leaned down and bestowed the gentlest kiss imaginable on her lips before giving similar homage to each eyelid and her temples. "I will never hurt you, little one."

"But you will. Mama said so."

"Your mother is hardly the person to go to for advice in these matters. She is, after all, married to your father."

He had a point, but, "Aunt Harriet and Thea said the same thing. The first time hurts, maybe even sometimes afterward."

"Bloody hell. There may be some pain, but I promise to minimize it all that I can. I will not allow you to suffer, little one. You must believe me. I want to pleasure you, not harm you."

She felt the need vibrating in his body, the hardness of his male member pressing against the juncture of her thighs through the barrier of his breeches and . . . she believed him. Her body relaxed slightly, but she still couldn't get enough air. He must have sensed her softening and her predicament because he rolled to the side, keeping their bodies in constant contact, but giving her the room she needed to draw a proper breath.

"Perhaps if you kissed me," she suggested.

He gave a short bark of laughter. "Yes, perhaps that would help." He released her wrist and lightly traced the line of her hip and waist, letting his hand come to rest to the side of her breast. "I have wanted you so long, sweetheart. It's all I can do not to ravish you."

She heard the chagrin in his voice and smiled. "It felt for a moment as if that was exactly what you were doing."

His black brows came together in a scowl. "I'm sorry, my love. I will try to go more slowly."

She reached up and smoothed the lines of his face. His admission and promise had quieted the last of her bridal fear.

"Don't go too slowly," she said softly.

He smiled and then dipped his head to take her lips with his. He tasted just as she had remembered, spicy and male. He moved his lips over hers with gentle urgency and she opened her mouth in a silent invitation to deepen the kiss. He did so and she slipped into a world of pleasure only Lucas could provide. He remained completely still against her as he kissed her with deepening passion.

She soon grew impatient and squirmed against him. She wanted to feel his hand on her breast and tried to tell him so without words by turning her body until his palm covered her. He took the hint and moved his hand in a circular motion against the hardened nub. It wasn't long before the relief she felt at his touch turned into need.

She broke her mouth away from his. "More. Please. I need more."

"What do you want, little one? Tell me."

Surely he knew what she wanted. He was the one with experience in this area, after all. She moved her head restlessly against the pillow, refusing to answer.

He chuckled and leaned up on his elbow so both palms now rested on her breasts, caressing her in leisurely circles. "Is that what you wanted?"

"Yes." It felt so good, but it still wasn't enough. "No."

Taking one nipple between his thumb and forefinger, he tugged and she arched off the bed. *"Lucas."*

"Ah, so that is what you want."

"Yes. Yes. Yes. Do that again. Please."

He did. Over and over again. He alternated pinching and pulling each nipple, then he stopped and instead of pulling, he rolled both nipples between his thumbs and forefingers at the same time. Heat and driving desire pooled low in her belly and she felt wetness between her legs, in her most private place. Once again tears burned her eyes, but they were not from fear. This feeling was indescribable. She needed more of him, but did not know what to ask for. She remembered the way she'd felt in the carriage and inspiration struck.

"Touch me. There. Between my legs." She thrashed her head on the pillow as she vaguely registered that her behavior was not at all ladylike, but she could not bring herself to care. She needed Lucas's touch and she needed it now.

He understood and obeyed with a husky sound of hunger. His big, blunt finger slipped into her most feminine place and glided over the swollen nubbin at the top, then he slid it inside her. She cried out at the intimate invasion, her entire body going rigid with shock and mounting desire. It felt so wonderful she wondered that she did not swoon from the pleasure of it.

"*Lucas.* Yes. Oh, please. Yes. That's so wonderful. Don't stop. Please, don't stop."

He didn't stop. His finger continued to work its magic until she was writhing against him. Then he slipped a second finger in and she protested. It hurt. But then his thumb caressed the swollen flesh above where his fingers penetrated and she forgot the discomfort. She forgot everything but the feelings spiraling through her.

Her body grew taut from the very tips of her toes to the top of her head. Her fingers curled rigidly into the bedsheet under her. She hung on that precipice for what felt like hours while she demanded satisfaction in a raw voice she only barely recognized as her own. Then she went over and screamed and screamed.

Lucas continued his ministrations while she bucked wildly trying to get closer to that tormenting hand while at the same time trying to escape it until her body finally went completely limp and his touch gentled to small sporadic caresses.

She lay still, staring at the ceiling in dazed wonder. How could she have been afraid of this feeling? Or have thought they should wait until night to experience it? Tears coursed down her cheeks and her hand released its grip on the sheet to come up and caress Lucas's shoulder.

She turned to meet his gaze and smiled through her tears. "Thank you."

His eyes were filled with pleasure in her response.

"Thank you, little one. You give yourself so completely, your pleasure robs me of my breath."

He leaned over and kissed her, his mouth betraying the need still lingering in his own body. "Are you finished with your fear?"

She nodded, her throat too choked to speak.

"Can I ravish you now?"

The mischievous light in his eyes could not disguise the seriousness of his question. Lucas wanted to know if she trusted him.

Again she bobbed her head up and down, but this time she managed to add words to the gesture. "I can't imagine anything I would enjoy more."

And after what she had just experienced at his hand, she meant it.

Seventeen

LUCAS ROLLED OUT FROM UNDER THE COVERlet and stood up. His body ached for fulfillment and yet he felt strangely satisfied in the pleasure he had given his wife. Perhaps even a bit smug. And who could blame him?

She lay like a satisfied feline sunning itself, her body boneless against the feather mattress of his bed. Her eyes were heavy lidded from spent passion, an expression he much preferred to her virginal fear.

He had not expected the latter, but he should have been prepared for the result of feminine myths. Unfortunately, too many ladies did experience very real pain on their wedding night, but he was determined that Irisa would remember hers with pleasure and delight.

He winced when he thought of the torn garments lying on the floor.

Her stunning wedding dress had not stood a chance against his need to see her beautiful body. That need had not diminished one whit since she dove headfirst under the bedclothes. Even in her currently relaxed state, she had the coverlet pulled up far enough to conceal even the uppermost curve of her breasts.

Damn but he wanted more than a brief glimpse of her

feminine attributes. He wanted to see the honey-kissed blond curls that covered her sex, and the way her nipples ripened like berries when he looked at her with the cravings of his body in his eyes.

"I'm going to remove my breeches now." He waited to see if she reacted to the news with a return of her fear, but she did not.

Her eyes opened wider, but with interest.

He took his time unbuttoning his breeches and pulling them along with his smalls from his body. He did not go slow merely for the sake of his new wife's sensibilities. He was so hard that one wrong movement could cause untold damage. Her gaze skittered from the flesh he revealed to his chest and up to his face and then back to his rock-hard erection. Her eyes remained focused on his lower body as he finished pulling off his breeches and kicked them away. He smiled to himself. She looked worried again, but he had expected it this time.

"Do not be concerned, little one. We will fit."

Her gaze snapped to his. "Are you certain, Lucas? It does not seem possible."

The hesitancy in her normally confident tones brought another smile to his lips. "I am certain. Trust me." Then remembering her concerns at Ashton Manor, he could not help teasing her a little. "Can we both agree that I'm not angry right now?"

She looked confused. "Yes." The word came out breathless.

He indicated his bulging shaft. "This is what *you* make me feel. I'm not angry and I want you so much it is all I can do not to take you this very moment."

But he would have her soon. Very soon.

Her eyes widened in comprehension. "You allayed my fears on that score in the carriage the other night." She bit her lower lip and then licked it with the tip of her little pink tongue. His manhood bobbed in response to the sight and her eyes grew round as a lady's open parasol. "It moved."

He couldn't help it. He laughed.

She scowled at him. "Are you amusing yourself at my expense?" she asked suspiciously.

He did not attempt to lie. "Yes, but don't be angry with me, sweeting. The charm of your innocence is very heady stuff."

As proof of his statement, his erection moved again.

"Oh."

He stepped closer to the bed, until his legs brushed the coverlet and his manhood stood out over the mattress. "You said I could ravish you."

She squinted at his sex. "I know, but I think we need to discuss this matter, Lucas."

He was well past the point of talking. If he had not found her reaction to his nakedness so amusing, he would already be on top of her, his hardness nestled between her spread legs.

"Not right now, little one. Perhaps later."

"But later will be too la—" Her words trailed off into a screech as he tugged the bedcovers away from her naked breasts.

She scrambled for a grip on the blankets and stopped them from moving any lower with just the tops of the pretty pink circles around her nipples exposed.

He bit back a frustrated groan. "I want to see you."

Her knuckles were white where they gripped the coverlet. He did not think he would survive another attack of virginal nerves.

"You've seen me," he reminded her.

She cleared her throat even as her gaze once again strayed to his manhood. "Yes."

"And you enjoy it."

She nodded, forcing her gaze to meet his. Her cheeks had a delightful crimson stain.

"Would you deny me the same pleasure?"

"No. Oh, Lucas, I want to give you the same pleasure you so generously give me, but I don't know how." Her earnest statement came bloody close to undermining the remnants of his self-control.

"Let me remove the bedclothes and I'll show you."

He could see her mentally preparing herself and then she released her deathgrip on the coverlet one finger at a time.

He waited until she had completely released it and then asked in guttural tones, "Are you sure?"

He did not know what he would do if she said no.

"Yes." It was a bare whisper of a sound, but he did not doubt she knew her own mind.

Heat coursed through his body as he gently, but inexorably, tugged the bedclothes away from her almost naked body. The air left his lungs at the sight of the female perfection lying in his bed. Bloody hell, she was beautiful. Her pale skin had a faintly pink hue, probably a blush from her embarrassment at being bare before him. Her nipples stood erect on perfect, rounded breasts. The indentation of her waist invited his hands to reach out and surround her, but by far the most fascinating object to him at that particular moment were the wet and glistening curls protecting her femininity.

He wanted her.

He needed to feel his sex buried inside her, surrounded by her liquid heat as his fingers had been. He could not wait to feel those slick folds of flesh tighten around him as she screamed her pleasure.

He reached out and trailed one finger from her collarbone on a path down over one breast, circling her nipple, then down her stomach, pausing over the indention of her belly button, then down into the little nest of curls. She moaned and he knew that though he had satisfied her, she was not sated. His incredibly responsive wife was ready for more pleasure.

He gently circled her clitoris. "I need you."

She gasped. "Yes."

Her garters had come untied and he took a moment to remove the last bits of clothing from her body. Then he climbed onto the bed and pushed her legs apart. He wanted to look at her, to study her feminine center, but he knew she was not yet ready for that intimacy. Perhaps later tonight. He contented himself with a glance at dew-kissed lips he desperately wanted to kiss and then settled himself between her thighs, allowing the broad head of his penis to push against her opening.

Her startled gaze flew to his. "Are you quite sure—"

"Yes." Impatience warred with regret that he would hurt her and a desire to minimize that pain. "I have done my best to prepare you, but it will hurt now, my love."

Her eyes remained locked on his. "I trust you."

If she knew how close he was to losing his hard-won control, she might not say the words with such conviction. He would be worthy of that trust, however. He moved to a kneeling position between her legs. He reached between them and caressed her with his thumb while he used his other hand to play with her nipples. She reached out and gripped his thighs, her small hands surprising in their strength. Within moments she was writhing on the bed and he felt as if he would shoot his seed into the air. He had to have her. Now.

He slid two fingers in her as before and mimicked the mating act while separating his fingers to stretch her tight passage. She groaned, whether from pleasure or pain he could not tell, but she did not ask him to stop. Then she started undulating against his hand. He pulled his fingers out and she made a protesting sound.

"Shh, sweeting, I'm not going anywhere."

He replaced them with his shaft and pushed inside until he felt her body's resistance. She whimpered and tried to sink farther into the bed. He withdrew and then repeated the forging in and withdrawal sequence over and over again while continuing his ministrations with his thumb. She stopped trying to move away from him and even lifted her hips toward his thrusting penis. He was careful to stop shy of her barrier with each inward thrust until he felt the first ripple of her climax.

"Lucas."

At the sound of his name on her lips, shouted in such

wild abandon, he surged into her past her maidenhead until his manhood was buried to the hilt in her silken softness. She cried out again, but moved against him as if seeking the fullness of her pleasure and he gladly gave it to her, pushing into her body with hard, fast strokes. He found his own completion and, with a loud groan, pumped his seed inside her in an act of possession unequaled by any other intimacy.

He collapsed on top of her and it was several seconds before he could raise his head far enough to check Irisa's well-being. When he did, he found her golden brown eyes awash in tears. He'd hurt her. Despite her response to him, he'd caused her pain.

"Irisa?"

She blinked and the crystalline droplets in her eyes spilled over, washing down her temples. "It was wonderful, Lucas. You are wonderful. I had no notion our coupling would be so profound. *Thank you.*"

He didn't know how to respond to her words. It *had* been profound. "I hurt you."

She shyly looked away from him. "Yes. A little. Not as much as I expected."

"I'm sorry."

She shook her head, turning her gaze back to his. "How can you apologize after giving me so much pleasure?"

He *had* given her pleasure. Her convulsing body and shouting had told him that, but he knew it paled in comparison to the satisfaction he felt at joining his body with hers.

"I love you, my darling, perfect wife." He lifted himself and gently withdrew from her body.

He reached down and pulled the bedclothes up to cover them and settled next to her.

She snuggled into his side. "I love you, too, Lucas, and I vow, I will be perfect for you."

"You already are."

She did not respond as she slid almost immediately into deep sleep, her body pressed securely against his own.

* * *

IRISA AWOKE TO DIM SHADOWS AT THE SOUND OF A light tapping on Lucas's bedchamber door. She reached out to touch him, but her hand encountered an empty bed. Then she heard his voice speaking in low tones and the indistinct replies of one of the upstairs maids.

As she came more fully awake, she realized he had closed the bed curtains and she was cocooned in darkness and privacy. Grateful for his consideration, she sat up, tugging the sheet with her, though no one shared the bed to see her nakedness. She winced at the tenderness between her legs when she moved.

It brought back a rush of memories of what had occurred in this very bed before she fell into an exhausted sleep. Lucas had made love to her with as much ardor as she could ever have hoped for. At times, his excitement had actually overwhelmed her. She blushed at the memory of her mad dash beneath the covers. She could not imagine what she had looked like running, naked but for her garters and stockings, across his bedchamber.

He had not laughed, though. He had followed her and soothed her and pleasured her until she felt as if she would die from it. Then he had pleasured her some more. She could not believe that all husbands took such care with their wives.

Lucas must truly love her, at least a little bit. No man would show that level of patience when his passions were aroused to such a pitch otherwise. Even if his love was inspired by a false impression of her perfection, it was worth every effort to keep it.

He was worth every effort and his lovemaking was something altogether amazing, but her reaction may have been more passionate than proper.

She let go of the sheet to cover her hot cheeks with her palms as she remembered how out of control she had been.

She had screamed.

More than once.

Had the servants heard? She knew Lucas had. She did not know if she could face him after her wild abandon. Did perfect wives respond to their husband's caresses in such a wanton fashion?

The curtains to her left opened, allowing light from the bedchamber to spill into the dusky shadows surrounding her. She blinked her eyes, trying to adjust to the light, and gathered the sheet closer to her body.

"I've had a bath brought up for you. You have time to wash before dinner and don that nightgown you were so intent on wearing earlier."

"Thank you."

Now that her eyes had grown accustomed to the light, she could see that Lucas was dressed. Sort of. He had a shirt and breeches on, but his feet and neck were bare. He held the curtain aside. Did he expect her to parade naked in front of him to reach her bath?

"Could I please have a nightrobe?"

Lucas chuckled as if her question amused him, but he dropped the curtain. He returned moments later with a black silk dressing gown. His. "Will this do?"

"Yes. Thank you." She reached for it and waited until he had once again left her in shadowed privacy before she put it on.

The sleeves fell past her hands and she rolled the cuffs before belting the robe and slipping out of the bed.

Lucas waited for her by the table against the far wall, his expression unreadable. "I suppose this means you will not allow me to play lady's maid and help you bathe?"

Was he funning her or was he disappointed? She decided that he had been teasing when she noticed the privacy screens near the fireplace. Her bath was undoubtedly on the other side. "I believe I can see to my own bath, sir."

He sighed, feigning regret. "I suppose you can."

She ignored him and walked toward the screen, wanting to get away from his too knowing eyes. Although his robe could wrap around her twice, she felt more revealed in it than she would have in her own.

"You're sore."

She stopped and nodded. "A little."

"I want you to soak until the water starts to cool."

"Will it help?"

He nodded and sat down, his attention immediately going to the papers spread on the table in front of him. She wanted to ask what they were, but craved the hot bath more than she did satisfaction to her curiosity.

For once, Lucas found it impossible to lose himself in plans for a new model. The intricate work required to build a ship inside a bottle usually served to settle his thoughts regardless of the cause of his disquiet. Then again, that cause had never before been the tantalizing, naked body of his wife on the other side of a privacy screen in his own bedchamber.

After the initial splashes indicating Irisa had stepped into the tub, he had not heard another sound for the last fifteen minutes or more. It would seem she had taken seriously his demand to soak. From the way she'd been moving, she needed it.

As much as he hated the thought, she would be better off sleeping in her own bed tonight. He did not think he could keep his hands off her if she shared his, and she deserved a chance to heal before he took her again. They would share an intimate dinner and then he would see her to her room.

Having made the self-sacrificing resolution, he still could not banish the image of her water-immersed flesh not ten feet away. He wanted to step behind the screen and do exactly what he had offered earlier . . . play her maid. He would wash her back—and the rest of her body as well. And when his hand dipped under the water to clean the folds of skin behind her feminine curls, she would make the noises that had driven him almost past reason before.

His flesh ached, and he swore. He was doing himself no favors allowing his mind to take this particular flight of fancy. He hoped dinner arrived soon and provided a distraction or he would not be able to follow through on his honorable intentions to leave his wife alone.

As if conjured by his thoughts, a discreet knock sounded on the door. He called permission to enter while gathering up his papers and putting them safely away. Pansy accompanied Jenny, one of the upstairs maids, when she brought the food into the room.

Pansy curtsied. She held a brush and ribbon in one hand and a nightrail draped over her other arm. "I thought I would ready milady for bed."

Lucas nodded his permission and Pansy went behind the privacy screen. The renewed sounds of splashing told him Irisa was finally finishing her bath.

She came around the privacy screen dressed in her nightrail and his dressing gown some minutes later. Her hair, which had been in wild disarray before, had been brushed and pulled back into one long, golden braid. She dismissed her maid and Jenny, who had finished laying out their food. He stood to help her into the chair opposite his own.

"Dinner looks lovely." She had not met his gaze since reappearing from her bath and now spoke to the plate in front of her.

"Irisa."

"Yes?"

"Look at me."

She raised her head, her expression wary.

He thought he understood the reason for her wariness. She was worried he would expect her to make love again and she was too sore to accommodate him. With the unexpected streak of shyness she had shown earlier, she was too embarrassed to bring the subject up.

He smiled reassuringly at her. "You still look tired. Once we have eaten, you can retire to your bedchamber for the evening."

Her expression went blank and she nodded. "If that is what you wish, Lucas."

IRISA COULD NOT SLEEP. FOR ONE THING, SHE WAS NOT tired. Lucas had spoken that faradiddle about her looking fatigued without blinking an eyelash. She had not argued because she knew why he had made the comment. He had not wanted her to sleep with him and pretending concern for her welfare had been his way of saving her the embarrassment of him asking her to leave the chamber.

Worry over why he had wanted her to leave the bedchamber would have kept her awake even if she *had* been exhausted.

She curled her feet under her on the cushion of the window seat and drew Lucas's dressing gown more tightly around her. She could smell him on the black silk and it comforted her, but it could not replace the warmth of his arms. Which was exactly where she wanted to be. She scowled at the pretty pink damask coverlet turned back invitingly on her bed.

She didn't want to sleep there. She never wanted to sleep in her own bed again. She wanted to sleep with her husband. It wasn't *proper*; she knew that. Ladies had their own chambers for modesty's sake.

If Lucas wanted her to be modest, then he should not have insisted on looking at her naked person in the afternoon light. How could he expect her to maintain strict decorum after that? He'd seen all there was to see. Not that she would march unclothed through their bedchamber, but surely he could not expect her to return to a cold and lonely bed after what they had experienced together in his.

Only that seemed to be exactly what he did expect. The evidence to support such a conclusion was irrefutable. Here she was, in her bedchamber. Alone.

She could only think of one reason for that—her behavior during their lovemaking had been too unladylike, too wanton and unrestrained, and she had failed her first test as his wife.

She wanted so much to be the kind of countess he desired, but he needn't make it so difficult for her. If he had not wanted her to behave wantonly, then he should not have touched her with such intimate pleasure. Didn't he know what a siren's call his body sent out? He probably did know and had expected her not to succumb. But if that were true, it was hardly fair. He should not tempt her beyond reason and then be disappointed when she could not live up to his expectations for the *perfect* wife.

Why, that was even worse than her parents. At least they had always consistently wanted the same thing . . . ladylike and biddable behavior. Lucas acted one minute as if he wanted her womanly responses, and then once she gave them to him, he rejected her.

She jumped off the window seat, her agitation too overwhelming to remain still, and glared at the door that connected their rooms. He was probably sleeping soundly, not caring at all that she was tormented with doubts, and worries that a lady should not be plagued with on her wedding night.

The cad.

Before she realized what she was doing, she'd crossed her bedchamber and thrown open the door to Lucas's. He wasn't asleep. For some reason that was even worse than if he had been. He sat at the table they had eaten at with some large pieces of parchment spread out in front of him.

He looked up when she entered. "Are you all right, my dear?"

He'd called her *my dear,* just like some old maiden aunt, and his attention was clearly still on the papers in front of him, though he pretended to look at her. The nerve of the man!

"I won't tolerate this sort of behavior. I really won't, Lucas. I'm willing to do everything I can to be the sort of countess you require, but I will not be tormented in such a fashion and you might as well know that right now."

He stared at her as if she had just spoken in Latin.

She glowered at him. "You needn't pretend you don't understand. Everyone believes you to be such a saint, but I know differently. You're a . . . a . . ." She couldn't think of what to call him and then it came to her. "You're a tease! Yes, you are. Leading me to behave in a perfectly wanton manner and then rejecting me for succumbing to your charms."

He stood up, concern and confusion evident in his features. "Irisa, what the hell are you talking about?"

She felt the tears that had refused to fall earlier prick her eyes and knew if she didn't get out of there, he would be witness to her humiliation. "I've said all that I meant to say. I will endeavor to remain more ladylike in future, but you must do your part and refrain from tempting me so thoroughly."

His mouth opened, but nothing came out.

"Good night, my lord." She spun on her bare heel and rushed back into her chamber, slamming the door behind her.

Eighteen

LUCAS STARED IN STUPEFACTION AT THE DOOR Irisa had just slammed. What in the bloody hell had she been talking about? One thing was certain. His bride was upset and it had something to do with their making love. What had she said? She thought he had rejected her. *She'd called him a tease.*

What kind of irrational nonsense did she have going through her head now? The only way to find out was to ask her. He felt no better equipped to deal with her current unpredictable mood than he had in handling her virginal nerves. He must have done a poor job with the latter or she would not be in such an unholy snit.

There had been tears in her eyes when she slammed out of his bedchamber. The thought of comforting his wife in a tearful state sent chills down his spine. He'd prefer to face Boney's entire army.

He went to the door and opened it. She was a small black lump in the middle of her bed. She hadn't bothered to get under the covers, but lay on top curled in a shaking little ball. Damn. She was definitely crying.

"Sweeting."

"Go away, Lucas," she replied, the words muffled against the coverlet.

"I can't, little one. Something has upset you and I want to know what it is. Was I too rough with you this afternoon?"

Her answer to that was to let out one loud, long sob.

He couldn't stand it. Crossing the room in a few quick strides, he sat down on the bed next to her and tugged on her shoulder. "Tell me what has upset you."

She erupted from the covers and threw herself against his chest. He held her while she cried, wondering what the hell had sent her into such a state. She had called their lovemaking wonderful. He could not believe she now regretted it. He rubbed her back in what he hoped was a soothing motion.

After what seemed an interminable amount of time, her tears finally abated.

"Are you ready to talk about it now?"

She shook her head against the now wet silk of his shirt. "I've said all I want to say on the subject, my lord."

He gritted his teeth. Irisa only called him *my lord* when she was distressed with him. At least now he could be sure it was something *he* had done. "Unfortunately for my peace of mind, I didn't understand much of what you said. Perhaps you would do me the great favor of repeating yourself."

She pulled away from him and gave him the same glowering stare she had when delivering her incomprehensible lecture in his chamber, although now through tear-washed brown eyes. "You needn't mock me, my lord. I'm well aware I failed to live up to your expectations this afternoon. However, I only think it fair to point out that it was your own fault. You have more experience in this area than I do, and if you wanted me to behave with more decorum, you should have refrained from touching me in such a pleasureful manner."

"You think I was disappointed?" If he had been any happier with his wife's response, he would have died on the spot.

"You've made your feelings quite clear on the matter." Two more tears spilled down her cheeks and seared his gut.

He reached out, meaning to catch them with his thumbs, but she turned her head aside.

Thwarted in his desire to comfort, he asked, "How did I make such feelings known?"

He could only remember telling her how much he enjoyed her. Perhaps he had said something over dinner that she had taken the wrong way.

She sniffed and rubbed her eyes and cheeks dry with the cuffs of his dressing gown. "Please don't play the simpleton with me, my lord. I'm not up to dealing with it right now."

"I fear it is the role I am destined to perform this evening because I don't understand how I gave you the impression I was disappointed when, in fact, I found our time together intensely satisfying."

"You sent me back to my own room to sleep in a cold, lonely bed." She sounded as if she were accusing him of treason.

He stared at her, not comprehending this fit and start at all. "It is customary for wives and husbands to keep separate chambers, and I didn't send you anywhere. I merely suggested you retire after dinner due to your weariness."

She glared at him. "I wasn't tired."

He had known that. Just as he had known that if she stayed in his room, he would bury himself in her soft body again. "Are you saying you want to sleep with me?"

If that was what had caused her tears, he would force his male desires under control and sleep chastely beside her. He would not have her cry again.

She turned her head away and shrugged.

He tightened his grip on her arms. "Answer me."

"Yes." She turned her head back to glare at him once again. "I want to sleep with you every night, but if that is not ladylike enough for you, then I will sleep in my own chamber."

In her *cold, lonely* bed, no doubt. "Why would you believe I would think it unladylike for you to want to sleep with me?"

She twisted the tie of his dressing gown in her fingers.

"It is accepted for a husband and wife to sleep apart among the *ton.* I know it is probably horribly improper of me, but I don't want to. Thea and Drake share a bedchamber. She keeps her clothes in the connecting room for propriety's sake, but they sleep in the same bed. I suppose Drake doesn't mind because she was raised in the West Indies. Aunt Harriet is always making excuses when Thea does something original by saying it is due to her being brought up in the wilds of the British Empire. Thea says that's nonsense. That some things are just silly the way the *ton* does them and she won't follow suit."

Irisa stopped speaking long enough to take a breath and he kissed her to prevent any more rambling on her sister's habits. For the first time that he could recall, Irisa did not respond to his lips against hers. She held herself stiff in his arms, and after a few seconds of him moving his mouth over hers, she actually sucked her lips into her mouth.

He pulled his head back. "What's wrong? Don't tell me you've stopped liking my kisses."

She released her lips and it was obvious she'd bitten them to keep from responding. "I don't want to give you a disgust of me."

"Is that what you believe you have done?" How could she be so ignorant of the pleasure he had found in her, of how much he wanted her now?

"You didn't want me to sleep with you tonight." She said it as if that fact explained everything.

"You were sore," he reminded her.

She blushed, but nodded.

"I wanted you again, and I knew that if you slept with me, I would take you. I didn't want to hurt you."

It was as if the sun rose in her eyes. She beamed at him. "I truly didn't disappoint you?"

"How could you doubt that I enjoyed our time together?" She had been there. She had felt him come inside her, had witnessed his loss of control.

"I got worried. I thought maybe I had failed my first test as your wife."

He stared at her. "There aren't any tests you have to pass, little one."

She ignored that. "Does this mean I get to sleep with you?"

"Yes."

Sleeping with his new wife and not touching her had been every bit as difficult as Lucas had imagined, particularly when she rubbed her soft little bottom against him in her sleep. He woke with a raging erection and contemplated how best to disentangle himself from her womanly curves without waking his wife or further aggravating his desire to claim her.

He carefully lifted the small hand resting on his chest and started to slide his body away from her, slowly extricating his shoulder from under her head and his legs from hers. She made a sound of sleepy protest and wrapped her calf over his thigh, her knee coming precariously close to doing damage. He stifled a groan.

Then that little leg moved in a tantalizing caress, brushing his manhood in a very dangerous but pleasant way. "Good morning, Lucas."

He turned his head and met her sleep-softened gaze. "Good morning, little one."

He still held her hand in his and she brushed her thumb against his palm. He felt the sensual jolt all the way to his manhood.

So did she if the sweet smile of satisfaction on her face meant anything. "You moved again."

He laughed although the sound ended on a strangled moan when she brushed her knee against his hard flesh a second time. "You've got to stop that."

He didn't really want her to. He wanted more than anything to finish what she had started.

"Why must I stop? Is it wrong for me to touch you?" She sounded genuinely worried.

"No. It is just dangerous right now."

"Really?" She pulled her hand from his in a wholly unexpected move and soon he felt hot little fingers curled around him.

He arched into her hand without conscious thought.

"Oh. Do you like that, Lucas?"

"Very much," he said through gritted teeth. "Caress it, little one. Please."

The words were out before he could stop them, though they would only increase his torment.

She lightly brushed his shaft down to the hilt and up to the head again. "Like this?"

"Yes. Just. Like. That."

Suddenly he could take no more and he pulled her hand away. Coming up on his elbow, he loomed over her. "Are you sore?"

She blinked up at him, her little owl eyes going wide.

"Answer me." He needed to know *now.*

If she was still too sore for making love, he hoped he had enough self-control to leave the bed. He was not entirely sure he did.

She blushed, but her smile was as old as Eve. "I want you to love me."

The words broke through the last of his resistance and he took her mouth in a hungry kiss, demanding admittance for his tongue and receiving it without protest. Unlike the afternoon before, Irisa had no fear and was not content to let him set the pace. When he attempted to be gentle and go slowly, she wouldn't have it. She tore off her nightrail and threw it from the bed in a move that left him panting.

She wanted to touch him all over and she did, to devastating effect. If she had not been so responsive, she would not have found her satisfaction because his came so quickly. However, she peaked even as he was shooting into her and her screams were like the loveliest of sonatas to his ears.

They spent the rest of the morning exploring their passion, and Lucas made sure that this time Irisa had no doubts about the delight he found in her uninhibited responses.

When a maid came to ask if they wanted lunch served in his chamber like dinner the night before, Lucas left the warmth of Irisa's body reluctantly. It could not be helped. He had several matters to attend to, some of which involved seeing to her protection.

As he'd promised Jared, Lucas had devised a strategy for investigating the peers on Irisa's list. He would begin by visiting his club and encouraging something he usually abhorred . . . gossip. That would attract less notice than visits to each gentleman would do, but even club gossip would help little in identifying whether or not Cecily Carlisle might be involved.

Servants' gossip could be both the bane of an investigation and a blessing. He was hoping that in this case it would be the latter. However, he first had to determine which of his servants could be trusted with the job. That would require consultation with his valet, a man who had been in Lucas's employ since his days as a spy for the Crown.

He would discover something today, he vowed silently. His lovely new wife had lived under the shadow of this threat for far too long already.

LUCAS WENT DIRECTLY TO WHITE'S. THE GENTLEMEN'S club betting book would be an excellent place to determine if the blackmailer had made good his threat to reveal the Langleys' secret. He experienced a certain grim satisfaction when he saw Owlpen, one of the *ton*'s most accomplished gossips, seated near the fireplace in the main room. If the betting book showed no evidence of rumors related to his wife, but such rumors existed, Owlpen would know about them.

And Lucas knew how to extract such knowledge.

Perusing the book elicited no signs that the Langleys' secret had become known, but there were a few entries of interest.

Lord R bets Lord Y £3 that The Saint will announce his engagement to Lady I before the end of the Season. Dated a week before Lucas had proposed to Irisa. Evidently his careful courtship had still led to a certain amount of speculation.

Lord O bets His Grace, Duke of C, £5 that the wedding date between The Saint and Lady I will be set at least six months into the future. Dated two days after the formal announcement had come out in the London papers.

Lord Y bets Lord G £10 that The Saint will call off his wedding to a certain notorious lady seen driving in the park with a former actress and His Grace, Duke of C, bets Lord K that Lord L will disown Lady I before the end of the Season. Both dated the afternoon of Irisa's infamous drive in the park.

F, Esq., bets Lord Y £2 that Lady I will cry off from her engagement to The Saint now that she's met C de B. Dated the day after Irisa had taken Clarice for a drive.

The bets in themselves were nothing extraordinary. Gentlemen among the *ton* bet on anything and everything, from the expected color a Diamond of the First Water might wear to a particular ball to how soon a gentleman would be expected to come up to scratch once his courtship of a certain lady became known. No, the topics of the bets did not surprise Lucas at all.

Nor was he particularly surprised that His Grace, the Duke of Clareshire, had participated in two of the bets. His dislike of Irisa was well known. However, the fact Yardley had been discussing her on at least three occasions in the past three months, and that those discussions had led to bets being made, was very interesting.

Yardley was one of the suitors Irisa had refused—perhaps her rejection had rankled more than she'd realized.

"Anything interesting going on?" asked a familiar voice from behind Lucas's left shoulder.

Lucas turned to find both Ravenswood and Drake waiting for an answer to the question. He didn't say anything out loud, but pointed to the different entries. His brothers-in-law came forward and leaned over the betting book to read what he indicated.

Ravenswood swore under his breath. "Who the hell is this Lord Y? I'll teach him to make bets about my sister."

Lucas almost laughed. Ravenswood's lack of Town polish didn't offend him at all. He wouldn't mind pounding Yardley into the dirt himself, but it would have to wait. He wanted the other men's opinion of the pattern he'd spotted.

Drake frowned. "Let's find someplace to discuss this."

So he had noticed the relationship between the bets as well.

Drake turned as if to go, but Lucas stopped him. "In a moment. I want to chat with Owlpen."

Ravenswood scowled. "Why the hell do you want to talk to that old gossip?"

"Because he'll know if there are rumors about your parents' marriage circulating among the *ton*."

"He's an old campaigner. He might even know the source," Drake added.

Ravenswood nodded. "Then let's talk to him."

At first, Lucas didn't think the discussion with Owlpen would elicit anything more than confirmation that Yardley seemed inordinately interested in Irisa's activities.

But then the older man rubbed the side of his nose and looked piercingly at Lucas. "Most gentlemen wouldn't have left their house so soon after the wedding, Lord Ashton. Your being here leads to a certain amount of speculation."

Lucas concealed the irritation that remark caused and affected nonchalant amusement. "What speculation might that be?"

"It's no secret that your lady behaves rather scandalously for the wife of The Saint."

Lucas could not let that slide. "My wife's behavior is above reproach."

He kept his voice firm but amiable. He wanted to keep Owlpen talking.

The older man snorted. "Perhaps for a woman of her birth."

Lucas felt the familiar thrill of imminent discovery he had often experienced when conducting intelligence investigations. "She's the daughter of an earl. Her birth is in perfect accord with her exemplary behavior."

Owlpen nodded his head with quick agreement, but his expression remained shrewd. "Yes. Yes. The daughter of an earl, but perhaps she has more *natural* aspects to her character than one might at first suspect."

Lucas could sense Ravenswood's mounting fury as the meaning of the other man's words became clear. Owlpen had very cleverly played on the word *natural* often used to describe the illegitimate offspring of a member of the *ton*. He had couched his comments in such a way that Lucas would be hard pressed to issue a challenge without first acknowledging the slight against his wife's honor. Lucas shot Ravenswood a look meant to warn the other man to retain his composure. Ravenswood acknowledged it with the barest inclination of his head.

Lucas turned back to Owlpen. "My wife's character appears to be of considerable interest to you, and perhaps to other members of the *ton*. Would it be too much trouble for me to inquire who they might be?"

The older man shifted nervously in his chair and hastily set down the cup of tea he had been lifting to his lips for a drink. "I do not wish to cause a lady grief by bringing her name to your attention, particularly when she was merely passing on comments raised by others."

"I assure you that although I find the passing on of gossip abhorrent, in this instance it is the originator of such speculation who interests me." Lucas almost smiled when Ravenswood crowded his chair closer to Owlpen and nodded in agreement.

Owlpen swallowed nervously. "Perhaps my wife could assist in naming such a person."

Lucas nodded. "I would appreciate that very much. In fact, such help would mitigate the implied criticism of my wife and negate the need for a dawn appointment, if you take my meaning."

Owlpen's head was now bobbing like an apple in a barrel on All Saints' Eve. "I'll go right home and ask her."

"Send word to my town house as soon as you hear."

For the first time, Lucas entertained the notion that the blackmailer might be a woman. He should have considered the possibility all along. Hadn't he seen firsthand how women could easily match men for deviousness during the war with Boney?

Before he would let Owlpen leave, Lucas added, "Perhaps you would be so good as to remind those who wish to participate in unwarranted speculation about my wife how I responded to such actions regarding my mother."

Owlpen's eyes had gone round and he agreed readily before dashing from the club, not at all filling the role of the dignified purveyor of tittle-tattle he usually played.

Drake smiled. "That was well done, Ashton."

Ravenswood asked, "How did you respond to gossip about your mother?"

"I issued challenges and kept dawn appointments." He had put bullets in three men's shoulders before the *ton* had figured out that The Saint did not tolerate scandal associated with his family's name.

"You can be a bloody cold bastard when you want to be." Ravenswood's lips curved in an approving smile.

They agreed to meet at Lucas's town house that evening to discuss the entries in the betting book and any information Owlpen's wife had managed to provide.

A visit to Tattersall's was the next item on Lucas's agenda before returning home. He wanted to buy Irisa a wedding present. The visit turned out to be profitable in more ways than one. He found Irisa a pretty little curricle with matching bays to pull it. Not quite as liberal as Drake, Lucas had no intention of buying Irisa a high-perched phaeton like Thea's.

When the gentleman selling the first set of horses Lucas looked at made a comment to the effect that providing a high-spirited lady like his wife with her own conveyance might be the act of an overly indulgent bridegroom, Lucas had the opportunity to make his stand regarding his wife clear to another interested party. The man had made a hasty apology before any challenges could be issued.

All in all, it had been a very productive hour.

IRISA HAD EXHAUSTED THE AFTERNOON TOURING HER new home and becoming acquainted with her household. She now assisted Pansy in going through her garments looking for those that needed mending or updating according to the newest *Belle Assemblée,* the arbiter of fashion for ladies among the *ton.* She had already discussed the condition of the staff's livery with the butler, the housekeeper, and the cook. She had also let each of them know that she wished to meet the staff under their supervision individually over the coming days.

Lucas had left the house right after lunch, saying he intended to visit his club.

She made a discovery about him during the tour of the town house conducted by the housekeeper. He built ships in bottles. She had remarked on the beauty of one gracing the library mantle and the housekeeper had informed Irisa that Lucas had built it. According to the housekeeper, it took Lucas sometimes more than a year to complete one model.

Irisa wondered if he would be willing to do a replica of Drake's first ship as a gift for her brother-in-law. She could not wait to see the others the housekeeper had told her about, displayed in Lucas's study at Ashton Manor.

Because of the many things vying for her attention, it took her several hours to realize two important facts. The first was that Lucas had clearly given instructions to the staff regarding her safety. She had not been alone for a single moment since he left the town house. The other salient truth was that no one had come to call. Although one might expect the *ton* to leave a new bride and groom in privacy, the fact still worried her.

Had the blackmailer made good his threats?

She refused to let the prospect ruin her disposition. She

would not give up the sensation of happiness that had cloaked her since waking in Lucas's arms that morning. That had to be one of the greatest pleasures she had ever known.

Even if he had been trying to sneak out of bed.

His motives for doing so had become clear when he asked with obvious desperation in his voice if she was sore. She smiled at the memory. Lucas had lost control and she had loved it. He had also told her repeatedly that he enjoyed her wantonness. Recollection of his words and her own wild behavior which had precipitated them made her blush, but her heart was filled with contentment.

It seemed that in some areas her husband did not wish to be married to a proper lady at all.

And that filled her with hope. If Lucas did not expect perfection in all things, he would not be as difficult to please as her parents. His love would not be so impossible to maintain.

Her bubble of happiness burst when Jenny entered the room carrying a salver with three envelopes on it, two of them addressed to Irisa and one addressed to Lucas. The white envelope in the center had become all too familiar, and with unhappy certainty, she knew it was from the blackmailer. The other one addressed to her was in a lavender envelope, sealed with the Langley crest. The handwriting looked like Mama's.

Coward that she was, she could not decide which to open first. She did not think she would like the message in either one. Forcing her hand to pick up the two unwanted missives, she asked Jenny, "Was the white envelope delivered by a street urchin?"

Pansy was by her side in an instant. "Is it another of those nasty notes, milady?"

Irisa shook her head in a quick gesture to let Pansy know she did not want to discuss it in front of the upstairs maid.

Jenny said, "I don't know how it was delivered, Lady Ashton. The footman gave it to me with the others."

"Please instruct the footman to come to me in the library.

You can leave the message for his lordship on the small table in his chamber."

"Yes, milady." Jenny bobbed a curtsy and left.

"Come, Pansy. We must go to the library to query the footman—and in answer to your question: Yes, I do fear this is another of the blackmailer's notes."

"You don't want your new staff to know about the threats, milady?"

"I think it is best to discuss the matter with his lordship first. He may wish to keep it from the other servants."

Pansy didn't reply, but followed Irisa to the library.

Upon interrogation, the footman admitted that he didn't know how the envelope had been delivered. It had been in the usual spot for calling cards and correspondence when he came into the front hall with the other notes delivered by the Owlpen and Langley footmen.

Irisa thanked and dismissed him.

Deciding the anonymous blackmailer would be easier on her nerves than Mama's recriminations, she took a deep breath and opened the white envelope.

Nineteen

THE MISSIVE WAS MUCH SHORTER THAN THE first letter had been.

Lady Ashton,

You will not find much joy in the title, I can assure you. You have made a grave mistake in going through with your wedding to The Saint. Such an unforgiving man will not tolerate the stain your birth is bound to bring to his name. Neither of you deserves happiness and you will not find it together. That I can promise you.

Once again the note was unsigned.

Irisa dropped the note on the small table by where she sat and hugged herself, having gone suddenly cold. She could not begin to comprehend the message. Who hated her so much they would be willing to hurt Lucas to prevent her happiness? She had made no enemies that she knew of.

True, there were the few gentlemen over the past four years her papa had refused when they asked permission to pay their addresses. She could not see one of them so moved they would go to the lengths the blackmailer had in order to get revenge for the rejection.

After all, had their passions been so strongly aroused, she might have been willing to entertain their suits. Only the duke had been furious when she refused to marry him. His pride had been pricked and he'd barely been civil to Papa and Mama, but why wait four years to wreak some kind of vengeance?

Which was exactly what Irisa told Lucas when he came into the library ten minutes later. She had not yet read her mother's missive, her mind still occupied with the personal and threatening direction the blackmailer had taken with his messages.

"It makes no sense. Why would someone wish me such ill?"

He reached out and brushed her cheek with reassuring fingers. "You forget that the author of this note has implied that I do not deserve happiness either. In fact, he or she refers to me as unforgiving. That is a rather personal indictment of my character."

Lucas read the note before tossing it back on the table with disgust. "We must consider the possibility that the blackmailer's original complaint is with me. The vitriol expressed toward you could easily stem from your association with me."

She did not agree. "The opposite could just as easily be true. If the blackmailer is trying to harm you, why send me the notes? Why not focus his attention on you?"

"Because the blackguard realizes I am more vulnerable to your hurt than I am to my own." Lucas picked up the lavender envelope. "Who is this from?"

"Mama. I'm nervous about reading it, if you want the truth." Which sounded perfectly ridiculous when she thought about it. The other note had been from a *blackmailer* and she had wanted to read it first.

He smiled and handed her the envelope. "You may as well get it over with. Putting it off will only make it worse."

The prospect of reading Mama's words did not have

quite the fearsome aspect they had had a half hour before. She knew the difference could be attributed to Lucas's presence. It gave her strength. She tore open the envelope and read quickly, unable to stifle a gasp of dismay at the words.

"You will never believe it." She met Lucas's concerned gaze, feeling stricken. "Papa has decided to take Mama on an extended tour of the Continent."

Lucas's face relaxed and he shrugged. "Many members of the *ton* have done so since the war ended. I'm surprised your parents have waited so long to join their ranks."

"Yes, but they are doing it in order to avoid the gossip. Mama says she does not know when they will return to England. They are leaving for Dover the day after tomorrow. She says that if I wish to say good-bye, I must call this afternoon, as they will be too busy to receive me this evening or tomorrow. The afternoon is almost over, Lucas."

"Then I suppose we must make haste and leave immediately." Lucas's voice lacked enthusiasm for the project, but he did not try to dissuade her.

Slipping into his Wellington role, he issued instructions to the servants and led her outside to the waiting carriage twenty minutes later. As he handed her into the carriage, even in her agitated state, she realized she had never seen it before. In fact, the pretty yellow curricle did not have Lucas's crest on the door.

"Did you buy a new curricle, Lucas?"

He handed her the reins and waited for her to set the horses in motion before answering. "Yes. Do you like it?"

"It's lovely." The bottle green squabs contrasted beautifully with the bright exterior.

"It's yours."

Surely she had not heard him correctly. "Mine?"

"Yes. A wedding gift, if you like it."

She almost dropped the leads and had to force her attention to the road in front of her in order to avoid running into a slow-moving pony cart. "But, Lucas, I thought you did not want me to drive."

He had been very kind about Thea teaching her, but she

had assumed it would take a great deal of cajoling before her husband would even consider her owning her own carriage.

"You have an excellent hand with the ribbons, and once this mess with the blackmailer is cleared up, you will want the independence of your own conveyance."

She was staggered by his trust in her.

MUCH TO HER SURPRISE, PAPA AND MAMA WERE BOTH in the drawing room when she and Lucas were announced by the Langley butler. Papa looked over papers while Mama plied her needle, the scene so similar to the one four years ago when Irisa had come to them intent on her own form of blackmail that she stopped motionless in the doorway. Lucas's grip on her arm tightened briefly.

She took a deep breath. "Papa, Mama, I've come to wish you well on your trip."

Mama looked up from her needlework, accusation in her lovely brown eyes. "One can only hope it will not be a permanent exile."

Papa did not look up from his papers.

Lucas led Irisa to a small sofa and sat her on it before taking the spot beside her. For once his overt possessiveness did not embarrass her. His warmth reached out to surround her and she felt able to face this new ordeal with her parents with a certain amount of serenity. "I'm sure it will not be so bad. You are bound to enjoy the travel."

Mama shuddered. "It will be a perfect nightmare if we find ourselves barred from the company of our kind."

"Mama, you are refining too much on possibilities."

Her mother's eyes narrowed. "I would expect you to have more sympathy for my plight, but you always were an unnatural daughter."

Irisa tightened her hands into fists. "I have been the best daughter I knew how to be."

"It's difficult to believe you could have caused us more grief if you had tried." Papa's accusation so shocked her that for a moment she sat in numb silence.

Lucas was not similarly affected. "Irisa has been an exemplary daughter to you, Langley, and if you are too much the fool to appreciate her, then you can bloody well keep your opinions to yourself."

Papa's face set in grim lines and he inclined his head in acknowledgment of Lucas's words before turning his attention back to the papers in front of him.

Irisa could not stand it. She jumped up, both hands fisted at her sides. "Was what I did so very bad? I tried so hard to please you, but I could not marry His Grace four years ago any more than I could cry off my engagement to Lucas four days ago. Is wanting to be happy such an unnatural thing for me to do?"

Mama's only answer was to burst into noisy tears and Papa pretended as if she had not spoken at all. Irisa crossed the room in a few swift strides and swept the papers from the table. Papa looked at her then, his face filled with disgust, and something inside her cracked.

"Why did you stop loving me? There was a time when you touched me with affection, when you smiled at me and noticed me. Then one day it was as if I no longer existed for you. Is it because I was the cause for Jared's scar? Was it the fact that I reminded you of your own failings? Did you come to hate me because I was too *natural* a daughter?"

Mama's outraged gasp filled the room. Irisa stopped speaking, her throat too clogged with tears to go on.

Papa was looking at her now, his expression unreadable. "When the wolf almost got both you and Jared, I realized I was vulnerable to losing you, just as I had lost Anna. There are so many things that can happen to a child. Illness. Accidents. I could not face the prospect of losing someone else I loved."

"So you stopped loving me?"

"Yes."

She thought he was going to leave it at that, but he didn't. "I do not regret that decision. The grief you have brought to me as your parent would be compounded if I cared for you as I once did."

The absolute selfishness and cowardice of her father's response left her breathless. "Do you truly believe I sent the blackmail notes myself and will now make your secret known to the *ton*?"

"Of course your father doesn't believe anything so ridiculous, but you chose to marry Ashton yesterday rather than protect your family from scandal."

She turned to face her mother. "What of you, Mama? Did you stop loving me as well?" But even as she asked the question, Irisa knew the answer. Mama had not stopped loving her. Mama had never loved anyone as much as she loved herself and her social position.

"I wish I had, but I cannot stop loving my only daughter, and that has increased my pain at your betrayal tenfold."

Suddenly Lucas towered beside her. His body radiated outraged fury. "Just how long do you expect your daughter to pay for your sin?"

Mama turned crimson and her mouth opened and shut in outraged shock, but nothing came out.

"It is not our sin at issue here," Papa said, his voice raised in angry protest.

"On the contrary. That is exactly the issue here. Irisa is not responsible for your past actions. You have succeeded in making her feel guilt where she has none. She is the only innocent in any of this and I bloody well won't allow you to make her the sacrificial goat for your own failings." He turned to her. "We're leaving."

Irisa shook her head. "There is something else I wish to say." She glared at both her parents, as she saw her past through the eyes of the truth Lucas had spoken rather than a hazy veil of guilt and shame. "My husband is right. I am not responsible for your current imbroglio. Refusing to marry him would not have been a permanent solution. One day, someone would have latched on to your secret, but what you both fail to realize is that it is *your* secret, not mine."

She met her papa's gaze head on. "Thea once said that your weakness tore apart our family. I didn't believe her at the time because I always mistook your harsh implacability for strength. She was right, though, wasn't she? You were too weak to admit your wrong to Anna Selwyn and save your first marriage. It was your actions that caused Jared to live without knowing the love of his mother." Irisa shifted her gaze to Mama. "A woman who cared more for her children, both of them, than she did for her own happiness."

"Anna had no right to steal my daughter and raise her in the godforsaken West Indies." Papa sounded every bit as unbending as usual.

Irisa turned toward him, rage filling her. "God did not forsake her. *You did*. Just as you forsook Jared and me when you were too afraid to risk loving us. Just as you are about to forsake your family once again because you are too weak to face the consequences of your past."

Silence reigned in the drawing room. Mama had even ceased sniffling. Irisa looked from Mama's shocked face to Papa's stoic one. "I suppose coming here today was a fool's errand. You showed me long ago that my only value to you was what I could bring into your life. The best I can do for you now is to leave it. *Bon voyage*."

She turned to go, knowing neither Mama nor Papa would call her back. She'd made her choice and they had made theirs.

WHEN THEY REACHED THE CARRIAGE, LUCAS HANDED her inside. But this time, he took the reins. The trip home went by in a blur of thought for Irisa. Once they reached Ashton House, Lucas led her straight to his bedchamber. Unlike the day before, she did not feel embarrassed. She was relieved. Emotions cascaded through her in one disturbing wave after another and she wanted nothing more than to be alone with her husband, his arms wrapped securely around her.

And that is exactly what she got. He shut and locked his door, then seated himself on a chair and pulled her onto his lap without a word. He held her, his hand rubbing circles on her back, and that gentle touch brought the tears.

She sobbed against his shirtfront for the longest time while he murmured soft words of comfort and reassurance. Her tears finally abated and she searched in her reticule, still dangling from her wrist, for her handkerchief.

After she had repaired herself as best she could, she looked up at Lucas. His eyes were fathomless blue pools and for a moment she forgot what she was going to say.

"Better now?" he asked.

She nodded, wadded up her handkerchief, and shoved it back into her reticule. "I've become a regular watering pot since our marriage."

His hand around her waist tightened. "You've had a very trying time of it lately, little one. It would be surprising if you didn't give way to tears."

"It hasn't exactly been a picnic for you either, but I don't see you turning on the waterworks."

He chuckled. "I have other ways to vent my frustration."

She rubbed her backside against him and felt his manhood stir. "Yes, but our first time was last night. What did you do before that?"

This time he laughed outright. "I build models. Ships in bottles. It takes my mind off things and helps me to focus."

So that was why he did it. It put a new light on the previous night as well. If he'd felt the need to resort to his models after sending her off to bed, he must have found it as difficult as he'd implied he had. "Have you always built them?"

"I started with simple models of ships right after my father died. I began putting them in bottles when I was fifteen or so."

"They're very beautiful. I cannot wait to see the ones you keep at Ashton Manor."

"Who told you about those?"

"The housekeeper." She nuzzled against Lucas's neck. "Lucas?"

"Mmmm?"

"Thank you."

"Are you going to be all right, my love?"

"Yes." She tilted her face up and kissed him, touching his lips lightly and gently with her own. "Thank you for going with me."

His eyes filled with familiar blue fire and he shifted under her until a hard ridge rubbed against her bottom. "Irisa."

"What?"

"I'm not angry."

It took her a moment to get his meaning, and when she did, she went off in peals of laughter. It didn't take him long to change her laughter into breathless desire, and her last coherent thought as he carried her to the bed was that she certainly liked it when her husband wasn't angry.

LUCAS MARVELED AT THE SWEET GENEROSITY OF THE woman snuggled into his side as he brushed the curve of her breast with his fingertips.

She stretched against him with a purr of satisfaction, pressing her soft flesh more firmly into his hand and licking delicately at his male nipple. "Lucas, are you *still* not angry?"

He heard the mischief in her voice and growled even as his body shuddered in response to that impish little tongue. "You are playing with fire, sweeting."

She nipped the hardened nub on his chest and then licked it again in a soothing gesture. "Do you promise? I like it when you burn me up, my love. I like it very much."

He flipped her onto her back and loomed over her, catching her wrists in one smooth motion and drawing them above her head. "Say that again."

She smiled up at him, her eyes no longer shadowed with pain as they had been in her parents' drawing room. "I like it very, *very* much."

He hadn't meant that, though pleasure shot through him at her words. "Call me your love," he commanded. She'd never done so before and he found he liked it.

Her smile faded, but her eyes remained warm. "You are,

you know. My very own love. I love you so much, Lucas."

What had been renewing interest turned into raging need with those few, short words. Using his knee, he pressed her thighs apart and pushed his throbbing erection into her damp and welcoming sheath. "You belong to me."

"*Yes.*" She squirmed under him, trying to draw him deeper into her body.

He accommodated her with forceful thrusts. Keeping her wrists locked together with one of his hands, he used the other to caress the breasts so tantalizingly displayed by the position he held her in and brought them both to shattering completion. Afterward, he barely managed to withdraw before collapsing by her side on the rumpled bedding.

She gave a lusty, very unladylike yawn. "This marriage business is exhausting, isn't it?"

He was too tired to reply.

HE AWOKE LATER, HIS BEDCHAMBER SHROUDED IN darkness. Irisa stirred beside him as the mantel clock struck the hour. Bloody hell. Ravenswood and Drake were due any moment and he was naked, lazing in bed with his wife. He untangled his limbs from Irisa and the sheets before jumping out of the bed. He quickly lit the lamp beside the washstand.

"Lucas?" Irisa's voice was still clouded with sleep.

"Your brothers are supposed to be here momentarily and I haven't even asked the servants if we've received word from Owlpen yet."

"Why are Jared and Drake coming over?" She sat up, tucking her unruly blond curls behind her ears. Her lush curves glowed pale in the dim light and Lucas had to fight the desire to rejoin her in the bed. "Will Drake be bringing Thea?"

He decided to answer the second question first as he rapidly washed his body with a towel dampened in the frigid water from the pitcher on his washstand. "I don't know if Mrs. Drake is coming."

He made quick work of pulling on a pair of breeches and shirt. He did not bother with a cravat or coat, but decided to don his waistcoat, stockings, and shoes. "We're going to discuss what we learned this morning regarding the blackmailer."

"You learned something?" Irisa jumped out of the bed and quickly washed herself as well.

He stopped dressing long enough to watch.

She laughed at him, but blushed all the while. "Stop leering at me and hand me my dress."

When he realized she planned to put it on without her petticoats, or anything else for that matter, he refused to give it to her. "You are not going downstairs half-dressed."

"Why not? You left off your collar and neckcloth, not to mention your coat."

"But I remembered my breeches. Now put this on, or you can stay upstairs while I meet with Ravenswood and Drake." He handed a shift to her. "You can leave your corset off."

The little baggage rolled her eyes at him and then pulled the shift over her head, speaking through the fabric while she did so. "Thank you so much, Lucas. You're the soul of reasonability."

"Stop baiting me or you'll find out just how *un*reasonable I can be," he warned her.

She yanked on the dress and turned her back to him, lifting her hair in a silent command to do up the tapes. He did so, brushing the silken skin of her back with his knuckles and wishing they had enough time for him to explore the area more thoroughly.

He finished the last tie and stepped back reluctantly. "That will do."

She turned to him and smiled. "Thank you. I think I would prefer to have you dress me than Pansy."

"*I* prefer undressing you."

Her cheeks turned a charming rose pink, but her smile did not abate. "That does sound more promising."

He could no more prevent himself from pulling her into

his arms and kissing that sassy little mouth than he could have prevented his lungs from drawing his next breath. She melted against him and opened her tender lips in instant response. He forced himself to stop kissing her when he realized his hands were in the act of untying the tapes he had just secured on her gown.

He retied the gown and pulled his mouth from hers, stepping away from temptation. "I need to speak to the servants."

"Why?"

"Owlpen was supposed to send word on a matter we discussed at White's earlier today."

She paused in the act of brushing the tangles from her hair. "What does Lord Owlpen have to do with the blackmailer?"

"Nothing, but he's a gossip and I believe he may know something."

She secured her golden hair with a ribbon, fixing serious brown eyes on him. "He would only know something if gossip had already started to circulate. Has it?"

Lucas didn't want to lie to her. Besides, she would know soon enough. "I have reason to believe it has."

"I see. Why didn't you tell me earlier? No wonder Papa and Mama have decided to leave Town. I suppose they'd heard about it as well."

He frowned. "Your parents' plans had to have been in the works before today, or they could not possibly be ready to leave as soon as tomorrow. I will not allow you to take responsibility for their decision to go."

She smiled. "It's all right, Lucas. I don't blame myself—and you are right. They must have made plans to leave Town the night we told them about the blackmail letter." Her expression grew concerned. "I am sorry for you, though. It will not be easy for The Saint to live down marriage to the natural daughter of an earl, and a not very well placed one at that."

"Your father's place in the *ton* is of no interest to me, nor is your former status as his daughter, natural or otherwise. You are now my wife, the Countess of Ashton, and that is all I care about." His status as The Saint could go hang.

She gave him a misty smile. "Thank you, Lucas. That is a very sweet sentiment, to be sure."

"It is not sentiment. It is the truth."

She nodded, but something in her expression said she didn't believe him. "I think Lord Owlpen may have sent the message earlier today. Jenny brought the envelope to me, but since it was addressed to you, I had her leave it on your table."

The nondescript white envelope that lay innocently on the well-oiled surface of the table held the answer to who had been tormenting his wife.

Twenty

Lucas broke the red wax seal embedded with the Owlpen crest on the envelope and removed two sheets of folded foolscap from the inside. He scanned the *sincere* apologies for any offense Owlpen or his lady may have caused in innocently repeating the *vicious rumor* of Lady Ashton's illegitimacy and likewise skimmed over Owlpen's assurances such scandal would not pass their lips again. Owlpen then went through a detailed description of how the vicious rumor had made it to his lady wife's ears. Lucas smiled with deep satisfaction.

He now had a name.

"Who is it, Lucas? What does it say?" Irisa was trying to read the letter over his shoulder, but the light from the single lamp had clearly not been sufficient for her to do so. "Is it Cecily Carlisle-Jones?"

"No." He smiled down at her. "Apparently Owlpen took my threat very seriously. He's traced the gossip to its source. He would have made an excellent source for information during the war."

She tried to shake his shoulders. "Lucas, I swear if you don't tell me who has been trying to blackmail me, I'm going to do you bodily harm."

She looked angry enough to mean it, but the idea of his

tiny and rather gentle wife threatening him was so ludicrous he laughed. Spurred by the elation he felt at knowing the identity of his quarry, his laughter grew louder.

His wife crossed her arms over the tempting flesh of her bosom and glared at him. "This is not a laughing matter, my lord."

Neither he nor Irisa noticed the maid standing in the doorway for several seconds. "Milord, milady, Mr. and Mrs. Drake and Lord Ravenswood are awaiting your convenience in the library."

Irisa's face brightened perceptibly. "Oh good. Thea did accompany Drake. Perhaps she will succeed in getting you to name the blackmailer. I vow my patience for the task is all but spent."

Lucas pressed a hard kiss on his wife's lips. "It is Lady Preston. Now come. We must discuss this new development with the others."

"Lady Preston? That spiteful, gossiping harpy. Why?"

Irisa peppered him with questions interspersed with dire opinions regarding Lady Preston's character all the way to the library.

He led her into the room and then held the letter up for his brothers-in-law to see. "We have a name."

"Who?" Ravenswood asked, his expression fierce.

Mrs. Drake's mouth opened in astonishment.

Looking as pleased as Lucas felt, Drake said, "It sounds like Owlpen took heed of your words earlier today."

Lucas nodded with satisfaction and then named their enemy. "Lady Preston."

"The notorious widow?" Mrs. Drake asked, her bewilderment as clear as Irisa's. "But why?"

Lucas did not have the answer to that question yet, but he would soon.

"What words? What threat?" Irisa again asked in a voice that demanded this time he answer.

He shrugged. "I merely made it clear I would not tolerate the passing on of scandal attached to my wife's name."

She did not look satisfied with his answer, but he did not want to go into his plan to protect her from gossip. He knew instinctively that Irisa would not see a dawn appointment in quite the same light as her brother.

He met first Drake's and then Ravenswood's gaze. "I believe it is time we called on Lady Preston."

"And Yardley," Drake added.

"Why Lord Yardley?" Irisa wrung her hands and sent Lucas a disgruntled glare. "I am the one being threatened and yet I feel as if I have been kept in the dark on important matters. I expect you to explain yourself, my lord, and from this point forward, you will do me the courtesy of fully disclosing all details."

Irritation filled him at her bossy tone and her obvious ploy to put him in his place for perceived wrongs committed against her. "I have not intentionally kept you in the dark, madam. If you will recall, I arrived home this afternoon to find you distraught over yet another letter from the blackmailer. And then news of your parents' impending flight from Town necessitated our leaving immediately so you could tell them your good-byes."

She was not placated in the least by his explanation if the stubborn tilt to her chin, fist on her hip, and tapping toe were any indication. "We have been home for several hours since then, my lord. You could have given me a report of your progress at any time."

The sheer outrageousness of her remark left him stunned for a moment and then he narrowed his eyes.

"Really?" he asked, allowing silky menace to filter into his voice. "When did you want the progress report? Perhaps you think I should have told you while you were busy moaning your pleasure, or later when you fell asleep from exhaustion?"

She turned brilliant crimson in the space of two heartbeats and gasped his name in horrified tones. "Lucas! How could you say such a thing in front of our family?"

"Pardon me. I thought you wanted me to answer your

question as to why I had not discussed certain issues with you this afternoon and I have attempted to give you my reasons."

She gaped at him while Ravenswood laughed. Drake smiled, but the frown on Mrs. Drake's face kept him from giving in to his mirth at Irisa's embarrassment.

Lucas sighed. He hadn't meant to say anything so provocative in front of her family. He quickly explained his discovery of Yardley's wagers in White's betting book and subsequent discussion with the gossip, Owlpen.

"You challenged Lord Owlpen to a duel?" Irisa asked in shocked accents. "How could you do something so caper-witted?"

"I did not challenge him. I simply let him know that a challenge would be forthcoming if he did not cooperate in certain matters." His mood did not improve upon hearing her opinion of his protection.

"Worked like a charm, too," Ravenswood said. "Your husband's got quite the reputation for dueling from his salad days. I'd say his threat to challenge anyone who passes on the gossip about your birth will go a long way toward protecting you from scandalmongers among the *ton.*"

Irisa turned stricken eyes to Lucas. "You threatened to call out anyone who gossiped about me?"

She sounded faint.

He sought to reassure her. "It's a very effective way to prevent unsavory rumors from floating around."

"Facing death is your answer to unsavory gossip?" She looked at him as if she'd never really seen him before.

"It worked very well with my mother's exploits, and she was far more notorious than you, my love. I trust you will place your confidence in my knowledge in these things."

"You have decided to handle being married to me the same way you dealt with having a mother who lived outside the bounds of propriety?" She whispered the question.

He shrugged. "It was effective once. I see no reason for it not to serve me well again."

"And if you die in one of these dawn appointments?"

"I am not going to die and I doubt there will be any duels. I have a certain reputation in such matters."

"How many duels did you participate in on your mother's behalf?" Her voice was barely above a whisper.

He would not lie to her, but he realized the answer was bound to upset her. "Three."

Ravenswood took a step toward Irisa and patted her gently on the shoulder. "If it will make you feel any better, I've spent the day letting it be known that I stand by your husband in this. He is not the only gentleman willing to issue a challenge if your reputation comes into question."

Irisa's face went from pale to sickly and her eyes darted from Ravenswood to Lucas. "You're both putting your lives at stake for my *reputation*? You lied to me. *You both lied.* You said it didn't matter." She turned burning eyes on Lucas. "You said you didn't care what the gossipmongers said. That I was Lady Ashton now and the circumstances of my birth were unimportant."

"They aren't important." How dare she accuse him of lying? He had never told her a falsehood, even when the truth would upset her.

"Then why are you letting it be known among the *ton* that anyone who speaks of me will have to face you over a brace of pistols?" Accusation laced her tone, and she seemed far more upset by his actions than those of the blackmailer.

Damn it. She didn't understand, but he'd be hanged if he was going to discuss this any further in front of a room full of people. "We will finish this conversation later."

Irisa closed her eyes in silence for a full three seconds before opening them and agreeing. "Yes. Of course. Right now, we must deal with the more immediate problem of Lady Preston."

"Isn't she the one who told you that Miss de Brieuse was Lucas's mistress?" Mrs. Drake asked Irisa in an obvious bid to change the subject.

Irisa bit her lip, her expression thoughtful. "Actually she told Mama, but it comes to much the same thing, as

I'm sure she must have seen me standing there. I suppose that was her first ploy to prevent my marriage to Lucas. And then for Lord Yardley to make a wager to that effect—I don't understand. It seems such a mean-spirited thing to do. Papa refused his suit on my behalf last year, but he hardly acted brokenhearted about it."

"Sour grapes, perhaps," Mrs. Drake said.

Irisa shrugged and looked at Lucas, the thoughtful expression in her soft brown eyes tinged with something he could not quite decipher. "It is Lady Preston who concerns me at the moment."

That look couldn't be jealousy. He had never had even the slightest association with Lady Preston. He noticed that everyone else in the room was looking at him with a certain amount of speculation as well.

"You can all stop wondering if the woman was my mistress. I haven't spoken two words privately to her. I have no idea why she became obsessed with ending my engagement with Irisa and I won't find out until I see her." He turned to leave. "Ravenswood, Drake, are you coming?"

"Lucas?" Irisa's voice held a tentative note.

He turned toward her and his anger melted at the look of concern and genuine fear in the warm brown depths of her eyes.

He crossed the space separating them in three long strides and took her shoulders in his hands. "All will be well, sweeting. Do not worry."

"Be careful. And Lucas?"

"Yes?"

"Please do not issue any challenges tonight."

He could not promise that. If he found Yardley and discovered the other man had been part of the plan to kidnap Irisa and blackmail her, Lucas had no choice but to do so. "You must trust me to know best."

Her mouth thinned in a straight, mutinous line. "If you do not promise me you will not issue any challenges, I will not let you leave."

"How do you propose to stop me?"

Eyes narrow, she asked, "Do you want me to be here when you get back?"

"You had bloody well better be." His jaw ached from tension.

"You have only two ways of ensuring that happens." She crossed her arms. "Either stay here with me or extract my word that I will do so."

"Are you threatening to run away if I don't give in to you?" he asked, sounding only mildly interested while his gut twisted with fear that she would make good her threat and fury that she'd had the nerve to threaten him at all. "There is another way to ensure you are here when I return, wife."

She glared at him, but did not rise to the bait.

"I can lock you in your bedchamber."

Mrs. Drake gasped, but Irisa did not so much as blink at his statement. "Promise me you won't challenge anyone tonight, Lucas. We are not finished discussing the matter, and until we are, you must not act precipitously."

"I cannot give you that promise."

"Then I cannot promise you I will be here when you return."

"I will trust in your strong sense of honor guaranteeing it. I refuse to believe you would do something so ignoble as to run away simply because you cannot have your way."

"Why should I be bound by my sense of honor when you are not bound by yours?" Her voice came out choked, and the pain he heard in it stopped him from losing his temper.

"I had thought to stay and keep her company while you gentlemen are gone," Thea said before he could reply to his wife's accusation.

Lucas turned his gaze to his sister-in-law. She looked like she would cheerfully have taken the fireplace poker to him. "You may stay and visit my wife as long as you like."

"Then I need not go to my bedchamber?" Irisa asked. Her sweet mouth turned down unhappily.

"Will you be here when I return?" he asked.

"You are certain my honor will prevent me from leaving. You don't need my pledge. You will not promise me not to challenge anyone, will you?" She sounded defeated.

"No. I am sorry if that upsets you, but I have no choice."

She shook her head, but said nothing and turned away.

He followed her and turned her until she faced him. "I will do my best to avoid challenging anyone," he offered by way of a compromise.

Her eyes filled with sadness. "I suppose I must make do with that."

He leaned down and brushed her lips lightly with his, wishing he could take the time to comfort her now. At least she did not pull away. "Yes, just as I will make do with my trust in your honor."

She said nothing and he and the other men turned to go.

Ravenswood stopped in front of her on the way. "Don't worry about your husband, brat. I'll watch out for him."

She twisted her hands together until the knuckles on her fingers had all gone white. "Who will look after you, Jared?"

Bloody hell. Lucas did not like leaving her like this. She was very upset. Perhaps her sister would calm her down, but from the look in Mrs. Drake's eyes, they would spend the time he was gone enumerating his flaws.

THEA SUGGESTED IRISA ORDER TEA AND SANDWICHES served to them in the library. Irisa had missed dinner, but could not bear the thought of food at the moment. However, she did as her sister suggested, having even less liking for another argument. She never used to argue with anyone. Meeting Lucas had changed her in so many ways; she just hoped he would not regret them.

She knew that the biddable creature she had once been, intent on earning her parents' and Lucas's approval, would never have challenged him over his actions as she had done tonight. She had meant to be the kind of wife that Lucas desired, but had discovered tonight that if that included approving dangerous schemes like the one he had concocted to keep the *ton* from talking about her, she could not do it.

Surely the main ingredient for the perfect wife was one who cared, not absolute submission and perfect propriety. Anyone could offer Lucas those things, but she would love him all her life, with her whole heart. Surely that meant more than the other.

She could only hope Lucas would agree.

Thea refused to discuss the evening's events over tea. Instead, she told an amusing story about her son's encounter with the kitchen cat. Irisa relaxed enough that she surprised herself by consuming several small sandwiches along with her tea and even found herself laughing at her nephew's antics.

"Lucas is rather autocratic at times, is he not?" Thea asked after the underfootman had taken the tea things away.

Something had pricked Irisa's memory as the underfootman walked away, but she let it go as she focused on Thea's question. "Yes. I try to remind myself that he means well."

"You're worried about this duel nonsense, aren't you?"

Irisa smoothed her skirts, dusting off crumbs from her sandwiches. "Very much. Oh, Thea. I could not bear it if either he or Jared was hurt defending my reputation."

Thea frowned, her startlingly blue eyes narrowed in thought. "I must admit that I know very little about this whole challenging business. It was not something the English gentlemen on my island ever participated in and Aunt Harriet never spoke of it in her letters. The only mention I ever heard of it before coming to England was the one my mother made in her diary in relation to Langley."

Irisa started with surprise. "Papa was in a duel?"

"No, but apparently he challenged the man he found kissing my mother in the garden. The blackguard apologized and that was the end of the matter. For him at least."

"It's a truly horrible practice and not at all legal any longer, but that does not seem to stop hotheaded gentlemen from issuing challenges."

"I would not describe Ashton as hotheaded."

Irisa wished she agreed with her sister. "I think he has a temper, it's just under control most of the time."

"I see." Thea looked deep in thought for a moment. "Do you really think he will challenge anyone who comments on your birth? Surely that would be going too far."

"I don't know." She wished she did. "It's awful to think that he feels the need to protect my reputation with the same drastic measures he used on his mother's behalf. He had little respect for her, I think, and even less affection."

Thea shook her head decisively. "In that you must be mistaken. No one, even a complete idiot, is going to risk his life for someone he does not care about."

Irisa couldn't prevent a small smile from forming on her lips. "Are you calling Lucas a complete idiot?"

"That might be doing it a bit brown, but it's obvious to me that his gentleman's pride is more involved than his head in this matter."

"And Jared?"

Thea shrugged. "Jared *is* hotheaded and will do anything he thinks necessary to protect those he loves."

"Yes." If only Lucas were similarly motivated.

It would not decrease Irisa's concern for his safety, but at least she would not feel like such a burden to her husband. The prospect that he saw her in the same light as his mother weighed heavily on her heart.

"People *will* talk. Does he truly think to challenge every man—or woman!—who disparages my birth? What am I to do?" she asked her sister in frustration.

"I don't know, sister mine. I'll talk to Pierson about it later tonight if you wish. Perhaps he will have some insight."

Irisa held little hope of that. It seemed to her that when it came to foolish things like duels, most gentlemen seemed to be of the same mind. She sighed with a certain amount of resignation. "I do not see how it can hurt."

Thea smiled. "Do not be so downhearted. It has been a difficult few weeks, but all will come to rights soon. I'm sure of it."

Irisa summoned her own smile, albeit with more difficulty. "I hope so."

The underfootman came into the room with a message from Thea's nursemaid asking her to return to the town house because one of the children had come down ill. Irisa promised to pray for her nephew and saw her sister to the door.

Thea stopped in the hall. "I am not certain I should leave you here alone. Perhaps you should come home with me until the men return."

Irisa smiled reassuringly at her sister. "Do not be silly. I will be quite safe here in my own home. Now go. Your son needs you."

Thea looked unconvinced. "Will you be here when Ashton returns?" she asked, her gaze still worried.

"Do I have a choice?" Irisa asked.

Thea's eyes turned dark with understanding. "Not if you love him."

IRISA WANDERED BACK INTO THE LIBRARY, HER thoughts on Thea's parting comment. She did love Lucas, enough that the very thought of him facing a pistol at dawn because of her sent shards of pain knifing through her heart. She looked up in surprise at the underfootman who had followed her into the room.

"Is there something you need?" she asked.

"His Lordship said you were not to be left alone, milady."

Irisa expelled an irritated breath. It was perfectly all right for him to face death, but she could not be left alone for one moment in her own home. Gentlemen could be illogical in the extreme.

"Very well."

She picked up a book and opened it, but did not attempt to read. What she needed to do was come up with a plan to stop Lucas from challenging anyone. For people were bound to comment on her base birth as the gossip became more well known. Some of them would even do so without any malicious intent, but simply out of curiosity or shock.

"Perhaps you would like a glass of ratafia with your book, milady?" the underfootman asked.

Considering the state of her nerves, the idea was an excellent one. The fruit liqueur was not her favorite drink, but it could have a calming effect as she had noted at her come-out ball, which had been the first and last occasion on which she drank it. "Thank you, that would be lovely."

He poured a glass and served it to her by the fire. As he walked away, her memory stirred once again. There was something quite familiar about the set of his shoulders and his carriage from the back. Some memory that wanted to come to the surface, but if she focused too hard on it, it would not.

She sipped the sweet liqueur, thinking it tasted even worse than she remembered, and tried to concentrate on the book of natural history she had selected from Lucas's shelves. Perhaps the elusive memory would come to her if she kept her mind occupied with something else.

Her eyes grew tired rather quickly and she wondered if she should not ask the underfootman to light another brace of candles. Brace of candles . . . A storm . . . So cold . . . As the almost empty glass fell from her fingers, she remembered why the underfootman seemed so familiar. He had been in the hall the day she sneaked into the tower room. She remembered being worried that he would tell on her.

She must ask him about it.

Just as soon as she woke up.

Her head fell back on the chair.

My, she was tired. She wondered why.

She hadn't even made love to Lucas.

Twenty-one

LUCAS WAS NOT IN THE BEST OF MOODS AS HIS carriage rolled toward Ashton House.

His quarry had fled London.

The servants Lady Preston had left behind to close her town house informed Lucas that she had returned to the country that very day. His search for Yardley had fared no better. Whether or not he had left Town with Lady Preston was undetermined, though the two had been seen together quite a bit of late. However, Yardley had not been at any of the gaming hells or clubs Drake and Ravenswood had visited.

Lucas had been forced to cool his heels in the carriage while his brothers-in-law investigated everything but Yardley's rooms and the gaming hells because, although he had called for a coat, collar, and neckcloth before leaving home, he was hardly dressed for evening calls by the standards of the *ton.*

Tired and frustrated, he did not look forward to continuing his argument with Irisa. Nor did he anticipate with any measure of pleasure telling her of his failure to find Lady Preston or Yardley.

Bloody hell. What a night.

To be so close to answers and forestalled by the simple

expediency of his prey fleeing to the country. He should have expected Lady Preston to make such a move. She had to know that Lucas would eventually be able to discover the source of the gossip. She would not have counted on Owlpen helping Lucas do so as quickly as he had, but she clearly had been unwilling to risk staying in Town. Lucas did not like the sensation that he had been outmaneuvered.

He could not begin to understand why she had targeted him and Irisa for her foul schemes, but he *would* find out. Even if it meant following her to the remote estate in the north she had shared with her husband prior to his death.

Ravenswood broke the silence in the carriage. "Hope Irisa's in a more logical frame of mind."

Lucas smiled grimly. "A pleasant prospect, to be sure."

Drake chuckled and spoke from the opposite squab. "After four years of marriage, I have come to the conclusion that ladies do not always agree with men on what constitutes logic."

Ravenswood smiled and the scar on his face turned white in the dim light cast from the carriage lamp. "I can see where living with Thea might lead you to that conclusion."

Drake fixed his brother-in-law with a wry look. "I've also decided that blood will tell. You and my wife may not have been raised in the same nursery, but your sister is every bit as stubborn and certain of her opinions as you are."

"Then the stubbornness must come from Langley's side of the family because Irisa's got her own fair share," Lucas said.

Ravenswood shrugged and lost his smile.

Lucas understood the reaction. His brother-in-law did not like the reminder that he had his father's blood in his veins. Langley's lack of honor must weigh heavily on his only son.

Lucas had often felt the same way when confronted with his superficial resemblance to his mother. She had had the same dark hair and uncommon shade of blue eyes. When people had commented on it, he had wondered how much more he shared with her, and had set out to prove that the one thing they did not have in common was her penchant for wild behavior.

He flipped aside the curtain on the carriage window to see how far they were from his town house just as the coachman reined in the horses. He let the curtain drop back into place and tensed in anticipation of seeing his wife again. No doubt they would argue, but then perhaps they would make up . . .

Drake and Ravenswood followed him into the house. The butler and one of the footmen came into the hall almost immediately upon their arrival.

"Are Lady Ashton and Mrs. Drake still in the library?" Lucas asked.

It was conceivable that Irisa and her sister had moved to the drawing room or Lucas and Irisa's private sitting room to increase their comfort while they waited.

The butler's face registered distress before the customary bland expression worn by proper English servants reasserted itself. "Mrs. Drake called for her carriage and left earlier this evening."

Lucas felt a shiver of premonition skate up his spine. "And my wife?"

"I am not certain of her ladyship's whereabouts, milord."

"What the bloody hell does that mean, man? Are you saying Irisa's gone?" Ravenswood demanded.

The butler looked pained, but did not have the chance to answer. Pansy came rushing into the hall, her mobcap askew and her expression clearly revealing a wealth of emotion.

She skidded to a stop in front of Lucas. "Oh, milord. She's gone! She is. I don't know what 'appened, but she's disappeared. I'm that worried, I am."

Rage boiled inside Lucas, but he forced his tone to remain even. "I left strict instructions for my wife not to be left alone."

"Yes, I know, milord. I don't know 'ow it could 'ave 'appened. One minute she were taking tea with her sister and the next she was gone."

"She threatened to leave, but I didn't think she would," Ravenswood said.

Lucas made a sharp movement with his head. Irisa would not have made good on her threat. He was certain of it. "She didn't."

He turned to the butler. "Are you sure she did not leave with Mrs. Drake?"

"Yes, milord. The footman who helped Mrs. Drake into her coach has already been questioned. He said she was alone."

"Has the house been searched?"

The butler did not get a chance to answer. "We've been searching for the last hour or more, milord," Pansy said, her voice breaking on the last word. She surreptitiously wiped her eyes with the sleeve of her gown.

Drake asked, "Why did my wife leave?"

"I do not know, sir," the butler responded.

Lucas turned and met Drake's eyes.

Drake answered his unasked question. "I thought Thea planned to stay until we returned. I don't see her abandoning Irisa to wait alone and I also don't think Thea would want to wait one moment longer than necessary to hear our news. She can be impatient. If she left, there must have been a reason."

Lucas nodded and turned back to the butler. "Who was the last servant with her ladyship?"

Pansy opened her mouth to speak again, but the butler gave her a quelling look and she subsided. "I believe that would be the underfootman, milord. Timothy. He is new to the household staff this year."

"Have him brought to me at once." Lucas turned on his heel and headed to the library. Drake and Ravenswood followed him.

"ARE YOU SURE SHE HASN'T RUN?" DRAKE ASKED LUCAS, clearly remembering the night Irisa had come to his wife for help in doing just that when faced with the first blackmail threats.

"Yes." He almost wished he could believe she had run. It was the possibility that she hadn't left the house under her own power which sent fear unlike anything Lucas had ever known coursing through him.

"You think she was kidnapped?" Ravenswood asked, his voice disbelieving, "From under the watchful eyes of your servants, from your own town house?"

Lucas clenched his fists in an effort not to hit something. "Their eyes obviously weren't watchful enough. Damnation. I should never have left her tonight. I should have locked her in her room with Pansy for her own safety."

Timothy entered the room along with the butler and Pansy. The maid had stopped crying, but looked as if she would start again any moment.

The underfootman stopped in front of Lucas, his servant's mask more firmly in place than the butler's. "You wanted to speak to me, milord?"

"You were the last servant with my wife?"

"Yes, milord. I had taken the tea things away. Then a message came for Mrs. Drake calling her home. I brought the message to her ladyship and Mrs. Drake and asked another footman to call the carriage round. I stayed with her ladyship after that because your lordship had given orders she was not to be left alone."

Lucas stared at Timothy. "Then how do you explain the fact that my wife is now missing?"

Timothy flinched at Lucas's tone, but otherwise remained impassive. "Her ladyship asked me to call her maid downstairs. I assumed Miss Pansy was in the kitchens as she often is late in the evening, visiting with the other maids." His disdain for such behavior in a lady's maid was apparent in his voice. "After searching the kitchens and maids' quarters, I found Miss Pansy waiting in her ladyship's bedchamber. When Miss Pansy and I returned to the library, her ladyship was gone."

"I thought, at first, she'd withdrawn to the water closet," Pansy inserted, her voice full of distress, "but she weren't there. She weren't anywhere, milord. Not anywhere!"

Lucas's gut told him that something wasn't right, but a commotion at the door caught his attention before he could question the two servants further.

Mrs. Drake had returned.

She rushed into the room and went straight to her husband. "Is it true? Is she missing? I've been terrified the entire trip back from our town house that I would arrive to find her gone."

Lucas didn't let Drake answer. "Why?"

She turned to face him. "I wasn't worried she'd run away, if that's what you're thinking." He ignored the angry retort and waited for his sister-in-law to go on. "I received a message that my son was ill and I was needed at home. But when I arrived, I discovered him sleeping soundly in the nursery and no one knew who had sent the message."

Lucas faced Timothy. "You said you brought the message to Mrs. Drake?"

"Yes, milord."

"How was it delivered?"

"A boy brought it."

"What do you mean a boy?" Lucas asked with forced calm.

Lady Preston had employed street urchins to deliver her foul notes to Irisa.

"Just a boy, milord. The young ones that will carry messages for a bit of money. A street urchin."

"Did you not think it strange that the Drakes' footman had not delivered the message?" He turned to Mrs. Drake before the underfootman could answer. "What about *you*? Didn't you think it odd that your footman had not come if there was an urgent need for your presence at home?"

His sister-in-law's eyes filled with remorse. "I should have thought of it, but the idea that my child was ill had rattled me. I didn't think anything odd until I got home to find things calm and my son safely tucked in the nursery."

Drake pulled his wife into his side and glared at Lucas. "It's all right, my love. You are not to blame for what has happened tonight."

Lucas gritted his teeth and did not disagree. The truth was, he had not protected Irisa well enough and now she would pay the price for his negligence.

Timothy had not answered his question and Lucas turned back to glare at him. "Well?"

"I did not think to question it, milord." His tone implied that the ways of Quality were not always reasonable.

Lucas wanted to throttle him. "Obviously."

"If you will pardon me for saying so, milord. Her ladyship acted peculiarly when she sent me to fetch her maid, as if she wanted to be alone." Timothy cleared his throat delicately. He had all the makings of a very efficient butler one day. "I, too, wondered if she perhaps needed a bit of privacy to attend to necessary matters."

"Are you implying you believe my wife left the house of her own volition?" Lucas asked in a dangerously calm voice.

Timothy's face took on a deferential cast. "It is not my place to say, milord. However, it would appear that if street thugs had entered the house and taken off with her, one of the other servants would have heard."

"I see. You have nothing more to tell me?" Lucas asked.

"No, milord. There was no trace of her ladyship or her shawl when we returned to the library."

Lucas nodded and turned to the butler. "It's late. Let the servants find their beds. We won't find my wife tonight, not if she left of her own volition."

Pansy let out a long wail. "Milady wouldn't 'ave left like that. She wouldn't!"

Lucas faced her. "That will be enough, Pansy. Go to her ladyship's bedchamber and see if any of her things are missing."

Pansy nodded and left, too upset to say anything else.

Thea opened her mouth to speak, but Drake hushed her. Ravenswood stood still as a statue near the fireplace, his intent regard on Timothy. Lucas dismissed the underfootman and the butler, watching to make sure they were safely headed to the kitchens before closing the library door tightly and facing the remaining occupants.

"Surely you don't believe she's really run away?" Thea demanded.

Lucas frowned. "No."

"Then why did you send Pansy to check her room? Why did you stop questioning the underfootman?"

"How are you at surveillance?" Lucas asked Ravenswood before answering Thea's questions.

The huge man shrugged. "I'm large, but I can be silent when I need to."

After their experience in the park, Lucas believed him.

"Go around to the mews and watch for him. I'll join you shortly."

Ravenswood made a brisk assenting movement with his head and left the room. Lucas did not hear the front door open and shut, but then he hadn't expected to. His brother-in-law knew what he was doing.

"I don't understand what is happening," Thea said.

Lucas turned to face her, knowing she shared his fear on Irisa's behalf. "It all comes back to that locked door to the tower roof."

"What?" Thea asked with bewilderment.

"At first, I thought your father had done it."

"But if he didn't, that left one of your servants as the culprit," Drake said.

"Right. And then there was the matter of the last blackmail letter. No one remembered its arrival. The simplest explanation for that would be that Lady Preston had someone on my staff in her employ."

"If it's such a simple solution, why didn't you come to it earlier?" Thea asked with some acerbity.

Lucas felt the weight of failure pull at him. "I damn well should have, but I made a tactical error and assumed the threat came from without, not within, my household."

"You believe Timothy is the culprit?" she asked.

"He was the last servant to see my wife. He said that she sent him in search of Pansy and then disappeared. We believe Irisa did not leave voluntarily, so that leaves the only viable alternative. Timothy lied."

Thea's face creased with anxiety. "Then why did you let him leave? Why have you not forced him to tell you where she is?"

Drake answered his wife's distraught questions this time. "We can't be certain he knows where she is. I think Lucas plans to follow him when he attempts to leave the house and meet with his other employer."

"But what if he doesn't leave the house?" Thea sounded close to the breaking point.

"He will." Lucas was sure of it.

He had made some mistakes in this fiasco, mistakes he could only pray had not caused his wife any true harm, but he trusted his instincts. And those instincts told him that Timothy would be reporting to his employer very soon.

His instincts proved correct when, an hour later, he and Ravenswood followed the underfootman as he skulked away from Ashton House wearing nondescript clothing that would never be mistaken for a footman's livery.

IRISA'S HEAD POUNDED AND HER MOUTH TASTED LIKE cotton wool. She tried to open her eyes, but it required too much effort.

A feeling of disorientation made it difficult to make sense of her predicament. She was lying down, but not in a bed. The surface under her body was too unyielding to be a feather-tick mattress, and too narrow as well. Her fingers could feel the edge of what might be a fainting couch. They brushed against the rough pattern of velvet, but she stilled them when two voices somewhere to her left became distinct as the haze receded from her brain.

The man was definitely not Lucas, nor any servant whom she recognized. "She'll wake soon," he said.

"Yes, and when she does, she will learn the full extent

of her mistake in marrying The Saint." The woman's vaguely familiar voice was full of venom.

Had they taken her from Ashton House? The room did not have the fragrances she associated with her new home. Instead it smelled of expensive perfume and dust. A strange combination, and definitely not familiar. She forced her eyelids to open and was unsurprised to see the beautiful young widow, Lady Preston, seated in a chair across a small table from Lord Yardley.

"The underfootman put something in the ratafia," Irisa said before she thought better of speaking at all.

Lady Preston turned her head and smiled mockingly at Irisa. "So, you have awakened—and rather more alertly than I expected. The drug is usually more debilitating."

Irisa believed it. She still could not move from her supine position on the fainting couch.

"You are quite right," Lady Preston continued. "Timothy put a small dose of sleeping powder in your drink."

"Why?" She did not mean why the sleeping powder. Clearly that had been necessary to kidnap her, but why kidnap her at all? Why hurt her family? Why hurt Lucas?

"We required your presence, Lady *Ashton.*" Lady Preston made Irisa's name sound like a curse. "How unfortunate—The Saint will return to his home tonight to discover that your honor was not up to the task of keeping you at the town house. Very distressing for a man who puts such store in his wife's integrity, don't you think?"

"But why?" Irisa persisted, ignoring the other woman's taunt. Lucas would not believe she left of her own will. He could not. Memories of how he had caught her trying to flee London, not once, but twice, during their engagement, rose up to haunt her. She pushed them away and chose to dwell instead on Lucas's own words of faith in her earlier that evening.

"Ah. You wish to know why I have done what I have done?"

Irisa nodded and immediately regretted the movement. The pain in her temples throbbed.

"What is that saying? Ah, yes. Hell hath no fury like a woman scorned. Your precious Saint hurt me unbearably, and he will pay for it."

"Lucas has never been your lover."

Lady Preston laughed, the sound a grating trill in Irisa's pain-ridden head.

"How naïve you are, Lady Ashton. Is that what he told you?"

"Lucas said you've never been his mistress and I believe him." It was difficult to affect disdain when lying on a fainting couch, but Irisa endeavored to do so just the same. "He has much more fastidious tastes."

Lady Preston's eyes glittered with fury. "I suppose you think you are so much better than me? That your prissy behavior puts you above my notice. Yet your once pristine reputation is not nearly so spotless as before. By now, all of London knows that you are base born."

"They know that I am Lord Ashton's wife and that is all that matters," Irisa responded with as much conviction as she could muster while feeling a distinct need to cast up her accounts.

"Ah, but he wanted a perfect wife. All of society knows it, and you are hardly that. You have consorted with actresses, been revealed for the bastard daughter you are, and now the *ton* will be titillated with the scandal of you running off with your lover the day after your marriage."

"I haven't run off with anyone."

"Ah, but that is not what the servants will say. You know how effective servants' gossip is. And my very dear friend, Lord Yardley, will have placed a wager in White's betting book to that effect by tomorrow evening. A week from now, your reputation will be in shreds and The Saint's along with it. After all, what kind of monster must a man be for his wife to run off the day after their wedding night?"

Irisa was appalled, not only by Lady Preston's words, but by the abiding hatred she read in the other woman's eyes. "No one will believe it. You must let me go eventually and I will return to my husband, giving lie to the rumor."

She refused to believe Lady Preston intended to murder her. If that were the case, wouldn't she already be dead?

"Oh, you will return, all right. In five days' time you will arrive at a well-known posting house, abandoned by your lover and recovering from the cruel treatment on your wedding night. Unfortunately, you will be unable to cover the fading bruises."

For the first time real fear coursed down Irisa's spine. "I have no bruises."

"You will." Lady Preston's gaze shifted to Lord Yardley. "After tonight."

He smiled, but his eyes remained quite chilling. "It is not often that I am allowed to indulge my little whims with ladies of the *ton,* and I have had my eye on you for quite some time. I assure you, Lady Ashton, I quite look forward to entertaining myself with you."

This time the bile could not be kept down and Irisa began retching. Lady Preston yanked her to her feet and shoved her toward the water closet, where Irisa was violently ill. Lady Preston had not allowed her to close the door, so she had no time to collect herself or her thoughts before being summarily forced back into the sitting room. At least this time she remained in an upright position.

"You must tell me why," she said, hoping to gain enough time for Lucas to find her before the beast, Yardley, made good his threats.

For Lucas would find her, she had no doubt. Until then, she must protect herself. In her current state, she could not hope to win a physical battle against both Lady Preston and Lord Yardley, so she must keep her wits about her. "You have threatened my family, driven my parents out of England, and terrorized me personally. Tell me the truth of why you hate Lucas enough to do so, if you can."

"I've told you why," Lady Preston said smugly.

"And I've told you that I don't believe you." Irisa clung to her faith in Lucas.

"Your husband is responsible for six years of hell in my life and I *will* see him pay."

"What do you mean?" Lucas would never hurt someone purposefully. The woman had to be unbalanced.

Lady Preston's face twisted with remembered raged. "In the last year of the war, your husband was responsible for the death of the man I loved."

"But Lucas was an intelligence agent for the Crown. He was not a soldier."

"I am aware of that."

Sudden understanding dawned. "He was a spy for Bonaparte. He was a traitor, and Lucas exposed him."

"He was a gentleman. A wonderful dancer, charming in every way, and we were going to run away together." Her voice was fierce, and the choked grief and rage in her eyes told Irisa that, for once, Lady Preston told the truth.

Irisa could almost have sympathy for the other woman, but even her grief could not justify the terrible things Lady Preston had done—or the terrible things she was planning to do.

"Nigel would have taken me away from the provincial little town in which I had grown up. He promised me trips to London and to the Continent when the war ended. We wanted the same things. He was everything a gentleman should be."

"Except loyal to the land of his birth."

Rage twisted Lady Preston's features. "What do you know of it? Politics have no place in matters of the heart. I would not have cared if he were French. I loved him and your husband killed him."

For Lucas to have killed, he must have had no other choice. "Your fiancé drove him to it."

"We needed money to live the lifestyle we dreamed of. His connection to France provided it."

"He was a traitor."

"He was a man living by his wits! But after his death, when my parents discovered I had been secretly engaged to an enemy of the Crown, they were appalled. They wasted no time in marrying me off to an aging peer before the secret could spread." Lady Preston shuddered, her revulsion unfeigned. "You cannot imagine the horrors of my marriage bed, those cold, dry hands groping me in the dark."

Irisa did understand. She remembered her disgust at the prospect of marriage to the Duke of Clareshire, a man old enough to be her grandfather. Then her gaze fell on Lord Yardley and she could not see how sharing a bed with him could be an improvement.

Lady Preston caught her look and she laughed. "As Yardley has said, he does not get the opportunity to exercise his particular passions on women of Quality like myself. We have far more mutually satisfying forms of entertainment."

Irisa shuddered. "Yet you will allow him to hurt me?" she asked accusingly.

Lady Preston sighed. "It will not be so bad. The bruises are necessary to my plan, so he will bruise you. But for all his talk, he does not like to truly hurt the women he beds. He just likes to scare them."

It was Lord Yardley's turn to laugh and the sound froze Irisa's heartbeat. "*Lady Preston* has a rather charitable view of me, does she not?"

Charitable or not, Irisa would fight to her last breath before she allowed the foul man to bed her. "You do not care if he tosses another woman's skirts?"

Lady Preston's laugh was mocking. "You really are naïve. There are many forms of pleasure to be had between two lovers. Watching Yardley force you to submit will do a great deal for my sense of vengeance and darker passions."

Irisa felt a strong urge to throw up again. "Lucas will kill you."

"I think not," Lord Yardley replied, standing and reaching out to caress Irisa's cheek.

His touch was nothing like Lucas's, and she was unbearably grateful that he still wore the gloves of a gentleman's evening dress. Without thought, she brought her hand up and slapped his arm away.

"You're a feisty little thing, aren't you? Does Ashton

know what a treasure he has in you, my dear? It's always such a pleasure to bring spirit to heel." He pulled off his gloves finger by finger, then curled one hand into a fist, his intentions clear. "He may challenge me, but all I need do is tender my apology. I will be most abjectly sorry."

"That will make you no less dead." Lucas's voice whipped across the room and caused Lady Preston to gasp and Lord Yardley to visibly start.

Twenty-two

THE SIGHT OF YARDLEY'S HAND AGAINST IRISA'S cheek sent blinding rage coursing through Lucas. He would not give the bastard a chance to touch her again. With two long strides he reached Yardley and delivered one solid blow. The other man collapsed in a motionless heap on the floor.

Lucas had been so intent on Yardley that he was unprepared for Lady Preston's attack.

She flew at him, her fingers curled in animalistic claws. "You bastard! You've ruined everything. I won't let you get away with it this time!"

He turned in time to watch in shock as his wife jumped up from the couch and swung her fisted hand in a wide arc, catching Lady Preston just below her right eye. "Leave Lucas alone, you villainous harpy!"

Irisa's punch was hardly that of a pugilist, but it knocked Lady Preston off balance. She fell back, landing with a thump in the chair she had been occupying. The chair's legs could not stand against the sudden pressure and they broke. Lady Preston tumbled to her knees on the floor.

Irisa looked at Lucas with eyes round as saucers and swayed on her feet. "I've never hit anyone before."

Lady Preston tried to stand, but her skirts were wrapped around her legs. Ravenswood stepped forward and unceremoniously lifted her to her feet, keeping his hands locked firmly on her upper arm as he did so.

She glared at him, her eyes slitted like a venomous snake. "Let me go, you great beast."

Irisa took a menacing step toward Lady Preston, ignoring the fact that she obviously was having trouble standing on her own. "I'm going to hit her again, just see if I don't."

Lucas wasn't letting Irisa near enough to the bitch to risk harm. He caught her arms and pulled her toward him, but it wasn't enough to have her against his side. He had to wrap both arms around her and press her body as close to his as he possibly could. And even that wasn't close enough.

He wanted her in his bed, naked and under him. The awful cold fear that had plagued him since learning of her disappearance would not be banished by anything less. He tried to speak, but could not say anything. He held her and let his body absorb the miracle of her nearness—something he had not been entirely sure he would ever feel again.

Irisa's arms wrapped around him in an equally tight embrace. "I knew you would come."

"I was almost too late." The prospect of her near miss made his chest tighten with emotion. "That twisted blackguard was going to hit you."

She shuddered. "I know. It was part of Lady Preston's plan to ruin your reputation and mine."

"I heard." Raw fury filled him and he looked away from the top of his wife's head long enough to meet Lady Preston's gaze.

She must have read the message in his eyes because she flinched and renewed her struggles against Ravenswood's hold. The giant man gave her one hard shake and said something low that put a look of terror on her face and stopped her defiant moves.

"Where's Drake?" Irisa asked, her voice muffled by Lucas's body.

"Outside with the guards and our former underfootman."

He'd tried to send Drake home with his wife, but Mrs. Drake insisted on staying at Ashton House until Lucas brought Irisa safely home. Lucas hadn't argued too much, realizing that he was bloody lucky Irisa's stubborn sister hadn't insisted on coming along on the rescue. He assumed if the thought had occurred to her, she would have.

Irisa nodded. "Just before I fell asleep from the draught he gave me, I remembered seeing him in the corridor the day I snuck into the tower room to be alone. He's been in on it all along, I think."

"Yes. He would have been one of the servants who traveled with me between the country and Town."

"That is how he was on hand to lock Irisa on the tower roof," Ravenswood said.

"He was also the one who found out about the Langleys' recent marriage and told Lady Preston about it. It appears that he and one of the Langley maids had gotten rather close."

Irisa tightened her hold on him. "Pansy told me. That's how we discovered your visits to Miss de Brieuse's home."

Lucas had surmised as much. "I should have realized something was up then. My servants are trained not to gossip about me. They know it could mean their instant dismissal—as it would have for him if I had not been sidetracked by other goings-on."

"You are not omniscient, Lucas. You could not have known simple servants' gossip hid something so underhanded."

He unwound Irisa's arms from his torso and pushed her a few inches from his body, needing to see her face. She looked fragile and pale.

"Are you all right?"

She actually smiled. "Yes, now that you are here. I knew you would find me, Lucas."

Her trust warmed places inside him that had gone cold at her disappearance.

"But what are we going to do with them?" she asked, indicating Lady Preston and the still unconscious Yardley. "They are too full of trouble to be ignored or set free without some measures being taken to ensure your safety. She's quite mad in her hatred of you, my love."

"I suppose I could kill Yardley in a dawn appointment."

Lady Preston gasped a protest, which Lucas ignored. However, he paid close attention to his wife's shaking head.

"I think not. That would require you fleeing the country, and unlike Mama, I do not fancy an extended tour of the Continent." Then Irisa's eyes lit up with familiar mischief. "I have just the thing."

Whatever it was, he hoped his wife's idea would not take too much time. He wanted to get her home and in his bed. "What?"

"Did you know that you were responsible for the death of Lady Preston's fiancé? It was during the tail end of the war with Bonaparte. He was a spy."

Lucas felt chills laced with guilt invade him. It was because of him that Irisa had been tormented and put at risk.

Irisa's voice continued in a musing tone. "I do not think Lady Preston would be pleased for the rest of the *ton* to discover that she was once engaged to an enemy of the Crown."

"No one will believe you," Lady Preston snarled.

Irisa looked at the other woman, her eyes filled with disdain. "You think not? You are mistaken to underestimate the influence of The Saint and his wife amongst the *ton*. Not only are others likely to believe me, but they will *care*. Once they hear how you helped your dear fiancé in his endeavors, every drawing room door will be closed to you. The *ton* can be forgiving about some things, but the war is too fresh in everyone's mind for them to ignore the taint of treason on a lady's character."

"I did not help him."

"We have only your word for that, Lady Preston," Irisa said, her voice hard.

The older woman curled her lip. "Do you think I care if you tell this silly story about me? I am not so concerned about what the *ton* thinks as your Saint."

"Ah, but it is one thing to be a notorious widow known for her fast behavior, and quite another to be reviled as a former spy. Every drawing room will be closed to you, every member of the Polite World will scorn you to your face."

Lady Preston's face paled, but she tossed her head with disdain. "I don't care."

"You will." Irisa sounded quite sure of it and Lucas was inclined to agree.

His own mother had been much like Lady Preston, though nowhere near as malicious. While she had courted notoriety, her enjoyment in life was reliant on Society's tacit acceptance. She needed her playground in which to play. Lady Preston was no different.

"You say you did not help him, but gossip will say something quite different," Irisa said relentlessly. "Scandalmongers will eagerly lap up the creamy dish of your ruin when it is offered by those with heavy influence in the Polite World. It will be your word against my husband's title, my brother's title, and let us not forget my brother-in-law's grandfather, the Duke of Pennington."

"What do you want?" Lady Preston demanded.

"Many members of the nobility are finding a tour of the Continent beneficial now that the war has ended. Some have even decided to live in permanent exile. I believe that you will be one of them, Lady Preston. So long as you stay out of England, your secret is safe."

"I see you are not exactly a stranger to the art of blackmail yourself, Lady Ashton."

Irisa shrugged. "One does what one must."

"And I must find myself content with life on the Continent?" Lady Preston asked.

"If you wish to keep your secret safe."

Lady Preston glared at Lucas and then at Irisa. "I've grown

tired of London anyway. Narrow-minded people pursuing tedious habits. A change of scenery will be welcome."

"Lucas?" Irisa asked.

"Yes?"

"I think your man of affairs should see about the sale of Lady Preston's estates in the north. We do not want her to be tempted to return eventually."

"I'll see to it."

Lady Preston said nothing, attempting an air of bored disdain for Irisa's plans, but her complexion had not yet regained its normal color.

"What about Lord Yardley?" Irisa asked.

Lucas glowered at the man, who was just beginning to stir. "Are you quite sure I cannot kill him?"

"I believe we should be fair-minded about this, my love. Can we not offer him the same alternative?"

"Life on the Continent, or death in England?" Lucas asked, knowing from the stiffening of the man on the floor that Yardley had heard him.

"Yes. I think that will do nicely." She turned to her brother, who had remained silent throughout the conversation. "What do you think, Jared?"

Ravenswood's smile was chilling. "I think, brat, that you have an excellent plan, but the Continent is not quite far enough away for my tastes. I would prefer to see them set sail on one of Drake's ships and disembarked on an island in the West Indies. Yardley is only a baronet. If his estate is not entailed, we can see to its disposal as well. Regardless, I believe I will personally escort them on their little venture from England."

Lucas liked how his brother-in-law's mind worked. "Excellent."

Yardley pulled himself to his knees and then woozily to his feet. "See here. I'm not going to some island in the West Indies populated by savages."

"I'm not going to the West Indies!" Lady Preston's façade of calm was beginning to crack.

"Drake's ships also dock in America. We can set you ashore there," Ravenswood offered magnanimously.

"Or I can kill you," Lucas said to Yardley, knowing that his eyes and tone showed just how serious he was.

The bastard had laid hands on Irisa. He clearly did not know how lucky he was to be breathing this very minute.

Lady Preston looked at Yardley, her self-confidence cracking around the edges. "Our lives are forfeit. I am willing to begin anew. There is nothing for me here, not with Lady Ashton's threats hanging over my head."

"You expect me to come with you?" Yardley asked.

Lady Preston shrugged. "It is your choice, but if you stay, you face a worse fate than the destruction of your standing among the *ton*."

Lucas could not help wondering how long this particular partnership would last beyond boarding the ship.

Yardley sat heavily in a chair, his head dropping into his hands while his elbows rested against his knees. "I will go."

Drake brought the guards and underfootman in, and it was decided that enforced sea duty on separate ships in Drake's company would adequately compensate them for their part in Lady Preston's plan. Drake left with Ravenswood to set their plans in motion, while Lucas took his wife home.

As she walked past Lady Preston, she stopped and reached out to point at the rapidly forming black mark on the other woman's face where she had hit her. "How unfortunate. It looks like you're going to have a bruise. I hope the other passengers aboard ship don't think Lord Yardley gave it to you."

IRISA CUDDLED AGAINST LUCAS IN THE CARRIAGE ON the way home, still too much under the influence of the sleeping draught to want to share in conversation. Lucas did not appear to mind. He seemed content to hold her on his lap, his arms wrapped tightly around her. When they reached the house, she found Thea and Pansy together in her bedchamber, the door locked from the inside.

"Your husband was not sure whom to trust in his household. He would only allow me to wait here for you if I remained in Pansy's company with your door locked," Thea explained while hugging her sister fiercely.

Irisa returned her sister's embrace and then hugged her quietly crying maid. "Lucas can be very protective."

"I didn't do a very good job of protecting you, little one." Lucas's eyes looked tortured with an emotion Irisa found quite familiar. Guilt.

She crossed her arms and gave him a very firm stare. "It is not your fault that Timothy drugged and abducted me, Lucas. None of us suspected a household servant was part of that harpy's plot."

"So Timothy *was* the culprit?" Thea asked.

"Yes," Lucas said. "Lady Preston arranged for him to apply for a position in my household in order to act as a spy. He was responsible for both Irisa's misconception that I kept a mistress and for the discovery of her parents' recent marriage."

"He kept Lady Preston apprised of developments and was in the perfect position to facilitate my abduction," Irisa added.

"But why kidnap you at all?" Thea asked.

Irisa repeated Lady Preston's complete plan. She was somewhat prepared for her sister and Pansy's exclamations of horror, but Lucas's increasing fury frightened her a little. He had not heard all the details earlier and going over them now was having a disastrous effect on his temper.

"I should have killed him."

She laid her hand on his arm. "All is well. I am unharmed and we have very neatly seen to their disposal."

His glare turned positively feral and she took a step back. "Lucas?"

"He was going to hurt you."

Yes. She knew that and so had Lucas. Why did she get the impression that the full extent of the situation was making itself known to Lucas only now? "Are you all right, my love?"

He made a visible effort to control the rage she could sense in him. "I am fine. It is you I am worried about."

"I am quite all right, but a bit tired, to tell the truth." She yawned and quickly covered her mouth. Very tired.

Thea stifled her own yawn and asked, "What did you do with Lady Preston and Lord Yardley?"

Lucas explained their plan.

Thea's eyes narrowed. "I hope Jared sees them disembarked on a deserted island without hope of rescue."

"I wouldn't mind if 'is lordship saw fit to throw them overboard, myself. I wouldn't," Pansy said.

Irisa understood her sister and maid's bloodthirsty attitudes, but was too fatigued under the lingering influence of the sleeping draught to work up any strong emotion at the moment. All she wanted was to curl into bed with Lucas by her side.

Thankfully her brother-in-law arrived within the hour, having left the villains under guard in one of his warehouses and Jared in his rooms preparing for a sea voyage. Drake took Thea home, promising to fill in any details Irisa and Lucas had left out of their explanation. Irisa sent Pansy to her room, wanting no one's help preparing for bed other than that of her husband.

Lucas returned from seeing Drake and Thea to the door. He walked into her bedchamber, his expression so intent that she felt her body tingle in awareness.

He didn't stop walking until he stood directly in front of her. "Bloody hell. Irisa, I never want to go through another night like this one."

She desperately wanted him to hold her. "Neither do I."

With an untamed groan, he swept her into his arms and carried her into his chamber. Pansy had started the fire and it lent a gentle glow to the room. Without bothering to light a candle, Lucas began undressing.

Irisa was not capable of doing likewise, feeling mesmerized both by his concentration and the effects of the sleeping draught. When he stood naked, his manhood proudly erect, he reached out and began removing her clothes as well. She stood like a doll, allowing him to do so without the slightest resistance or assistance.

Once she was as bare as he, Lucas lifted her in his arms again and placed her gently in the center of his bed. He then came down on top of her, covering her entire body with his own. They both shuddered at the impact of their flesh touching from shoulder to ankle.

"I love you, Lucas." They were the only words worth saying at the moment.

Lucas groaned. "Say that again, my love."

"I love you, Lucas. I love you. I love you. *I love you.*" She kept repeating it as he explored her body with his lips, showing her his feelings without words. He began at her temple, dropping soft kisses and licking her skin with small darts of his tongue. By the time he reached her breasts, she had forgotten her tiredness and writhed under him.

"Yes, my love. Please, kiss me there," she pleaded with him as his lips hovered above her almost painfully erect nipples.

Then he lowered his mouth and suckled first one and then the other. The pleasure bordered on pain and her head tossed from side to side on the pillow. Then he released her nipple with a small popping sound only to move to the underside of her breast, licking, kissing, stroking with his tongue and nipping with his teeth. As that devilish mouth moved down her stomach and played erotic games with her belly button, her thighs spread of their own accord.

"Lucas. What are you doing to me?"

Even when they had made love before, he had not made her feel these things. Her entire body felt drawn tight like the string of a bow. She restlessly tried to touch him, but he was moving lower and then his mouth was there. Right where she most desired it to be. No. She could not want it. Not there. Surely, he didn't mean to kiss her there. But he did—with his tongue. She screamed and tried to close her legs, but his head was in the way and the feel of his hair against her thighs was more tantalizing than anything she had ever known.

"Lucas. You mustn't do that. I can't . . . It isn't . . ." And then she did. And it was. And she cried, sobbing out her pleasure as wet tears tracked down her temples into her hair.

He continued his tormenting kiss until she convulsed again and finally went as limp as a rag doll. She fell asleep with the sound of his love whispered against her temple and the vague realization that something wasn't quite finished.

LUCAS SOFTLY CARESSED IRISA'S MILK WHITE SKIN, waiting for her to awaken. Light filtered into his bedchamber through a crack in the window draperies, proclaiming the morning far gone. Surprisingly, as excited as his body had been, he had not found it difficult to follow Irisa into sleep. Having her back in his arms had been satisfaction enough for his mind to find the solace of sleep, but now he throbbed with the desire to be inside her and to tell her of his love.

This time, he would make her understand he loved the woman she was, not the woman she believed she needed to be to keep his affection.

Her eyes fluttered open and her lips tilted in a sweet smile of greeting. "Good morning, Lucas."

He kissed the sleep-softened mouth beneath him and pressed his hardness against her thigh. "Good morning, sweeting."

Her eyes opened wide. "You didn't . . . Last night . . ." Her face turned pink and she quit talking.

"Oh, but I did. How can you deny it when you shouted your release so clearly?" he teased her.

She closed her eyes and then opened them again, her cheeks now the color of raspberries.

Lunging up and over him, she found the ticklish spot above his collarbone. "You, sir, are a rogue."

He laughed and squirmed under the tortuous caress of

his wife's wicked little fingers. "If you are intent on touching me, I can think of an area that is longing for your attention," he gasped out between chuckles.

She stopped tickling him and sprawled across his chest, her head resting on her hands. "This area?" she asked with wide-eyed innocence as she thrust her pelvis against his manhood.

The feel of her soft curls caressing his sex pushed all humor from his body and replaced it with rampaging desire.

"Yes." He reached down and slipped his fingers past her buttocks to test her readiness. He had to remind himself that his wife would not wake prepared for love as he had. Only . . . she was wet. Very wet. And soft. And swollen. "What did you dream about last night?"

She grinned shyly. "You."

"Would you care to take a riding lesson this morning?" he asked as he gently but inexorably separated her thighs until her legs rested to either side of him and his penis pressed against the opening of her sex.

For a moment she looked confused. "Riding lesson?" But his wife was very intelligent, and as he rocked against her, understanding lit her face. "Oh, I think I would like that above all things."

And she did. So did he. She proved to be a most apt pupil, and soon brought them both to a very noisy completion. Afterward she collapsed against him.

She lay there drawing patterns with her fingertips through the hair on his chest. "Lady Preston tried to tell me you had been her lover."

He felt his body tense under her. "She lied."

"I know." She kissed his male nipple. "You told us you had never even had an intimate conversation with her, remember?"

He did remember, but that didn't mean Irisa had to trust him. "You believed me."

"Of course I did." She drew the pattern of a heart around the nipple she had kissed. "I love you, Lucas. That means I trust you completely."

His heart expanded at her softly spoken declaration. He wanted to give her an equally valuable gift. He wanted to say just the right thing. His beautiful, faithful wife deserved it. "I knew you hadn't run away."

She snuggled against him. "You trusted me."

"I love you, Irisa. That means I trust you completely," he said, repeating her words back to her. "And I do mean I love *you,* not some perfect paragon."

"Are you saying I don't have to be perfect to keep your love?"

"You are perfect," he vowed.

She shook her head and her honey blond curls tangled with his chest hair. "I'm not. I've discovered that I have strong opinions and I plan to share them with you when necessary. I won't let you go through with this crack-brained notion of challenging anyone who mentions my illegitimacy. I do silly things like driving through Hyde Park with the woman I thought was your mistress, or trying to run away rather than fight a blackmailer. Are you sure you love *me*?"

"Yes." He pulled her head down so their lips met in a fierce, possessive kiss. "I love *you.*"

She sighed, the sound full of deep contentment. "I'm not a paragon, you know."

He laughed. "I'd figured that out, believe it or not. Please remember, I wanted to marry you after discovering you had dressed as a stable boy to spy on me and had gone driving with Clarice, showing yourself to be a hoyden hiding in a paragon's proper wardrobe. But, Irisa?"

She cocked her brow at him. "Yes?"

"You *are* perfect for me and that is all that matters."

Tears washed into her eyes. "I thought you only loved the proper part of me."

"It hasn't been much in evidence of late, and my love for you grows minute by minute."

"Oh, Lucas, I do love you so very much."

"I love you back, and I will never stop."

"Even if the hoyden shows herself more frequently?"

"She will undoubtedly give me gray hairs, but I will never stop loving her—because she's a part of you."

And then he showed her just how deep the love in him ran, their bodies in one accord as only two people who love beyond limits can know.

Epilogue

IRISA CONVINCED LUCAS TO TAKE HER TO THE Continent to visit the newly wed Clarice. However, they could not go until Jared had returned from his ocean voyage. With both Jared and Lord Langley out of the country, Lucas had to oversee the Langley estates as well as his own. Irisa waited until they reached France to tell him the happy news of his impending fatherhood.

He wanted to strangle her for letting him take her out of the country, but ended by making love to her instead. As promised, she nagged him about his threat to challenge those amongst the *ton* with wayward tongues regarding her past, but he remained adamant. However, as he had tried to assure her, his reputation with a pistol served its purpose and the *ton* found other things about which to gossip than his wife's murky past.

The most interesting bit of scandal among the *beau monde* surrounded the Lord Beast, or so the *ton* had nicknamed Viscount Ravenswood, who had been seen of late quite often in the company of the Angel, an altogether beautiful young widow.

Scandalmongers speculated incessantly about the relationship, but all agreed on one thing. It would be inconceivable for such a gentle, quiet, and lovely creature to accept courtship from the giant, scarred man.

Irisa had her own thoughts on the matter. She believed it was time that her dear brother found a love as great as the one she shared with Lucas, a love that filled her life with joy and had succeeded in finally dispelling all the ghosts of her past.

Turn the page for a special preview of
Lucy Monroe's next novel

Take Me

Coming September 2006 from Berkley Sensation!

Ashton Manor
Summer 1825

LORD BEAST.
Viscount Ravenswood.

A very dangerous man.

Calantha watched the huge man cross the small ballroom toward her with both anticipation and dread. His black and white evening clothes clung alarmingly to his well-muscled, oversized body, and he carried himself with an easy grace that belied his size. Watching him move demanded all of her attention. The play of muscles under his tight-fitting breeches fascinated her, as did the way others hastened to move aside as he approached.

This inexplicable reaction to him had so startled her on the first night of Lady Ashton's house party that Calantha had fled with the flimsy excuse of a headache as soon as the ladies left the gentlemen to their port after dinner. She had not returned since. Until tonight.

She had promised Lady Ashton that she would attend tonight's ball, and Calantha always kept her promises.

Besides, she liked the friendly Lady Ashton. So, she had come. And now she watched the man the *ton* referred to as

Lord Beast with the same absorption she reserved for her studies, her painting and her gardening. Yet, none of those things made her tremble with pleasure-laced dread at the thought of being in the same room with them. Nor did they make her pulse race.

In truth, nothing made her pulse race. For such a reaction was an emotional one, and she had long ago learned that life was safer if lived without emotional excesses and turmoil. Her heart was a frozen ball of ice in a soul that shivered from the cold winds that howled across it . . . if she had a soul at all.

"Oh, no. He's coming this way. He has not forgotten our dance. Oh, what shall I do? *What shall I do?*" A young debutante standing directly in front of Calantha spoke.

Ah, so he was coming over to dance with the deb. A mixture of relief and disappointment flowed over Calantha. Of course he would not be desirous of making her acquaintance. She was beautiful, but boring. She had overheard herself referred to as such, and thought it accurate. A woman who hid her true self could not be interesting, but she could be safe.

Everyone knew that Lord Beast spoke only to people that interested him. It was rumored that he gave his own father, the Earl of Langley, the cut direct. And now he intended to dance with the simpering chit in front of Calantha.

She would not have to talk to him. She would not be required to refuse his offer of a dance, or even worse, as she very much feared she might . . . accept.

"Calm yourself, Beatrice. 'Tis only one dance. Lord Beast isn't going to eat you on the ballroom floor," replied another young lady, sounding not in the least sympathetic to her friend's plight.

"That's easy for you to say. *You* don't have to dance with him. I'm at sixes and sevens at the thought of him touching me," complained the silly Beatrice. "I mean that awful scar. And he's so *big*."

Calantha understood her own fear of Ravenswood, but why would the debutante fear him?

Could she not see that under the brute size and glaring demeanor was a man who knew gentleness? Calantha had taught herself to watch others closely in order to assess their true natures after making the colossal mistake of marrying a duke who had been well named after the devil.

It was not difficult. Not really. She was quiet. She remained in the background, another protective behavior she had learned during the years of her marriage. From her vantage point on the periphery of any gathering, she gathered and analyzed information on the people around her.

The first night she had seen Ravenswood, she had been unable to focus on anyone else, and her intent regard had revealed some unexpected facts.

He cared deeply for his sisters and respected the men they had married. In his own way, he was even quite patient. It did not seem so at first, but he had an incredible ability to ignore the rudeness of the many who responded to his scar rather than to his person or his position.

Rumor had it that Ravenswood had fought with a wolf as a very young man to save his sister's life and that is how he had become scarred. Could not the foolish Beatrice and the rest of the *ton* see the beauty in that, the courage and selflessness that such an action would require?

Even the servants were very nervous around him. However, at one point during the previous dinner party, a maid had come close to spilling a tureen of soup on him. He had not berated her, or demanded her punishment as many of the *ton* would do. Instead, he had saved her, and so very carefully that he had not added to her upset.

He was not infinitely patient however. She had also seen him send footmen running with a look and had heard him raise his voice in argument with a local squire she found particularly set in his outmoded opinions.

Beyond everything else she had noticed about him was the truth that he was a man of power . . . perhaps even enough power to melt the ice that encased Calantha's own heart. The thought sent chills of fear skating down her spine.

If that were to happen, there would be pain, great rushing waves of it that would drown her once and for all.

Perhaps the debutante feared Ravenswood because she too could sense this power, though Calantha had difficulty crediting the chit with such insight. After all, her voiced complaints amounted to nothing more than window dressing. Like so many others, she was bothered by the scar. Foolish child.

Calantha could have told her that true evil lurked within, and had nothing to do with physical imperfection. That sort of evil had the power to hurt beyond bearing. Her dead husband had taught Calantha that lesson very well.

Ravenswood stopped in front of Beatrice and put out his hand. "Come."

Beatrice's companion's eyes widened at the peremptory command. Gentlemen of the *ton* did not order their partners to the dance floor. They made suitably bland comments and requests to which a lady could easily respond in the negative.

Beatrice gasped and Calantha watched with interest as her face drained of all color. "I couldn't possibly, my lord. I've . . . I've . . . I already promised this dance. My partner is over there." She waved her fan in the direction of the other side of the room. "He's waiting for me."

Had Calantha seen hurt in his gaze before his eyes narrowed? Had the hastily made-up excuse pricked his pride or damaged his ego? For some reason she could not fathom, she could not bear the thought. She tried to ignore the stirrings of compassion she felt—compassion toward a man who logic said would not be touched by such a silly girl's foolishness.

Calantha had pushed away such reactions early in her marriage, when she realized that allowing herself to care for others put them at risk. It gave her husband further opportunities to punish her many imperfections by hurting those she loved. She tried, but failed, to suppress the memory of her one dear friend, Mary.

Calantha had befriended the girl in the first months of her marriage only to discover that when her husband's anger burned brightly toward her, he was capable of all manner of evil toward those she held dear. She still believed her husband was responsible for Mary's disappearance the second year they were married. She did not believe her friend would have left without a word, otherwise.

She still regretted her lack of vigilance on Mary's behalf, just as she bitterly repented so many of the weaknesses that haunted her.

It was definitely a weakness of mind that made her feet move forward and caused her to say, "Excuse me, please," as she stepped around Beatrice to face Ravenswood directly.

"If you are not otherwise engaged, my lord, perhaps you would consent to escort me onto the floor. I am weary of stillness." *Liar. Liar.* Her brain screamed at her, but she could not pay it any heed. She danced rarely and never grew weary of motionlessness. It was a condition of excellence when one existed on the perimeters of life.

His eyes widened and once again the deb gasped, this time with clear surprise. Calantha waited in frozen silence for him to answer. She had learned not to shift nervously when confronted with a potentially explosive situation, and that training came in to play now. She waited.

And waited.

Finally, convinced he would refuse, she began to step back toward the outskirts of the room, as embarrassed by her behavior as she was confused by it. She could feel heat stealing up her cheeks and she wanted to cover them with her gloved hands. This man of power would have no interest in dancing with a weakling like herself.

But he was willing to escort that brainless twit, Beatrice, her mind taunted her.

Calantha could not believe how that knowledge had the ability to hurt her. She forced away the pain and summoned a smile that meant nothing, just as she had done so many times in the past. She did not remember the last time she had smiled with any true feeling behind it. She opened her mouth to speak.

JARED WATCHED THE ANGEL'S FACE TAKE ON THE QUALity of a porcelain doll, the little emotion that had been revealed, now wiped clean from her features. She was backing away, not because she feared him as so many others had, but because she believed he would refuse her invitation to dance. He had seen the knowledge in her eyes and it seared him because he instinctively knew it had caused her pain.

He hadn't meant to stay silent, but he, who was used to shocking others, had been completely taken aback by the actions of the Angel. Ladies *did not* ask gentlemen to dance, and yet she had asked him. She had opened her mouth to speak again, but nothing had yet emerged.

He forestalled her speech by bowing low toward her and said, "I would be delighted by the honor, your grace."

Blue eyes, the exact shade of an English summer sky, widened and she stopped edging away. Mary had had blue eyes, but even after what she had gone through with the duke, they had never shimmered with quite the wariness the Angel's did.

Beatrice, the simpering miss his sister had arranged for him to partner, stared at them with fascinated awe. She no doubt could not believe that any lady would willingly partner him. With her trumped up story of another partner, she'd made it clear she wouldn't.

The Angel's willingness to do so surprised him as well. As did the fierce urge to hold her, even if it was for something as fleeting as a country dance. He had not expected anything resembling this response to the woman when he made his promise to Mary.

He reached out to take her arm, unsurprised but disappointed when she flinched from his touch before seeming to gather her courage and allow him to pull her toward him. He led her to the other dancers as the musicians began to play. They joined a set and she went into the dance steps with polished style.

But then, that was no less than he expected of the Angel. She looked and acted like the epitome of feminine perfection, her beauty ethereal in its flawlessness. Tall for a woman, she still gave the appearance of fragility.

Her blonde hair had been dressed in a Grecian knot, accentuating the slender column of her neck and further encouraging the perception of her as an otherworldly creature. Along with her translucent skin and composed features, it gave the impression of a marble statue of a Greek goddess, rather than a mere mortal woman.

Her blue silk gown matched the shade of her eyes perfectly, and exposed the upper swell of her small breasts without being vulgar.

Perfection.

Why had she asked him to dance? It did not fit with his image of her, neither the cold-hearted bitch he had assumed she must be, nor the Angel the *ton* believed her to be. After all, an angel did not dance with a beast.

He knew what the *ton* called him and did not care. He was used to the reaction of others to his scars. As he'd grown older and bigger, much bigger than most gentlemen amidst the *ton,* that reaction had only intensified.

Hell, the only two men of his acquaintance that approached him for size were his sisters' husbands, and they were unique in other ways as well. Neither one had ever shown the slightest fear of him, and they'd both been courageous enough to marry strong-willed women. His sisters had stubborn streaks that matched his own.

Why had the Angel asked him to dance?

He frowned in thought, and the lady now facing him forgot the complicated steps involved in this portion of the dance and tripped. Jared's hand shot out to steady her. Her eyes flew to his and he read surprise in her gaze as he gently righted her and continued the pattern of the dance. When he once again faced the duchess, he did so with relief.

"You are not staying at Ashton Manor?" he asked her, knowing the answer, but wanting to hear the melodic voice that had asked him to dance once again.

"No. I live nearby, and your sister graciously invited me to attend tonight."

He knew that Irisa had invited the Angel to come for all of her planned entertainments, but the duchess had only shown up for two. She had come to dinner the first night of the house party and Jared had covertly studied her, making plans to corner her and talk to her after the gentlemen rejoined the ladies. However, he'd been disappointed to learn that she had left early with a headache.

He had waited for her to appear again, but she hadn't, and he'd resigned himself to seeking her out at her home. He wanted to discern what kind of person she was before he kept his promise to Mary. His original plan had been to attend the tail end of the Season and meet her then, but Hannah'd had a small accident playing in the garden and had not been able to travel.

When he had learned his brother-in-law's primary country estate was near the duchess's home, and that his sister planned to invite her to the house party, Jared had shocked Irisa by accepting his own invitation. Although he was always happy to see both of his sisters and their families, he preferred his own estates, as his sister was well aware.

He found the *ton* and its superficial ways irritating. It wasn't just the way people reacted to his appearance, thinking him a beast because he didn't fit the *beau monde's* idea of a gentleman. He hated the way truth and honor got shoved aside in order to maintain appearances. It had happened in his own family, and he couldn't stand the sight of his father because of it. He hated the fact that both of his sisters and the mother he had never been allowed to know had been hurt by his father's cowardly actions.

The country dance ended and the Angel followed him off the floor.

"Would you like a glass of champagne or punch?" he

asked her, wanting to prolong their encounter, needing some answers to the questions that continued to grow in his mind.

"A glass of champagne would be lovely." The musical quality of her voice washed over him and he wanted to keep her talking, but he had to find the footman with the champagne tray.

Calantha sat in the chair Ravenswood had escorted her to, her back ramrod straight. She feared that if she let even one muscle relax, she would lose control completely. Dancing with Ravenswood had been more dangerous than she'd anticipated. Much more.

Lucy Monroe is the award-winning author of more than thirty books. She's married to her own alpha hero and has three terrific children. The only thing she enjoys more than writing is spending time with them. Write to her at lucymonroe@lucymonroe.com, or visit her website at www.lucymonroe.com.

Also available from
BERKLEY SENSATION

Master of Wolves
by Angela Knight
The *USA Today* bestselling author whose werewolf romances are "torrid and exhilarating"* returns with more werewolves—and a handler who's too hot to handle.

0-425-20743-9

The Spirit of the Wolf
by Karen Kay
To break the curse that keeps his people enslaved, Grey Coyote must gain ownership of something belonging to his enemy. And he does: a golden-haired beauty named Marietta Welsford.

0-425-20920-2

Whispers
by Erin Grady
Not only has Gracie Mitchell inherited the Diablo Springs Hotel, and with it the curse that has haunted her family for years, but now the man she has tried to forget has mysteriously returned to town.

0-425-20890-7

Wicked Nights
by Nina Bangs
In an adult theme park, the Castle of Dark Dreams is home to three extraordinary brothers who promise ultimate fulfillment for any woman bold enough to accept their sensual challenge.

0-425-20370-0

**Best Reviews*

Available wherever books are sold or at penguin.com